EDDIE MANN

Messenger

First published by Titan InKorp in 2018

First edition

ISBN: 978-1-78520-117-2

Editing by Hillary Crawford
Cover art by Fraser Price

This book was professionally typeset on Reedsy.
Find out more at reedsy.com

Dawn, my ever loyal and supportive wife. The woman, who made me see how wrong I was about the original title for this book.

Mark, Dee, Tony, Sian, Elaine and Vicky who continue to make me feel like a real writer, thanks to their supportive words. Thank you for being my original fan club.

The problem with messages is that the information that the writer wants to convey, is often misunderstood by the person interpreting those messages.

Contents

Acknowledgement

Steve 'Shuffler' Dawson

Thank you so very much for your story which became the basis for a critical character.

Amy Wintle

For offering to practice your proofreading skills on the first manuscript.

Months Lost

The curved plastic deflectors surrounding the bright neon lights, did nothing to deter the eyes from them. The lights burnished agonisingly onto the person below. His eyes flickered and briefly opened, quickly shutting again due to the intrusive artificial light. The surprising thing was that the blinds covering the external window, and those that hung down over the large windows surrounding his room, were all closed. Outside, the sun shone brightly, which would have enabled cooler, natural light in to the clinically clean room.

The man lying in the bed endeavoured to open his eyes again, gradually this time. He squinted so that his eyelids offered some protection from the painful brightness. A shadow crossed his eyeline from left to right. He heard a door being opened and a male voice spoke out.

"Nurse, he is waking up."

The word "nurse" indicated that he was in a hospital, which in turn meant he was alive. He looked around the room; his vision was blurred and out of focus. Machines, obviously medical, stood on both sides of the bed. From one, a plastic tube led into his arm, the entry point of which was covered by a dressing. He attempted to move to get a better look around the room and immediately regretted it. The pain that shot through most of his body was so excruciating, that he immediately fell back into a state of unconsciousness.

Regaining consciousness around three hours later, Grant made no attempt to move. The lights had been turned off. Enough natural light was being allowed into the room through the now partially opened window blinds for him to see reasonably clearly and without pain. A nurse was checking readings from one of the machines attached to him. She removed a plastic peg from his finger and smiled at him as she noticed him open his eyes.

"Hello, sleepy. Welcome back to the land of the living," she said.

Grant tried to talk, but his throat was as dry as sand. It hurt as he said in a gravelly low voice:

"Didn't realise I had ever left it."

"Several times by all accounts," said a male voice from the area of the room at the bottom of his hospital bed, beyond Grant's vision.

Grant looked at the nurse and despite the discomfort from speaking, asked, "Nurse, could I be sat up a bit, please? And some water, if possible?"

The nurse smiled once more and moved to the side of the medical bed. Leaning forward, she pressed a switch at the side of the bed and it began to rise at the head end. Releasing the switch after a second or two, she moved up toward Grant's head and helped raise his head and neck, so that she could better position the pillows for comfort.

"Back with us for less than a minute and demanding services already. I am going to have my work cut out with you I can see," said the nurse.

She pulled a table over the bed and placed a plastic cup filled with water onto it.

"The jug is on the bedside locker if you need a refill. I am sure your friend will assist you if necessary." She smiled at both the occupants of the room and left to attend to her other duties.

Grant looked up toward the area of the room from where he had heard a male voice moments earlier. A shadowy figure sat in a plastic hospital chair against the far wall. The lights were turned off. Despite the light shining through the partly opened window blinds, the darkness was sufficient to prevent Grant from seeing any facial details of the stranger.

"So, who is my friend?" he asked the stranger.

"Well," the unknown male replied, "before we get into that, allow me to inquire as to how you are feeling? That was one hell of a beating you received; it would have killed most men."

"According to you, it did, several times apparently," replied a very suspicious Grant.

"It did indeed. Once on arrival at the hospital, and once in the operating theatre, but you have been stable for the past few weeks," the stranger informed Grant.

"Weeks?" exclaimed Grant.

He lifted his arm to look at his watch, as if that would somehow confirm what the stranger was saying. His wrist was bare, and the tube stuck into his arm tugged at the flesh, making him wince in pain.

"How many weeks?" he asked.

"Well, months to be totally accurate," replied the stranger remaining seated. His gaze never left Grant as he continued. "Three months in total. They put you into a medical coma after the operations to put you back together completely. Ordinarily, you would have come out of that coma after about a month, but we stepped in and made sure you stayed asleep for a bit longer, to give you the extra time to recover, so to speak. The doctors were becoming quite concerned, so we eased up, and that is why we are speaking now."

"Stepped in, eased up?" said Grant, confused by what he was being told. "Who the fuck are you?" he asked.

"Who are *we*, to be accurate, Grant?" the stranger replied.

"What do you want?" Grant was tired and any pain relief that he had been receiving was beginning to wear off.

The stranger eventually stood and approached Grant. He came to a standstill at the foot of the hospital bed. He was approximately five foot eight inches. He was wearing a white V-neck shirt and a black jacket. He had dark hair. All in all, he was non-descript.

"That can wait," the stranger said. He placed a small card on the table in front of Grant. "We like your style and believe you could be useful to us." He walked toward the door, pausing only to say, "And don't think about leaving this place."

Grant shouted, "Wait!" The man stopped, but remained facing the door. "If you like my style, then I assume that you know what I am capable of. So what's to say that I don't decide to just kill you when I next see you?"

The man laughed quietly.

"Don't be deceived by my outward appearance, my friend," he replied. "I have more experience in terms of killing than you will ever know. I could have you dead within five minutes of leaving this room, and all the tests in the world would only show that your heart gave in and you gave up on life."

He turned around to face Grant. The stranger's face held no expression as he declared, "You've lost your family, your best friend and the one thing you seemed to hold dearly, your bike. Be sensible, Grant. Rest up, and we may just give you something back that is worth living for again."

Grant closed his eyes, trying to make sense of what he was hearing. Seconds later, when he opened his eyes, the man was gone, and Grant was alone again.

About ten minutes later, the nurse returned to the room. She looked at Grant, who had beads of sweat on his forehead and face.

"Are you in pain, my dear?" she asked.

Grant nodded. The nurse walked across to one of the machines and pressed a button twice.

"Let me increase that dose a little bit for you," she said and then added, "Where has your friend gone?"

Grant didn't respond. He closed his eyes as he felt the effects of the strong pain medication surging through his veins. As he started to drift off again, he was roused by distinct images entering his mind. A kaleidoscope of memories in no order. Boots striking down on him; a room soaked in blood; faces of friends, family and enemies flashed through his mind, incorporating acts of evil committed by him and others. Eventually, the strong medicine took hold and Grant fell into a deep morphine driven sleep. The images invading his mind were more vivid, enhanced by the drugs, teasing and torturing his mind, not allowing it to rest.

Hours had passed by the time he awoke again. The room was darker. The lights had been turned low and the window blinds had been partially closed. It was also now evening. The table remained in place over his bed, but had been moved farther away from him. It sat over the lower part of his legs and the cup of water had been placed next to the water jug. On the bedside table next to it, lay a business style card. Grant reached for it and held it in front of his face. As his vision came into focus, Grant slowly read the simple script written upon it—four letters and a number—each separated by a full stop and a company name. That was it. No phone number, no name. *What kind of business card was this?*

C.O.R.T.
The Bloom Foundation

He thought back to what the stranger had said before leaving. *We like your style. You could be useful to us.* The words *we* and *us* indicated a team or organisation of some kind, he thought, but why would he be useful to them? What style did they like? He wasn't even aware that he had a style. He briefly thought about pressing the call button to summon a member of the nursing staff as the pain was beginning to intensify. He stopped himself from doing so, deciding that he needed a bit more time to think things through and consider the bits of information he had at hand.

He had never expected to wake up after the beating he had received from the Crippens. In fact, he had welcomed the darkness as it wrapped itself around him. He remembered thinking at the time, that he had literally nothing to live for, having lost his family and his best friend. Death had seemed like an acceptable companion. No matter how much he tried to scour his memory, he could not remember anything between having accepted death as a fait accompli and waking up from what he now knew to be a medically induced coma.

The mental pictures he was trying visualise from the time of his final liaison with the biker gang were neither clear nor vivid. He attributed this to either the drugs or the beating. Grant's mind wandered to the possibility of having suffered some minor brain damage, or maybe worse. Had this stranger's organisation administered some previously untested drug during his long sleep that prevented any memories from returning? There were too many questions, and absolutely no answers. He reached for the call button that had been placed on the side of the bed by his left hand. He reached for the red button at the centre of it. After a few minutes of waiting, the nurse arrived, the same one he had seen earlier that day.

"Hello, sleepy head, what do you require now?" she said. The same smile was etched on her face, which seemingly became more fake each time Grant looked at her.

"I need to know what has been going on. Why haven't I been seen by a doctor yet?" he asked.

The nurse made her way to the other side of his bed, and once again began to mess around with the machines he was hooked up to.

"No!" exclaimed Grant. "No more pain killers, please. I need answers." His voice became increasingly imploring with every word he uttered.

"They will come with time. Let us look after you and then we will talk to you," replied the nurse, her smile now gone. As Grant once again felt the heavy weight of drug-induced sleep fogging both his pain and his mind, he mused as to whether the nurse was talking about hospital staff when she referred to "we" or "us."

The nurse softly stroked his forehead saying, "It will all make sense when we think you are ready."

When Grant eventually arose again, it was the next morning. He felt groggier than ever before. It took a few seconds for his eyes to focus. A different nurse was removing an empty tube from the machine to the left of his bed. She replaced it with another, filled with white liquid. This nurse didn't have a smile on her face. In fact, she looked quite concerned about something.

"More drugs?" he asked, his voice raspy and dry.

"Morning," replied the nurse, acknowledging Grant with her reply whilst making no eye contact. She remained focused on the job at hand. Happy that she had done what she had to, she turned and looked at Grant. "Sorry," she said, "yes more drugs, but a different one. The doctor will be in to see you very soon."

"Something wrong?" asked Grant, keeping his responses and questions short, given talking remained painful.

"The doctor will answer all your questions I'm sure," the nurse answered, the perturbed look remaining on her face.

"Where's that other nurse? The one here last night?" He reached for the cup of water and sipped at it eagerly.

"I have been on duty all night, sir. There has been no other nurse caring for you for the last," pausing to look at her watch, "fourteen hours."

"I saw her, twice, and the man who visited me yesterday."

The nurse looked confused. "I promise you, sir, there have been no other nurses caring for you, and you have had no visitors since you arrived here weeks ago," she said.

"Okay," replied Grant, still feeling too disorientated to continue with the questions. "However, there is no need to call me sir, a bit formal for the NHS surely? I thought the policy was to call patients by their first names." He tried to smile, but discovered even that smarted.

"Sir," the nurse started to say, correcting, then continuing.

"Mr. Grant, firstly, we don't know your first name, and secondly, this is not an NHS hospital. It's a private Institute."

Here we go again with the Mr. bloody Grant, he thought to himself and closed his eyes. The nurse took that as a sign that the conversation was over, and left the room.

Grant looked at the feed line that was attached to his arm. Removing the tape that held the needle in place, he slowly pulled it out. Blood quickly began to pour from his arm. He pulled the tape back to cover the blood seepage, with little effect, as the blood easily soaked through it. He looked around the room, but could see nothing to use to stop the blood flow. He removed the light purple hospital shirt and wrapped it around his arm.

Slowly he sat up. The pain was dire, but Grant fought through it and got himself into a sitting position on the edge of the bed. He placed his feet on the floor. Despite his extreme discomfort, the first thing he noticed was that the floor was warm. *Under floor heating,* he thought. Certainly not an NHS building. He looked down at himself and was shocked at how much weight he had lost. He was neither gaunt nor skeletal. In fact, he thought he looked quite good. His paunch had disappeared. This made Grant think that with just a bit of work, he would be able to develop a six-pack for the first time in decades. He tried to stand, but a milky swaying feeling filled his head. Given the fact that it was obvious that his legs were not ready yet for weight bearing duties, he remained in the sitting position.

A deep smooth voice from behind him said gently, "Standing is not recommended. Sitting up is a minor miracle, but in my humble but very knowledgeable opinion, I would suggest that laying back down on the bed would be best for your health right now."

Grant turned slightly and winced as additional pain shot through his ribs and chest area. A mousey blonde-haired man stood by the room door. His blue eyes were piercing. Under the white coat he was wearing, that suggested to Grant that this was the doctor, he wore a very expensive and exquisitely tailored suit.

"Doctor," said Grant, the word delivered more as a statement as opposed to a question.

"Stanridge," replied the medical man. "Martin Stanridge to be precise."

Grant looked at the name badge on the white coat worn by the man. It clearly read Dr. Martin D. Stanridge.

"Are you the man responsible for keeping me alive?" asked Grant.

"I am one of a rather skilled team, but yes, I am the main man," Dr. Stanridge replied, smiling widely in a bid to reveal himself as humorous.

"Suppose I should say thank you," said Grant.

"Only if you think we did the right thing. You did try your hardest not to live," said the doctor.

Grant didn't respond. Clearly not a fan of uncomfortable silences Stanridge asked, "So, would you like to know what we know?"

"And more," replied Grant. Satisfied that the medical advice received seemed more than reasonable, he lay back down on the bed.

"Let me just call a nurse to put that line back into place," began Dr. Stanridge. Before he could do or say anything else Grant intervened.

"No more drugs. I need a clear head. If that means

tolerating some pain, then so be it."

"Okay," said Stanridge. "How about she just cleans up the mess you have made then, both to your arm and the bedding."

Grant looked at his arm and for the first time he noticed that the blood had soaked through the hospital clothing. It had been dripping all over the bed sheets and probably the floor.

He nodded his head, adding, "And then some answers."

"Certainly," replied Stanridge, waving toward a nurse through the door he held open with his foot. To the nurse he said, "A quick clean-up of patient and room please, Alice." Turning his attention back to Grant, he continued, "I promise you a story of unanswered questions, a medical genius, and a bit of mystery. As for answers, I cannot promise anything."

The nurse patched up Grant's arm using a wad of cotton wool and some bandaging. Having wiped up the blood splatters on the floor, she excused herself, telling Dr. Stanridge that she would return later to change the bedding. She declared she would require assistance in order to get the patient out of the bed. The doctor nodded his approval. He thanked the nurse who left the two men alone.

"Well?" asked Grant the second the door had closed behind the nurse.

"Where shall I start?" asked Stanridge, who seemed to be questioning himself as opposed to Grant.

"Try the beginning," responded Grant sarcastically. Dr. Martin Stanridge commenced.

"Circa three months ago, you arrived here at The Bloom Institute in the back of a private ambulance. You had been beaten to a pulp. You suffered numerous broken bones to all limbs, spine, ribs, and multiple skull fractures. The minute I saw you, I considered you to have two options. Permanent brain damage resulting in a life being spoon-fed baby food and pissing into a nappy. The second was death. We rushed you into theatre and worked on the more serious of your injuries. Of prime importance was alleviatung the pressure on your brain and repairing the two fractures in your spine. It took us six hours just to do that and technically you died twice in theatre. It took me nearly three minutes to revive you the second time. A colleague called it twice telling me to stop." Stanridge stopped, as he was interrupted by Grant.

"Who brought me here?"

"All in good time. You wanted to know what happened and I am trying to tell you...from the beginning," he said, mimicking Grant's level of sarcasm.

"Over the next month, we operated on two more occasions to reset bones in your arms and legs. A bit more tinkering was done to fix the jigsaw puzzle that was your skull. For the rest of the time, you have been monitored. You remained in a medically induced coma for much longer than we anticipated. In fact, we expected you to come around at least a month ago, given we stopped administrating the drugs that kept you in a coma nearly five weeks ago. The current professional opinion is that your brain is of the belief it craved more recovery time. We kept you unconscious until we felt your brain was primed. That moment occurred yesterday."

"At that precise point, one of your nursing staff was meddling around with a machine. Call me a conspiracy theorist if you want but that is a bit of a coincidence," Grant interrupted.

"The only drugs you have been on for the last five weeks have been painkillers. To accuse one of our staff of interfering with the care of one of our guests is a serious allegation. Furthermore, there is no proof, except for your deluded tale concerning a nurse, who was not on duty overnight, and a visitor that we have no record of. Therefore, they hold no merit. May I suggest these were merely fragmented thoughts of a mind that has been through severe trauma recently?"

"The unknown visitor told me that *they* had assisted in keeping me in a coma. The imaginary nurse told me that I would get answers when *they* were ready to give them. Explain that!" Grant's response was one mixed with anger and confusion.

"I just have," answered Dr. Stanridge. "Think about it. From the moment you have been awake you have wanted answers, which is to be expected. All of your dreams or uncalculated thoughts have seen you subconsciously looking for a source for those answers." His voice remained calm and as smooth as liquid chocolate.

"And what if you are also one of *them*? You are bound to say all this stuff," said Grant.

Stanridge laughed quietly and stated, "I think a little time spent with one of the psychological consultants might be of some benefit."

"Oh, so now I am just fucking mad?" shouted Grant, regretting it immediately as the tension in his body caused the pain to rise up another notch.

"Mr. Grant, the trauma you have suffered would send most people mad. However, I do not think you are mad. I just believe that talking things through with an impartial professional could establish further clarity within your mind," replied the unfaltering doctor.

"Will you get my name right? It's just Grant." Tiredness was tangible in Grant's response.

"That proves my point! After three months of knowing you, I have learned something new about you. I'm not the one whose brain has been dented and pulped. Perhaps talking this through will help to clear things up in your mind. It will enable you to learn things whilst clarifying the old." Stanridge, always the constant professional, looked at Grant. He raised both eyebrows as if asking Grant whether or not he agreed.

"Whatever," responded Grant and dropped his hand back down onto the pillows. "When do I learn to stand up again?"

"The physiotherapist will be your next visitor, Grant. Now, are there any more questions?"

Grant opened one eye, "Any chance of some food, preferably not baby mush?"

Dr. Stanridge smiled. "I will send the nurse back in to take your order."

"I take it that it will be the typical standard hospital food from a very small menu," said Grant, caustically. This for Grant was usual form.

"You can order anything you like, Grant. We have no menu at the Bloom Institute," replied Stanridge, obviously proud of the service they provided.

Turning to leave the room, Stanridge was momentarily delayed as Grant asked, "Doctor, may I ask who is paying for this top-notch service?"

"I have no idea. All I'm aware of is that you are to receive the best treatment and service. The bill is covered. Clearly, somebody cares about you. I have no idea why...must be your charming personality." On that note, Dr. Stanridge left the room, leaving Grant annoyed that he hadn't had the last word.

——— ———

About an hour after Dr. Stanridge's departure, the door opened slightly, and in strolled the apparent figment of his damaged brain. The male stranger was dressed almost identically as before, except this time, his shirt was a dark blue colour. Grant wondered if purely imaginary creatures changed their clothes.

The man spoke before Grant could.

"Hello again. You are looking much better today."

"Apparently, you are not real. The only person who ever sees you is me, or possibly my damaged brain. Therefore, a conversation with you would seem to be a pointless exercise," replied Grant.

"Oh, I am real, Grant. Surely the fact that you are in possession of my calling card is all the proof you need," said his visitor.

Grant realised that he had forgotten all about the business card. He became inwardly angry with himself for not showing it to Dr. Stanridge as a form of evidence.

"So, are you here to give me some answers?" asked Grant, now boring himself by repeatedly asking the same question.

"Not right now, no," came the response. "I am here merely to advise you to work hard in your physio sessions. They will be difficult and very painful, but they are the key to your release from this place. You are very important to us, Grant. We have already invested in you with abundance. We would like to receive something back for this venture."

"Who the hell is *us* and before you say later, or you can't say right now, remember this: If I am that important to you, whoever you are, you need to know that without answers, I ain't doing anything." Grant was determined to get something from this annoyingly un-giving stranger.

The man pondered for a short while prior to responding.

"Grant, you need to think hard about your predicament. As an organisation, we have been involved in your life for longer than you can imagine. How do you think you got away with what you did? How come the police were not the first people you saw when you woke up? How did information come your way that led you to suspect members of the Crippens were behind the crimes against your family? We are the reason you were successful in getting the revenge you desired. We are responsible for you being here, and therefore, we are the reason you are still alive.

"We created the vision, the mask from behind which you are able to hide. We can destroy that protection just as easily as it was created. You need to be just a little more grateful. Alternatively, you can be your normal coarse self and tell me to fuck off. I can guarantee that this will result in you living your life in a prison cell for the next thirty years being someone's arse bitch—being passed around among his mates like a human pass-the-parcel. I cunningly suspect that you are more aware than most of how easily the human sphincter can be destroyed."

Grant was beaten, he knew it, but had one final question.

"Just tell me who *you* are?"

The stranger smiled and shook his head. "We don't believe that you are ready for that information yet, Grant. When we think you are ready to come on board with us, then you will get some of the answers you desire. Until then, decide, my friend. Get fit or get packed for prison."

With that, the stranger left the room, leaving Grant with

more questions and fewer answers than he had had before the man arrived.

Within seconds, another man entered the room. This one was obviously hospital staff. He was dressed in black trousers and a black smock type top, the words "Bloom Institute" embroidered on the upper left side of the smock, in plain and simple white text.

"Hi Grant, my name is Pete and I am your physiotherapist. You ready for some exercise?"

"Tell me you just saw a bloke leave my room," Grant pleaded.

Pete the physio looked blankly at Grant. "No, I didn't see anyone," he replied.

"Oh, fuck off. You couldn't have missed him," he snarled.

"Grant, please. I just work here as a physio. Believe me, I love working here. A, because the working conditions for physiotherapy are second to none, and B, well, to put it simply, the salary is way above what I should be earning. The main reason for that embarrassingly high salary is to ensure that I don't see anyone I am not supposed to see. I hear nothing that I am not meant to get wind of. I don't answer any questions that may suggest otherwise," replied Pete, looking behind him just to ensure that the door was fully shut.

"I think you just answered my question," said Grant.

The next forty-five minutes were spent by Pete explaining to Grant what the physiotherapy treatment would comprise of. He showed Grant a few exercises that would initialise some progress beyond his bed.

"It's going to be painful Grant," advised Pete. "My nickname in this place is the Pain Ninja." Grant sensed a certain level of conceit in Pete's voice as he disclosed this information.

"I've been known to hand out a fair bit of pain too during

my time," said a smiling Grant.

Pete rubbed his hands together and laughed. "Ooh I love a challenge! The first session is tomorrow at ten o'clock. I will come to collect you." He left the room. Immediately, Grant started to do some of the exercises that he and Pete had discussed.

He stretched his toes upwards and turned his feet inwards and outwards. Whilst doing this, he thought about what the stranger had said to him. He had put some relevant questions to Grant, particularly in relation to the absence of the police and how the information regarding the Crippens involvement had come to him so easily. At the time, he was nonchalant about it. Prior to being assaulted, Grant had been hurting, angry and hungry for revenge. The police were progressing way too slowly. When a man he vaguely recognised as being a neighbour suddenly engaged in a conversation with him, he had listened intently. His *neighbour* had mentioned seeing three bikes riding away from his property, and continued describing the back patch of the bikers quite accurately. Thinking about it, the description of the bikers' colours was too accurate, considering the time of night and the poor street lighting. That said, it was precise enough to enable Grant to complete some basic internet searching and discover the identity of the bike gang.

Grant rubbed the side of his face; the remaining scar left on his face was itchy. The thin long patch of skin grafting that had been used to repair the gash caused by the ripping of the bike chain felt strange to his touch. It didn't feel like hisown skin. He hadn't asked where the skin graft had been taken from, as he hadn't wanted to be told that he had a piece of his own arse now sitting on his face. With that in mind, he stopped scratching the wound that would serve as a constant daily reminder of the beating he had taken and miraculously survived.

The agony the basic stretching exercises caused momentarily broke him away from his thoughts. Grant persevered with the exercises. He was driven by his determination to get back on his feet.

As he exercised, Grant considered the second question—the police. He had killed at least three people, blown up a building in the middle of a town, and been involved in a gun battle in an open street. In addition, Ian's best but poor efforts to clean up the evidence left behind at the building in the woods would be incriminating. The only logical outcome should have been the police guarding his hospital room door, awaiting his return to the real world.

The reality, was that there were no police. There was, however, a strange man who knew way too much. He appeared to be the representative of some organisation that had somehow, for unknown reasons, guided Grant on his path of targeted revenge. Thereafter, they had cleaned up the aftermath or at the very least, cleared up the mess that the Crippens had left him in.

He pulled up the bedside rails and used them to assist him in doing short sit-ups. Having only completed three, he stopped. He may have lost quite a bit of weight, but his abdominal muscles had not magically strengthened. His back was burning with pain. Grant reached over to the bedside table and retrieved the business card. Laying his head back down on the pillows, he held the card up in front of his face by the two bottom corners with his first fingers and thumbs.

It would seem to him that C.O.R.T. ensnared him. He could

not see any other option but to work with these people. Death had let him down by rejecting his many applications to join the assemblage. It was possible that his future remained in the land of the living.

He placed the card into the drawer of the bedside table. The effort of doing so caused more pain to shoot through his broken body. He was tired once again, but he knew that this cycle of thinking, sleeping, asking questions, and sleeping again had to be broken.

Grant had to get out of this place, which would involve hard work and an abundance of pain. He grabbed the bedside rails once more and started to do more sit-ups. Three images in his head somehow provided him with additional strength and determination. It seemed that if only spiritually, his wife, daughter and best friend were still there by his side.

The Pain Ninja

The following morning, Grant awoke from a good night's slumber. Sleep had been assisted by a liberal dose of painkillers. The breakfast that faced was fit for the tables of any five-star hotel. He ate like a man who had been deprived of food for a lifetime. He would have willingly asked for a second breakfast, had he not quite liked his new sylph body shape.

Grant was assisted into the sit-down shower in his room's en-suite bathroom by a very attractive, and thankfully very professional, nurse. She must have realised why he had lowered his hands to cover his manhood whilst she rubbed a soapy sponge over his body, but never said a word, or showed any visual acknowledgment on her face. Once cleansed, he decided to tell the nurse that he would attempt to dry himself off. She made him promise to pull the assistance cord if he needed her to help before she left the room.

It took Grant almost twenty minutes to fully dry himself with the soft, luxurious towel. It was almost as long as the time required for his semi-erection to dissipate. Even though he was alone in the bathroom, he still blushed with embarrassment. He imagined what the nurse must have been thinking about him. A fully-grown man who couldn't control himself while being bathed by a medical professional. He was still a man though, and a man who had not had a sexual encounter for well over a year. This had been his decision he reminded himself.

He sat, still naked, in the wheelchair that the nurse had helped him into. He wheeled himself back into the main room. A pair of dark blue shorts, white socks and a white T-shirt had been laid out on his bed, which he spent ten minutes struggling into. Grant moved the wheelchair toward the door, in the realisation that after the third attempt at putting his socks on, the assistance was required.

He turned the door handle and was surprised to find it locked. He had never heard the door being locked when other people had left the room. There was no keyhole on the inside of the door or the round door handle, leaving Grant to assume that it had been locked from the outside. He fully intended to ask why this had been done, and get the assurance that it would never happen again.

He spun the wheelchair around to make his way toward the call button at the other side of his bed, when he saw a small oval indentation in the door just above the handle. He studied it closely. A plain, dull black plastic or glass covered the indentation. Its shape was like the pad of a fingertip. He placed the first finger of his left hand against it and the colour of the glass turned red. He removed his finger and the pad slowly returned to its original dull black colour. He went through this process with both thumbs and every finger of both hands. On every occasion, the result was the same.

Fingerprint recognition locking devices, he thought to himself, *in a hospital!*

He continued with his planned task. A few minutes after pressing the call button, the nurse who had bathed him entered the room.

"All ready, Grant?" she asked.

"Need help putting my socks on, love," replied Grant. A sense of shame pervaded his spirit. He was dependant on assistance with a task that an average three-year-old child could accomplish. The nurse picked up the socks from the bed and kneeled in front of Grant, gently pulling the socks one by one onto his feet. Standing up, she smiled and asked Grant if he was now ready for his physiotherapy session.

"Just tell me where to go and I'll be on my way," he said.

"Sorry, patients are taken everywhere in the hospital. It's a health and safety thing I think," replied the nurse.

Grant knew immediately that she was lying. In the short time he had been conscious within this building, he had established that the staff knew why everything happened as it did. This nurse would have known whether the transporting of patients was for health and safety purposes, or for some other reason.

"The doors being locked by fingerprint pads. Is that also for health and safety?" he asked her.

"Pure safety, Grant. We have patients here who would be endangering themselves should they try to get anywhere by themselves," the nurse replied. *Another organisational answer,* he thought.

"Not a danger to others I hope?" asked an inquisitive Grant.

The nurse simply smiled saying, "I'll go and tell Pete that you are ready for your session."

As she left, Grant was able to watch her deftly place her thumb against the small pad. It turned green, allowing the nurse to turn the door handle and leave the room. As the door shut behind her, Grant waited and listened. A second or so after the door closed, he heard the quietest of electronic clicks. He knew that once again he had been detained in his room. Imprisoned in the highest quality of medical care, but incarcerated nevertheless.

Pete, aka the Pain Ninja, collected Grant not long after the nurse had left his room. When he arrived, Grant's head and face had been glazed in a mist of sweat, caused by the effort he had put into the exercises. Pete had been pleased, but also warned caution, telling Grant that the path to recovery was going to be slow. Grant was going to have to show a level of constraint so as not to delay his recovery, which would mean being in hospital for longer.

"Like hell I will," Grant had whispered under his breath. In a bid to show this youngster he was up to the job, he sat up and swung himself around to a sitting position on the edge of the bed. He did his best to conceal the dizziness he suffered from the head rush he experienced, as the blood rushed away from his brain, as a result of sitting too quickly.

"Get the damned metal chariot," said Grant, nodding toward the wheelchair.

The young physiotherapist helped Grant into the chair and moved to grip the handles to push it forward.

"I can move myself," Grant hissed, turning his head slightly to look at Pete.

"It's some distance to the gymnasium."

"Part of the pain process then. You should be in favour of that, Mr. Pain Ninja," replied Grant, grabbing the wheels of the chair, making his point by moving it forward. Pete walked to the door, raising his eyes to the ceiling and thinking that yet again his bosses had handed him an onerous patient. Once again, Grant witnessed the placement of the thumb onto the fingerprint reader, before Pete turned the handle and opened the door.

"Follow me, warrior, to the pain clinic," said Pete with a smile, disappointed that he received no response of any kind from his patient. Grant was too busy taking in as much information about his new surroundings as he possibly could.

Just a few metres down the corridor stood a nurses' station. There stood two female nurses, studying a computer screen. The corridor was quite long, at least a hundred metres, with doors on both sides. Grant assumed there were more rooms for patients. The entire area was spotless and an almost blinding white: White walls, white floors, white ceilings. Nothing broke up the artificial arctic landscape. The doors to the room were a slightly duller shade of white.

The only respite from this incessant white, were the black uniforms worn by the staff and the odd flash of green, provided by the few large potted plants placed uniformly down each side of the corridor. Grant took his time wheeling his chair behind Pete, in order to memorise as much as he could. Pete was no stranger to this kind of reaction from patients on leaving their rooms for the first time.

"Just like any other hospital, Grant," Pete said in a monotone voice.

"Not quite," replied Grant. "No visitors. When is visiting time in this place?"

"Not my area," said Pete, evasively.

The rest of the journey was completed in silence. Grant didn't see the point in asking questions to someone who clearly had no intention of answering them truthfully. They travelled past about six other rooms before Pete came to a halt at the doors to a lift. Again, he placed his thumb on a fingerprint reader, which turned green instantly. The lift doors slid open, smoothly and silently. They both entered the lift, Grant turning his wheelchair around to face the lift doors. He waited for them to close but they didn't. Pete placed his thumb against another fingerprint pad, inside the lift. Beneath the pad, Grant saw five other buttons, which were obviously led to different floors. They were numbered 4, 3, 2, P, L and B. All were lit up a dull yellow except for the buttons 4, 3 and B. Pete pressed the button with the letter P on it. Grant watched it turn blue and then felt the lift smoothly start to move downwards.

"Well, that makes me feel better," said Grant.

"What's that?" asked Pete, expecting yet another question or disparaging statement.

"The fact that two of the buttons bulbs are not working. It makes the place feel more like a real hospital," said Grant, smiling once more.

"Nothing's broken. The buttons not lighting up just means I don't have access to those floors," replied Pete. The response was more natural than previous replies indicating that Grant had, at last, received a truthful answer, as opposed to a lie or a well-rehearsed organisational response.

"So why don't you have access to levels three and four or the basement?"

"Because they don't have patients on them, I suppose," responded Pete, wishing the elevator would hurry up. "The basement is for supplies, level three is administration and the suits work on the top floor. I have no reason to go anywhere unless there are patients, physiotherapy facilities, or a way out."

"And why do the lift doors have card readers next to the

fingerprint pads?" asked Grant hoping not to arouse suspicion with his endless questions relating to security.

"The security staff have swipe cards as a back-up in case the fingerprint pads fail to work in an emergency. Should anything kick off, security staff are obliged to attend the situation no matter what," Pete replied, with no hint of suspicion.

"But no back up system on the doors of the patients?" asked Grant.

"No," replied Pete firmly. "Fingerprint access only to patients' rooms."

Grant decided he had asked enough questions for now. He remained silent for the rest of the elevator journey.

A recorded female voice gently announced, *"Physiotherapy Department."*

"Any more questions before the fun begins?" asked Pete, who looked more comfortable now that he was back in familiar surroundings.

"Is it really going to be fun?" asked Grant, with an annoying grin returning to his face.

"No," replied Pete, "follow me."

Grant followed Pete down a corridor, a short distance passing three consultation rooms along the way, the physiotherapy office, and then straight, before going through an open door into a large gymnasium.

Grant perused his surroundings. The gym complex was large. Grey walls surrounding a dark brown floor, which appeared to be made of soft impact material. He could only think that was to soften the fall of any patients, should they take a tumble. An array of machinery was selectively spaced around the area. It included three jogging machines, two cycling machines, a walkway with balance bars on either side of it to support its users, and a set of steps at each of its ends. Other apparatus included exercise units designed for users to strengthen the different parts of the body—legs, arms and every other body part—Grant imagined. All the equipment was very high-tech.

There were devices that measured the amount of weight being moved and the level of effort put in by the patient, explained Pete. Large exercise balls were stacked up against one of the walls on a cleverly designed rack system. It appeared as if the balls were hovering in mid-air. Grant, however, was no longer looking at the machines. His focus was fully on the far wall. A huge glass window spreading the full width of the gym and floor to ceiling, revealed a view over a beautiful lake surrounded by well-maintained grassed areas.

"Where the hell is this place?" he asked.

"We are out in an isolated and tranquil part of Berkshire. The peace allows our patients to fully focus on their rehabilitation without any distractions," replied Pete proudly.

Grant was allowed a few moments more to observe the view, given that it was possibly his first sight of anything other than the inside of the hospital facility for months.

"So, you ready to begin, or are you planning to stay in that wheelchair and hope that the Para Olympic wheelchair basketball scouts come visiting?" said Pete.

"What's first on the menu?" asked Grant, his gaze transfixed on the view.

"The walkway is as good a place to start as any. Don't worry, I won't expect too much during your first visit," said Pete, smiling and clearly more confident in his own domain.

The implicit challenge in Pete's invite did the trick. Grant stood up and walked slowly, yet wobbly on occasion, toward the walkway. He negotiated his way up the first set of three steps. Refusing to use the handrails, he began to walk his way toward the other set of steps. He only made it halfway, before stopping and grabbing hold of both rails to prevent him from collapsing to the floor.

"Easy does it, Grant. This is not a race," said Pete.

"For you, maybe not, but for me, I want out of here sooner rather than later," replied an exhausted Grant, who was doing his best to mask the pain that was shooting down his back and into his legs.

"If you don't follow my advice, you will be here for a long, long time," responded Pete.

For the next thirty minutes, Grant walked back and forth along the walkway, stopping several times. At one stage, he asked Pete to bring the wheelchair over so that he could sit down. Instead, Pete took one of the larger exercise balls from the wall and told Grant to sit on it instead, explaining that it would help with his balance and core strength, whilst allowing Grant to rest for a while.

"The wheelchair is for getting here and leaving here whilst you need it," clarified Pete.

Grant sat on the large silver ball, but keeping his balance was harder work than he had imagined. After nearly five minutes, it struck him that he was getting no rest at all.

"Any chance of a drink of water then?" he asked.

Pete nodded over to the door. "It's over there…yours to use whenever you want it."

Grant glanced toward the door. He saw a water fountain. A funnel of disposable cups was attached to its left side.

"You doing the honours?" asked Grant.

"I'm not the thirsty one and I am certainly not your nursemaid." Pete was very much in charge now.

Grant raised himself from the ball awkwardly, almost falling at the first attempt. Finally achieving an upright position, he managed about seven or eight steps before falling to one knee. He steadied himself by placing both hands on the floor. He looked up toward Pete and said, "Happy now?"

Pete was emotionless with his response. "You have a choice. Get up and go get that drink you want, get up and get back on the walkway, or stay down and give up. If you choose the latter, you will be returned to your locked room. I will retreat to my office to enjoy a nice cup of green tea before my next client arrives."

Grant pushed himself up to a kneeling position. With a huge amount of effort, he managed to stand up again. At some point during this process, he had whispered the word "prick."

Pete laughed and simply responded by saying, "Pain Ninja my friend. You are the prick who can't even walk a few metres to a drinks machine."

Grant turned around to face the young physio and shouted, "I will walk over there and kick your fucking ass, you insignificant little sprog."

Once again Pete laughed, "I very much doubt it, old man, but give it a try. I won't move. In fact, if you manage to reach me without falling over or stopping and breathing like an eighty-year-old I will allow you one free punch."

Grant put all his efforts into walking toward the cocky young man. Once again, he ended up falling forward about three feet away from his quarry. This time, he ended up face down on the floor. He heard Pete clapping his hands together steadily in a mocking style applause.

"You bastard," gasped Grant. "Is this how you get your kicks, you sick fuck?"

Pete stopped clapping and dropped to one knee close to Grant's head and face. "No, Grant. The applause was genuine. That determination you just demonstrated is what I want to see every single session. Together we will get you out of here. Shall I get you that cup of water now?"

Grant dropped his forehead onto the floor and gave Pete a thumbs up sign with his left hand. He had to admit the little prick knew what he was doing.

——————— ———————

For the next weeks, Grant's days merged together into a fog of painful physio sessions, and solitary periods spent in his locked hospital cell. During this time, the stranger did not return. Grant's physio sessions intensified, lasting longer. He felt himself getting stronger with each visit. He was no longer falling over or walking like a wobbly old age pensioner.

His back still served as a constant reminder that he still had a way to go. He suffered bouts of painful spasms that would either shoot down his arms or his legs, depending on where the pain in his back started. Pete's only response to Grant telling him about his enduring pain was to give him more exercises. The Pain Ninja certainly deserved his nickname. He was relentless.

On the Friday afternoon of the fourth week of physio sessions, Grant once again found himself in the now very familiar surroundings of the gym. Pete had given him a different exercise to do. It involved bouncing up and down on a small trampoline. He rhythmically richochted up and down, ensuring he was facing the large window so that he could enjoy the view.

Over the past week, Pete had also introduced some music on occasions. It wasn't the heavy metal that would have been Grant's choice. However, in a situation where there was nothing but boring repetitive exercises to do even '80s pop music offered a welcome mental distraction.

A band was singing in the background about being as hungry as a wolf, when Grant noticed a small object on the floor. Whilst insignificant in itself, what made it momentous was that it was the first time Grant had witnessed anything out of place. He stopped bouncing and sat on the edge of the trampoline, placing his foot over the small piece of plastic. He quickly pulled at the laces of his training shoe so as to undo them before Pete realised that he had stopped exercising.

"Whats wrong, old man? Do I need to get the wheelchair out of the store room for you?"

Grant pointed at his shoe. "Health and Safety, boss. Need to fasten my shoelace."

Tieing his shoelace, Grant quickly lifted the hidden piece of plastic from beneath his foot. He placed it down the side of his shoe, keeping a discreet eye on Pete to ensure he wasn't being watched.

Grant got back onto the trampoline and began to jump up and down again, occasionally hopping from one leg to the other. "I'm getting good at this, look, Pete."

"Yeah, very flash," replied Pete, his interest seeming to have diminished. "You don't seem your usual self, Pete. What's wrong mate?" asked Grant, still bouncing around like a juvenile.

"Just a bit tired. Went to a gig last night and it finished later than I expected."

"Anyone I may have heard of?" he asked, now getting rather breathless from combining talking and jumping a bit too enthusiastically.

Pete laughed a strained laugh saying, "I doubt it, just a cover band. I think they were called Spandex Gold. Pretty good though."

That explained the guitar pick now secreted inside my shoe, thought Grant. *Silly sod must have allowed it to drop from his pocket.*

"Shall we call it a day then?" The question surprised Pete. He turned around to give Grant attention for only the second time during the training session.

"Are you all right, wanting to return to your beloved cell early?"

"Well, after all the kindness and compassion you have shown me over the past few weeks, the least I can do is give you a break when you obviously need it." Grant's contempt was returning almost as quickly as his strength and agility.

"Well, if you don't mind, yeah, that would be good. I have so much paperwork to catch up on. Thanks, Grant."

They made their way up to the next floor, using the stairs as had been the case for the past few days. Halfway up, Grant stumbled, landing onto one knee.

"It's okay, I'm fine, carry on," he called to Pete, using the opportunity to retrieve the piece of plastic from his shoe. Grant caught up with the physio, keeping a steady flow of pointless dialogue in order to keep Pete engaged.

Upon reaching his bedroom door, Pete placed his finger

against the fingerprint recognition pad. The door opened. Grant reached past Pete and placed his hand against the door.

"Got it, thanks. See you tomorrow, usual time. Enjoy that paperwork," he uttered. He placed his body between the door and its frame, squeezing past Pete, and as he did so, Grant licked the guitar pick and stuck it to the black metal strip that covered the entire inside of the door frame. He hastily looked over in the direction of the nurses' station and called out, "Sarah, I will skip tonight's meal if that's okay. Still got a sandwich from lunchtime and I'm going to have an early night."

"You sure, Grant? Not a coffee or anything?" replied the nurse.

"No thanks, darling. I have some of that healthy green juice stuff left. I'm just tired. This git is wearing me out," he said.

"Okay," replied the nurse. "I will leave you in peace tonight." She returned to the PC screen to continue with her work.

Pete walked away. He waved his hand in a goodbye gesture, turning back the once to check that the door had closed. What he did not notice was that the fingerprint pad remained illuminated.

Grant sat on his bed and waited. He was unable to avert his eyes from the green glow of the fingerprint pad. He waited for the moment that someone else would see it too.

Daylight faded to dusk, which turned to the darkness of early night. For Grant, every minute dragged way beyond the scientific rules of time. He stood up and walked toward the door, still uncertain that his intervention had worked. He grasped the door handle and gently pulled it toward him. It opened, much to Grant's surprise. The guitar pick remained stuck to the metallic door frame strip.

Grant pulled the door open just an inch, so that he could glimpse through it toward the nurses' station. Sarah was sitting behind the PC screen and upon seeing this, Grant's heart sank. He slowly allowed the door to close again, controlling it carefully to the very end. He then watched in hope that the fingerprint pad would remain green. Thankfully, it did.

Occasionally, Grant checked the time on the wall clock, which led him to wondering about his trusty watch. He had not seen it since waking. It had not been returned to him when his few personal belongings turned up in a blue plastic bag. He would make a point of asking about that at some stage.

He lay down on the bed, once again reminded of how many injuries his back had sustained, by sending a sharp pain shooting down toward his hips. He closed his eyes and the three familiar facial images filled the blackness. Grant knew that this was probably something that he would have to endure for the rest of his life. He felt that it was his inner conscience producing the images. The guilt of not being home that night, which could have resulted in an alternative outcome, and his contrition with regards to the reason why he was not home that night.

"Gotta work a bit late, darling. Really sorry. I should be home by about eleven. Midnight at the latest," he had told his wife on the phone.

He had eventually arrived home at around four in the morning, to find it surrounded by police officers and crime scene tape. He had turned up that late, because his twenty-four-year-old nubile and extremely irresistible work colleague had wanted sex *just one more time*.

He wiped the tears of culpability from his face and opened

his eyes. Checking the clock, Grant was surprised to discover that he had been lying on the bed for just over an hour.

He returned to the door and repeated the process of opening it, only to find the nurses' station empty. He slipped his head out just far enough to check in both directions of the corridor: Deserted. He entered the hospital corridor gently closing the door. It was quite dark, as the hospital had entered into night mode. This meant that all lights were off unless they were required for the night shift staff, and even these were dimmed.

The first thing Grant noticed was the luminousity of the green pad on his door. He was pushing his luck with this too far. He had to do something about this problem. He suddenly remembered something. Grant re-entered his room and retrieved a length of black physio support tape from his bedside table. He ripped off a length, approximately an inch long.

He re-entered the corridor whilst pulling off the backing tape. He stuck the black tape over the glowing light. It worked. The glow had completely vanished.

Looking around once more, Grant ensured he was still alone. He decided that it was time to investigate his surroundings without the usual escort.

A Walk of Discovery

Grant made his way past the nurses' station and down the corridor, in the direction of the lift. He knew that it was not going to be possible to leave this floor because of the security devices in place. He headed for the first door on his left that he had always assumed would be a patient's room just like his. He could see nothing through the heavily frosted glass panel in the middle of the door. It was so well fitted, that there were no gaps down the sides allowing him to snatch a glimpse of anything on the other side.

He pushed against the door. As he expected, the door did not move. Knowing that he did not have the luxury of time on his side, he hastily moved onto the adjacent door with the same result. He decided to try the doors on the other side of the corridor. This was to no avail. He reached the last door that was the nearest to the nurses' station, resolute that his plan had been both pointless and fruitless. Not wanting to be discovered outside of his room, thus revealing he had a means of escape from its confines, he started to head back to it, when he was stopped in his tracks.

A voice whispered from the other side of the last door.

"Nurse?" it asked.

Grant stood still and silent, not sure whether to speak or

not. Eventually, he threw caution to the wind and replied with one simple word.

"No."

"Staff?" came back the reply.

Once again Grant replied by saying no.

"How did you get out of your room?" the faceless voice asked.

"That isn't important right now. Who are you?" asked Grant.

"My name is Jim. I am what they describe as a patient in this place. Do you work for the company?"

Grant was confused by the question at first and asked for clarification on what this person meant by the company.

"The company," came a frustrated reply, "the damned company. You do, don't you? Is this some kind of test? I remain loyal to the company, I promise." The person's voice had become apprehensive, then became anxious and imploring.

"Listen pal," replied Grant, "I don't work for any company. I am just a patient here working hard to get out."

"They will never let you out until you prove yourself. Once you do, they will bring you back here and lock you away again," replied Jim.

Grant could only think that this man was suffering from a mental illness. He opted to stay for a while longer, purely because this was the first person he had spoken to that did not work for this hospital.

"Why are you here?" he asked.

"Open my door and we can get out of here together," replied Jim.

"I can't open your door. Surely you know about the

fingerprint security," said Grant.

"You got out of your room. Don't fuck me around." Jim's voice was becoming exasperated.

"I'm not fucking you around, mate. I got lucky and managed to circumvent the fingerprint devices. I don't have a lot of time. The nurse will return soon. Tell me why you are here?" Grant surveyed the corridor in both directions, grateful that there remained no sign of Sarah.

"Use the computer system. Get your fingerprints on the security database. I heard a nurse talking to a new member of staff about it a few months ago," replied Jim, in a drastic manner.

"A few months ago? How long have you been here?" Grant asked his fellow patient.

"About a year, I think," came the shocking response.

Grant was about to reply when he heard a soft thud to his left. The lift had just halted at that very floor.

"Got to go, Jim, the nurse is returning. I will try to return later."

Grant headed back to his room, quickly snatching the strip of tape from the fingerprint pad. He looked back toward the lift and saw the glow from the fingerprint device turn green. Entering his room, he removed the guitar pick from the metal strip on the door frame. He gently closed the door behind him, just as Sarah exited the lift accompanied by another nurse and walked toward the nurses' station.

Despite, weeks of intense physiotherapy and exercise, Grant's body bemoaned this recent spate of exertion. He leaned against the door, analysing the information that had just materialised. He could only conclude that Jim must have suffered extensive injuries to have been kept in here for a year. Grant summarised they must have been head or brain injuries. He certainly didn't articulate like a sound of mind person.

The more he replayed it, the clearer it became that an opportunity to outwit the security pads could present itself. This meant another sojourn outside. It also denoted the necessity to access a computer system, of which he had no knowledge. He knew it was a long shot, especially as he recalled his daughter trying and failing to explain how Twitter worked. She was defeated after an hour, walking away laughing and saying, "Dad you are impossible. Stick to using pen and paper."

Grant heard voices coming from the corridor area. Having not witnessed anyone exit from the lift, he had just assumed that it had been Sarah. Evidently, there was another person with her. The sound of voices suggested it was another female. He pressed his ear against the door, straining to hear what they were saying.

"Thanks for letting me come down here and spend some time with you Sarah. That upper floor spooks the hell out of me. I hate working nights up there. I'm just glad they aren't capable of leaving their rooms."

"It's okay Dee. We've all had to do our time with the freaks," stated Sarah.

"I just don't understand why we are not allowed to enter their rooms. Why do they sound like they are in so much pain when the doctors are present? I am a nurse. I became one to care for people. Up there I am nothing more than...well, a guard if I'm being honest." The unknown nurses voice was filled with vexation.

"Just do your time, ask no questions and never enter any

of the rooms Dee. You will soon be reallocated to this floor. Nobody works up there for very long," replied Sarah.

"I hope so. I'll have a quick cuppa and then go back to listen to their screams and groaning," the nurse responded. She was obviously not enthralled by the idea of returning to her post.

"Put your earphones in and listen to some music. That's what I used to do. You can't help them, so you may as well try to block them out of your head," said Sarah.

"Yeah, I'll try that, thanks Sarah. I'll put the kettle on."

Grant walked to his bed and sat down. There was no alternative. He had to try to do what Jim had asked him to do. After what he had just overheard, it was essential he access the floor above. Grant knew that this undertaking tonight would be too risky. He reclined on the bed and placed his head on the pillow. Sleep did not come readily that night.

—————— ——————

For the next three days, Grant continued with his normal regime. He worked hard in his physio sessions, but his mind was focussed elsewhere. The nights were frustrating, as Sarah never left the second floor other than to make a coffee, toilet visits and the occasional visit to a patient's room. Grant studied her habits and movements, through hours of intense listening through his door.

Her customary use of headphones had obviously continued, following her transfer from the "freak ward" to the second floor. Occasionally, Grant would hear her singing along to whatever song she was listening to and she was clearly a big fan of Cher and the song, "If I Could Turn Back Time," which was frequently listened to.

As Grant reached the end of the fifth week, after rousing

from his medical coma and the beginning of his fifth month of being a *guest* at the Bloom Institute, he was awarded a break in the form of a shift change.

Sarah popped into his room one morning to say that she wouldn't see him for a week, as she was finishing her cycle of night shifts and now had five days off.

"Okay," said Grant. "Thanks for letting me know. You got anything planned?"

"Let my hair down, party and forget about you lot," replied Sarah, with a big happy grin across her face.

"Thanks," said Grant. "I'll miss you, too. So who are you handing my care over to?"

"A nurse named Wendy is on for the next week, an elderly lady. Not as attentive as me, but at least you won't be disturbed by regular nightly checks," replied Sarah, smiling to reveal her jocular nature.

"Well, in case I'm not here by the time you return to work, thanks for everything Sarah," said Grant, genuinely grateful for the kindness she had shown him.

"Oh, you'll still be here, trust me. You're not ready to leave yet," she countered, in a matter of fact tone. She left his room and Grant reached into the pocket of his shorts pulling out the guitar pick. "We'll see about that," he uttered.

He placed the pick back into his pocket, crossed his arms behind his head and rested upon them, humming the tune to "If I Could Turn Back Time." He bloody hated that song, but couldn't get it out of his head.

For the next two nights, Grant followed the new night nurse's pattern. He had it worked out by the first night, but wanted to double check to ensure his first thoughts were flawless. The second night served as confirmation that they were. Wendy was an older nurse, nearing the end of her working career. She was just pleased to be earning such a strangely high salary for her job.

Simultaneously, it had become clear to her that working nights in this place was a doddle. Nobody checked on her; she worked, and was free to as she pleased. For Wendy, this didn't involve working too hard. It also included getting her head down for a couple of hours during every night shift.

After the second night when Pete turned up to take Grant to his physio session, he feigned feeling a bit off-colour. He asked Pete to return that afternoon, which he did. The change from a morning to an afternoon training session allowed Grant to place the guitar pick into place later in the day, giving it less of a chance being of discovered. On this occasion, he also placed the sticky physio tape over the fingerprint pad.

The perfect opportunity presented itself when Pete stopped to have a quick chat with a pretty new nurse. Possibly the one he had overheard talking to Sarah a few nights earlier. Grant sat in his room for the next few hours, fearing his little additions to the security devices would be discovered. At eight, he heard the familiar voice of Wendy completing her hand over from the day staff.

He relaxed in the strong belief that he had evaded being caught yet again. The trust in the building's security, combined with staff complacency, had allowed him to get around the high-tech security devices with considerable ease and very basic materials. Grant knew that tonight was the night he had to make more of a dent into this organisation's electronic systems. He didn't have faith in his run of luck lasting much longer.

After hearing the day nurse saying her goodbyes, Grant

settled himself down on his bed and waited. He knew that Wendy would now be logging herself onto the hospital's computer system. She would then complete her one and only check on the patients. This did not include entering the rooms or checking the doors. She simply walked the length of the corridor. As long as everything was quiet, she ended her patrol at the kitchen, where she made herself a cup of coffee or tea. Grant wasn't sure which.

For the following two hours or so, she would play computer card games. Around 11 p.m., it was time for her nightly nap ,which lasted between two and three hours.

Grant lay and waited. Each minute dragging by. Every hour seeming like an eternity. The hour hand of his wall clock eventually clicked into place, indicating it was eleven in the evening. He made his way to the door and pulled it open a centimetre of a gap, for which to glance through. Wendy was still sat at the computer screen. He lingered, glancing occasionally back toward the clock. Finally at 11:06 p.m., Wendy stood up, stretched her short stubby arms skywards and made her way out of the nurses' station and toward the staff restroom.

It was time. He slipped out of the door and, stooping down slightly, made his way to the curved semi-circular shaped nurses' station. He hid below the level of the desk. Raising his head slightly above the desktop, he looked toward the staff restroom. To his horror, he saw the elderly nurse walking back toward the nurses' station. Working hard to control the blind panic that was threatening to overcome him, Grant cleared his mind and focused.

The workstation's desk had a wooden drop front, which followed the curve of the desktop. One gap which allowed the user to sit in front of the PC and pull the chair closer, was the only exception. Grant scrambled through the small gap and found it hollow behind the wooden frontage. He pulled him self inside and hid away just, as Wendy sat back down in front of the PC.

"Now where was I?" Grant heard her quietly ask herself.

Cramped beneath the tight space of the desk in the tightest of places, Grant felt the pain building up in his back and down his legs. Meanwhile, the nurse finished off her game of solitaire on the computer.

About five minutes later, which to Grant and his ailing back felt much longer, he heard her exclaim:

"Beat you, you little bastard."

Standing back up, Wendy made her way to the restroom. She began to make herself comfortable on the elongated sofa that stretched itself along the longest wall of the room. Grant crawled out of the space under the desk, biting his lip to stop himself from squealing. The multiple stabs of pain all round the thoracic and lumbar areas of his spine were untennable.

Crawling out on all fours, he turned himself over and lay on the hard floor on his back and stretched out his spine and back muscles. *Should Wendy return now, he was fucked,* he thought. At that moment, he couldn't have cared less. He lay in this position for around ten minutes, waiting for the pain to abate. Eventually, he raised his head above the desktop. He was relieved to see that the restroom door had been pushed forward until it was almost fully closed. The light had been turned off.

He slid silently into the chair and shuffled it forward on its plastic casters to bring him closer to the PC. This allowed him also to be slightly more hidden behind the computer screen. The screen remained lit up, indicating that the nurse had not logged off or locked it. As Grant studied the screen, looking at the different files dotted around the desktop, he noticed a small black box with a fingertip shaped indent in the middle of it. A cable fed itself from the back of this box to the computers hard drive.

It took him several minutes to find a folder titled "Security Systems." Upon opening it, a selection of other files appeared on the screen. One of them read "New User–Fingerprint Recognition." He opened it. A grey box appeared in the middle of the screen asking him to enter the administrator's password.

"Shit," he whispered to himself.

In an act of amateurish desperation, he typed in the word "fingerprint." He received the warranted response, "password not recognised." Grant halted and contemplated his conundrum further. He had to assume that the nurse currently sneaking in an unauthorised nap would never have been granted administration rights. The responsible nurse for which he had some respect would be the candidate for that level of respect and trust from an organisation level. He had seen Sarah supporting and mentoring new nursing staff for a while. On the back of that he struck the keyboard five times, "Sarah." The same response appeared on the screen.

He searched the murky depths of his brain for any clues. What conversations and observations had he experienced with this member of staff? He recalled the last conversation with her, remembering her divulging that she was going to "let her hair down." Maybe she was just simply a party girl. He slowly typed in the letters p-a-r-t-y. A split second before hitting the enter key, he stopped himself and held down the backspace keyuntil his last entry attempt had disappeared. Repeating his last entry he capitalised the first letter, "Sarah." Surely it couldn't be this. Closing his eyes he pressed the entry key.

Opening just one eye, he was surprised and elated to see that the screen imaging had changed. He was now being instructed to "instruct new user to place right thumb on scanner." He positioned his right thumb on the fingerprint reader. An orange ray of light scanned across the underside of his digit. The systems instructions asked him to do the same with his left thumb. He did, and once again the orange light did its stuff. Finally, the screen issued the instruction, "enter username." He paused and gave this part of the process some thought, recalling his physio mentioned not having access to the upper levels., which was the level of access he wanted. He typed in the name "Martin Stanridge" and the screen issued its next instruction box. "Dr. M. Stanridge is an existing user–do you wish to update records?"

Two boxes, one containing the word "Yes," and the other the word "No," were displayed. Grant moved the mouse and placed the cursor over the "Yes" box. He clicked the left mouse button. The screen turned black and for a few seconds nothing happened. Grant instinctively held his breath, staring at the screen, fully expecting something dramatic to occur, like the system shutting down or alarms going off all around the building. The screen lit up white again. A grey text box appeared in the middle stating, "User Record Updated."

Grant let out a long sigh of relief. He quickly returned the computer to its original state. Pushing the chair slowly backward, he stood up and advanced down the corridor toward the area of the lift.

As he passed the first room on his right, he heard Jim's familiar voice. The patient he had spoken to a few nights earlier, whispered "Grant, have you done it? Let me out."

Grant immediately approached the door and whispered back, "Shh, you'll wake up the sleeping dragon. I'll be back soon."

He didn't wait to hear the response. There was too much to do and probably nowhere near the time required to do it. Reaching the lift doors, Grant took a deep breath and placed his thumb against the security finger pad. He watched it turn green. The doors silently slid open in front of him.

He took a step away from the doors; their instantaneous movement had taken him by surprise. For some reason, Grant had assumed that he would have to wait for the lift to make its way to his floor. Thinking about it, the last person to have probably used the lift would have been the night duty nurse. He entered the lift, turning to face the empty corridor outside of the open doors, he looked down at the numbered buttons. Above them was the fingerprint pad, which he placed his thumb against. The doors began to close. All the buttons lit up a dull yellow. *Access all areas*, thought Grant to himself. Something as a rock fan, he had always desired but never achieved.

He pressed the button that would take the lift to the third floor. It moved silently upwards to the floor that Grant had been informed was the administration level. The lift came to a subtle halt. Grant waited for the doors to open. Remembering the security systems, he pressed his thumb against the fingerprint reader.

The doors slid open and Grant glanced out looking quickly left and right, only to find a corridor very similar to that which he had left just moments before. This one had fewer doors on either side. He walked out of the lift and toward the first door that stood opposite him, slightly off toward the left. Happy that this floor appeared to be empty, he looked at the door's name plate and was disappointed to read that it stated, "Surgical Administration."

He headed down the corridor, discovering that every door had an identical name plate. He walked past the "Stationary," "Cleaning Products," "Tina Aulton–Administration Manager" and finally "Dr. M.D. Stanridge–Senior Surgical Consultant," where he now stood. He could see a sign ahead of him, a sign attached to the ceiling. A printed upwards arrow was accompanied with the words "Surgical Theatres." Farther down the corridor were closed double doors. Grant assumed this was where the operating theatres were subsequently located.

Very much like any hospital, he thought, *just not as many doctors*!

It appeared to Grant that Pete had not been misleading him. Barring the operating theatres, this floor seemed to be exactly what he had said it was—an administration level. He walked back to the lift. The doors remained open and Grant realised that he had forgotten to use his thumb to close the doors behind him. He wondered if this meant that the lift could not be called from the other levels. He made a mental note to himself not to commit such a schoolboy error again.

He entered the lift and placed his thumb onto the pad. Once the doors had closed, he pressed the subtly lit number four button. Opening the doors once the lift arrived at what would seem to be the top floor of the building, Grant immediately sensed a difference about this level. It smelled more surgical, more like a hospital. Also, it somehow felt different. He walked into the corridor. He was immediately hit by the lower level of light. Other than that, it appeared to be laid out exactly like the floor where he resided.

He walked slowly down the corridor observing each door. It occurred to him the frosted glass panels were absent. Instead, in each small hinged door were observation panel covers, each with a keyhole in them, located at eye level. The other differences that Grant noticed were that the doors were not numbered. Unlike his own room door, nameplate slots presided. So far, he had witnessed what appeared to be cardboard or plastic nameplates slid into them. Making his way farther down the corridor, Grant was convinced he heard occasional noises emitting muffled indistinguishable sounds from behind some of the doors. For some unfathomable reason, he felt afraid. He noticed that the hairs on his arms were standing up and he felt a chill all over his body.

In the distance, Grant could just make out an identical nurses' station to the one on his floor and made his way toward it. He could see that the station was unmanned. As he got closer, he wondered if whoever was in charge was also having an unauthorised sleep. Constantly looking in every direction, Grant cautiously made his way to the station and stood in front of the lit-up computer screen.

The screen glowed in contrast to the badly lit area. The screen display had a blue background and above a logo he did not recognise, were the words "The Bloom Institute—excellence and discretion in all that we do." He grabbed the mouse and as he moved it, a voice made him jump backward away from the computer. The surprise and fear made him move so far back that he slammed into the wall behind him.

"Hello Grant. As resourceful as we hoped you were."

Grant looked over to his left and saw a shadowy figure, arms crossed, leaning casually against the wall. He could not make out the man's face, but he had instantly recognised the voice of the stranger who had visited him twice before.

Recovering from the initial shock, Grant asked the question, "Do I get answers now?"

The man, prone against the wall, uncrossed his arms and stretched out his right arm, the hand of which found a wall switch. He pressed it, increasing the dull lighting of the floor.

"I suppose you have now earned that right," he replied. "Come Grant, walk with me and let me explain the work that we do."

The stranger pushed himself away from the wall and began to walk toward the corridor from which Grant had moments earlier emerged. Grant followed the man, keeping a few feet between the two of them, just in case he needed a bit of reaction time.

"Do I get to know your name?" asked Grant.

"Certainly," said the stranger, "you can call me Fox."

"Oooh intriguing, animal codenames," replied Grant sarcastically.

"Not at all Grant. My surname is Fox and everyone addresses me as just that," responded Fox, with no hint of a reaction toward Grant's sarcastic tone.

Fox by now had reached the end of the corridor. He came to a stop just before reaching the lift. Grant noticed that once more he had left the lift doors open. He shook his head in disbelief at his stupidity.

"So, what is it exactly that you and your organisation do?" he asked.

"Well...," began Fox, "we bring about a balance of justice against wrongdoings. To put it simply, we address a wrong that has been committed against our clients. Clients, which may I add, pay a hefty price to ensure that justice is served."

"Saviours of the world, eh?" The acrimony was once again very noticeable in Grant's response. "As long as the world has the money to be saved," he added.

"Grant, with justice comes a price. You of all people know this. That price may well be a life, a change of lifestyle, a drastic change in a person's attitude or indeed a financial price," said Fox, the tone of his voice not faltering once.

"So no justice for the poor?" asked Grant.

"The poor receive the so-called justice that the law of our beautiful country provides. The people who we serve desire a justice that does not end up with the perpetrator of the wrongdoing being waited upon in what we laughably call prisons." Fox walked toward the first door that Grant had seen when he had walked out of the lift. "Let me show you an example of justice and our work."

Fox produced a small key attached to an extendable cord, which could be reeled out of a small circular metal holder attached to his belt. He used the key to unlock the observation panel cover in the door. Grant switched position to better see what was behind the panel. From his position, a few feet behind Fox, Grant saw a panel of thick toughened glass. There was a circular metal device in the middle of it and a small silver button a few inches to the right.

Fox pressed the button and a red light lit up to the right of the circular metal device. Grant stepped a pace or two closer. He recognised the metal insert as being similar to what was inlaid into the safety panels still used by some banks. It allowed the person on one side of the barrier to talk to the person on the other. The only difference with this one being that it could be activated or deactivated with the press of a button.

"Please Grant, come and take a look. I promise that I will not attempt to cause you any harm," said Fox. "Allow me to introduce you to Mr. Harry Cornwell."

Grant moved forward and stood adjacent to Fox. He looked through the thick glass into the room. The room contained only a hospital bed surrounded by two large pieces of medical equipment. Using tubes and wires, these machines were connected to a body laying on the bed. The body was that of a man who was violently shaking and twitching. Grant looked at the man's face and saw that it was one portraying immense pain.

"Who the fuck is Harry Cornwell and what the hell is happening to him?" asked Grant, now looking directly into Fox's face.

"Well," replied Fox, his facial expression emotionless, "Harry is an interesting character. In his previous life, he was the gardener to a rather well-off family. Over the two-year period of his employment, Harry sexually and physically abused the two children of the family who so kindly employed him and paid him an over the odds salary. He was an exceptional gardener by all accounts. However, he was a much better paedophile. The family did not suspect a thing until one day, their seven-year-old son, whose behaviour in school had been getting progressively worse, was called into his House Master's office, whereupon the House Master began to deliver a lecture to the young boy about his deteriorating behaviour. At one point in that lecture, the teacher asked the young man how he was going to demonstrate to him that his attitude and behaviour would improve. It was at this moment that Harry's little secret was discovered. The young lad asked his teacher if he sucked his dick would it mean he wouldn't be punished."

Grant, having listened intently to Fox's tale shrugged his shoulders and said:

"So okay, the police were called and this nonce was arrested. So, how and why did he end up here? What is this place? Some kind of mental institution?"

"No Grant, the police were not called. We were."

Grant looked confused. Upon seeing this, Fox continued to explain.

"You see, the House Master happens to work for us. He called us and we introduced ourselves to the family. We explained how we could be of service and what we could achieve for the right price, of course. We knew that this was easily affordable to the family. Once the alternative outcome of a comfortable life in prison for Harry was pointed out, the family, especially the father, was more than eager to pay the price for justice."

"And what is that justice?" asked Grant inquisitively, now quite intrigued.

"Nothing more and nothing less than what the client wants," replied Fox, matter of factly.

"All right, enough of your cryptic answers. I'm not a fan of fucking crosswords, so just answer the question." Grant had reached the point where Fox's game of "who is the clever bastard here," had gone beyond boring. It was now just plain infuriating.

"Well," responded the still, outwardly in control Fox, "let's take Harry for instance. Our clients, the parents of the children robbed of their innocence, wanted Harry to suffer for the rest of his existence. They wanted that existence to be lengthy. Our sexual deviant here spends his days, and nights, in a perpetual nightmare. A horror where children have the power over him. An ordeal in which he is continuously taunted by children who he cannot harm. Basically, he is in a state of permanent sexual frustration."

Grant stared at Fox, waiting for him to crack and break out in laughter and announce the punchline. The climax to the joke never came. Fox remained as composed as he had always been on every occasion that he had been in Grant's company.

"And how the hell is that possible?" asked Grant eventually.

"The institute that you are currently in the care of, the Bloom Institute, is a research facility. It is highly regarded within the medical and scientific world. Its research into the development of life-changing drugs and treatments is unrivalled by any other company in its field. It maintains a low profile, insisting on the highest level of confidentiality from the organisations it works both with and for. As well as the drugs that have been put into public and open scientific use, the Institute also works on other mind-altering and controlling drugs and techniques, such as the one you can see being used on Harry."

Fox stopped talking and for the first time the expression changed on his face. He smiled. "The doctor who saved your life is also one of the world's most intelligent medical researchers. He develops advanced drug technology, at the same time as being one of the craziest sociopaths you could ever wish to meet."

Grant stood silently outside of Harry Cornwell's room. He looked once more through the glass observation panel at a man who he should find despicable. Yet at the same time, Grant could not help but feel a small amount of pity for him.

"This is fucking sick," declared Grant. "Why not just kill the filthy bastard?"

"Because, Grant, that is not what the client wanted or indeed paid for and continues to pay for."

Grant could not believe what he was hearing, yet the evidence was apparent before his very own eyes.

"So what use do you have for me?" he asked. "I'm not a scientist."

"Not all of our clients require a level or type of justice warranting the involvement of the Bloom Institute and Dr. Stanridge. Some of our clients, for instance, just want to watch the individual die in front of their own eyes. Most of these requests crave the perpetrator suffers a violent death, and let's face it Grant, you have proved your ability to provide such a service and there is one other thing about you that, as an organisation of our type, we believe you have." Fox once again fell silent and waited for the inevitable question from Grant, who he found to be quite predictable. The question duly came.

"And what is that?"

"We believe that you possess the ability to scrutinise a situation such as, let's say, a crime scene or a criminal investigation in a non-institutional way. Putting it bluntly, you don't always stick to the recognised rules. You neglect to let the normal regard for moral or legal standards cloud your viewpoint," said Fox, like a man who had delivered this response on numerous occasions.

"A bit of a sociopath then?" said Grant.

Fox indicated with a sweeping arm movement that it was

time to move on.

"Now, the next competitor in the 'dork behind the door' challenge, you are going to love," stated Fox, repudiating Grants last question.

"Hey, if you want time alone to get your rocks off in the company of these freaks, I am quite happy to return to my room and leave you to it. It would appear their deviancy is rubbing off on you Fox," said Grant, now moving on from affirmed derision in the hope of getting a reaction out of this robot.

It worked, as Fox for the first time, showed a glimmer of emotion as he scowled at Grant. A look resembling anger flashed momentarily across his face.

"Fine," responded Fox, the anger apparent in his voice. "Why don't we discuss why we have recruited you and the job that we are interested in you taking on?"

Grant laughed at Fox.

"I haven't been recruited. I'm not interested in anything to do with you or this grotesque freak show set up," he retaliated. "How about I just tell you all to fuck off and take the first opportunity I find to get out of here."

"It will never happen Grant. You have no idea what hold we have over you," said Fox, in a menacingly confident tone.

"Well, how about I take my chances on a one-on-one with you, and if I get lucky I can just leave now." Grant moved his body position to emphasise the seriousness of his proposal.

Now it was Fox's turn to laugh. Once he had finished, he looked at Grant saying, "Three things wrong with that plan Grant. Firstly, I would probably kill you. Secondly, there are three members of our security team between you and the exit, any one of them capable of crushing you without a second thought." He paused again, waiting for Grant's response.

"You said three things," stated Grant.

"Oh well, now you will have to come with me. I have to show you the third reason." Without another word, Fox walked down the corridor back toward the nurses' station.

He stopped briefly to use the phone. Grant deduced that he was talking to the security staff when he said, "Yeah, it's Fox here. Go to the second-floor staff room and wake that useless skin carrier of a nurse and escort her from the building. Tell her that she's sacked and will never work anywhere as a nurse again. When you've done that, call in Katy. Tell her that she will get the usual short notice bonus." Placing the phone back into its cradle, Fox continued walking down the corridor.

"Come on Grant. Let's meet reason number three."

The Deal Clincher

Fox ambled farther down the corridor than Grant had managed to venture. After just a few metres, he came to a stop just before a door on the right-hand side and turned to face Grant.

"Before we see the last reason and the one that makes me so confident that you will work for us, I think I should tell you a little bit of history about us," he said to Grant.

"Oh fantastic, a freak show followed by a history lesson. If only my school had been this entertaining, I may have attended more often," retaliated Grant, feigning indifference. He was, however, eager to hear more about this organisation.

"Back in the early 1980s, the world appeared to be fairly settled. The Cold War was over, the peace plan with the IRA was already secretly being discussed and agreed. The Falklands War had united the British people, whilst telling the world not to fuck with us, even over a piece of worthless rock in the middle of God knows fucking where, but at home things were not all beach, barbeque and beer. Crime was at crisis levels, including all levels of crime and especially violent crimes. This increase meant that, of course, there was more chance of the rich, famous and powerful being personally affected by it," Fox paused for effect. Having seen Grant's blank reaction, he continued.

"In 1984, a very powerful businessman, who had a huge amount of influence over the government at the time, had his daughter kidnapped, tortured and murdered. He insisted that there was to be no police involvement. Using his influence, he spoke to a member of the cabinet, who happened to be a personal friend. This MP formed a small working group. Soon after, our organisation was assembled. At that stage, there were just six of us, all serving members of the armed forces, and more importantly, all problem cases for the military. We were mavericks. We refused to be treated as just another number by the military. We had all played an enthusiastic part in the shoot-to-kill policy in Northern Ireland. The military was chuffed as fuck to be able to remove us from their books." Fox paused again, but this time he went quiet to reflect on his own memories of those days. Grant watched the man as in the depths of his thoughts, a smile appeared on his face.

"They were crazy days, months even. We were an instant success. We found the kidnapper and took him to a secret location, a military location may I add. The father of the victim was invited to meet the man who had killed his daughter. He instructed us to hold the man down, which we did. He then beat the man to death with his bare hands. He broke all of his knuckles doing it, too. Finally, when the kidnapper lay dead on the floor, he kicked and stamped his balls to a mush. When it was all over, he shook the hands of each and every one of us. Apparently, he reported back to his friend in government and insisted that 'The Revenge Squad' should be kept operational."

"The Revenge Squad, really?" asked Grant, a look of scorn on his face.

"His nickname, not ours," replied Fox. "We didn't care what we were called, we were just happy to be providing a service that we thought worthwhile without having the constraints of the military holding us back. The political working group, comprising of four people secretly working without government knowledge with the exception of the then Prime Minister, gave their approval. With that Covert Operations Revenge Tactics was born. Over the past thirty years or so, we have dealt with hundreds of crimes and more notably, the perpetrators of those crimes, behind the scenes. Furthermore, neither the public, nor any government since, has had any awareness of this. The only thing we recieve from them is the finances, contacts and facilities. The only rule applied to us is that we work for those who can afford it, AND those who move in the right social, political or business circles to warrant receiving our services."

"As I said, a secret police force for the rich and famous," stipulated Grant.

"Well, actually we would rather not work for the famous. They can't be trusted to keep their mouths shut," replied Fox. It was clear that he personally had no time for celebrity clients from the tone of his voice and the look on his face.

"Right, come on then, disclose what is behind door number two," said Grant, becoming increasingly impatient with the self-indulgence of Fox.

Fox smiled.

"Ah well, this one is a doozy." Fox stepped aside so that Grant had a full view of the door. It was no different to any of the others.

"Recognise the name Grant?" asked Fox.

He stared at the nameplate and disbelief came across

Grant's' face, quickly followed by anger.

He turned toward Fox and in a flash he had grabbed him by the throat and forced him backward against the wall behind him.

"Is this some kind of sick joke?" shouted Grant.

His raised voice provoked a reaction from a small number of the "residents," some of whom began to yell out. Others simply groaned and moaned as if they had been awoken to yet again face some unknown agony or living hell.

"Answer me you piece of shit," demanded Grant.

Despite the pressure being applied to his larynx, Fox continued to smile. Grant's eyes were so focussed on the Fox's face, that he didn't notice Fox dip his hand behind the flap of his jacket and produce a gun from a rear lower back holster. It was only when the tip of the barrel was pressed against his forehead, that Grant acknowledged the weapon.

Grant released his grip slightly and the colour of Fox's face rapidly returned to its normal colour.

Fox's voice was slightly raspy as he addressed Grant. The gun's muzzle was still firmly pressed against his forehead.

"You ever do that again, my friend, and I promise you that the pain you will suffer will be prolonged and agonising." Fox rubbed his other hand over his throat, trying to ease the pain caused by Grant's tight grip.

"It can't be her. This is impossible. What the fuck is going on here?"

"Read the name Grant. It is her."

He looked once again at the nameplate, JULIA RICHARDSON. He was staring at his dead wife's name.

—————— ——————

On the floor below, two security guards in plain black uniforms were escorting the now very much awake nurse down the corridor, toward the lift. They did not speak a word as Wendy protested her innocence.

"I was just having a quick lay down. I had a headache you see...please tell me what is going to happen to me? Am I being sacked?"

So concerned was she with her own plight, she did not even notice that the first door in the corridor to her right was slightly ajar. It was not open enough for her to see the scene behind it. Jim's body lay on the floor, his necked snapped, his eyes bulging out of their sockets, an indication of the last horrors he experienced, as the two security men walked silently into his room. He knew that his fate was sealed before the larger of the two grabbed hold of his head and turned it sharply and violently to the right. He dropped instantly to the ground, free at last from the organisation that had been planning to keep him securely locked away in that room for the remainder of his life.

Wendy walked into the lift, through the already open doors, a burly and serious looking security agent standing each side of her. The one nearest to the control buttons closed the doors and pressed the button marked B.

"Why are we going to the basement?" Wendy asked them. The only response she received was silence

—————— ——————

"I don't believe my wife is in that room," muttered Grant, his voice quieter now.

Fox didn't say a word. Walking to the door, he once again

unlocked the observation panel door and stood to one side. Grant gazed through the toughened observation glass.

Lying on her side in the bed was a woman in her late forties, dark hair about shoulder length. Her eyes were closed, but Grant did not need to see them to know, that beneath those eyelids, were the softest brown eyes he had ever seen in his life. The last time he had seen his wife, she had been sporting blonde hair, in a bid to look younger and more fun, she had said. Over the past, nearly, eighteen months, her natural colour had returned. Grant placed both hands onto the sturdy door, on either side of the glass panel, and placed his forehead against the glass. A tear ran out of one eye as he whispered, "J."

"She can't hear you Grant, and she wouldn't know who you are," said Fox. For the first time a hint of emotion peppered his voice. It was as if he actually felt for this man who stood at the door looking at a woman, through tear-soaked eyes, he had believed to be dead.

"I want to speak to her," pleaded Grant.

"Pointless and impossible," replied Fox, the emotion gone once again. "She doesn't remember a thing or anyone since before *that night*. Her mind has locked itself away in the now. We are trying to help her, please believe that, with advanced drugs we hope to help her return to the person whom she once was with no recollection of the traumatic incident."

"She died," said Grant, turning now to face Fox. "I was told...the police...they told me, she died."

"Clearly not," replied Fox. "The police told you what they knew, what they had been told by our people, our hospital staff, our coroner's office people."

"There was a funeral. You couldn't fake that, I was there."

Grant looked back toward his wife, appearing to be sleeping so peacefully. A smile appeared on her face, fleeting and then gone.

"Our funeral directors," responded Fox. "When will you see that we can influence whatever we want whenever we need to?"

"She died, I buried her, you bastards." Grant's tears flowed once more.

"She nearly died Grant. Her mind as good as perished. We are fixing it and hopefully...," Grant interrupted him.

"My daughter?"

Fox did not even have the emotional capability or the respect just to lower his head. Looking directly at Grant, then replied.

"No, she is absolutely dead."

Externally, Grant didn't react to Fox's disdainful reply. Internally, another small piece of his heart disappeared.

"What now?" asked Grant.

"That bit is easy Grant. You now work for us," said Fox.

"What makes you think I can be of any use to you?" asked Grant. "I did what I did because I thought I had nothing to live for." Grant's voice and stance were that of a broken man.

"Yes," said Fox, once again his smile returning, "and imagine what you are capable of now that you have something to live for once again?"

Fox closed and locked the observation panel door and began to walk back down the corridor. Looking back over his shoulder he said, "Let's take a walk Grant, outside...I think a bit of fresh air is well overdue."

Grant placed one hand on the door of his wife's room. "I'll see you soon, babe," he whispered and reluctantly walked away, joining Fox.

They walked down the corridor in silence and stood by the lift doors. It took longer than usual to arrive on this occasion. The silence continued throughout the lift journey down to the lobby floor. The doors eventually opened, and Grant took his first glimpse of the "public" reception area of the building, which was plush, to say the least.

A curved reception desk stood about twenty feet from the lift. The rest of the area was filled with comfortable looking sofas and small square and rectangular shaped glass-topped tables. A huge sign on the wall announced a welcome to "The Bloom Institute for Medical and Scientific Research."

As they walked across the huge area, Grant nodded toward the writing on the wall, saying, "Misleading wouldn't you agree?"

"Not at all Grant. That is exactly what we do," replied Fox.

"And what about the rest of the stuff? I don't see you proudly announcing the work being done on the upper floor."

"Oil companies state quite correctly that they provide energy to the world. I don't ever remember hearing of one of them saying anything about killing wildlife and simultaneously destroying the environment," said Fox vehemently. "The work we do with our, let's call them guests, is in fact a form of medical and scientific research."

"Wrap it up how you like, you are still a bunch of murdering twats," replied Grant curtly.

"You won't get a reaction of guilt from me, if that is what you are searching for. Maybe Grant, it is your own feelings of guilt that are driving your anger," said Fox, purposefully poking a provocation stick at Grant.

Grant looked at Fox. The look on his face clearly demanding an explanation from Fox for that comment. He didn't remain disappointed as Fox, now standing still just before the exit doors of the building, said:

"I saw you at your wife's funeral. I saw the tears of loss and grief. We watched as your anger drove you to seek, and then hand out the revenge you needed and deserved. I have just seen your emotions flood out of you, seeing that your wife is still alive. But I ask you this: Is it love, anger or is guilt the driving force behind what you did? Let's get it out in the open, shall we?" Fox waited for a response, but only got the same blank look from Grant, and so he continued.

"Okay, we both know that on the night that your wife and daughter were brutally raped, violated and murdered, well your daughter at least for that final act of crime, you were sharing a bed in a cheap hotel room with a young and, may I add, very sexy work colleague who you had been having an affair with for several weeks."

Grant's face tensed with anger and both of his hands formed themselves into fists.

Fox simply nodded his head and lowered his eyes briefly to his right hand, which still held the gun he had earlier produced.

"What you going to do Grant? Punch me? Grab me by the throat again?" Fox then sneered. "Try to kill me?" He paused for a moment and then added, "Guilt is a fucking bitch, isn't she? Which is why I don't do guilt."

Grant relaxed his body and hands. He was beaten and literally outgunned.

"I could do with that fresh air," he said. "It stinks in here."

Fox turned to the door, reaching into the inside pocket of his jacket. He produced a plastic card, which he swiped through a card reader. He then pressed his thumb against yet another fingerprint recognition security device. Finally, he stood still facing a dark strip of plastic or glass which scanned his eyes. The doors clicked and silently fanned outwards. Grant felt the refreshing air hit his face and breathed it in deeply.

Outside, it was a dark and cloudy night. The air was predictably cold given it was the early hours of the morning. The well-maintained gardens were lit up by subtle lights hidden behind and within the shrubbery, plants, trees and rockery.

Grant walked relatively free around the outside of the building. He knew it was pointless trying to run. He guessed that Fox was a good shot and anyway, what was the point of escaping from a building and an organisation that held his wife as a hostage and patient? Fox gave him the freedom he thought he required, but remained alert and never more than a few metres from his charge.

"If, as you say, I am so wanted by this organisation because of my direct approach to dealing with problems, why aren't you worried that I will just try to take you on?" asked Grant suddenly.

"I never said I had no misgivings. I'm just not scared of you. I am always wary of you Grant. You can be unpredictable, sometimes I'm not convinced even you are aware of what your next move will be," replied Fox, slightly surprised at the question. "Take that question for example, I never expected that. A question about your wife...yes. A question about what we want you to do....absolutely."

Grant shrugged his shoulders and said, "Let's start with the latter."

"No problem. It's simple really. We have a target that we are having a problem tracking down. We need a new approach, your kind of approach. The type that looks at things with the untrained eye. One that will, hopefully, see what we have been unable to."

"What have you done with Wendy?" asked Grant out of the blue.

"You see, there you go again, the unpredictable, the unexpected question. That is what we need. She has been dealt with," replied Fox.

"You do know that when this is all over, I am going to kill you?" Grant turned to face Fox, hoping he would be able to see that he meant business.

Fox just smirked back at him. "You know, under any other circumstances, I think we could have a pint and a laugh in a pub Grant."

"Yeah, so that I could smash the pint glass and grind it into your face," replied Grant.

"It's good to see that you still have that desire to hurt people that you hate. Let's go back inside, and I will tell you more about this individual we need help finding. I promise you, by the time I have finished, you will be so repulsed by him you will want the job of finding him. Anyway, I need you to meet one more person before I return you to your room."

Fox walked back inside, stopping only to ensure that Grant walked through the doors first. He had meant it when he had told Grant that he was wary of him, and he had no intention of turning his back on him. Fox knew that Grant would have no problem carrying out his threat and would, given the opportunity, try to kill him.

Back inside, the first thing that Grant noticed was two large men dressed all in black, who sat behind the large reception desk. They had not been there when he and Fox had first arrived in the reception area. One of them stood as Fox walked into the building.

"Good morning, Mr. Fox. Is there anything you need?"

"Good morning, Kelly." Fox cast an eye at him, and then looked at the guard who had remained seated. "Morning Johnson." Johnson nodded his head but said nothing. *The silent type*, thought Grant.

"Could you fetch the Inserters file for me, Kelly? Bring it to me in the small meeting room, if you wouldn't mind please."

Grant made a barking noise under his breath and quietly said, "Go fetch, Butch."

Fox frowned at Grant.

"Please Grant, more respect if you don't mind. Mr. Kelly here could kill you so quickly, you wouldn't even know it had happened."

"His bollocks better be made out of marble then, because I would send them fuckers into orbit before he did it," sneered Grant, not looking at Fox. Instead, his gaze met that of the scowling security guard. He beamed at Kelly, a big childish smile. "Just a joke Kelly," he said.

The security guard made his way from the reception desk, following a circular path that disappeared behind the reception wall. He maintained his pace and did not react in any way when Grant added:

"I wouldn't kick them into orbit, I would tear them off and juggle with them."

Fox placed his hand lightly on the top of Grant's shoulder and guided him away from the security staff. They headed toward the other side of the reception area, toward a small office which they entered in silence. Fox closed the door behind them and invited Grant to take a seat.

The room was plushly yet sparsely furnished. Three comfortable looking chairs accompanied a table. A large plant was in the corner and there was a drinks machine, well a water dispenser, to be precise.

Fox sat in one of the chairs on the other side of the table from where Grant sat.

"Who or what is the Inserter?" asked Grant.

"All in good time." Before Fox could add any more, Kelly entered the room with a brown file, about two inches thick.

"Thank you Kelly. Would you arrange for a clean-up team to be called in? I want everything back to normal before Mr. Bloom arrives," Fox instructed the security man. Kelly nodded and left the room.

Grant leant forward upon hearing Fox mention Bloom, the man after which the Institute was named.

"Do I get to meet Bloom?" he asked.

"No Grant. Nobody gets to meet Mr. Bloom. He is here to meet with an important client. In fact, the one you will be indirectly working for. The client wants an update report and neither he, nor Mr. Bloom are going to be too pleased with the lack of progress. However, the news that you are now on board should improve the mood of both men."

Fox placed the file, which Kelly had handed to him, on the table and opened up the front cover. Inside, Grant could see a thick collection of paperwork, and from what he could see of a corner of one of the sheets, suggested there were possibly photographs, too.

"Let me tell you what we are dealing with," said Fox to Grant. "The Inserter is the nickname we have given to an individual, who we believe to be male. He is taking and killing young people. His style is unique in many ways. His targets do not appear to be connected in any way. There is no pattern to the timings of the snatching and killing of the victims that we have worked out at least. We have had two of the country's leading criminologists and our own expert profilers working on this case. Yet we are no further forward than we were from when it was handed to us."

"And when was that?" asked Grant, hankering to look at the file.

"Just over a week ago, when our perpetrator took the child of our client," responded Fox.

"He or she been found dead yet?" inquired Grant, still transfixed on the file like a child gazing at presents under a Christmas tree.

"Yes," said Fox.

Grant reached for the file and attempted to slide it over to his side of the table. Fox placed his hand firmly on the file, preventing Grant's attempts to access it.

"You read this file Grant and you are in! There is no way out until this person is caught and dealt with to the satisfaction of our client," said Fox firmly.

"You know I'm in. You have my wife, and to be honest, even if you didn't have that hold over me, I think you would kill me if I refused." Grant looked once again at the file and then at Fox, "So?"

Fox moved his hand and Grant slid it toward him and started to read its contents.

It took a while for Grant to read, or more accurately, critically scan through the documents. As he came across a photograph, he quickly turned it over and placed it to one side. Fox watched with interest at Grant's style of studying the information.

"The pictures too graphic for you Grant?" asked Fox, after about ten minutes of observing him making his way through the case file.

"Oh yeah! After what I did to a few members of the Crippens, you must have worked out that I am a very queasy person," reciprocated Grant immediately, regretting his typically contemptous response. Cynicism had always been ingrained in Grant's personality, much to the annoyance of his wife.

"Well, we did find evidence of you having vomited at some stage outside the building in the woods. You have not looked at one of those photographs yet. You can't blame me for being inquisitive." For once, Fox's response was less business-like, demonstrating a personal interest.

"I prefer to separate factual reports from explicit pictures, I find mixing the two can result in mixed emotions, which in turn, can complicate my thoughts," replied Grant, turning to the final document held within the file.

"Any initial thoughts?" Fox waited patiently for Grant's response.

"Plenty," replied Grant, "but none worthy of mention right now," he lied.

"Maybe you need some assistance," said the C.O.R.T. agent.

A light frown appeared on Grant's forehead and his eyes closed just very slightly, demonstrating his annoyance at this suggestion.

"I work alone, you should know that," he retorted.

"Really, do you?" replied Fox. "What about Ian, Murphy, Emma? Even Ordnance. They were all part of your last team."

"With the exception of Ian, the rest were just accidental inclusions," said Grant, annoyed by how much this man knew about him.

"So you accept that you don't actually work alone? Which is good." Fox stood up, walked toward the door and holding it open, waved his hand toward the reception area. "Bring the file with you, if you like. I am sure you will want to read it in more depth. Right now, let's go and meet your new team member."

Madness to Catch Evil

Grant followed Fox to the floor where they had met a few hours earlier. He remained subdued, deep in thought. In just a few hours, he had discovered that his once thought dead wife was alive. It was highly probable that he was directly responsible for the death of an innocent woman, due to his sneaking around the building and the information he had just briskly absorbed about a person who was clearly mad and murderous in a way that made him see that his innovative ways of extinguishing someone's life were fairly tame in comparison.

It had been immediately obvious why the killer had been given the nickname the Inserter. The first body to have been found was discovered on some waste ground in an area of London that Grant could not recall, because his skimming through the information had been so quick. The body, a young male, had been found with his lower abdomen and groin area eaten from the inside out. Medical examinations revealed that the victim had been cut open whilst alive, presumably under some kind of anaesthesia. A live rat had then been inserted into the stomach cavity. The body had been sewn up. It is then believed that the victim died from the horrific effects of the rat eating his way out of the man's body. The post-mortem indicated that this had occured whilst the victim was awake and not in receipt of any painkillers. Grant could only imagine that the death was prolonged and agonising.

There was no other evidence of any torture or other physical brutality having taken place. In fact, the only other findings were that the victim's nails and fingers were torn and cut. This suggested an attempt to possibly break open something wooden. And finally, that those same fingers and nails were covered in particles of the victim's own flesh and blood. It would seem that as the rat eventually began to break through the upper flesh and skin of the victim, and he had himself assisted the rat's escape by tearing open his own body. One of the strangest findings that Grant could recount from the medical report was that, for some reason they mentioned, through DNA findings from rat saliva and hair had proved, the rat to be female.

At some point after death and before dumping the body, the killer had stapled a small piece of paper to the ripped flesh of the young man. The words on the note were clearly defined in Grant's memory bank. This was one of a couple of facts in the report he had read several times. In tiny scrawled handwriting the note read:

> ***And our adversaries said, They shall not know, neither see, till we come***
> ***In the midst among them, and slay them, and cause the work to cease.***
> ***For now they will not grow in numbers, but dwindle to nothing forever.***

During a tedious period of Grant's army life, he had spent

three months in the back of a vehicle box body, maintaining and monitoring equipment that sent out signals to block the attempts of the IRA to set off bombs using mobile phones to detonate them. Over those very lonely solitary months, Grant recalled doing only two things: Reading a lot and masturbating. One of the books he read was the Bible, and that is why he recognised the words as being from Nehemiah.

The second body to be found was that of the client's daughter. It was discovered floating in a canal a few miles from where the first body had been discovered. It seemed to Grant that this was the point at which the organisation had become involved. It had ensured that the two murders were not connected. The press had reported that the poor girl had died by drowning, following a night out partying with friends. It had made in all the national papers, which was to be expected, considering that the girl was the daughter of an MP in the current British government. Grant was led to conclude that it was this person who was the client Bloom would be meeting later that morning.

This second victim had been alive and, it was thought, conscious when the killer inserted a human penis deep inside her vaginal cavity, so deep that the tip of it was touching the bottom of her womb. The insertion had caused so much internal trauma and bleeding, that the victim had *simply* bled to death. The young girl had been found with a long-handled metal hook in her hand, which had been curled around the metal handle and held into place with thick black tape. Neither the medical team, nor any other members of the organisation's investigation team, were able to comprehend the significance of this.

Another note in the same tiny handwriting had been found

rolled up and wrapped in a condom inside the girl's vagina. It read:

> ***And Adam said. This is now bone of my bones, and flesh of my flesh: she shall be called Woman, because she was taken out of man.***
> ***Therefore shall a man leave his father and his mother, and shall cleave unto his wife: and they shall***
> ***Forever more be of one flesh***

Grant knew, and assumed that many others would also recognise, that these words were from Genesis.

"Two things before you introduce me to my new partner," said Grant, seconds after Fox had pressed the lift button to the fourth floor.

"Go," replied Fox.

"Firstly, I want to go back to my room and study this file in more depth. Secondly, I want to speak with Jim," said Grant.

Fox looked at him for a second or two. "No problem with regards to your first request. As for the second, sorry Jim is no longer with us. He was discharged a short while ago."

"Discharged?"asked Grant quizzically.

Fox nodded his head, and as quick as a flash, Grant hit the red emergency stop button. The lift halted with a shudder and slight sideways movement.

"Define discharged," demanded Grant.

"Let go, released, disappeared," retorted an emotionless Fox. His ability to give nothing away with facial expressions impressed Grant.

"Killed?" challenged Grant.

Fox did not reply, verbally or visually.

"Back to reception, now, and don't argue," said Grant. Fox could see that the man was in no mood to be argued with. Pushing his luck, Fox asked what the reason for this was.

"Forgot my manners," said Grant, with a rye smile.

Fox pressed the button labelled L, and the lift began its journey back to the lobby. Grant pressed the button to open the doors, but nothing happened.

"We corrected your access rights back to, go nowhere," explained Fox, pressing the button himself.

Grant walked out of the lift and headed toward the reception desk, where the two security guards were sat. Both stood as Grant approached and both looked as surprised as each other, as Grant walked around the reception desk, directly toward Kelly, and offered to shake the security man's hand.

"I think we got off on the wrong foot mate," he said to the guard who in turn held out his own hand, whilst giving Grant a smug look.

Grant grabbed his hand and immediately tightened the grip and dug his thumb into the small indent at the base of the security guard's thumb, pressing downwards and inwards.

Kelly released a sharp breath and a noise that sounded like *aaargh* emerged from his body. He dropped to one knee in front of Grant, who applied more pressure to the security guard's wrist to increase the level of pain.

"This is for Jim," he said, looking down at Kelly's pain stricken face. "The next time we meet, you will end up sporting a bruise three inches up inside your arsehole, just about at the point where the tip of my boot ends, you little fuck."

Kelly tried to stand, but was forced back to his knees. The

slightest amount of pressure applied, resulted in Kelly being prostrate on his back. He applied even more pressure to the base of his thumb and seconds later, he was flat on his back with a split lip caused by the punch he received from Grant.

Grant let go of the floored security man's hand and walked away. When passing the other security guard, he slapped him on the shoulder saying:

"He'll probably need an ice pack for that, or you could kiss it better for him." Grant puckered his lips and made two squeaking noises imitating kisses, and then walked back to the lift.

"Back to my boudoir please," said Grant to Fox. "And remember this: If you ever feel the need to discharge me, come and do it yourself."

Fox let Grant out of the lift and allowed him to walk alone down the corridor toward his room.

"Your door has been wedged open," he called after him. "When you are ready, go to the nurses' station and call 400. I will come back down to get you."

Grant simply waved his hand in the air to acknowledge that he had heard him, and continued walking toward his room. He laid down on his bed and opened the file, letting out a huge sigh and pictured his wife's face. "This is for you, darling," he whispered and began to read.

———— ————

On the floor above, Fox had disembarked from the lift and made his way down the corridor to the very last room., one which was just a bit farther on from Julia Richardson's room and on the opposite side. He slid open the observation panel door and pressed the button to allow a conversation to take place.

A shadowy figure sat on the bed inside the room, his back to the door.

"Doesn't want to see me I guess?" the raspy, gravelly voice of the occupant enquired.

"He will be up soon. He wants to get up to speed with the details of the case first," responded Fox.

"Does he know it's me that he will be working with?" the man inside the room asked.

"No, not yet," Fox answered. "And you will not be working with him. You will merely be advising and offering your, shall we say, expert opinion."

The man turned to face the door. The moonlight shining through the high window caused his bald head to illuminate. His dark goatee helped Fox notice that the man was smiling as he replied, "He won't see it that way."

------ ------

In his room, Grant read and re-read the case file for just short of two hours. He studied the very graphic crime scene and autopsy photographs, which only confirmed what the written words told him.

From the information in the file, he was certain that the murderer must have at least some medical knowledge and/or training. The sutures on the male victim were neat. It was as if the killer had almost taken pride in his work. From the autopsy report, Grant had learned that the positioning of the rat had been no accident. It had been placed in the perfect place to allow the animal to successfully escape from its human prison.

Details of the two victims were sparse, largely ascertained from interviews with their family members and a few friends. The only connection that Grant could make, was that both had been described as being distant and withdrawn. The two recently changed their circle of friends and both had been described by their sets of parents as rebellious before suddenly deciding to leave home and move to either live with friends or to their own place.

The 22-year-old male victim had been living with his parents in Kent. He had no criminal record. There had been no social services involvement during his life, and no evidence of drug or alcohol dependency.

Similarly, the female victim, daughter of the organisation's client, was age 23, had resided in London in, as expected, a quite exclusive area, but had decided to move to Kentish Town to bunk up with a couple of friends. The autopsy divulged cannabis use, but no other traces of drugs were found in her body.

After finally deciding that he had deduced all that he could from the reports, Grant dropped the folder onto the floor and laid his head on the pillow. *Questions,* he thought to himself.

Firstly, what about the third victim?

Secondly, no trace of any drugs, other than the cannabis, was found in either of the victims. What did the killer use as anaesthesia? Surely he could not have performed these vile acts on a conscious victim.

Third and last, what was he missing? Where was the connection? Serial killers always seemed to select their victims because of similar traits. Their background and upbringing could not have been more different. They were of similar age. Their recent behaviour had coincided, but was not abnormal for people in their early twenties, thought Grant.

The hook taped to the girl's hand confused Grant. There had been no weapon or tool found in the possession of the male victim. The only tangible similarity started and ended with the method of killing, or to be more accurate, within the killing process. Both bodies had something embeded within them.

It was time to call Fox and meet this mysterious person he was expected to work with, maybe they had some answers to his questions. Grant made his way to the nurses' station, which was still without a nurse in place, and picked up the phone and dialled 400, as Fox had instructed. The call was answered after just two short rings. Fox's familiar voice spoke quietly.

"On my way down." He ended the call without a further word. Grant placed the phone's receiver into its cradle, convinced that he had heard a voice in the background. Distorted yet still distinguishable, saying, "tell him."

Fox was angry with himself for forgetting to switch off the microphone system on the patient's door. He returned to the man once more. Again facing away from the door.

"Mortimer, you ever speak again without permission, the pain that you have suffered so far during your short stay will seem pleasurable," said Fox angrily.

The man stood and raised his arms, holding them out away from his body, so that they were parallel to the ground.

"You cannot hurt me. The pain that I have suffered in the name of my master, has long prepared me for any earthly pain you can administer." Mortimer did not look toward the door as he spoke his words.

"Fuck you freak, just shut the fuck up until I tell you to speak," screamed Fox. He walked toward the lift, this time leaving the microphone switched on intentionally.

Grant stood by the lift doors as they opened. He walked in, turned around to face the doors and waited for them to close. As the lift ascended yet again to the floor above, he glanced toward Fox.

"Tell me what?" Grant asked.

Fox looked him, appearing confused.

"No idea what you are on about Grant."

"Do you have to believe that your words are true to be able to lie so well?" Grant asked him.

The lift came to a stop, which gave Fox the reason he needed not to continue the conversation Opening the doors, he stepped out and said to Grant:

"Come with me. I will introduce you to the person with whom you will be collaborating with on the case."

Grant followed Fox, perplexed as to his use of the word "collaborating." His bewilderment continued as he watched Fox walk past the nurses' station and toward the last door on the left side of the corridor. He had expected to be meeting up with another agent waiting at the station or maybe in one of the staff areas.

"Where are we going Fox?"

The agent stopped beside the door and beckoned Grant toward it. Grant slowly sauntered forward, looking briefly to this right as he walked past the door of the room where his wife slept peacefully.

"I would like you to meet Mortimer Church, the person who will be assisting you as and when required." Fox stepped away from the door so that Grant had plenty of space to look inside the room.

Mortimer Church was once again sat on the bed. A voice, slightly distorted by the communication system, the voice that Grant had heard just minutes ago, spoke.

"Hello, Grant."

Grant had heard this voice before, not just a few minutes ago, but way before that, but he couldn't quite place it. He looked at Fox.

"Who the hell is Mortimer Church?"

The man inside the room stood and slowly began to turn toward the door. As he did, he spoke and the words sent a chill of horror through Grant's body.

"There is no need for such formality Grant." As before, the man held out his arms, "call me The Priest."

------ ------

It was 3:10 a.m. The narrow alleyway only served to give the impression that the night was pitch black. The wall at the end of the alleyway was the back wall of a local flower shop. The man pushing the wooden cross down the narrow space stopped suddenly. He listened intently, waiting for the noise he had heard, or perceived to have, sound again.

It was five minutes before he moved, slowly continuing to push the cross. Beneath the head of the cross was a tiny wheel, propelling the full sized cross smoothly, despite the dead weight of the body secured to it. The preparation for this macabre scene had been completed the evening before in what he lovingly called his "Church of Change."

The dark van parked on the road, just metres away from the entrance to the alleyway, that had enabled him to transport the cross the short distance from his area of preparation, stood silently where he had parked it. All the maker's marks had been removed, the distinctive Mercedes badges and the model decals no longer a part of the vehicle. The number plates were the originals and had not been tampered with. The reasoning being that false or altered plates would only arouse police suspicion, should he ever be stopped for some minor traffic offence.

Of more importance, was the fact that the man was extremely confident that he would never be caught. He was protected by the higher power for who he was doing the work. He was dressed completely in black clothing, similar to that worn by surgeons in theatre, including the surgical head cover and mask. These last two items had been donned once he had entered the protection of the alleyway. On his hands, he wore two pairs of black surgical gloves.

The body of a young man was secured to the cross by two large nails through his wrists and one through his feet, which had been crossed one over the other. The unusual thing was that before securing the feet, the killer had wrapped his victim's legs and feet around the cross, so that the feet were secured to the reverse side of it, the nail entering through the soles.

He reached the end of the alleyway, and with immense effort, stood the cross upright yet upside down, so that the victim's head was closest to the ground. He had practised this several times before, so that he knew he had the strength to do it, and also so that the body was well secured to the cross. The evidence of these previous attempts was evident all over the victim's body. Blood trails ran from the dead man's groin, down over his stomach and chest, streaming down and around his neck and shoulders, ending under his chin. A few dried blood drops sat on the underside of his nose and his forehead. The blood was the result of the man's penis having been hacked off, and the last thing this unfortunate victim watched as he slowly bled to death, was his own penis being forcibly placed inside the vagina of a screaming young woman.

The perpetrator of these horrendous rituals reached into the waistband of his elasticated trousers. He removed a small wooden wedge, which he placed under the base of the cross to hold it in place. He stood back and admired his work. As he bowed his head, he whispered:

"In thy name Lord, I send thee another who has changed from the path of deviation."

He walked back down the alley. Just before entering into the street, he removed the surgical head cover and mask and then the gloves, folding the latter around the first two items.

Climbing into the van, which he had left unlocked to prevent attracting unwanted attention as the indicator lights flashed on and off in the locking and unlocking process. He placed the rolled up gloves into a small orange medical waste bag, which he retrieved from under the driver's seat and quickly returned it to the same place. Along with his surgical scrubs, they were to be disposed of when he arrived back to his secret lair.

Starting the engine, he quietly and slowly proceeded down the empty road, turning left at the junction onto the main road. He glanced toward the hospital building as he left it behind him and nodded his head in its direction, whispering once more, "Save the unblemished children and waste those who wear the marks of sin."

He disappeared into the early morning duskiness, his mind now focused on his next mission for the Lord.

―――――― ――――――

Grant stared into the room at the smiling face of his old adversary. He closed his eyes in the hope that when they next opened, the abomination he was faced with had proved to be just a figment of his imagination or, even better, a terrible nightmare. He opened his eyes, only to find the Priest still standing there. His smile had diminished and his arms were now down by the side of his body.

"How are you doing?" asked Mortimer.

"Fuck off," riposted Grant, pointing his finger toward the Crippens president for emphasis. Snapping his head in the direction of Fox, he said, "You must be fucking joking me."

"Finding out that your wife is still alive was no joke, and neither is this Grant," answered Fox. "We believe that Mortimer will be able to give you an insight into our killer's mind that nobody else is capable of."

"Call me The Priest," whispered Mortimer from inside his room.

"One more word Mortimer and I will kill you myself," said Fox savagely. "You are not a Priest. You are nothing more than a majorly fucked up mental case who has no respect for anything or anybody."

"I bet he has esteem for your elusive killer," stated Grant sharply.

"How wrong you are Grant," said Mortimer, ignoring Fox's threat. "I hold him in no more regard than I do you. He works for a different master than I."

Grant ignored the man inside the room. Walking away from the door, he leant against the opposite wall and once again looked at Fox.

"I am not working with that...," Grant struggled to find a suitable word settling on "thing."

"No problem," replied Fox, his response surprising Grant, until he added, "so take one last look at your wife and I will return you to your room. Who knows, we may even consider moving you to this floor. See if we can help you with that troubled mind of yours."

Grant walked toward Mortimer Church's room again and pressed the button shutting off the communication system.

"What happens to him when the job is done?"asked Grant.

Fox smiled looking amused. "Well, at the moment, he is what we call *unowned*. He was bought here on the advice of one of our criminologists. Should he remain in his current state once the job is complete, he will be set free."

Grant shook his head and then, neither to himself or Fox, he said, "You people are more insane than the fucktards you lock up."

He turned to face Mortimer's door again to find the occupant licking the inside of the observation glass. His long tongue leaving a trail of drooling saliva in its wake. He wiggled his tongue left and right in a suggestive manner toward Grant and then laughed. Grant was thankful he could not hear the sound. He could only envisage that it was one of frenzied merriment. A cacophony only a person akin to The Priest could produce.

Grant turned to face Fox.

"That fucking psycho and his leather-clad arse bandits tried to kill me....this....this here...it's a bag of wank," shouted

Grant.

"Your choice," replied Fox, his vehement tone doing nothing to improve Grant's mood.

Grant looked once again at the crazy ex-biker president and current incumbent of a facility holding and torturing other equally insane and evil excuses of human beings. His eyes may have been fixed on Mortimer, but his thoughts turned to his wife.

A voice whispered inside his mind, "Dad, do it for Mum. You always said you would do anything for Mum."

Grant whispered back, "Okay darling." He turned his head toward Fox.

"Three things, that is all I ask," he said.

"Okay, hit me," said Fox, and then quickly holding up one finger he added, "as long as hitting me isn't actually one of your three requests."

Grant didn't smile at Fox's attempt at humour, he responded curtly.

"One, my fee is the amount of money it takes to keep this freak locked up until the day he dies. Two, I decide the treatment he will receive until that day arrives and three," Grant paused for a second before saying, "once it's over, my wife and I walk away safe in the knowledge that we shall never again encounter either you or one of your gorillas again."

"Mercenary approach, I like it Grant," a smiling Fox sneered.

Grant held out his hand to shake on the agreement, but Fox merely let out a short burst of laughter.

"After watching what you did to Kelly I think I will choose not to shake on this one."

Grant lowered his hand.

"Do you miss anything?" he asked.

For the second time that day, Fox's response astounded Grant.

"Just a peaceful life."

The two men made their way to the floor below back to Grant's room. A new nurse was sat at the nurses' station. Fox nodded his head toward her saying, "Thanks for coming in at short notice Katy. Poor Wendy really isn't feeling too well. By the way, this gentleman's door can remain unlocked tonight."

The nurse, taken aback, looked at Fox a tad concerned. Fox simply smiled assuringly.

"Don't worry, he is no danger to you. Grant is a colleague who is using the hospital for a short while to recuperate after a nasty accident."

Katy smiled back. "Certainly sir. Can I get you anything Mr. Grant? A coffee maybe?"

Grant shook his head to indicate he didn't need anything and then said, "It's just Grant."

Fox followed Grant into his room, and watched as Grant sat down and retrieved the case file from the floor.

"Giving me the key to the kingdom, eh? Risky," said Grant.

"Not at all Grant. I'm merely allowing you the small amount of freedom that you deserve. After all, you are one of us now," replied Fox.

"I will never be one of you Fox. I have worked for organisations that control people with no regard to the dangers they face. You are nothing more than a robot, programmed to think in a particular way. This is exactly why you need me, a free thinker, a roaming spirit," Grant continued trying to get under Fox's skin.

"Read the file some more Grant. Then get some sleep. I will return in a few hours and you can start your work with Mortimer. After that, you will need to learn your cover story so that your investigations can really begin." Fox's skin remained firm.

Fox turned to leave the room. The last words he heard from Grant as he did so made him smile.

"Call him the Priest."

A Journey Through a Crazy Mind

Mortimer lay on his bed and licked his lips with anticipation, as he thought about coming face to face with Grant again. He also anticipated getting to know more about this ambiguous killer who was proving to be so elusive. What he had said to Grant about having no respect for this individual, couldn't have been further from the truth. He had to keep up this pretence to ensure everything worked out in his favour.

He got off his bed and kneeled down, clasping his hands together and upright.

"My Lord, give me the ability to lead this sinner to his death at the hands of the enemy's servant. Service me with the knowledge of the path to your kingdom." He started to stand and then stopped, returning to his kneeling position.

"One last thing, my Lord. Allow me one opportunity to deal with Fox, for my Lord, he is a disbeliever and a heretic." Mortimer stood and then lay back down on the bed.

"He's also a fucking cunt and deserves to be well and truly fucked," he mused as he fell asleep with a smile on his face.

——————— ———————

-

Grant placed the file onto the bed. Having repeatedly

examined it each time, digesting more of the information within it, he only had more unanswered questions. He stood up and walked out of his room.

Katy, visibly jumped in her chair as Grant asked, "any chance of that coffee please?"

"Good God," she said, her voice shaking slightly. "Don't ever do that again."

"Sorry," he replied, "didn't mean to frighten you."

She stood and began to walk to the small kitchen/staff room. Grant followed her. As she entered the kitchen, he leaned his shoulder against the door frame. As the nurse made the coffee, Grant couldn't help himself. "Why do you work here and not, let's say, at a normal hospital?" he inquired.

"Simple really," she replied without looking in Grant's direction, "I am a qualified mental health nurse. I hope to learn more about the research side of things, and they pay really well."

Higher than normal salaries seemed to be a recurring reason, thought Grant.

"Ever worked on the floor above?" he continued.

Katy laughed. "Yeah, I love working up there. They don't allow as much patient interaction as I would like, but I learn a lot about mental health just by listening and observing. There are some interesting cases up there."

"Why did you laugh? Did I say something amusing?" Grant asked, bemused by her initial reaction.

"No, not at all. It just made me think of the nickname we have for that ward," she said, giggling again.

"Go on then, enlighten me," Grant said.

"We call it the 'puddled to fuck' ward." Her face blushed in a way that only happens when someone uses a bad word when foul language was not part of their everyday vocabulary.

"What about the woman in the end room on the left? What do you know about her?" asked Grant, trying his best to sound innocent.

"Oh, she is an interesting one. Apparently, her husband tried to kill her. She is now suffering from 'locked-in syndrome,' a condition that I am really interested in learning more about."

Grant held in his rising anger. "Really?" he said. "So why is she up there? Surely she is not dangerous or a threat to anyone?"

"Well," said Katy, turning to face Grant, "the reason her husband tried to kill her was because she killed their daughter by slitting her throat."

She handed Grant his coffee.

"I'm sorry," she said. "I have said too much already. Please don't tell anyone about this, especially Mr. Fox. It's just been nice to talk to someone about a subject that really interests me. The chance does not usually arise. They are so hot on discretion and keeping your mouth shut."

Grant smiled at the young nurse and used two fingers to simulate zipping up his mouth and throwing an invisible key over his shoulder.

"My lips are sealed," he said gently, "however, before you seal yours, what about me? You don't seem one bit worried about being here alone with me."

"Why should I be?" she said, surprised by the question. "You were really badly hurt in a car accident working for the company. You aren't a mental case."

Grant sipped on his coffee. *Little do you know girl,* he thought.

Returning to his room, Grant finished his coffee and lay down on the bed. He fell asleep surprisingly quickly and even more miraculously managed to get a few hours of sleep without the awful nightmares or horrific memories. The first thing that he was aware of was Katy waking him up and informing him that Fox had just called to say that he would be about thirty minutes.

Grant rubbed his eyes and glanced at his watch, 0705 hours. He slowly got out of bed, still feeling tired. He made his way to the bathroom in the knowledge that Fox would not be a second late. He wanted to be ready for when he arrived.

—————— ——————

At 0700, a small gathering of people began their strange ritual beneath the streets of Camden Town, although they had no idea where they were. Three of the group of four huddled together like a gathering of very scared small animals. The three had experienced this ritual several times already. For one, it was his first experience.

The room was lit up by a dozen or so large candles, giving it an even more eery feeling as the flickering flames threw up shadows that moved each time a flame was caught by an occasional breeze. The room resembled a sinister medieval dungeon, reeking with years of mouldy disuse. Leading from the large opening were four large, but low arched tunnels, each of which led to a maze of derelict, mildewed smaller archways and tunnels. Some trailed off to dead-ends. Others led to enormous cavernous areas, similar to the one where the four young people now assembled.

They were all dressed in identical long, white gowns and

stood in front of a long stone trough containing a milky white coloured liquid. The candlelight occasionally glinted off a bejewelled gold cross that hung on the large dank wall in front of them, sending shards of light around the chamber.

The dark cloaked figure stood in front of the cross. His face was hidden behind a black plastic mask giving the image of a featureless human being. The man behind the mask issued his simple, yet almost demonic, instructions. His voice echoed slightly off the walls of the room.

"Derobe and wash, cleanse yourselves of the sinful marks you disfigure yourself with."

The three who were already familiar with the practice began to lift the robes upwards and off their bodies. The two girls and one man were visibly shaking, but not as much as the newest member of their throng, who began to sob.

"Stop it and be quiet or you will be punished. Do as he says," one of the girls whispered to the crying young man.

The man wiped his face and bit his bottom lip, hoping that it would help to stop his sobbing. He began to lift the white robe from his body. All four now stood naked and vulnerable. The space they occupied became visibly smaller, as they clustered together even closer than before. The young man dropped his robe to the floor, not noticing that the other three had held onto theirs.

The second girl from the ritual experienced group of three, sucked in a gasp of air and muttered, "Shit."

The man's voice rebounded around the room as his anger intensified:

"Pick up your shroud of Christ, you unholy creature of hell. How dare you dirty the sacred cloth with the filth of this world?"

The boy looked around, confused, not sure to whom this man was talking. It was then that he noticed that the other three were still holding their robes. He quickly picked his up from the damp floor.

"KNEEL," the man yelled, his booming command resounding off every solid surface. All four dropped to their knees. The newcomer only a split second after the others.

Their masked captor made his way toward them, using an indirect route by following the walls of the large area. When he left the areas that were lit by candlelight, he disappeared into an all-encompassing blackness.

Seemingly from nowhere, he emerged behind the kneeling figure of the man who, having initially dropped his robe onto the floor, now clung onto it as it it were a comfort blanket. The first he knew of the presence of the menacing tormentor came when a cold, surgical glove covered hand was placed on his forehead, pulling his skull backward. The young frightened man screamed.

Holding the head firmly in place, so that it was pressed against the lower part of his abdomen the masked man said, "Number three, stand and face this heathen."

The young girl, who had earlier pleaded with the boy to stop crying, stood up and turned around.

"Closer," her captor commanded. She stepped forward, so that she stood about two feet in front of the kneeling boy.

"Open your legs and present your passage of birth," he told her. Without thinking, the girl did as she was told.

The young man felt something press into his shoulder blade. It was a subtle pressure, not painful. The man behind him said, "Enter her, feel her natural desire."

The young man had no idea what was expected of him.

"What do you mean?" he asked. At first, he felt no pain, but as the scalpel was twisted inside the back of his shoulder, he released an agonising scream. His entire body tensed and he threw his clenched fists upwards. The left one struck against the inside of the thigh of the young girl in front of him.

He felt the warm breath of the masked man, through the dark plastic veil, as he whispered close to his ear, "Yes, feel her, enjoy the beauty of the Lord's natural creation."

The boy began to understand and reluctantly, but with no other choice available to him, he reluctantly uncurled the fingers of his tight fist and slowly pushed a finger into the girl's vagina. The hand that had been holding his head tightly now relaxed and he felt it stroking his forehead.

"Now taste Eve's liquid that eases the passage of birth," ordered the masked man.

The boy knew instantly what was expected of him as he withdrew his finger from the girl and moved his finger toward his mouth. He stopped momentarily and turning his eyes downward, he looked at his finger. It was tipped with blood.

"I'm sorry," whispered the standing girl, "I'm having my monthly." A tear trickled down her face.

The boy gagged, and once again the man behind him gave the one-word command of, "Taste." At the same time, he once again twisted the scalpel.

The boy's finger instinctively shot into his mouth and he bit down as more agony ripped through him. He was unable to distinguish between the menstrual blood of the girl and his own. Both struck his taste buds. The metallic taste of blood, mixed with the sweet taste of her other juices, were distinct from one another as he sucked on his own finger.

Further pain was endured as the scalpel was pulled out of

his shoulder and he felt the warmth of his own blood running down his back.

"You are blessed, child," said the man known as the Inserter. "You have tasted Eve, both natural and sin mixed, while feeling the pain encountered by Christ as the spear pierced his own body." He let go of the boys head. The boy slumped forward and despite his suffering, his only thought was to keep the robe from touching the floor.

The man made his way back to his place in front of the cross, and once there, gave a familiar instruction to three of his throng.

"Now hang thy robes of Christ and cleanse your filthy carcasses."

The newcomer followed the actions of the other three, hanging his robe on a row of wooden pegs that were part of a wooden plinth that had been bolted to the stone wall to their left. Picking up a white flannel from the edge of the stone trough, he began to wash his body. Then, he noticed that the others were bathing each other. The water from the trough, heavily mixed with bleach, stung his skin but it was nothing compared to the electrifying smarting caused by the girl washing him, sweeping her wet flannel over the open wound on his shoulder. The blackness of his mind fused quickly with that of his surroundings. He fainted, collapsing from the dire soreness supplied by the heavily bleached water entering the stab wound.

------ ------

Right on cue, at 0735 hours, Fox entered Grant's room. Grant was in the midst of brushing his teeth following a speedy shit, shower and shave. With a mouthful of foamy toothpaste, Grant looked up and seeing Fox said, "Hello Fox," but given the brimful of teeth cleansing fluid, it sounded more like *"Hello Fucks."*

Grant spat out the liquid into the sink and smiled at the agent.

"A true gentleman, as always," responded Fox.

"Killed anyone since we last spoke, or do you lock your apes up at nighttime?" Grant found it impossible not to rile Fox.

"No, but it does seem like a new victim may have been taken," responded a now serious looking Fox.

Grant figured it was probably time for a break from his little game. He grabbed a towel and wiped his mouth and face.

"Are we sure?" he asked, realising that he had used the term "we" whilst asking the question.

"Fairly certain. The victim appears to fit the profile of our perpetrator." It was clear that the lack of progress was getting to Fox. "Young, recently left home, new found friends and a strained relationship with his parents before moving out of the family home."

"When do you suppose they were taken?" asked Grant.

"Well," replied Fox, his mood appearing to slightly elevate, "this is where we seem to have struck a bit of good luck for a change. The lad's disappearance was reported by his two flatmates at around 0200. They became worried when he didn't return home by midnight. Apparently, he is a habitually predictable creature. He stays in every night except for Fridays, when he always returns home by midnight, without fail."

Grant suddenly realised that he had no idea what day of

the week it was. Thinking about it, this was not something he had been concerned with since waking up in this place.

"So, I take it today is Saturday?" he asked just to make sure.

Fox nodded to confirm that it was indeed the day that Grant had enquired about. Grant walked past him and made his way to the narrow wardrobe in the corner of the room. He opened the single door and stared at the selection of T-shirts that had been provided by the hospital. They were all plain ranging in colour from black, white and a purple colour that Grant would never be seen dead in for anyone, his wife included. At the bottom of the wardrobe was a plastic bag, which contained the remnants of his personal belongings. Grant could only assume that whoever had retrieved his broken body from the road where the Crippens had left him, had also retrieved the contents of his leather panniers. He rummaged through the bag and eventually pulled out a creased T-shirt. He held it up to his face and gave it a sniff. Stale was an understatement. Undeterred by its odour, he pulled the shirt on over his head and turned to face Fox. The shirt was baggier than the last time he wore it.

"What do you think? Am I presentable to meet your esteemed guest?" asked Grant, obviously referring to Mortimer Church, aka the Priest.

Fox stared at Grant and the faded, grubby T-shirt.

"Who'd have thought it?" he said. "Never had you down as a fan of the Clash."

"Fucking hate the punk scum, but it was a *borrow* from a good friend," replied Grant. In the world of Ian and Grant, a borrow was a term they used for any item that one took from the other with the intention of never returning it. This was certainly the case with this particular item.

"Awww sentimental," said Fox, happy to be the one supplying the sarcasm for a change.

"Fuck you, prick," replied Grant smiling. "Now, talking about knobheads, let's go and talk to The Priest."

"Why do you refer to him by the name he loves so much?" Fox asked.

"Only when not in his presence," replied Grant. "I just can't get my head around him being named Mortimer. However, to his face it will be Mortimer all the way. It's no wonder he killed his parents," Grant winked in the direction of Fox, who shook his head in disbelief at what he had just heard Grant say.

The two men made the now all to familiar journey to the floor above them. They did not speak until halfway through the lift journey, when Fox asked Grant if he would like to grab a bit of breakfast before they started.

"No thanks," said Grant. "It's bad enough that I have got to share the same air as Mortimer without running the risk of throwing up."

"Are you sure?" asked Fox. "A splendid breakfast has been laid out for our client in the executive lounge."

"Only if I can stay and meet Bloom," said Grant.

"Give it up man, it will never happen." Fox had to admire Grant's persistence.

"Never say never Fox," said Grant. He smirked for few seconds prior to delivering the punchline. "Hey didn't some secret agent once say that? Right up your street…man!"

Fox opened the lift doors and they walked steadily down the corridor toward Mortimer Church's room. Fox looked inside before going through the sequence involved to unlock the door. Grant heard a familiar click and placed his hand against the door. He pushed it inwards and walked in.

The Priest was laying on his side, facing away from the door. Before Grant or Fox had a chance to say anything he spoke.

"Good morning Grant, you smell…mouldy this morning. Almost like…a decaying dead body."

Unconsciously, Grant touched the T-shirt he was wearing and sniffed his hand, though he didn't react, other than to say, "Morning Mortimer, and before you say it, no I will not be calling you the Priest. I will call you by your given name, the name given to you by your parents, God rest their souls."

A brief angry expression flashed over Mortimer's face, unseen by the other two men in the room, but it was gone as quickly as it appeared. In the time it takes a heart to beat twice, he spun upwards and around, resulting in him sitting on the edge of the bed facing the two men.

"How's the wife?" he asked Grant.

"Doing better than your mum," responded Grant quickly.

Before Mortimer could open his mouth, Fox interjected.

"If you two boys have finished comparing dicks, can we get on with the business at hand?"

"Yes, let's try to work together, Grant. I had such a stomping time at our last meeting," Mortimer glared at Grant through half closed eyes.

"Yeah, I got a kick or two out of it too," Grant retorted, not willing to give up this battle of words.

Fox grabbed the door and slammed it shut. In its unlocked position, it slammed into the door framing and bounced back open again.

"Next time, both of your heads will be in the way. This shit stops right now. There is a killer out there, who last night potentially took another victim. Let's see if your mixture of direct thinking and sheer madness can make a difference," Fox snapped at the other two men.

Mortimer was the first to break the visual standoff between Grant and himself. He looked toward the frustrated agent.

"Another victim, tell me more." Looking at Grant once again, Mortimer nodded his head in the direction of the file that Grant had brought with him from his room. "And I want to read that too."

Fox refused to tell Mortimer any details of the latest youngster to be taken, but indicated to Grant that he should let him read the file. Grant threw it onto the bed next to Mortimer. Both men stood firm, while the bald headed psychopath read through the information contained within the case file, Grant noticing how long he lingered over the pictures. After ten minutes, Grant broke the silence.

"So, you got any ideas or were you just uploading the images into your warped mind to put into your wank bank for later?"

Ignoring the insult, Mortimer read a few more lines of information, and then placed the file back onto the bed. He looked up at Grant and then toward Fox.

"Well gentleman, we do have a true believer and a skilled tradesman out there, don't we?"

"Killing isn't a trade," said Grant.

"Trade," scoffed Mortimer, "a commerce, a business, a job, a calling. Killing is a trade, just not one that you get legally paid for in this blinkered world. For our individual, it is a calling. I am sure you have both worked that out already. He works for his master, and whether or not you choose to believe if that is totally irrelevant, the fact is, he believes it and he is very passionate about his work."

"It sounds like you admire this freak," said Grant, still

disgusted with the situation of having to work with the man who tried to kill him. "But you would, because he, just like you, hides behind a mythical being to protect himself from any self blame regarding his actions."

"You are right Grant, I do admire him…or her. None of you are really sure yet are you?" Mortimer looked for a reaction from them. The lack of one proved that he was right. He continued speaking.

"So let's look at what you do know and just for the purpose of this exercise, let us assume that our killer is a man. He snatches his victims, but you have no idea exactly where from. He takes young people who are troubled for some reason. Geographically, they have no connections or similarities. He takes men and women. When you find the bodies, there appears to be no logical pattern for where he leaves them." He waited a few seconds to see if Fox or Grant had anything to say. They both remained silent.

"You are assuming that the first body you found was the first person taken, but you don't really have any evidence to back that up. The confusing bit for me is that there is no mention of your third victim."

Grant knew exactly to what he was referring.

"I picked up on that too. We are still awaiting a body of a male victim who will be lacking a penis," he said.

"Yes Grant, well done," said Mortimer. His tone was one of a proud adult congratulating a young child on achieving a simple task. He turned to Fox and asked, "Has this one turned up?"

"No, and I haven't heard it talked about during any of the operation meetings that I have attended," replied Fox. Internally, he was feeling embarrassed because this was something he had given no thought to.

"Well maybe there isn't a body. Perhaps our killer just went to a local butchers and purchased a human penis," and then attempting a stereotypical London accent Mortimer added, "Morning guvnor, do you have any 'uman knobs in today? Average length will do mate, but would prefer it to be caucasian if you know what I mean. Luvverly day for buying a cock ain't it Mr. Butcherman?"

"Yeah, okay Mortimer, you've made your point," Fox responded, obviously annoyed at this oversight.

"Call me Priest," said Mortimer, once again.

"Over my dead body," said Grant, becoming angrier on each occasion this request was made.

Mortimer smiled at Grant and said, "Oh no my friend, I intend to curl out a huge steaming turd over your dead body."

Grant broke. He hurled himself toward the sitting ex-biker president, knocking him backward, flat on to the bed. He clambered up his body, ending up with one knee on Mortimer's throat, pinning him down. He managed to land four punches to Mortimer's face before he felt himself being pulled backward, ending up on his back on the floor. Looking up, he found himself staring directly into the barrel of a handgun, Fox's handgun to be exact.

"I will fucking kill both of you." This simple but clear statement of intention Grant could find no reason to disbelieve.

Grant stood up, Fox following his movement with the gun, the muzzle never moving more than an inch from Grant's forehead. Grant looked beyond Fox and saw Mortimer Church moving into a sitting position. His nose had been broken. He would definitely be sporting a meaty blackeye sometime in the near future. A couple of punches had split his lips open.

Grant watched him, as Mortimer raised his hand and put two fingers into his bleeding mouth. His hand moved side to side slightly. Then, Mortimer retracted his two pincered fingers. Between them, he held a bloodied tooth. Mortimer began to laugh. A huge belly laugh, filled with evil and insanity. He held the tooth high in the air toward Grant and smiled. The new gap in his line of teeth was very obvious.

"Does my new look suit me Grant?"

Fox grabbed Grant by the top of his shirt and dragged him out of the room. Back in the corridor, he slammed him against the wall and returned the muzzle of the gun back to the front of Grant's face. He locked and secured the door to Mortimer's room.

Grabbing Grant again, he pulled him across the corridor and shoved him in front of the door to the room where his wife, Julia, lay in bed sleeping soundly.

"Say goodbye," he said.

"Why?" asked Grant, straightening his T-shirt in a futile attempt to make the old faded piece of clothing look more presentable, given its treatment at the hands of the agent.

"Why? Because I punched that freak? Because I fucked up the face of a prick who has no intention of helping with this case of yours? A man who only wants to taunt me for his own pathetic pleasure?"

The two men stared at each other, neither willing to look away.

"Fine, unlock the door and I will say goodbye. I lost her a lifetime ago and I never believed that you would allow her to come back to me. Fuck you, Fox. I hope you never catch your killer. I hope that he finds someone that you love and kills them. I want you to feel just one percent of the pain that I did when I lost everything that mattered to me."

Grant approached the door and placed his hand on it, trying hard to feel that bit closer to the woman he loved so much. He choked back the developing tears and swallowed them back down his throat.

"But remember this. Make sure you keep me secure. Make sure you never turn your back on me, because I promise you this...I will kill you. I will kill you in such a way that studies by psychologists and psychiatrists will be performed for a millennium," he said to Fox, while still looking through the door at his sleeping wife.

Fox didn't say a word, but just moved toward the door and edged Grant out of his way. He unlocked the door and walked in. With a quiet and gentle voice, he said, "Good morning, Julia. It's time to wake up my dear."

The sleeping woman slowly woke and turned over to face toward Fox. Grant walked in behind Fox and looked at his wife. He stood no more than eight feet from her—the closest he had been for over a year.

Julia Richardson rubbed her eyes and a small smile broke out on her face.

That face, that oh so sweet face, thought Grant. His heart was pounding inside his chest. He felt it would stop and never beat again, as his wife said.

"Good morning, Mr. Fox. Who's your friend?"

Fox looked at Grant, who was almost convinced he could sense pity from the agent.

"He's a new colleague of mine, Julia. I am just showing him around the place. I couldn't resist bringing him to meet my favourite patient."

"Good morning Mr. Fox's friend. Do you have a name?" Julia said, looking at Grant.

Grant had so many mixed emotions racing around his body, colliding with one another, that he could hardly get a word out of his mouth. His first sentence to his wife in ages stuttered out of him.

"Err…yeah, it's…," but before he could finish Fox interrupted.

"This is Mr. Grant, Julia."

"Well nice to meet you Mr. Grant," replied Grant's wife and smiled at him. Grant felt his legs weaken beneath him. He was convinced that he was going to collapse. Fox must have sensed it too, for suddenly he grabbed Grant's arm, steadying him and leading him from the room, turning to Julia and saying, "I'll arrange for breakfast to be brought to you Julia. Lovely seeing you again."

"Mr. Grant…" Grant spun around as he heard his wife say the words.

"Yes Jay," he used his pet name for his wife.

"Have we met before?" she asked.

Grants heart broke again, something he had deemed impossible after everything he had suffered.

"No Julia, I don't think we have."

Grant left the room without requiring any assistance or guidance from Fox. He had to get out of that room.

Outside, he leaned against the wall and slid down it, eventually sitting on the floor, a sad slumped figure of a broken man. Fox secured the door and stood over Grant.

"Okay, you win," said Grant. "I will do what you want. Just don't put me through that again."

Fox walked away, leaving Grant to suffer alone. Fox also

needed the solitude as, for the first time in an age, he felt guilt.

The silence was broken within seconds, as Fox's mobile began to ring. He took the call, grateful for a reason to focus on something else, other than the feeling of remorse that was starting to make him feel very uncomfortable.

Grant heard Fox say, "Okay, well get if off there. Get our IT people on to it immediately. If it's not gone in thirty minutes, you can tell them they will all be looking for new jobs." Fox ended the call and returned his phone to his pocket.

"It looks like your penis donator has turned up," he said to Grant.

"Where?" asked Grant.

"No idea," replied Fox. "It was discovered by a member of the public, and right now, the images and videos are streaming out on every social media network."

Within minutes, both men were standing in front of the computer screen, scanning through the social networks. Images flashed of what appeared to be a man upside down on a cross, his body splattered with blood. The majority of the images were poor due to the lighting, caused by both the time of day that they were taken and the devices they had been taken with. The videos, however, were in the main, very clear and extremely graphic.

Thirty seconds into watching one video on YouTube, it stopped playing. When Fox tried to replay it, a message flashed up on the screen announcing that it had been deleted.

"Looks like your people are on to it already," said Grant.

"Yeah maybe," replied Fox. "Probably also the people at the organisations as well."

After each search, Fox cleared the browsing history and looked again. Every attempt resulted in fewer images and videos being displayed.

"Damage dealt with by the looks of things," said Grant, more hopeful than confident.

"No, it's out there now. The internet freaks will have been all over it within seconds, copying and downloading them. As each one is deleted a new crop will be uploaded and shared," said Fox. He looked and sounded exhausted.

"Bad night's sleep Fox?" asked Grant.

"No." Fox was rubbing his temples. "Just trying to imagine how pissed off Bloom and our client are going to be."

He stood up straight and switched off the computer screen. Puffing out his chest and tucking his shirt tightly into his trousers, he announced, "You have about an hour to memorise your cover story, because that is how long it will take us to get you to the police station."

"What fucking cover story?" said Grant.

"The one we have already created for you," replied Fox matter-of-factly. "The one that says you are a criminologist and criminal profiler with an unhealthy predilection for serial killers."

Grant looked genuinely surprised, saying, "I only agreed to work with you people a while ago, how have you done all of that in such a short space of time?"

"We haven't. We started on it a month or so after your broken body arrived here. You have a website, have published two books, not best-sellers. Sales have increased over the past few months...amazingly! Your new documents such as driving license, bank cards, you know all that normal shit along with a document file all about you, is waiting for you down in the car." Fox started to walk toward the lift, stopping only when Grant spoke again.

"Woah cowboy. I cannot become a new person in one hour. I can't take that much information into my head. This brain is full of shit that I cherish, to cram more in some of the old stuff will have to go. Seriously, I need more time."

Fox looked at him with that now all too familiar expression that said, *why are you wasting time when you know I am going to get my own way?*

"Firstly Grant, we don't have the time. As this has got out, the police will be panicking like shit and will be doing everything to up their game. You need to get in there and disrupt their efforts, by leading them down the wrong path." Fox began to walk again.

"And secondly?" Grant called after him.

"Secondly Grant, you don't have a choice. There is a new suit in your room. Get changed and be down in the lobby in ten minutes. The car is waiting for us. Your freedom rights have been extended to allowing you movement between the entrance level and the one where you once resided."

Grant remained stood in the same position, totally overwhelmed by the whirlwind of information he had just been hit with, not to mention what was now expected of him. He began to walk quickly down the corridor to catch up with Fox, who had arrived at the lift doors.

"I don't wear suits AND I certainly DON'T travel in fucking cars," he shouted.

—————— ——————

After travelling down in the lift, Grant left Fox to go his own way, making his way back to his room. He thought about what Fox had just said, *the place that you used to reside. Was this the last time he would see this room?*

Packing his few belongings, and choosing not to select anything that the hospital had given to him, including the suit laying on the bed in its plastic zipped cover. Grant's thoughts once again turned to his wife. Being here had made it a little bit easier, knowing that he was only a few metres from her. Although he couldn't interact with her, he felt at least his presence provided her with a little protection. He didn't want to leave her here, in the supposed care of this place and these people, especially Stanridge. However, he knew that the only way of getting her out of here was to do this job.

Dressed in scuffed boots, his usual style of band tour T-shirt, jeans and leather jacket, all of which carried the evidence of the trauma of coming off a bike and the kicking he had endured, he made his way down the corridor and into the lift.

Grant had no idea where this journey was taking him, but he had been here before, out of his depth, no real detailed plan, just a desire to sort out a bad bastard. The only difference was that this time, he was not driven by revenge. This time, it was love. The love he had for his wife and the need to have her back in his arms and to take her home, wherever that now may be.

Another Mask to Hide Behind

Despite his protests, Grant sat in the back seat of the car parked outside the entrance to the Bloom Institute. Fox was already at the car awaiting his arrival. With a look that said, "why do I bother?" written all over his face as he looked at Grant's clothing, Fox handed him a thin file.

"Read it, digest it and become it," he said.

"You are what you read, eh?" Grant replied and opened the file.

A white envelope contained a driving license, bank and credit cards, an NHS medical card, even a few store cards and loyalty cards, the type with which points could be received on making purchases.

Fox handed him a black wallet, a chain was hanging from its corner with a securing clip at its other end. Grant took it with raised eyebrows. "Does a bike come with it," he asked.

"Read the file," was the only response he got from an agitated Fox.

Grant didn't argue or respond with one of his trademark sarcastic comments. He looked down at the file again.

The first single sheet of paper disclosed the basic information of his new identity.

Name: Dr. Colin Garside
Profession: Criminologist and Profiler
State information such as NHS number and NI number, which Grant had no intention of trying to remember.
Marital Status: Unmarried, no children
Qualifications gained at the University of Birmingham and the Southern New Hampshire University in the U.S.
Published Literature: "A Map of the Mad Mind" and a couple of papers that resided in several university libraries, the title of one that intrigued him, "The Insanity of a Biker's Life."

"Who wrote this shit?" Grant asked.

"A few of our researchers put it together over the past few months," replied Fox. "I don't think they would appreciate their work being described as shit."

Once again Grant raised his eyebrows.

"I didn't mean my new identity, although I do not see myself as a Colin. I meant who wrote these publications?"

"The same people," responded Fox, his mind clearly somewhere else.

"Are they any good?"

"Who bloody cares? The only people who will read them will be real criminologists just so they can criticise them. Oh, and potential serial killers looking for ideas. They are the people interested in reading these things. Now, will you please read your fucking profile?" Fox snapped back at him.

"Manners and foul language, not many people can carry that one off," Grant's sarcasm did not staying hidden for too long. Fox didn't bite, he remained mute, his thoughts his only companion.

Grant decided to leave him alone and returned to the file. The second two sheets of paper contained information about his professional career. A job working at a university teaching criminology, several jobs assisting police forces around the country with murder cases. He was currently listed as a writer working on a new book. The last paragraph described a rather pathetic personal existence. Two failed relationships, which had brought his sexuality into question. He lived alone in an apartment in London, no pets.

"I'm a pufter?" asked Grant.

Fox exhaled a huge sigh.

"No Grant. You are a well-respected professional who would not use such politically incorrect terminology."

"Wrong again Fox," said Grant. "I am someone who has served my country for years and doesn't deserve to be told by any wanker that there is a need now to be politically correct."

"Are you ready to become Colin Garside yet?" asked Fox. His level of patience for Grant's contempt now reaching a dangerous level.

Grant looked down once more at the meagre information. He had expected so much more. At the same time, he was grateful that there was not.

"Yeah, you guys haven't given me much to work from, but I am a good blagger, so I will run with it and make it a success," he said, forcing a smile in an attempt to raise the mood.

"You know what Grant? There are times that I wish, that at the moment just before your conception, your mother had decided to swallow." Fox felt that maybe a cruel comment might shut up this man for a short while. How wrong he was. Grant instantly opened his mouth.

"Fuck off. I applaud my parents every day for creating a fucking legend," said Grant, the smile on his face now not a forced one.

The majority of the rest of the journey was spent in silence, only occasionally broken by a phone call either taken or made by Fox. Grant perused his file once again. It was sparse and probably had been designed that way just in case a situation like this arose, one giving very little time to remember a large amount of detailed information. Grant listened to the last words of Fox's phone conversation.

"Yes, we will be with you in five minutes."

"You going to tell me where we are heading, or is it all sneaky beaky, need to know, on her majesty's secret service sort of crap?" Grant asked.

"We will be arriving at Paddington Green Police station very soon. How about you lose yourself in to your character, please?" came the genuine plea from an increasingly nervous Alex Fox.

"Do I get a phone?" asked Grant. "A criminologist would have a phone wouldn't they?"

Fox reached into an inside pocket and tossed a mobile phone toward Grant. Catching it, he looked down surprised to see a battered old model, new enough to have all the necessary applications, but old enough to make him look like an out of date old man.

"You're old school and not a massive fan of technology," said Fox, before Grant could say anything.

"Where was that information in the file?" said Grant.

"I made it up. Blagged it as you would say." Fox smiled for the first time during the car journey.

Grant beamed back, "Colin says thank you, kind sir."

The car came to an abrupt stop and Grant looked out of the window. A drab, grey 1960s style office building loomed over them. Grant found it hard to believe that this building operated as the most important high-security police station in the United Kingdom.

The driver got out of the car and opened the door for Grant. For the first time, Grant saw that the driver was the security guard who he had forced to his knees by applying a bit of wrist pressure.

"Hello Kelly, how are you my good man?" Grant added a wink for good measure.

"Very well thank you, Dr. Garside." Even Grant admired that level of professionalism.

Grant got out of the vehicle and was joined by Fox, who asked Kelly to return in two hours to collect him. As Kelly returned to the driver's seat and drove away, Fox dangled two sets of keys in front of Grant's face.

"Keys to your apartment and your new transport," he said.

"Don't tell me, a dull hatchback in line with my boring new identity," replied Grant, grabbing the keys and placing them into his jacket pocket, zipping it closed.

"You will find out later, now come on, they are waiting for us."

They both walked up the few steps arriving at the front door and pushed the button to gain access to the building.

"Identity please," said an electronically distorted voice through the metal speaker on the wall.

"Dr. Colin Garside and Mr. Alex Fox. We are here to meet Detective Inspector Gamby," Fox answered.

A buzzing noise followed and Fox pushed the door open.

—————— ——————

The two men watched Grant climb into the car outside of the Bloom Institute.

"You are hanging your hopes on that?" asked one of the other.

Both men were dressed in expensive suits, top quality that showed their standing. One was CEO of a hugely successful global company and the other a powerful cabinet office civil servant, not an MP as Fox thought.

Godfrey Lambden looked at Professor Arnold Bloom, waiting for a response.

"My people tell me that he is capable of more than even he thinks he is. He has a real instinct for our kind of work Godfrey."

"He better be Arnold. Just remember that my father was one of the people who helped to create this organisation, gave it the freedom to do what it wants. Don't ever forget that you will always work for us." There was a level of threat in what the senior civil servant said, which managed to intimidate the usually unflappable Bloom.

"How can I possibly forget that fact Godfrey? In a few months, you are to be announced as the new head of the security services, a position that I hope will give us even more power."

"The rise or fall of your organisation, Bloom, is not reliant on my position of power. Catch the deviant who killed my daughter, or the collapse of your company will be talked about in the business world for years to come," said Lambden.

He sipped on his coffee and spat it back into his cup.

"With the money you are getting from us, I would suggest

that you replace this dishwater before I return here again."

He walked away and sat at the large table that dominated the executive boardroom.

"Catch my daughter's killer or kill that reprobate you have hired," he said as he sat down. His tiredness and stress was exceptionally obvious. "Don't worry Godfrey, we will and as for Grant…well, he is dead either way."

——— ———

DI Dave "Gambo" Gamby raced down to the police desk the second the call was received in his office three floors up and at the back of the police building. The murder squad had been allocated a room well away from the normal police duty areas, allowing them to focus totally on the case in hand without too many distractions. Not that it had made any difference to their success rate so far.

He burst through a set of double doors and made his way directly toward Fox, holding out a welcoming hand and saying, "Dr. Garside, great to meet you. Thank you for coming on board." His sentence was rushed, a result of the amount of black coffee he had been drinking all night in an effort to keep himself awake and alert.

Fox did not return the hand gesture offered to him, but swept his hand out in the direction of Grant.

"May I introduce Dr. Colin Garside," he said.

The DI stopped in his tracks and looked toward Grant.

"Oh," he said, giving Grant a visual once over. "Sorry," he continued, "I didn't realise. Really sorry I just assumed the suit, well you know, the leather jacket, err…unusual, well unexpected."

"No need to apologise. I often get that reaction. I dress to please myself not others and please drop the title. Doctor makes it sound like I save lives," said Grant, getting straight into character and impressing Fox immediately.

"Well, we hope that is exactly what you are going to do Doctor, sorry Mr. Garside," replied Gamby, trying his best to slow down his speaking pace, and failing.

"It's just Colin," said Grant, and held out his hand, grabbing the policeman's firmly and giving it a welcoming shake.

"Yeah fine, no problem and please call me Gambo. Everyone else does, including the chief."

The DI looked tired. Dead on his feet if the truth was to be told.

"Having a rough time at the moment I guess?" Grant asked him.

"Tougher than you can imagine, mate. Pressure from heights that I didn't know existed," replied the stressed Gamby.

"Okay, let's go to the investigation room and you can tell me about your progress," said Grant.

"Oh, that's an easy one to answer Doctor, fuck sorry, Colin," the DI, exasperated with himself for getting his guests preferred title incorrect and for then swearing. He slapped his own forehead. "We have made no progress. In fact, if I'm honest, I feel we are further back now than when we started."

He walked toward the door from which he had first made his whirlwind entry and nodded to the desk sergeant indicating he would like the doors to be opened.

"Follow me please. Let's see if you help us take a step forward," he said.

Grant and Fox followed him through the doors.

"Sorry," said Gamby, "we will have to use the stairs. The damned lift is broken, bloody government cuts! However, as one of our victims is the daughter of a member of the government, the money has suddenly been made available. It should be fixed tomorrow."

As they made their way up the flights of stairs, Grant tried to analyse the man leading the way. Old school obviously, long time in service undoubtedly and, the government cuts comment suggested, cynical. *Probably cannot wait for retirement to arrive,* thought Grant.

Gamby swiped his ID card through a card reader next to a solid metal door at the top of the sixth flight of stairs. He led the two men down to the end of the corridor where the murder squad office was located.

The first thing Grant noticed were the two photographs of the dead victims on a whiteboard on the far wall. The board was almost the full length of the wall itself. Their names were inscribed below their pictures. Next to them, was a third picture. Although blurred and badly pixelated, Grant could still make out that it was a picture of the third victim, probably printed from one of the internet images.

He looked around the room. There were approximately twelve desks, all with PC screens and a telephone. There was a small office off the main room, which Grant assumed would be where Gamby based himself.

Two detectives sat at their desks, one looking at images on the PC screen, the other typing information onto an electronic form.

"Where is the rest of the team?" asked Grant.

"Our other two are down at the crime scene of the latest victim, or shall I say what we assume to be our latest victim," replied Gamby.

"You only have four team members?" Grant was shocked so had to ask the question to clarify this fact.

For the first time since incorrectly being mistaken for Dr. Colin Garside, Fox spoke.

"Shall we go to your office Detective Inspector ,so you can bring us both up to speed?"

Gamby looked at Fox. It dawned on him that he had led this man into the most secure police station in the country and hadn't checked his identity.

"Sorry, who are you?" he said.

"My name is Alex Fox. I am an associate of Dr. Garside," replied Fox.

"Just consider him to be an assistant of mine," said Grant, unable to conceal his smugness at seeing Fox's facial expression having been described as Grant's assistant.

Now, they stood in Gamby's office. Fox invited all parties to sit and then to Gamby, asked,

"Please, could you bring us up to speed so that Dr. Garside can get a grasp on the case?" Gamby was urged.

DI "Gambo" Gamby spoke for about thirty minutes. Gradually his pace of speech slowed and reached a normal level. Neither Fox, nor Grant interrupted him. Fox took a few notes and Grant paid heed to everything that was said: "And that's your lot," ended the detective, now looking expectantly in Grant's direction.

Fox remained silent, curious to see how Grant would handle the situation.

"So let me summarise," began Grant. "You have no evidence whatsoever to lead you to any potential suspects. You have two dead bodies, sorry now three, no DNA of any persons other than the victims themselves. There is no connection linking the victims. You cannot fathom how the killer is selecting his prey. You don't know where they are being taken from. There appears to be no pattern to the drop sites. All you ostensibly have is a nickname for the killer."

"We have the notes left by the killer," replied Gamby defensively.

"Well maybe you should have called him the Note Writer," said Grant sarcastically.

"Why haven't you made more use of the press to get this out there?" he asked the detective.

"Two reasons. We don't want to invite claims to be the killer from cranks and we didn't see the benefit in causing panic among the population when we really have nothing to go on. We would effectively be admitting that we were clueless and anybody could be his next victim." Gamby sounded agitated as he answered Grant's question. He had expected solutions from this man, not more problems, and certainly not criticism. Gamby then quickly added:

"Sorry, there is a third reason. We were advised not to involve the media too much at this stage."

"By who?" asked Grant.

Fox cleared his throat.

Immediately, Grant knew that Fox's people had influenced this decision.

Grant raised his hand. "It doesn't matter, it is what it is."

He took a few seconds to think. He stood and walking around the small office, eventually stopping he said:

"What you have created is the perfect scenario for this serial killer. Let's make no mistake that is exactly what he is. This individual does not crave publicity or fame. He sees this as his vocation, for reasons I do not know at this precise time."

Fox wondered if these were Grant's tangible thoughts about the situation, or if he was just trying to get into character. Grant continued and the other two men listened intently.

"As far as the public is aware, what has occured here are two tragic accidental deaths of young people, one of which just happens to be the child of someone who works in the government. Nobody out there suspects murder. Not a soul is aware that there is a serial killer somewhere out there, possibly in their community You have handed the killer a level of freedom he could only dream of. Whoever advised keeping the truth out of the press is a total prick." Grant cast his eyes over to Fox just to make sure that the agent knew the last part of that sentence was directed solely at him.

Gamby slammed his fists down onto his desk.

"So what do you fucking suggest? Also, let's not forget, I don't think we can call this third one a tragic accidental death!"

"I don't want to read any of your evidence thus far. It will only prove misleading and useless," said Grant, ignoring the detective's comment about the third victim, and now thoroughly enjoying being in command, thanks to the position Fox himself had placed him. "I want to speak to the parents of the three victims. This should help determine a connection between the three fatalities. Believe me gentlemen, that is the key to this investigation. If I can find out what connects these young people, I can begin to think like our killer." Grant looked at the other two men.

Gamby looked affronted. Fox was expressionless, although internally quietly impressed, while still a little annoyed at being called a prick.

"Fine," said Gamby eventually. "I'll get a police officer to drive you to their homes."

"No need," replied Grant looking at Fox, "apparently, I have my own transport."

The three men, led once again by Gamby, travelled back down the stairs. On reaching the bottom, Grant turned to his right and headed toward the door that led back to the front desk.

"Dr. Garside," said Fox, "your transport is in the secure car park at the rear of the station. This way please." Looking at Gamby he added, "I presume."

"Give me a moment please. I noticed something out front when we arrived. I would like to take another look," replied Grant, standing at the double doors waiting for them to be released. Gamby opened them and without a word, Grant made his way outside. Fox stood at the top of the outside steps and watched as Grant crossed over the road outside the station. He headed toward a small group of five people.

Fox immediately recognised them as being reporters. "Oh shit, no," he said to himself.

Grant determinedly approached four men and one woman, who were stood together chatting with one another. He supposed their presence outside of the police station was to get a story, not necessarily any specific news.

"Good morning lady and gentlemen," he said with the confidence that comes with being successful in your field of expertise. "I assume that you are members of our esteemed press corps?" he asked.

The five people just looked at him. They were aware he wasn't a member of staff from the station. They had loitered outside this place for long enough to know everyone who worked at Paddington Green.

"No," replied one of the male reporters, "we are police groupies." The rest of his group laughed loudly.

"Oh, I do apologise. I didn't realise that you were just hanging about in the hopes that you would get the opportunity to suck on a coppers dick. You won't be interested in a breaking story then. Could you point me in the direction of somebody who would be?" said Grant, now fully assuming his role of Dr. Colin Garside, esteemed criminologist.

Fox arrived at Grant's shoulder just as one of the reporters asked, "Oh yeah, what story would that be?"

"Colin, could I have a word please," asked Fox.

Grant ignored him and pressed on.

"Folks, get out your notebooks and prepare to be elevated to the top of your profession. This by the way," he pointed at Fox, "is a detective. He will happily let you suck his cock once you have made your notes." He looked at the reporter who had tried to be funny moments earlier. "Assuming, of course, that you are in fact groupies and not professionals who live for news."

The reporters reached into their bags looking for a pen, a notebook or a voice recorder, anything to help them document what this strange man had to say. Fox looked at the ground, knowing that his attempts to refrain Grant had failed. He remained only to listen to what Grant was about to say, hoping that he would be able to repair some of the damage he was certain Grant was about to create.

The female reporter held out a voice recorder, a very modern one that was voice activated, in the direction of Grant's face.

"Could you start by telling us who you are and then tell us

what you have to say?" she asked.

Grant began.

"My name is Dr. Colin Garside, a criminologist and profiler with an interest in serial killers. I have been invited by the police to assist them with a number of murders that have occurred recently. I believe them to be the work of one individual. Thus far, we are aware of three victims, the latest having being discovered during the early hours of this morning by members of the public. You may have seen some of the images on the internet."

The reporters nodded their heads in unison.

"The first two victims you have been led to think died as a result of tragic accidents, one of those poor individuals being the daughter of a government official."

"Godfrey Lambden?" asked one of the reporters.

"Indeed," replied Grant, who was now fully absorbed into the developing character of the newly created Dr. Garside.

"The killer, who I am certain is male and working alone, has been nicknamed the Inserter by the police, for reasons I am not willing to disclose at this time."

The tightly huddled group had now increased by one, as DI Gamby arrived at the scene. He concentratred on what was being said by the person who he initially had hoped would be his team's saviour in utter disbelief. Grant continued speaking, unaware of the detective's presence.

"I implore the general public to be vigilant and careful, especially late at night and during the early hours of the morning. It is my theory that the killer snatches his victims at these times. If anyone has information that could assist the police and I with our investigations, I request that they call the murder investigation team here at Paddington Green police station."

The recording devices were suddenly removed from Grant's face as the reporters shifted toward Gamby. They all clambered around the detective shouting, "Anything to tell us, DI Gamby?" "Can you confirm what Dr. Garside has just told us?"

DI Gamby hurriedly returned to the police station repeating the phrase, "no comment," as the throng of reporters followed him.

Grant and Fox now stood alone. Fox squeezed and rubbed the bridge of his nose with two fingers.

"What have you done Grant?"

"I've done what you brought me in to do," he replied. "To shake things up, to look at this situation differently and act instinctively without the constraints that control you, despite your denials that such restrictions exist."

"Okay, just tell me the point of what you have just done," said Fox, still perplexed by what he had just witnessed.

"I have just put our killer into a position that he doesn't want to be in. He doesn't want attention, don't you understand that? He doesn't wish to be caught. He doesn't want a book written about him. For some reason, he believes he is working for a greater good. The only way to encourage him to make mistakes, is to get him out of his comfort zone. I have just done that, or at least I will have, the minute the papers are printed and this is blasted out from every news channel."

"This had better work Grant, or I fear you are a dead man," said Fox.

Grant glared at Fox and said, "I couldn't give a flying fuck about your death threats Fox and the only rat's ass I am aware of, dug its way out of the first victim's abdomen." Getting no reaction or response from Fox, Grant then asked, "Now, where is this crummy vehicle you are giving me?"

They passed the group of reporters, who now were all stood at the bottom of the steps leading to the entrance of the police station. They ignored the two men, as all of them were making phone calls to their newspapers and any other media organisation they could get a response from. The sense of excitement among them was electric.

Fox and Grant entered the police station and walked toward the double doors. Fox swiped a card through the reader and opened one of the doors.

"Wow, I am impressed. Did you pick Gamby's pocket?" asked Grant, looking at the security swipe card.

"I've had it all the time, just didn't want Gamby to know. I was in this police station before his murder squad was put together. It was my idea that they be based here. The security gives them protection from the press, or at least it did until today."

"Oops, bad me," replied Grant, placing his hand over his open mouth. "So, who do you have on the inside?"

"One of the murder investigation team, he is currently at the crime scene of our latest victim, a uniformed police sergeant and the Chief Inspector," replied Fox.

Grant didn't say it but he had to admit he was impressed by the network of people this organisation had at their disposal.

They walked through the police station unchallenged and emerged back into the daylight at the back of the building into the car park area. It was secured by a high metal fence and security gates that required a pin number to be entered on a small keypad to enter and exit the car park. This was controlled by security or police staff, via the usage of

CCTV cameras. Grant looked around the area. As expected, there were marked police vehicles, a few standard vehicles that could have been unmarked police cars or the personal vehicles of the staff. Grant continued scanning the car park, looking for which vehicle he had been allocated by Fox and his people. And then he saw it. He tried to hide his surprise and excitement, but was sure he had failed.

He knew that his attempt was in vain as he looked at Fox and saw the big cheesy smile all over his face.

"You are joking me?" said Grant.

"No. It's yours, in your name. Not a loaner," replied Fox. "Consider it a demonstration of the belief we have in you, despite what you have just done."

Grant looked again at the black motorbike parked about fifty metres from where he stood. He walked over to it and stroked his hand over the Indian Chiefs head emblem emblazoned on the side of the tank. The Indian Chief Dark Horse was 1800cc of pure cruising power. Grant pulled out the keys that Fox had handed to him earlier. Glancing at them he didn't recognise any of them as a bike ignition key.

"No need for a key Grant, as long as the fob is on your person when you are near the bike, you just have to press the ignition button. This will provide a quick getaway, should you decide to let people shoot at you again," said Fox, throwing in the reference to the last time Grant needed a quick exodus and had failed to get it quite right.

"I don't think our killer is a gun type person," said Grant, still beaming ear to ear.

Fox laughed and said, "I know of pacifists who would be quite willing to shoot you within thirty seconds of meeting you."

"This doesn't mean we are friends," said Grant.

He quickly pressed the ignition switch and revved the bike loudly, drowning out Fox's response. He didn't need to hear it to know that it was something abusive. He continued to rev the bike, falling more and more in love with it with every turn of the throttle.

Fox tapped him on the shoulder, Grant released the throttle and let the bike tick over.

"I'm going to see how Ganby is doing following your press release and then return to Bloom's," he informed Grant. "Built in GPS on the bike, three addresses already programmed into it. The first two are the homes of the parents of our first two victims, the third is for your apartment."

"Okay, thanks," shouted Grant, even when just ticking over the bike was still quite loud.

"I will text you any information I think you may need to know about the latest victim once I get some." He patted Grant on the shoulder, "Don't fall off," he said, returning to the police building.

Grant picked up the helmet hanging from the front brake handlebar. Inside the black flip up lid, he could see that a Bluetooth communication device had already been fitted. He retrieved his mobile phone and switched on the Bluetooth option. Within seconds his phone recognised the device ID in the helmet and gave him the option to connect to the new device, Grant didn't bother.

"Fuck that, having to listen to his voice whenever he wanted to call, that would alone make me want to fall off," he said aloud to himself.

He donned the helmet and made his way out of the car park. The heavy barrier and sliding gates opened seconds after he became visible on the many cameras covering the exit area.

Riding through the streets of London was not the best place to get used to a new bike, especially a cruiser type. Twice he clipped the kerb on the inside of roundabouts, once having to place his foot so solidly on the floor to keep his balance, he was certain that he was about to come off. Thankfully, he stayed shiny side up and decided to pull over quickly to activate the GPS.

The system took him east and thankfully he remained mainly on the larger roads. Within a short time, he was leaving the busy streets of London behind him. His first destination was southeast of Maidstone. He remembered the address from the file he had read—Nettlefield. He decided to follow the GPS instructions and followed the M-20 for most of his journey.

It was just over two hours later when he arrived outside the new build property. It was probably about twenty years old and very well maintained. A small white fence with a gate in the middle separated the small lawned frontage from the pavement. Grant switched off the bike and looked at the house. It looked so normal, not the sort of place that you visit, to question people about their dead child.

Grant checked his phone before approaching the front door. He saw that he had two missed calls from Fox and one voicemail. He listened to the voicemail, a permanent smile on his face as he heard Fox's vexed voice explaining to him how he and the police were trying to sort out the clusterfuck he had left behind. They wanted him back at the police station later that evening for a press conference that they planned to hold.

Probably won't make that, Grant thought to himself.

He placed his phone back into his pocket, double checking it was in silent mode. Clearing the smile from his face, he made his way to the door of the house and rang the bell.

The man who answered the door looked tired. He hadn't shaved for a few days and was generally dishevelled. He simply said one word.

"Yes."

"Hello Mr. Nickel, my name is Colin Garside." He held up his fake ID card for the man to look at although the man barely bothered to. "I am working with the police investgating the death of your son. May I come in and have a short chat?"

"I've said everything that I need to say to the police, several times actually mate. I have nothing more to add," said the empty Mr. Nickel.

"I appreciate that sir," replied Grant, "but I am a profiler and expert on serial killers. I don't believe that your son died accidentally. I think he was actually a victim of a serial killer. You would really be helping me, and possibly your son, too, if you would just allow me a few minutes of your time.

Making the Link

The medical staff, the on scene doctor, forensic officers and the police all had to concede that the fire service would be required to remove the young man from the wooden cross, so securely and uniquely had he been secured to it. The public, of which there was still a few dozen, were being held back by police crime scene tape and a couple of police officers. TV news camera vehicles were at the scene. A reporter was interviewing a man who was claiming to be the one who had found the body. The same man was eagerly showing some of the photographs he had taken on his phone to the young female interviewer.

"Look, someone has cut his cock off," the man cried.

A uniformed police officer walked away from the scene, making his way around a corner. He removed a mobile phone from his trouser pocket. Locating the number he wanted, he pressed the call button. It rang four times before being answered.

"Mr. Fox, hi it's PC Dylon. This is a messy one sir," he said. "Civvies have been all over it before we got here, but the body is with your people. What do you want doing with the cross?"

Fox responded from a quiet corner of the office at the police station.

"Well, the fire service says they will take it to the police station. What can I do?" he asked.

Fox's words were obviously not what the police officer needed to hear.

"I will do my best sir," responded PC Dylon, having no need to end the call. Fox had already done that with an angry tap of the red phone symbol on his phone.

PC Dylon made his way back to the crime scene and had a short conversation with one of the forensic officers, who he knew was working for Fox, too. In turn, a member of the forensic team, all of who were employed by the Bloom Instititute, working directly for Dr. Stanridge, made his way to the fire officer in charge. Their exchange was heated, but the fireman had to give way to forensic needs, as it was explained to him that he would be reported to his superiors for interfering with an item that could provide vital forensic evidence.

The blood-smeared cross was placed into one of the forensic team vans. The van and the ambulance left at the same time ,both making their way to the Bloom building where Dr. Stanridge would be waiting.

—————— ——————

Grant sat on a sofa, having accepted the offer of a cup of coffee. He looked around the room. Absolutely nothing out of the ordinary could be seen, except for a large photo, which stood on a round wooden table, surrounded by candles of all sizes and descriptions. Their flames flickered light against the glass front protecting the photograph of Jamie Nickel. Given the circumstances that had ripped this family's life apart, this was only to be expected Grant supposed, a feeling he knew all too well.

Mr. Nickel returned with two cups of coffee, handing one to Grant, who stood to accept it from him. He sipped the hot drink and then asked, "When did Jamie leave home?"

"About a month before they found his body," replied Mr. Nickel, holding his cup of coffee so tightly you could be forgiven for thinking that it somehow represented his son. His forever lost son, who he had let go of.

"Could I look at his room please?" asked Grant cautiously.

"Already been done, more than once," the heavily grieving father replied.

"No Mr. Nickel, it has been searched. I want to look at it," responded Grant.

"What's the difference?" Mr. Nickel asked.

"Care," was the simple answer.

Mr. Nickel took both cups of unfinished coffee, returning them to the kitchen, and then led Grant up the stairs. He stood outside of the first door they came to, not saying a word or moving toward it.

"Is this Jamie's room, Mr. Nickel?" asked Grant.

"Yes," the man replied, his eyes beginning to glisten as the tears of loss began to form again.

"Leave it to me sir," said Grant, with real genuine empathy.

Mr. Nickel began his slow descent back down the stairs, stopping halfway to say, "Please don't leave it like the coppers did. I have had to put it back to how he would have wanted it twice now."

"Trust me, Mr. Nickel, I will treat your son's room with the utmost respect," replied Grant.

The man proceeded down the stairs. Grant grabbed the door handle, turned it downwards and pushed the bedroom door open.

The inside of the bedroom was unremarkable, to say the least. A few music related posters on the walls, Jamie clearly had a penchant for '80s music. Madonna, Depeche Mode and Spandau Ballet, amongst others, could be viewed as well as more up to date ones, which included a few posters of Pink. The music law according to Grant was, that if you didn't have a rock band poster on your wall, you had bad taste.

He carefully looked through drawers and wardrobes, finding nothing of any significance. Jamie had taken the items that would have proven useful with him. There was no laptop, no journal or diary, nothing that would have given Grant a personal insight into the lad.

Grant left the room. On his way out, he noticed a sticker on the inside of the door proclaiming "I am HPY," with a rainbow motif above it. *You probably were once,* thought Grant. He returned downstairs, where Jamie's dad was standing in front of the window looking out through the net curtains. He had obviously heard Grant walking down the stairs as, without turning around to acknowledge Grant's arrival back into the living room he stated:

"The police said they weren't absolutely convinced that Jamie had been killed, that he may have been the victim of a mugging or robbery that went badly wrong. You used the word killed with a certainty that suggests you know he was. What are the police hiding from me?"

Grant sat down and invited Mr. Nickel to do the same. Remembering the man's first name from the file, Grant began to speak.

"Phil, may I call you Phil?" Phillip Nickel nodded his head to affirm that he was fine with that.

"Thank you. Phil, you are going to hear and read things in the press over the next few days and weeks that will probably shock you. I have no doubt that your son was a victim of a serial killer. What I don't know is why he was selected by that killer." Grant waited for a reaction of some kind from the man, but got nothing.

"Is there anything you could tell me about Jamie that might help me? Anything about him that could have possibly made him a target?" he asked.

"Why would anyone want to kill my boy?" Phil Nickel was clearly shocked by the information that Grant had told him. His head continually shook left and right, a negative symbolism that reflected his disbelief.

"He was a nice boy, liked his music, kept himself to himself, only had a few friends and they were nice kids. Worked hard at college too you know, not there just to skive for a few years."

Grant nodded his head, not because he wanted this man to know that he was in agreement with him. After all, how could he be, given he had never met Jamie Nickels? Grant just wanted him to know that he was listening and being attentive.

"You told the police that Jamie's behaviour had changed before he left home. How did it change, Mr. Nickel?" Grant needed to bring this back to a conversation that might provide him with some information, rather than a journey down memory lane.

"He became more reclusive, staying in his room all day and night. Stopped going to college, spent all of his time on the damn fucking computer," replied Phil Nickel. His mood changed to one of restrained anger. "I asked him, tried to speak to him, but he said nothing that could explain the change in his behaviour. He just kept telling me and his mum to leave him alone, declaring that we didn't and never would understand. I just put it down to his age, you know, hormones and all that shit, and then he just upped and went."

"Did he say where he was going?" asked Grant.

"Just said he was off to live in London. Attempted to convince us that he had enrolled into a college there to start a new course. I didn't believe him. I knew he was hiding something; he had never lied to us before that," replied Jamie's father.

Grant very much doubted that. A father himself, he knew that children lied to their parents all the time.

"Did he keep a diary?" asked Grant.

"Not that I know of, just typed a lot on his laptop, caught him a few times. Chatting to people, you know having conversations like kids do these days." Phil Nickel stood up and Grant took that as a signal to leave. He stood up and shook the man's hand.

"Thank you for your time, Phil," he said.

The man led him to the front door. "Thank you for being honest with me," he said to Grant.

Grant was not used to that response. Normally people didn't really appreciate his level of brutal honesty. Referring back to something that Mr. Nickel had said just moments earlier, he asked, "Did Jamie write a blog?"

Phil Nickel looked confused.

"I don't know what one of those is."

"Doesn't matter," replied Grant, and went to shake the man's hand again. Phil Nickel's hands remained at the sides of his body.

"When can I have my son back?" he asked.

"What?" countered Grant, with genuine surprise.

"We want to bury our son. When can he come home?"

Grant had no idea why this family had not been allowed to bury their son by now.

"Errr, that's not my area Mr. Nickel, but I promise that I will ask about that and make sure the information gets back to you."

He walked out of the front door that had been opened for him by Phil Nickel, hearing it close behind him swiftly after his exit. He took in a deep breath of fresh air and walked to his bike. He began to unlock the helmet lock, with which he had secured his helmet on arrival. He retrieved the phone from his pocket. Two more missed calls from Fox but no voicemails this time. Maybe Fox was starting to learn that Grant spoke to people when he wanted to, not when they decided he should. He pressed the call button and held the phone up to his ear. Fox answered almost immediately.

"How's it going?"

"Fucking wonderfully! Speaking to grieving parents is what I live for," replied Grant, not knowing what it was about Fox that brought out his scurrilous side so easily. "What do you want?"

"Just checking that you picked up my voicemail," replied Fox.

"Yeah, I won't be there." Grant's reply was short, sweet and nonchalant.

"Yes, you will be there Grant." Fox's response was less sugar coated.

"NO, I fucking won't be. Listen Fox, you brought me into this shit to find your killer. Attending a press conference littered with by-the-book quotes for the press to print will not bring this bastard out into the open. I am doing this my way, which is why you recruited me, don't ever forget that." Fox knew that he wasn't going to win this one.

"Well at least tell me what you are doing," said Fox, beginning to realise that he was losing control of Grant already, a feeling he intensely disliked.

"Gotta see a man about unearthing a worm," was Grant's cryptic response.

"Don't ever forget that we have your wife! You will work for us as long as that remains the case," said Fox, desperately trying to reclaim some control over this maverick.

"And don't you ever forget that you have no idea where I am, but I can always find you." Grant felt the emptiness of his implied threat the second that he uttered it.

"Grant, I will always know where you are," replied Fox, the confidence back in his voice.

"Good," replied Grant, "so you will always know when I am coming for you! Enjoy your time with the press rats." Grant ended the call, switched the phone off and placed it back in his pocket. Unlocking his helmet, he put it on and mounted his bike.

"Right," he said out loud. "Let's see how good my new credit line is."

He gunned the bike into life. Taking one last look back toward the house he had just visited, he could just about see Phil Nickel through the thick net curtains. He raised his hand up to the side of his bike helmet, delivering a two finger, Boy Scout style salute in the man's direction. He nodded his head and rode away, heading back toward London.

—————— ——————

The boy sat up on the mattress that he had been laying on. He remembered being naked, starting to wash his body with a liquid that stung like hell and then nothing. He was once more wearing the white gown. His shoulder felt tight. He reached his hand back over the opposite shoulder and just about reached far enough to feel something soft and padded. He could only assume that someone had dressed his wound. He slowly got to his feet, taking his time to allow the dizziness to slowly dissipate.

The heavy dark chain attached to the manacle around his ankle rattled. He looked around: dark walls, dark ceiling and most strangely, no door on the room in which he was contained. He tentatively walked toward the opening, the chain rattling again, this time, louder as it moved against the stone floor. It had been perfectly measured so as to reach its maximum length, halting him about a foot from any potential open escape route. He stretched forward with his arm, in a hopeless attempt to reach outside of the open doorway, as if it would make him feel free somehow. As he did so, he noticed words stencilled on the wall to the left of the opening. Its message was simple.

Be silent or be repentant at the lord's hands

He returned to the mattress, sat down and started to think, *how did I get here?*

He remembered being in the toilets, standing to have a piss. His new friend had just finished washing his hands and had walked out shouting, "I'll see you in a minute." He recounted experiencing pain and then nothing. He searched his memory banks, trying to remember what had caused the pain, something solid around his throat, a sharp pain in the side of his neck, then nothing.

The memories were sketchy at best: *a night out, new friends but how did he end up here, like this? Was this some kind of sick initiation? Would his new social circle really do this? No, they wouldn't cause him physical harm as part of some kind of prank, unless it was a test.*

"Hello, is anyone out there?" he shouted.

A few seconds passed before he heard a quiet, nervous whisper. The words, the voice full of fear, was a girl's voice, pleading, "Please, please be quiet. He will hurt us all."

"Are you the one I touched? Why did he make me do that?" the boy retorted in a whisper.

Nothing came back, no response. Just silence.

He heard the words before he saw the dark figure standing a few feet away from the opening he had tried to reach before. His presence was surrounded in blackness, barely visible.

"I cleansed his body Lord, but I cannot cleanse his soul. This one cannot be saved and needs to be released. Show me how to deliver his soiled soul to your keep my Lord," said the shadowy figure.

"Yes, yes, please," shouted the young man. "Let me go. I won't say a word I promise, I won't tell anyone."

The shadowy figure disappeared from his view. The boy sat and waited in silence, hopeful that he was going to be released. He sat like that for about five minutes before the girl's voice whispered to him again.

"You are next."

—————— ——————

Grant, aka John Richardson, aka Colin Garside, rode his way back to London enjoying getting familiar with the handling of his new metal steed. Braking was a little sharper than he was used to, which had almost caught him out twice.

The first time, was much to the anger of a car driver who almost ran into the back of him. The driver's tirade of abuse had been acknowledged by the well-known hand signal that had told the driver that Grant thought he was a wanker. On route, Grant had spotted a bike dealership and pulled up outside of it. The dealership had its own little coffee shop outside, of which were several riders, a few of whom came over to look at the 1800 Dark Horse in admiration. This was one of the many things that Grant loved about the biking world. Its members were always appreciative of a well-maintained, nice-looking bike.

Grant entered the shop and immediately found the items he wanted. A black, open-face helmet with integral sunshades, a pair of summer riding gloves made from thin comfortable leather with a bit of knuckle and finger protection built in, a pair of cruiser riding boots, and a lightweight riding jacket that he fell in love with the moment he saw it. He tried all items for size and was happy that they all fitted fine. At the last moment as he approached the sales desk, he spotted a display rack full of sunglasses and face shields. He selected a half face mask in plain black and a pair of round-lensed glasses that were blue mirrored.

The man monitoring the till was almost bursting with excitement as he scanned each item. He then went into the stockroom behind the sales desk, returning moments later with boxed versions of the helmet and boots.

"That comes to £348.99 sir," he informed Grant.

Grant slid his new bank card into the payment machine. He then briefly paused as he tried to remember the pin number that had been included in the pages of information that Fox had given to him. The smile on the sales assistant's face disappeared briefly.

"Is there a problem sir?" he asked Grant.

"Sorry, new card and new number," replied Grant honestly.

He tapped in four numbers followed by the green button on the keypad and mentally crossed his fingers. Within seconds, the payment had been approved and the screen was instructing him to remove his card. The smile returned to the young man's face.

"Thank you, sir, nice bike by the way."

"Yeah, she's not bad," replied Grant. "She'll do for now I suppose," winking at the man to show that he was just joking.

Grant placed the helmet and gloves that had been provided by the Bloom Institute on top of the sales desk saying, "I don't need these. Do what you like with them."

The sales assistant looked confused. It was apparent that the helmet and gloves that had just been placed in front of him were brand new. He looked at Grant quizzically.

"Erm, we can't take those off you sir and we don't buy used items."

Grant looked over his shoulder. A man in his mid-thirties was busy looking at helmets, or to be more precise, at their price tags.

"Hey fella," called Grant to him.

The man looked around toward Grant. Surveying the shop, he realised that the stranger was talking him.

"What?" he said to Grant, "are you referring to me?"

"Yeah," replied Grant. "Could you make use of these?" asked

Grant, pointing in the direction of the helmet and gloves. He picked up the gloves, placed them inside the helmet and lobbed it in the direction of the surprised customer.

"Try them on for size," said Grant. "They're free if they fit, sell them if they don't."

Grant proceeded to remove all the price tags and labels from his new purchases and put them on. He left the bike shop, carrying his old jacket, which he just could not part with but leaving his old boots on the floor where he had taken them off. Reaching his bike, which still had a few admiring guys looking around it, he asked, "Could we disband the nice bike appreciation society fellas? Need to get back on the road."

Most walked away with a smile and a wave or a thumbs up. One left with a look on his face that said he thought that Grant was an arrogant twat. Grant didn't care; he needed a few moments of privacy.

He hung the new helmet containing the new pair of gloves from one of the bike handles and once again pulled out his phone. After a minute or so speaking with an operator, he ended the call and waited. A few seconds later he received a text. The message simply containing the number he had asked for. Before calling it, he saved the number into the phone.

"Good afternoon, Milton Dryton Police, how can I help?" Grant didn't recognise the voice.

"Sergeant Murphy please," he replied.

"May I ask who's speaking sir?" replied the voice.

"You may. It's DI Gamby from the Met," lied Grant. One of the many useful things he had learned in life was if you believed your own lie, most others did too. Throw a huge amount of confidence into the mix and you could get away with quite a bit.

"I'll see if he's available sir," the voice said. The line went quiet until a very familiar voice spoke down the phone.

"Hello, Inspector Gamby. How can I be of service today?" asked Sergeant Murphy.

Grant smiled, and his thoughts briefly returned to the first time he met up with this police officer. His response identified his identity to Sergeant Murphy immediately.

"Well Sergeant Murphy, you aren't my father or my old Sergeant Major, but I bet you are still a cunt."

"What the fuck?" he responded, followed by silence. "It can't be." Further silence ensued before he stated, "Rumour had it you were dead."

Grant laughed and said, "Just occasionally, Gus. When you ride with the devil, he gives you a second chance to get it right."

"Bloody hell mate, it's great to hear your voice again," another period of silence followed before Gus continued. "However, I am guessing that your call means that I am about to be poured into a whole bag of shit again."

"Not this time my friend. You have a family now," replied Grant. "But I do need a favour. A couple of calls, that's all and then once again forget you ever knew me."

"Forgetting you is impossible, but you gave me my daughter back, so a small favour is the least I can do mate. Just ask." The sincerity and gratitude shone through the copper's response.

"Thanks Gus. First, I need you to find an old acquaintance of mine," said Grant. "He's an ex-con, known by a few names. Either his real name, Stanley Dawson, or one of his road names, Wolfie or Shuffler."

Gus Murphy hurriedly wrote down the information on

a notepad. "And the second thing?" asked Gus, fearing the worst.

"Get the word out to the wrong people that I am still alive and can be found most days around the area of Paddington Green police station," replied Grant.

"Are you asking me to tell the Crippens that you are alive and well?" asked Gus, bewildered at this second request.

"Well, I am guessing they haven't moved on too far and, don't ask me how, but I happen to know that they will have a new leader. I am hoping that whoever it is, will want to do what his predecessor couldn't," said Grant.

"Yeah, they are still around, moved out of my area I am happy to say, but they are successfully rebuilding elsewhere as far as I am aware. No idea who is in charge now," replied Gus. "But why the fuck do you want to mess with them again? Look what happened last time Grant."

"Gus, as much as I want to chew the fat with you and explain myself, I really don't have the time." Grant moved his helmet from the bike handle to the bike seat. "Just tell me, will you help me again?"

"I already said that I would Grant. How do I get the information to you?" replied Gus.

Grant read out the number of his mobile phone and Gus jotted it down.

"Thanks Gus," he said. "Let me know when it's done, and I would appreciate it if you could do some fast work on finding Dawson."

"I'll do my best Grant." Thinking that the conversation was over, Gus was surprised when Grant asked, "How's Emma?"

"She's fine and you stay away from her," replied Gus, laughing.

"You need to keep the horny bitch away from me mate," said Grant, laughing as loudly as Gus was.

"Yeah, she did tell me that she went through a period of wanting to take you to bed. Apparently, it was her effort to support the elderly." The laughing had stopped, but Gus was still smiling broadly.

"Speak soon Sergeant Major," said Grant, and ended the call.

—————— ——————

Fox sat in his car outside of the large police station in Paddington Green, drained having just ended a marathon phone conversation with Mr. Bloom. Whilst bringing Bloom up to date with current events, it had emerged that he was on speaker phone, when the voice of the client suddenly became involved in the conversation. Neither men were happy, the client especially. The news that Grant had spoken with some hack reporters had not gone down well.

"Bring him back in," Bloom had demanded, but Fox convinced him to let Grant continue.

"Let him find our target and then we will take over and serve our client in the way agreed sir," he had pleaded. "I can control this Mr. Bloom. I will be limiting the damage later at the press conference."

During the conversation, Fox had learned that the client was, in fact, a senior civil servant and not a serving MP, as he had initially been told. Without a doubt, it was clear that whoever this man was, he was extremely important to Bloom. The call had ended with Godfrey Lambden, reminding Fox that any failure would result in him spending the rest of his career cleaning toilets. This existence would occur in an unimportant office building. His most important responsibility would be counting the little yellow cubes that were thrown into urinals to hide the smell of piss.

"There'll be toilet fresheners then sir?" Fox had asked, adopting some of Grant's sarcasm.

The call had come to an abrupt end after Lambden informed Fox that he needed to remember that he was about as important as a fart in a hangar. This had about the same impact, which apparently, Fox had learned at that moment, was very little.

Fox placed his elbow on the armrest and pressed his finger against his temple, leaning his head onto it. He closed his eyes and rubbed his temple roughly. He had always known that keeping Grant in check would prove to be difficult, but the unpredictability of the man made it almost impossible. He really couldn't wait for the moment to arrive when he could kill him.

Looking out of the vehicle, Fox could see that the once small group of four or five hopeful reporters, had transformed into a camp of news channel vehicles, smartly dressed TV and radio reporters and presenters, and a host of journalists and photographers. The circus had certainly arrived outside of Paddington Green, and now two police officers had been posted outside of the main entrance doors.

You had better know what you are doing Grant, Fox thought to himself.

He made one more call. This one was directly to the office line of Dr. Stanridge.

A harsh whisper answered the phone with the word, "What?"

"Dr. Stanridge?" asked Fox, not recognising the voice who had replied.

"Sorry, Dr. Stanridge. How can I help you Mr. Fox?" said Stanridge, his voice returning to its normal tone.

"You okay doctor?" asked Fox.

"Yes, yes…tired that's all, what can I do for you?" replied Stanridge.

"No more meds for Mortimer Church please doctor," he said, a statement rather than a request.

"Are you sure Fox? He is a dangerous man on them, without them I will not be held responsible for what he might try," asked Dr. Stanridge.

"I know," replied Fox. He ended the call and got out of the car, ignoring the barrage of questions being shouted out to him from the news circus.

—————— ——————

Stanridge stood outside of Mortimer Church's room, looking at the man inside. He turned on the speaker system, not because he desired to converse with the man on the other side of the door, but because he knew that Mortimer would want to speak to him.

"What do you want my brother?" Mortimer asked.

"Just thought I would let you know that Fox wants you off the meds," the doctor replied.

"Big deal, I have been off them for weeks, you saw to that," replied Mortimer with a smile.

"What do we do next?" asked Stanridge.

"We do what we have been doing, my brother, nothing has changed," said Mortimer.

"But, what about Grant?" Stanridge was clearly worried by Grant's inclusion into the mix.

"An added bonus, we have no need to concern ourselves with him. Now, return to your work, write your patient reports and let me do what I do best." The Priest had not moved from his position. He was lying on his side, facing away from the door throughout the entire conversation. He did not want to look at the individual outside of his door. The sheer thought that he was actually loosely related to this bottom feeder made him cringe.

—————— ——————

Grant rode his bike through the streets of St. John's Wood following the satellite navigation system to the address of the family of the most recent victim. The postcode had been sent to him by Fox on a text message. Grant had responded to that text with a simple request:

"I need to speak to your client."

He had so far received no response.

Grant steered his bike into the small resident's car park that stood at the front of the brown bricked block of flats on Grove Road. Largely untouched since it was first built, the block was a rectangular building with four floor levels, all containing a frontage of windows and doors. One entrance door led to a flight of stairs, which led to each floor of the building. These, in turn, would lead you to the concrete walkway that allowed access to each flat.

Grant was familiar with this type of building. His wife's grandparents had lived in something similar for years, in a community quite close to this one. He knew that there would be a shared garden at the back of the building, and each flat would have a small balcony, just about large enough to squeeze two chairs onto them. Estate agents would describe them as art deco requiring modernisation.

Grant would have used more suitable words. Locking his bike and taking his helmet with him, he walked into the building. The main door was wedged open making the buzzer system redundant. He made his way up the enclosed stone stairway, which was pleasantly clean, graffiti free and didn't smell of piss like Grant had expected. Leaving the stairway, he reached the external walkway on the second floor. He made his way down it, following the direction indicated by the metal sign that pointed you toward two groups of flat numbers. He headed left toward flat numbers 48-64. He was looking for 52.

Finding the relevant flat, he pressed the doorbell and waited.

A large man wearing a white vest and dark blue trousers opened the door. He gave Grant a quick visual once over and said, "S'pose you had better come in then."

Grant stepped through the open door watching the man walk down the narrow hallway.

"Are you Mr. Gardner, sir?" he asked. "Mr. Frank Gardner?"

"That I am, and you must be the detective that I was told to expect by the two rozzers who left here about an hour ago," replied the gruff large man, rather bluntly.

"I'm not the police Mr. Gardner. My name is Colin Garside. I am a criminologist and…," Grant was not given the time to finish his self-introduction.

The man turned around sharply and with a rough, growling

tone said, "Listen pal, ask what you want, take what you need and then fuck off and leave me the fuck alone."

This was neither the response, nor the demeanour that Grant had expected from a parent who had recently been informed of his son's death. He followed Mr. Gardner through a door that led left from the entrance hallway into a small sitting room. It was largely filled by a long three-seater sofa, a small coffee table and a long table up against the wall that the sofa was facing. This held one thing, an extremely large television that Grant estimated to have at least a 90-inch screen.

Frank Gardner dropped his huge bulk onto the sofa, landing in the centre of it. This allowed no room for anyone else to sit without being in physical contact with him. He picked up a small bottle of whisky from the table and took a large swig from it.

"Mr. Gardner," said Grant, genuinely concerned by the way this man was acting, "are you okay?"

"Look, he's dead all right, I get it. Don't surprise me one bit if the truth be known. It was never going to end well, what with his shady new mates he was hanging around with. I fucking told him so, not interested one bit, he wasn't. He was the death of his mother, you know. Now he's left me all alone. Ain't he, the selfish little bastard?"

"Mr. Gardner, I know how you are feeling sir, please believe that," Grant started.

"Lost a fucking child have yer?" said Frank Gardner angrily.

"Well," replied Grant, "actually, yes I have. My daughter was murdered." Grant meant to continue with more detail, how long ago it happened, that type of thing, but he found that he couldn't talk about it.

"Lost a little girl did yer? The apple of your eye, eh? Your little China doll. That must have hurt. Sorry for your loss." Frank Gardner's tone changed from bitterness and uncaring to empathy toward Grant.

"Girls is different though, ain't they? Not like lads. They are born to fucking disappoint. We…I knew our lad would let us…me down. Turned into a right twat in the months before he moved out. I couldn't wait to see the back of him. His mum died two weeks later, broken heart it was, I tell ya that for nothing."

Grant felt for this broken man who was hiding behind a defensive emotional wall, hurt and let down. Grant knew exactly how he was feeling. He had been there. Grant was saved from having to say any more empty and useless words to Frank Gardner, who continued speaking.

"Those weird new friends of his were trouble, not the drugs and beating people up type of trouble mind, just fucking trouble. Dressed weird, they did. Hair all bloody colours, always hung about outside on the road waiting for Geoffrey to join them. Wouldn't come up here or come into the flat; knew I would tell 'em exactly what I thought about 'em."

"How long had he known these new friends, Mr. Gardner?" asked Grant.

"A few months, maybe a bit longer. Started to dress like them, he did. Them tight jeans and baggy T-shirts, some with no sleeves. It's not a fucking T-shirt if it don't have sleeves I told him, just a bloody rag. All colours they were. Never saw him wearing anything that wasn't black before them fuckers came into his life." Frank took another large slug from the whisky bottle.

"Did you talk to Geoff about it sir?" asked Grant.

"It's fucking Geoffrey not fucking Geoff," barked Frank at Grant. "They called him Geoff. Probably thought it was spelled with a fucking J too and yes, of course, I tried to talk to him. He was my…he is my fucking son. What kind of father do you think I am?"

"I'm sorry Mr. Gardner, I didn't mean it that way," apologised Grant.

"Yeah, I'm sure, like him you are. Said I would never understand. Said I was blinkered and stuck in my ways like I was thick, uneducated or something. I'm an ex London cabby you know. A proper one as well, did the knowledge and everything. Not a cabby now though. Not enough work out there anymore. Too many of them private taxi things and illegal ones too. It's all them muzzys and bloody Russians they're letting into the country. That's why I'm an ex London cabby. I met all kinds of people in my cab over the years. I was able to speak with all 'em, understand all 'em. My son knew better though. I embarrassed him, that's what it was really." Another huge gulp of whisky. Grant looked at the bottle as it was thumped back down onto the table. Frank Gardner had consumed half of the small bottle in the time that Grant had been there. Frank picked up the bottle again and tilted it in the direction of Grant.

"Forgetting me manners I am, would you like a glass?" he asked Grant.

"No, I'd better not, duty and all that Mr. Gardner, but thanks anyway," replied Grant, secretly wanting a quick nip of the amber liquid.

"Call me Frank, all my customers called me Frank. I told 'em all, call me Frank," said Frank.

"Thanks Frank," Grant paused, wondering if it was the right

time to approach the subject. Deciding that he was now uncomfortable enough he did not do so. He just wanted to get out of this flat. "Frank, can I have a look around Geoff…reys room?" He hoped that Frank hadn't noticed his quick correction of his son's name.

Frank waved his hand in the air and raised the whisky bottle to his mouth with his other.

"Yeah fill yer boots. Look at whatever you want, take whatever you have to. He's gone now, don't need any of it anymore."

Grant grabbed the opportunity eagerly and left the chlostra-phobic sitting room and returned to the hallway. Four other doors were in the hallway, one of which was open showing a grubby and messy kitchen. The sink was overflowing with dishes covered in dried food remains. He opened the door nearest to him and found himself looking into a small bathroom. A sink, toilet and small bath, not long enough to allow the average person to stretch out in it, filled the room. He closed the door and went to the door at the far end of the hallway. As soon as it opened, he knew he had found the room that he had been looking for. Grant found himself looking at posters once again. No '80s era music posters for Geoffrey though. His walls were covered in posters declaring his adulation for club music. An old '60s style wardrobe, a double bed and a desk were all that occupied the room, mainly because nothing else would have fitted. On the desk was an item that Grant could never have hoped to find. A laptop with its top lid open. Its black screen reflecting his face back at him.

Sensing both excitement and anticipation, Grant rubbed his finger across the built-in mouse panel, hoping that the screen would burst into a bright and colourful life. He was disappointed. He noticed that the power button light was not illuminated. He pressed it, holding it for a second until he heard the familiar whirring sound of a laptop powering up.

It took the laptop several minutes to come to life, time that Grant used to search through the small desk drawer. A box of condoms still sealed in its cellophane wrapping, a few pens, a watch and a strip of photo-booth style photos. This last item he pulled out of the drawer, looking at it closely.

He still had no idea what Geoffrey Gardner looked like. The images and photographs on the internet had not been clear enough to make out the features of the young man's face. Grant guessed that the man in the photograph at the back of the three people who had crowded themselves into the photo booth, was Geoffrey Gardner, such was the similarity to this father.

He placed the strip of four photographs onto the desk next to the laptop. He stared at the empty white rectangular box in the centre of the screen. Grant would require a password.

"Shit," he said out loud.

He could only hope that someone in the organisation had the skills to break through this barrier. Picking up the strip of photographs and the laptop, he saw a flash of colour coming from the top of the laptop lid. He had just seen another similarity between Geoffrey's and Jamie's bedrooms.

The sticker on the top of the laptop was a rainbow with the words, "I am HPY" beneath it.

Grant was no detective, but neither did he believe in coincidences. He was looking at what he could at last call a link, even it was a tentative one.

He grabbed the laptop, taking it and the strip of photographs back into the sitting room. Frank Gardner was still occupying more than his fair share of the large sofa. The whisky bottle was now empty and the television had been switched on, although the sound was muted. Jeremy Kyle could be seen on the large screen on a stage with a group of no-hopers. Secretly, Grant smiled, remembering how he used to chastise his wife for watching this trash and recollecting her reply when he had asked her why she watched such rubbish.

"It makes me feel better about myself," had been her answer.

"Frank," he said to the ex-London cabby. "I need to take Geoffrey's laptop and this strip of photographs if I may?"

Once again Frank waved his hand nonchalantly, saying, "Told ya already, take the fucking lot, I couldn't care less."

"Do you know when these photos were taken?" asked Grant.

"No idea," replied Frank, not even looking at the photographic strip. "Never seen them before."

Grant could only hope that they were recent ones. He held the photos in front of Frank's face.

"These other people in the pictures. Old friends or new ones?"

Frank looked up and briefly looked at the photographs, his gaze returned to the television screen, as he stated, "Two of the new ones."

"Thanks Frank. You going to be okay?" he asked, before leaving the room.

"Always have been and can't see that changing." Grant knew that the drunk man would be asleep on that sofa within minutes of his departure.

He began to walk back toward the hallway when Frank asked, "Could I have them photos back when you have finished with them? I don't have any others of my boy."

"I'll bring them back personally. You have my word."

Grant left the flat, closed the door and stood for a moment on the walkway. He just hoped that the distraught man he had just left would remain alive long enough to receive the photographs back.

Shuffler

Grant stood by his bike, having checked that it hadn't been messed with during his absence. He secured the laptop in one of the large panniers, locking it before once again checking his phone, having switched it back on. He was not surprised to see that Fox had called him three times and left one voicemail. He had also received a text from Gus, it simply said: "CALL ME!"

He listened to the voicemail first. Fox informed him that a meeting had been arranged with their client. He stipulated that Bloom would not be there before he asked, and that the client was giving him fifteen minutes and no longer. He called Fox back.

"Where have you been?" asked Fox, answering the call immediately.

"Oh, shut up, you're not my mother. Listen, tell your client that if he gives a shit about who killed his daughter, he will give me what I need, otherwise he can stick his fifteen minutes up his arse. I will see you at the Institute tomorrow morning, fifteen minutes before the meeting. I have a laptop that needs hacking into. I'm sure you have people with the ability to do that," he said.

"I'll pass on your request," replied Fox. "How was Frank Gardner?"

"How do you know I have even seen him yet?" asked Grant curiously.

"Oh, just guessing," Fox sounded elusive in his reply.

"He has lost his son twice effectively, and in between that, lost his wife also, but he is doing brilliantly, found a new friend called oblivion kindly provided by Mr. Walker," replied Grant, predictably sarcastically.

"Who is Mr. Walker?" asked Fox.

"Johnnie, you dumb prick. See you tomorrow morning." Grant ended that call and straight away called Gus.

The conversation with Gus was a mixture of good and bad news. The good news was that Gus had managed to track down Stanley Dawson, aka Shuffler, and that it had been easy to do so. Even better news, was that he was living in London, something that Grant had fully expected. The bad news, was the area where he lived. The moment that Gus mentioned the notorious part of East London, Grant recognised it. During his time in the prison service, the famous estate was well known for providing a regular supply of residents to the local prison. In fact, the joke was that if the estate hadn't existed the jail would probably have had to close. Grant knew that the problem was that the residents of this estate did not take kindly to strangers making an appearance. He also knew that some of those residents were the type who you didn't really want to get on the wrong side of. Even the police stayed clear. If they had reason to enter, they did so mob-handed, otherwise, they stayed away.

Grant could understand the appeal for someone like Shuffler to live there. The lack of police presence would suit him just fine.

Grant had first met Stanley Dawson while working in a

North London prison, very early in his prison service career. He had already had an interesting life. By the time of his arrival at the prison, he was suffering from the injuries that had earned him his new road name. Without constant sips of Oramorph, Stanley could hardly walk for more than a few minutes before agonising pain kicked in. His injuries consisted of several fractured vertebrae, a smashed up pelvis, a double hip replacement and many other minor fractures throughout his body. These had been caused by being chained to the back of a motorbike and dragged around the streets for about five minutes.

He had been involved in a bike gang turf war. Members of his own group of bikers had eventually fled the battle, outnumbered and out-weaponed. Stanley was on the losing side. His biker life ended at that moment. Twice during the many operations, it took to pin and fuse him back together—his life had actually ceased.

Prior to finding brotherhood in the murky world of the biker gangs, he had found solace in the brotherhood of the military, having served nine years with the Royal Artillery. Life hadn't been easy for Stanley after leaving the Army, finding it difficult to settle into civilian life, and it was this need for rigid order in his life, that had led him to a bike gang.

After a year recovering from his injuries, Stanley's life became a whirlwind of chaos. A lot of it was caused by head injuries, mixed in with minor brain damage, that changed his personality. He tracked down the biker who had dragged him around from the back of the bike and burned his house down.

Whilst resisting capture for that one, he developed an infatuation with fire and arson. Eventually, and inevitably, considering how many fires he had instigated, Stanley started and completed his first custodial sentence. He only got sent down for eighteen months as the court took into account his past history, his mental state and condition. During that first sentence, his warped opinion of the world had time to develop and he quickly came to the conclusion that the whole world was against him.

Conspiracy theory started to rule his life. Two days after being released from prison, he burned down the house of the judge who had sent him to prison, and both the judge and his wife were seriously injured in that act of arson. It was at this point, the beginning of his five-year sentence, that the lives of him and Grant crossed.

During twenty-five years in the service, Grant could count on the fingers of one hand, the number of prisoners who he considered to be fairly decent blokes, one of those four was Stanley Dawson.

As Stanley had arrived on the wing, Grant was leaning against the railings of the twos landing. He watched this little shuffling old man trying to carry a bag full of personal belongings. After only a few yards, Stanley threw the bag to the ground exclaiming loudly, "Fuck this for a game of fucking soldiers." Grant continued to watch as the conversation between the locating officer and Stanley developed, the smile on his face getter bigger as each verbal punch was thrown between the two of them.

Officer: Pick up the bag fella and get you and it up to your cell on the threes.
Stanley: Does it look like I can walk three flights of stairs? I can hardly walk three fucking steps.
Officer: Well, I ain't carrying it for you fella.

Stanley: Guv, I wouldn't expect you to. You have enough on your plate carrying that huge belly around.
Officer: You are heading for a short, painful journey to the block.
Stanley: Better get a couple of mates Guv, cuz you will be fucking carrying me. Better get an extra one to carry my bag, too.
Officer: The second you are in your cell, I am going to paint the fucking walls with your fucking claret.
Stanley: Well at least I will be in my cell. Don't forget to come down and get my bag for me, will ya Guv?

At that stage, Grant had got involved. It was a hot day, and he really wasn't in the mood to get hot and sweaty, wrapping up some old dude who looked as if he would have difficulty getting out of bed.

"It's all right, Mr. Docherty, leave him there. You locate the others and I will deal with the old boy," Grant had shouted down to his colleague. He made his way down the stairs to the ones and stood in front of Stanley, who was just looking down at his bag of belongings.

"What's your name pal?" he asked.

"Stanley," came the reply.

Grant looked up at the ceiling and asked again.

"Your other name."

"Shuffler," said Stanley.

"No shit," Grant rubbed his eyes and asked once more, "what's your surname?"

"Dawson, Guv," replied Stanley, giving the answer that he knew Grant wanted from the beginning.

"Well, Dawson, firstly, you need to know that we aren't a

progressive jail, none of that first name shit here. Secondly, Mr. Docherty there, well he may look like a lump of lard, but he can hurt you in ways you can only imagine, something that I am quite proud of, because I taught him everything he knows. And one other thing that may be useful to keep in mind, I didn't teach him everything that I know. Now, what's your problem?"

"I can't do the threes, Guv. By the time I get down here from there at mealtimes, you would have finished dolloping out that horseshit you call food," he told Grant.

There was something about Dawson that Grant liked. He couldn't put his finger on what it was, but he had warmed to him immediately.

"How would you like a cell on the ones and a job working for me on the hotplate? Serving up our first class, grade A horseshit?" enquired Grant.

Dawson looked at Grant suspiciously. No screw had ever offered him anything other than a sharp tongue.

"I ain't no grass, Guv," he replied.

"Good," said Grant. "I don't want no grass working my hotplate."

"So, what do you want?" asked Dawson. "You screws always want something."

"Nothing. Call it my one kind act for the year," replied Grant, smiling at the likeable con. "Now, cell two over there is sitting empty, think you can make it that far?"

"You going to carry my bag for me?" asked Dawson cheekily, smiling back at Grant.

"No," replied Grant liking this man's quick wit, "but I am willing to help Mr. Docherty carry your sorry ass down to the block."

Within two months, Shuffler had been promoted to number one hotplate orderly. Everyone called him by his nickname, including all the staff, even Mr. Docherty, and he and Grant developed a healthy officer/convict working relationship. Whenever Grant was doing an evening duty, and it was quiet on the wing, he would quite often sit with Shuffler, listening to his stories, many of them wild and crazy about how he knew he was being watched by secret agencies, about how it was dangerous to own a mobile phone because it could be tracked and they had technology that could read your mind.

Despite the craziness and probably because he had learned about Shuffler being ex-military, although he never disclosed anything about himself, Grant enjoyed talking with the old con. Some of the most interesting chats were those about Shuffler's love affair with fire. He would talk for hours about the stuff he had read about it. He knew how fire worked, how it thought about where to go, how it could hide away for hours, then burst into life at the worst possible moment. Overall, his conversation rested on the different ways to burn a place down. Those were the stories that had resonated with Grant the most. The fact that Stanley Dawson was unhinged and had committed crimes, he struck Grant as a nice guy who had been given the wrong breaks, literally.

"Hey Grant, you still there?" Gus's voice broke Grant's connection with his memories.

"Yeah, sorry Gus and thanks for helping me out with this," he replied.

A voice in the background shouted out to Grant.

"Hey trouble! Hope you are keeping out of bother. Sorta glad to hear that you aren't dead," shouted a giggling Emma.

"Listen mate give her a big hug from me," Grant told Gus.

"Gotta go. I'll be in touch…maybe."

"Okay Grant," Gus replied, not happy with the "maybe" at the end of his friend's sentence. "You be careful. Oh, the other thing has been done as well. I don't think they will be interested in you, but just watch your back."

Grant ended the call and put the phone away. He looked at his watch, which now had a small crack at the top of the glass face. Another remnant of his final involvement with the Crippens, but it still worked. It was getting late and Grant was tired. His recovery had gone well, but his body still ached after periods of prolonged activity.

He thought briefly about visiting Shuffler now, but decided that maybe the best time to visit the estate where he lived would be in the morning, when the residents would almost certainly still be sleeping off the effects of the activities of the night before. He decided instead it was time to head off to his new apartment gifted to him by Fox, or at least the Bloom organisation, or maybe it was C.O.R.T. Grant imagined they were one and the same.

—————— ——————

The room used for press conferences at Paddington Green police station was packed to the hilt. This station had been involved in many high-profile crime investigations, but nobody could remember a press conference attracting such a crowd. There were at least one hundred reporters representing local and national newspapers and television channels. The shrieking resulting from the multiple conversations being had, as they waited for the conference to start, was deafening. People began to walk onto the raised platform at the front of the room, headed by the Chief Inspector. The last person to appear was Alex Fox. He positioned himself at the rear of the area, choosing to stand in the background rather than sit at the row of three tables placed at the front. The level of chatter slowly diminished to a silence fuelled with anticipation. The Chief Inspector began to speak:

"Ladies and gentlemen, thank you for your attendance, especially considering the short notice that you were all given. We thought it necessary to hold this press conference in order to present the facts. In turn, we have faith that they will be reported accurately."

He paused and scanned the room with accusing eyes. He knew many of the reporters who sat in the room this evening. He was only too aware of their ability to misquote an innocent word or phrase.

"A new team member assigned to the case, which we are currently working, has made a surprising disclosure. It, therefore, appears pertinent to ask for the assistance of the press and public. May I also add that the new team member's purpose is one that is strictly advisory."

Fox stood at the rear of the line of seated police staff, fully aware that the Chief Inspector was hiding a level of anger and frustration capable of causing him a heart attack. During the ensuing meeting, held between the two men about thirty minutes after Grant had finished his little chat with the small group of reporters, the Chief had demonstrated anger in monumental proportions that Fox had only ever witnessed from Mr. Bloom. He was screaming, shouting, swearing and threatening, and finally demanding that *this Garside character* be removed from the team. Fox was to make sure that the man never got near a police investigation again, unless he was the suspect.

Fox explained that whilst Colin Garside's actions appeared to be unorthodox, he was a highly respected profiler, recognised in his profession as being one of the country's best serial killer experts. Fox couldn't remember the last time he had told so many lies in one sentence. The Chief had responded by saying that he had been in the police force for thirty-two years, and he had never heard of him and he didn't want this potential train disaster to be his swansong. A statement, Fox thought, only went to confirm the rumours that the Chief Inspector was considering retiring.

It had taken Fox forty-five minutes to convince the Chief Inspector to allow his profiler to remain involved. His last resort was to remind him that it was what the organisation and more importantly what Mr. Bloom and their high-profile client wanted. They had discussed the content of the press conference. Once the content was agreed, the station's Media Officer was then engaged.

Fox stood behind and to the right of the Chief Inspector, concentrating on his opening address. He did not remember agreeing to the bulk of what had already been said. As he listened to the Chief, he blamed Grant for putting him in his current position. Fox focussed back on what Chief Watkins was saying.

"My investigation team has, for some time now, been working on what we believe to be a number of disappearances and murders, possibly connected to one individual. We have no leads to date as to who that person could be."

Hands were raised into the air by the more experienced reporters, all hoping for the nod from the Chief Inspector, who would indicate that they could ask their question. One less experienced and less polite reporter, who had been one of the group who Grant had spoken with that morning, didn't bother with the expected protocol.

"Chief Inspector, your so-called expert, a Dr. Colin Garside I believe, seemed to confirm that this was the work of a serial killer. I didn't detect any doubt in his statement. Can you confirm that London has a serial killer roaming its streets at night?"

Chief Watkins shuffled in his chair uncomfortably, thinking about his words before speaking.

"It is the personal belief of Mr. Garside that the two victims found to date are the work of a serial killer. A minor amount of evidence suggests that this may be the case. However, I need to point out that my investigation team is not excluding the possibilities that they could also be the victims of unfortunate accidents, or crimes committed by one or more perpetrators, not intent on killing, but rather some lesser crime such as robbery."

He nodded toward a reporter he recognised from a national newspaper. The reporter looked toward the hack, who had just asked the previous question with disgust before she spoke.

"Thank you, Chief Inspector. Can you confirm that one of the victims is the daughter of Godfrey Lambden, a senior civil servant from the Home Office, and are you able to confirm the names of the other two victims?" she asked.

"Thank you for your questions, Gabrielle," the reporter, Gabrielle Newsome, smiled at the Chief. "I am able to confirm that Alice Lambden, the daughter of Mr. Godfrey Lambden, is indeed one of the victims. The second person whose death is being investigated as part of this ongoing case is James Nickel."

"What about the third victim found in the early hours of this morning?" Chief Watkins could not see who had shouted the question from the back of the room.

"I cannot comment on that particular crime scene at this moment in time. There is nothing to suggest at this time that this is in any way connected to the serial killings, if that is what they are," he responded.

A bead of sweat began to trickle down the side of his forehead. He wiped it away and pointed to another reporter. He regretted this action immediately, when he recognised the reporter as being a representative of a national newspaper well known for sensationalising everything.

"Why is the killer being named the Inserter?" the reporter asked with a big childish grin on his face.

"This unauthorised name has not been associated with this investigation or the team working on it," the Chief replied sharply.

"Your expert profiler used those words," shouted the unidentifiable reporter, again from the back of the room.

"As I said," countered Chief Watkins, clearly annoyed at this line of questioning. "It is not a term that any member of my investigation team can relate to."

At that moment, DI Gamby, who had been sat silently next to his Chief Inspector, leaned toward him and whispered something into his ear. The Chief addressed the press.

"Ladies and gentlemen, that concludes this press conference. Once again, I would like to thank you for your attendance. I hope that the facts of this case, few as they may be, are reported accurately and responsibly. We do not need to spread panic amongst the public. We would welcome any information the public can provide that they believe would help us with our investigations."

The eight people who sat at the front of the stage, stood in unison, with the exception of the Media Officer. He remained in his seat, in order to do his usual job of mopping up the inevitable further questions. The majority, if not all, he would swat away by stating, "no comment at this time." As the Chief Inspector walked past Alex Fox he quietly said, "Get your new puppy dog under control." He left the stage grim-faced and still fuming at the position in which he had been placed.

—————— ——————

Grant rode his bike down the short ramp that led into the underground car park of the apartment block that his satellite navigation system had guided him to. The metal security gate slid open as he approached it.

He stopped the bike at the back of the car park close to a door on which was a sign stating, "Residents Only," locking the bike, but deciding that the place was secure enough to leave the contents of the side panniers where they were, he walked toward the door, pushing it to open it as he reached it.

Unsurprisingly, the door was locked. He spotted an intercom box to the right of the door and pressed the small black button located at the bottom of the box. A buzzing sound declared that the door's locking system had been unlocked and Grant pushed the door again. Before he stepped across the threshold, he looked behind him and scanned the area, and saw two security cameras positioned to view the door from the left and right.

He walked through the doorway, finding a flight of stairs

to his left. The door slowly closed behind him as he made his way up the steps. The one at the top of the stairs had no such intercom box. On opening it, Grant found himself inside a plush, but small reception area. Behind the reception desk stood a man in a black suit with red trim around the jacket collar.

"Good evening, Dr. Garside," the man said, looking up the moment that Grant entered his domain. "Or would you prefer to be called Grant during your stay?"

The man was short but extremely stocky. The well-fitted suit did not disguise the outline of a well maintained, strong body beneath it. His hair was cropped short and his upright, straight-backed standing position suggested that he could have come from a military background.

"Grant will do fine," he answered.

"Good, my name is Oliver. Please do not address me as Ollie or any other shortened version of my name. If there is anything you need while you are here, you only have to ask. It is my duty to make your stay here a comfortable and stress-free one. What goes on outside of here is no business of mine. Please do not speak to me about that side of your life."

He extended his arm. In his hand he held a credit sized white card.

"This is your swipe card. It will allow access to your room, which is room number seven on the first floor. It will not permit you to enter any other room, so please do not try. If you do, I will know. Please do not bother any of the other residents. Their business is none of yours. Do you have any questions sir?"

Grant approached the man and took the card from his hand.

Leaning on the reception desk, he extended his neck slightly, so that his face was only inches from the concierge's.

"I'm guessing you are ex-Guards Regiment Oliver," he said.

A slight movement of the mouth and a squinting of the eyes were the only reactions from Oliver. Without moving an inch from Grant's attempted intimidating positioning, he replied, "Sir, do not dishonour my service background. I served with a real fighting force. I was a Royal Marine."

"A fucking Bootneck," replied Grant. "I should have got that one."

The keeper of the reception desk still held on to one corner of the apartment door swipe card and Grant felt his grip on it tighten.

"Grant, if you ever refer to me again as a Bootneck, you will find yourself flat on your back with my boot on your neck." His reply came across as more of a promise than a threat.

Grant smiled and moved away slightly, allowing for a more comfortable space between them.

"I like you Oliver," he said.

"Sir, my feelings toward you are ones of indifference. Your existence is insignificant to me." He released his clasp on the swipe card, allowing Grant to take full ownership of it. "Now as I said, you are in room number seven. Please feel free to use the lift if one flight of stairs has already proved to be too much for you. Oh, and be careful you don't trip over that ego of yours on the way up."

Grant walked toward the lift. Noticing a green sign with the word "Stairs" written on it, he changed direction and headed for it. Subconsciously the ex-Marine's last remark had impacted Grant more than he realised. As the door began to close behind him, Grant called out:

"Thanks for the welcome Oliver. I will call if I need room service."

The concierge sat down behind the reception desk and smiled. It made a change to have a guest with a set of bollocks and a sense of humour.

The décor of Grant's room was of a high standard while simply furnished. It was ample for a more than comfortable stay, but not somewhere you would want to live the rest of your life. Removing his jacket and throwing it along with his bike helmet and gloves onto the bed, Grant explored his new accommodation. By hotel standards, it had to be described as superior quality.

An added benefit was a full supply of clothes. Grant could only assume that Fox had given some input in the selection, given it consisted of mainly T-shirts and jeans, a pair of sturdy boots and more underwear and socks than Grant had ever possessed at one time in his entire life. The suit that Grant had left on his bed at the Bloom Institute was now hanging inside the built-in wardrobe, still in its protective cover, and exactly how it would remain, if Grant had anything to do with it. The last time he had worn a suit had been at his wife's fake funeral, and he fully intended that it would remain the last time, too.

He lay down on the bed. Within a few minutes, he had fallen asleep, still fully clothed. His time during the medically induced coma and recovery time at the Institute, seemed to have cured his need for medication to assist him in getting a good night's sleep. It hadn't, however, stopped the vivid mental images invading his resting mind.

His daughter, Shannon, whizzing past him on a roller coaster, screaming with excitement and waving crazily in his direction. He watched her disappear out of view as the track took the carriage around the ride. He waited patiently for her to complete the circuit and whirl past him again.

The second time, she wasn't waving but she was screaming, full of fear, "Dad, help!" she shouted as she held her hands around her bleeding throat, the blood pouring all down the front of her, a stream of droplets flying backward with the rush of the ride.

The third passing, showed his daughter slumped in the carriage, secured by the over the shoulder restraints. Her head lolled back, exposing the open, bleeding wound that travelled from ear to ear. He turned away, not wanting to see his dead daughter's body flying by, only to be confronted by his wife, pale faced with a bleeding wound down the side of her face. "Where were you? Why weren't you at home to prevent it?" she mouthed.

Grant tossed and turned, as the horrific images replayed themselves repeatedly, until he awoke in a cold sweat, the modern pendulum wall clock letting him know that it was 0430.

The Messenger(s)

It was 0450. A man sat in the front of his dark coloured van, only identifiable as being a Mercedes upon close inspection. Spread out on the passenger seat were that morning's newspapers broadsheets and shitsheets, as he was prone to describe the latter—what he considered to be the lesser quality media gossip mongers.

He had been performing this very same ritual every morning for weeks. He helped himself to the newspapers from a variety of shop fronts and businesses, libraries and public service buildings, once they had been dropped off by the delivery vans. Obtaining them legally would have been too risky. It could give a newspaper vendor the opportunity to identify him, or at the very least, make him memorable as the man who bought a copy of every national newspaper, without exception, at stupid o'clock each morning.

This morning had been no different until now. Sat in darkness of the driver's cab, he read the headline emblazoned on the front page of the newspaper propped up against the steering wheel for at least the third time. Every morning, he had scoured each page, except for the sports pages, of nearly a dozen newspapers. He searched for any type of report that could, even tentatively, be connected to his work. Prior to this very moment, he had been confident that he had gone unnoticed. This, he had considered to be, a mark of the high-quality job that he was performing. The headline, in what he would refer to as one of the less sensationalising tabloids, scorched his very existence.

> ***London Terror as the Capital's Streets are Stalked by Serial Killer!***

The first few lines of the report filled his entire being with pure, unadulterated rage.

> ***London has a new murderer, dubbed the Inserter by the Metropolitan Polices' top profiler, Dr. Colin Garside. Garside, who has been drafted in to assist the investigation team based at Paddington Green police station said: "At least three victims had been killed in a way that would suggest that the attacks had been sexually motivated..."***

Incensed, the man threw the newspaper into the foot well of the passenger seat, and frantically dragged each newspaper, one by one, toward him. His rage more potent as he read headline after headline all about one subject—himself, or at least what the police thought him to be. Each paper was disposed of in the same manner as the first. Every headline cut a further sliver of hate into his brain, which was reeling with questions, inaudible to everybody except himself. Ones which seemed unanswerable even to him.

Serial Killer?

Sexually motivated?

"How fucking dare you?" he screamed. Staring at the name

that had appeared in almost every newspaper report, his voice lowered into a morose, deep, animalistic growl.

"Who, the fuck, do you think you are, Dr. Colin Garside?"

He leaned forward and searched his way through the pile of discarded newspapers, until he found the copy of The Guardian, a paper he respected and had read regularly for many years. Their headline read:

A New Killer in the Capital?

The article reported on the apparent words used by this highly respected criminologist and profiler, a well-read expert on serial killers. Even in this newspaper, the opening lines of the piece appalled him.

> ***Jack the Ripper, the Lambeth Poisoner and the Devil's Disciple now have a new addition to their deathly ranks in the form of the Inserter. A spokesperson for the Metropolitan Police today confirmed that London has a new serial killer at large. The news will undoubtedly strike horror into the heart of every London citizen.***

How dare they associate him with these vile murderers, cold-blooded killers, with no purpose to their deeds? he wondered. He threw the newspaper to one side. Then speaking out loud asked the question:

"Who in hell's own carnage is the Inserter?"

He gazed at the discarded newspapers. From the middle of the pile, one paper caught his eye. He snatched at it. A small picture was placed in the midst of the written report. It featured a bald man with a greying goatee beard. Underneath the name was written—Dr. Colin Garside, police profiler. In the darkness, he smirked, while still looking at the face of the man who had just become his enemy, he whispered:

"So, Dr. Garside, you think me a paedophile. You mock my work with your words and defile me with your names. My holy deeds will be the end of you. But first, let the Messenger demonstrate how the words of one can cause the suffering of another."

His smile became a deep chuckle, which in turn, transformed into a deranged laugh. He threw his head back, banging it against the headrest, which only made him laugh louder.

Less than forty-five minutes later, the van was quietly being parked up into a small lockup near to the arches of Camden Market. The area was still quiet due to the early hour, although a few traders were starting to arrive. The majority grabbed a quick coffee and a breakfast roll before setting up their stalls for the day.

The driver made his way, unnoticed away from the market, toward the railway line that ran adjacent to the Horse Tunnel Market. He stood for a few minutes between a line of thick trees, checking repeatedly that his planned disappearance down the short steep bank toward the railway tracks could go unnoticed. Happy that the coast was clear, he backed farther into the cover of the trees, before turning around and heading down the grassy slope.

Reaching the bottom, he hugged the side of the bank, heading west alongside the train tracks. Making his way as quickly and carefully as possible, he reached a section of the embankment that was hidden behind a dense bushy thicket.

Only very close inspection would have uncovered a small break in the dense line of thorny bushes, which he quickly disappeared into.

Squatting down, he waited, checking to see if his entry into this hidden place had been noticed. The main rail line was clear. No trains or track workers were present. He continued his familiar journey, sliding down a worn track in the bank behind and through the bushes. There had once been a few of these entrances, but over the years, most had been blocked up to prevent entry into the hidden world behind them: A clandestine world of underground tunnels and vaults that had not been used for decades.

He eventually reached a small wooden door, worn and scarred by age, but solid, thanks to the 19th century craftsmanship, by which it had been originally created. Slowly, he opened the door just enough to create a gap by which he was able to slide through, and once on the other side, he pushed it again, this time back into its closed position.

Darkness descended around him as he was plunged into an almost blindingly black world. Two things aided his progress from his entry point farther into the catacomb world that spread out before him. First, the small amount of light that filtered through the darkness, light that was allowed to penetrate to the distant edge of this underground world by the existence of airflow outlets, was built into the ceilings of the tunnels. His second aid was his knowledge of the layout of his secret surroundings.

He headed toward a distant shaft of light and after just a few hundred yards, entered a low-ceilinged tunnel, which headed off to his left and right for as far as the eye could see. Open areas on each side of the tunnel were divided only by short narrow bricked arches, that formed part of the foundations of the vast subterranean construction. He never failed to be impressed by the standard of the building work that had allowed for this massive structure to remain largely intact for so long. The only parts of it that were no longer accessible, had been demolished during the redevelopment of the area above.

The complex array of tunnels had originally been built to house pit ponies and horses, that had been used to shunt railway wagons. They ran beneath the Euston mainline as far as the goods depot at Primrose Hill. From there, they went all the way to the warehouse buildings on the edge of the Regents Canal and under the entire area of Camden Lock market.

Despite redevelopment and some filling-in work, a few distinctive cast-iron grilles that had originally been set at regular intervals, remained visible in the road surface above. At one time, they had been the only source of light for the horses below. Now, they provided light for him and the new residents of the Camden Catacombs.

He relaxed as he made his way down the tunnel, content that he now had little or no chance of being discovered. He only knew of two other entrances into this cavernous world. One that was only accessible by the most adventurous of people, an underground canal basin close to the Camden Lock. The second, was one he had created by himself, without which his vital work would have proved almost impossible to complete.

He reached a bend in the tunnel, a sign hanging lopsidedly from the brick ceiling read "Emergency Exit." A large red arrow pointing off to the left indicated in which direction that exit had once existed. Beyond this sign on the right-hand side of the tunnel was a large and heavy black-brown wooden door—its keyhole typical of its age.

He removed a loose brick from the wall at the side of the door, behind which was a hidden a heavy metal key. He removed the key and before inserting it into the keyhole, he carefully replaced the brick, wiping it with brick dust from the floor in a good attempt to hide the evidence of its removal.

The key squealed slightly as he turned it into the lock. He winced and mentally reminded himself yet again that he must do something to stop that noise. It only served to announce his arrival to his guests. He locked the door behind him and looked around the large expanse that existed behind the door, an area that he could only imagine would have been used as some type of storeroom. Smaller spaces, which could be considered to be rooms, jutted outwards from the larger room, entry into which was through door-less gaps in the brickwork.

From the inside of one of these smaller rooms, he heard a shuffling noise and suspected that his noisy entry had woken one of the sinners who he now held captive. He remained calm in the knowledge that the individual would make no noise, would not shout out or scream, and content that it was not the one who he had come for today.

—————— ——————

Grant rose early that morning. His mind was totally focused on his meeting with Bloom and the client. He showered and dressed, not trying to impress. Donning his normal style of jeans and T-shirt, he chose his old, battered leather jacket as an extra mark of disrespect. He stood by the large window of his temporary accommodation, looking out over London and sipped on his coffee, followed by a long drag on one of his favourite miniature cigars.

On the ceiling, he noticed a smoke alarm. Placing the coffee cup and the cigar on the edge of the wide window sill, he walked to the area beneath the smoke alarm and pulled his knife out from the boot, where he had secreted it while dressing. Reaching up, he stabbed the knife into the white plastic casing and twisted it, so it was angled to the left.

Ripping the knife downwards, the alarm came away from the ceiling. It hung from a couple of wires that were connected to the battery housing. Stretching up again, he ripped the alarm from the wires and replaced the knife back into his boot. He returned to the window, and picking up the cigar, took another long draw on it and exhaled a huge cloud of grey-blue smoke. Smiling to himself, he put on his jacket, took one last mouthful of the lukewarm coffee and dropped the stub of the cigar into what remained in the cup. He collected his helmet, gloves and bike fob, then left the apartment.

The ride out to the Bloom Institute was a good forty-five minutes, but he wanted to have a ride out and freshen his mind before arriving. There was no better way of rejuvenating the mind than having the wind in your face.

Reaching the lobby floor, he noticed that Oliver was still on duty behind the reception desk, his back was turned toward Grant. He was busily leafing through some papers in a large filing drawer. Seconds prior to turning around, he said,

"Good morning Grant. Out and about early this morning."

"Christ," replied Grant. "You booties must have eyes in your arse cheeks."

Oliver did not bite at the use of the military nickname for members of the Royal Marines. He simply nodded in the direction of the area just below the reception desk.

"Cameras," he said, "cameras everywhere."

"I do hope you weren't watching me in the shower Oliver," replied Grant, giving his usual cheeky wink.

Oliver walked back toward the front of the reception area, and Grant noticed a slight limp in his gait.

"You are not my type Grant, not enough muscle definition or hair," he replied, sitting himself down in his chair. Grant was not sure if the ex-military man was joking or not, but refused to lose yet another battle of wits with him.

Grant teased, "Oh sorry! I didn't know you were a fully paid up member of the fairy club, didn't allow them in the mob in my day."

The ex-marine looked up toward Grant, who immediately knew that this time he had gone too far. Oliver stood up and leaned forward, laying his hands flat on the top of the reception desk.

"Grant, your quick wit, and shit-mouth responses may be acceptable in the underbelly world in which you have placed yourself, but I suggest, and politely request, that in my presence you show a little more restraint or I will not. This organisation may have you down as some kind of big shot, but I will fuck you up for fun if you don't change your tone when talking to me in future."

Grant took a few seconds to digest and consider the warning from the man, who for some reason, had gone from the glory of being a Royal Marine to nothing more than a well-dressed hotel doorman for some unseen secret organisation. Grant walked toward the desk in an effort to demonstrate that threats didn't impress him, in spite of knowing that Oliver was more than capable of carrying out his threat.

"Would your gammy leg not slow you down?" Grant pried sarcastically.

Oliver stood back and began to roll up his trouser leg revealing a modern looking prosthetic.

"It's not gammy Grant, it's reasonably new and very capable of holding my weight while I use my other leg to stamp your head into the ground," he responded, letting go of the trouser leg, allowing it to fall back into place.

"Afghanistan, Iraq?" asked Grant, quickly adding "Vietnam?" to try to lighten the mood.

"Unfortunate accident during my initiation into the fairy club," replied Oliver, this time with a smile on his face.

"Tough crowd," called out Grant, walking away from a conversation that he was now uncomfortable with. "See ya later Marine," and he made his way down to the car park.

Fully dressed for the ride, he started the engine of the Dark Horse, which rumbled smoothly, the noise from the pipes echoing around the underground car park. Much as he liked the sound, it lacked the growl of his old Midnight Star. Sitting on the bike, Grant took out his phone and sent a text to Gus, before putting the bike into motion and riding into the early morning London air.

As Grant left the apartment building, heading in the rough direction of the Bloom Institute, two other bikers were passing the junction for Luton Airport on the M-1. Two every day bikers seemingly heading for a day out somewhere south. They did not have club colours, nothing to suggest anything out of the ordinary...except for the look of determination and hatred worn on the faces behind the helmet visors.

―――――― ――――――

Grant had cruised for about ninety minutes. He had not followed any particular route but had just headed out of London, found some countryside and allowed the reasonably, empty lanes to lead him, confident that no matter where he ended up, he had the Bloom Institute location in the satnav system. He entered that location and allowed the system a few seconds to map his course. It quickly informed him that he was sixty-two miles from his destination and an estimated travelling time of seventy-three minutes. This would allow him to arrive about fifteen minutes before his meeting was scheduled to start.

In the last ninety minutes, Grant discovered that as well as not sounding as meaty as his last metal steed, the Indian wasn't as comfortable either. He did, however, have to admit he could not be certain if that wasn't also down to the injuries his body had sustained, and partly due to looking through rose-tinted glasses. He throttled the bike a little more, knowing that it was capable of much more, and also just to see if he could reduce that travelling time.

―――――― ――――――

The Messenger walked silently to where his target restlessly slept. He allowed the syringe to slip slowly from his grip, allowing it to glide into place so that his thumb fell softly onto the top of the plunger. His drug of choice always presented a bit of a risk, given he basically used an educated guess system when deciding how much to use. A formula based on the body weight of his victim, too much succinylcholine would cause a level of muscular paralysis that would cause the victim to asphyxiate as the muscles used for breathing failed. On the other hand, too little and he ran the risk of the victim being able to struggle and in turn possibly scratch him or do something else that could result in a bit of his DNA being transferred to that person. Both of these risks were uncomfortably high. Yet the beauty of this drug was its ability to become virtually undetectable in the human body after a short time.

He stepped closer to the young man lying on the floor and leaned down toward him, he only awoke as he suddenly felt his head being held down. A sharp stinging sensation penetrated the side of his neck. He grabbed toward the source causing the pain and his hands brushed against surgical glove covered hands. Genuine sleep was quickly replaced by one that was anaesthetically induced. A black featureless face looked down at him as his vision faded. He slurred out the words, "No, please don't."

When, just minutes later, he awoke he found himself unable to move, he had been bound to a table of some description. His face looked up at the ceiling, not through choice, but because his head was secured into place by leather straps over his forehead, chin and neck. Additional straps bound his chest and hips. His arms were entrapped inside those two body harnesses. The lower half of his body was secured by three further straps around the middle of his thighs, his knees and his ankles. He could not move an inch.

A voice, to his left, spoke calmly. A voice he instantly recognised.

"Today my child is your day. You will today enter the holy kingdom, because today your sins will be forgiven for allowing your filthy vessel to be used to convey the words of our Lord."

"Please, I beg you just let me go. I haven't seen your face. I have no idea who you are. I promise I will not utter a word to anyone. Please don't hurt me. What have I done?" he asked his captor.

The voice continued, undeterred by his pleas.

"Unlike the beasts that you surround yourself with, you will receive the blessing of the righteous, the rapturous welcome that heralds the arrival of the clean and virtuous. Something that a creature like yourself should never have expected but, with my help, will achieve."

"Let me fucking go you fucking freak," screamed the desperate panic-stricken youth.

A gloved hand pressed down on his mouth and when he tried to speak again, the hand pressed and gripped even harder.

"Mephistopheles decays inside you, he tempted you and you accepted his evil. He and his fork-tongued blaspheming will be forced out of your body and soul as I prepare you for your next journey. You are the lucky one, no longer forced like I to walk in this land of lepers and outcasts."

He removed his hand and moved to the top of the table where he lit a large candle, repeating the process at the foot of the table and then pulling a large black leather chair, which sat on castors, toward the table, he sat next to the boy's head. He leaned to his left and pulled a silver dish sat atop a silver pedestal, this also on tiny wheels, toward him. He looked at the contents of the dish—a small metal hammer, one end of its head covered by a film of plastic coating and a large bright silver nail, approximately twelve inches in length. Only the mask that he was wearing stopped him from licking his lips in anticipation.

Lifting the nail, he placed it into the auditory canal of the young man's ear. He tried to move as he felt the cold steel touch him, with zero success. He screamed again, a mixture of pleas and obscenities, at one point wailing out his love for his parents. As the nail was held in place, the Messenger reached for the small hammer. He lightly struck the head of the nail saying, "Be silent now horde of Hades."

The sharp tip of the nail just penetrated the eardrum in the middle ear and the victim screamed an agonising scream of excruciating pain. The masked man placed the hammer back into the silver dish and sat back in the chair.

"Let us be patient while I enjoy the releasing of the first of the seven demons who reside within you, and you enjoy the journey to your redemption."

The young man continued to scream and deeper in the catacombs, shackled inside their Victorian bricked prison-like tomb, the other young captives covered their ears and silently screamed with him.

------ ------

Grant arrived at the Bloom Institute building twenty minutes ahead of the start time for the meeting. Fox stood outside of the main entrance doors waiting for him. Without a single exchange of pleasantries, Fox said, "Caused a right stir down at the police station, your little press stunt has had an immediate effect, one that most aren't too happy about."

Grant shrugged his shoulders.

"It was always about the impact, whether or not the act is

pleasant, or otherwise people will always remember you and the place you were when your actions took place," he retorted.

"They have had to increase the number of staff on the investigation team," responded Fox, who looked tired. "They have received over a thousand calls, most from scared members of the public and quite a few pretending to be our serial killer. One memorable caller asked if we could call him the Dick Sticker and not the Inserter!"

"Catchy name," said Grant, his childish grin returning to his face. "Bloom and the client here yet?"

"Waiting up on the top floor for you," answered Fox.

"Good. Let's get this done," said Grant, walking toward the glass entrance doors before adding, "Oh, there's a laptop in the pannier of the bike. Any chance one of your IT hacks can break the password and get access to its contents for me?"

"Shouldn't be a problem. Looking for anything in particular?" asked Fox.

"Everything," answered Grant, as he walked into the building.

Fox followed him, and together they walked toward the lift. One of the security staff who sat behind the reception called over asking Grant to sign in, but Fox waved his hand dismissively without saying a word.

Fox followed the usual security protocol to allow the two men to enter the lift and once inside, he pressed the button for the fourth floor.

"Fourth floor, eh? The level of the gods," said Grant, interweaving his fingers and bending them enough to make a cracking sound from his knuckles.

"Grant, this is not a war. You wanted this meeting. Mr. Bloom and our client reluctantly agreed so if you act in a way that upsets or disturbs them in any way, the meeting will be stopped," warned Fox.

Grant rotated his head left and right, then up and down, and finally in a circular motion, his neck cracking on several occasions.

"Don't be so naive! Of course it's a fucking war. That cunt runs an organisation that has imprisoned my wife. A woman, up until recently, I thought was dead. He has manipulated me covertly and then imprisoned and blackmailed me into working for him. I want a few fucking answers and they won't all be connected to this fucking case."

Fox didn't respond. One of the many things he had learned about Grant was that when the swearing reached this level, there was no reasoning with him.

The lift arrived at the top floor. To Grant's surprise, the doors opened immediately without anyone having to press their finger against a fingerprint scanner. He walked ahead of Fox, straight into a large room that contained a huge oval conference table around which sat about twenty chairs. At the far end of the room stood a set of double doors. Seeing Grant looking at the doors, Fox said, "Mr. Bloom's office, but this meeting will be conducted in this room, not in there."

Grant ignored him and walked past the conference table, heading straight for the double doors and, grabbing both handles, he twisted them downwards and pushed the doors open.

Bloom, who had been sat behind his huge white marble desk, immediately stood upon seeing the doors swiftly open. The man sat opposite to him, however, remained seated and did not even look around to see who had entered the room as if he already knew.

"How dare you barge in here," started Bloom, but stopped speaking as he saw Grant rapidly approaching him. Before he knew it, the man who he had ordered to be kept imprisoned and in a forced medical coma was upon him. Grant had skirted around the defence of the large desk and was now gripping him by his necktie. Fox yelled out a warning.

"Don't Grant."

It was the man who had remained seated and silent who halted Grant's planned intentions.

"Mr. Grant, I suggest you release Dr. Bloom immediately or, well, or else."

Grant, still gripping onto Bloom, looked toward the seated gentleman. He was pristinely attired in a white shirt, pure silk yellow tie and a dark grey suit. Grant had no doubt that it was of Saville Row standard, even though he had never stepped one foot down that London street.

"Firstly," he responded, "or else does not impress me and secondly, it's just Grant not fucking Mr. fucking Grant." The last four words of his statement were virtually spat from his mouth.

"In my world, we honour a gentleman with the title of mister. Prove that you are one and release the good doctor," the man, who still remained seated, asked Grant.

"In my world, we call a man by the name he deserves or desires," replied Grant, who at last released his grip. Bloom straightened his tie while backing away from his attacker. Grant eyeballed the seated man, who in turn stared, steely-eyed, back at him.

"And anyway, weren't you one of the groups that insisted that prisoners be called by the title mister? I never met any gentleman during the years that I spent behind the wall. Then again, what would you and your kind know about that?" asked Grant.

Godfrey Lambden stood up. He was six foot two inches tall and slim. The well-tailored suit gave the impression he was stockier than he actually was. He studied the man in front of him—a man he would not normally have encountered in any of his recent social or business circles.

"I think you would be surprised by some of the places that I have been to and many of the things that I have seen. I am a great believer in getting to know your enemy before taking them on. I am up to date where you are concerned. It would appear, however, that you have not paid me the same respect. I would advise you to tread cautiously and not make me an enemy." Lambden's voice was steady and confident.

"Mr. Lambden," replied Grant, "I can also type shit into Google. You are a senior civil servant and the only reason that Professor Albert Bloom is kissing your ass is because you are soon to be announced as the next head of the Secret Services. This effectively will make you his boss. Now, if you have really done your homework on me, I would seriously suggest you don't make an enemy of me."

Lambden smiled and sat back down. He looked at Grant and then at Bloom.

"It would seem that we have more in common than losing a daughter."

Grant sat down in Bloom's chair. Leaning back, the chair tilted slightly.

"That and the fact that this modern-day Dr. Frankenstein is holding my wife hostage are the only reasons I am here. Now, given you brought up the delicate issue of your daughter, why don't you see if you can tell me something about her that might lead us to finding her killer?" asked Grant.

For the next fifteen to twenty minutes, Godfrey Lambden spoke about his daughter. Most of the information was in the form of memories of her childhood, her upbringing and successes, both sportingly and academically. More up to date matters revealed nothing to Grant. In fact, she could not have been more different from the other victims. She had not left home. She had not had a recent change of friends and other than the occasional spoiled little girl tantrum, she had not changed her attitude or behaviour toward her parents.

"When she went out with her friends for the evening, where did she go?" asked Grant.

"The homes of friends, a couple of quiet wine bars," replied Lambden. "She was always followed by one of my security staff, although I don't think she realised it. Perhaps you should speak with him."

Grant stood up and looked toward Fox.

"Get the family bodyguard in. We need to speak to him. In fact, arrange for him to meet us at the police station, Fox."

He walked toward the door and just before leaving the room, he turned and addressed both Lambden and Bloom.

"Mr. Lambden, I will do my best to find the person who murdered your daughter, not because I care about you or the loss of your daughter, but purely because I want my wife back, unharmed. Bloom, if anything happens to Julia, no amount of government protection or numbers of staff like Fox here will stop me putting you through an amount of hell that would make what I did to certain members of the Crippens look like playtime with unwanted toys."

He left the room and before following him, Fox looked at Dr. Bloom quizzically, mentally asking if there was anything he was required to do other than accompany Grant. Bloom nervously straightened his already perfect tie, ignored the look from Fox and walked toward a cabinet against the wall of the room. The cabinet contained bottles of top quality alcohol, and despite it still being well before 11 in the morning, Bloom needed a stiff brandy. Before Fox left the room, Lambden said, "Tell Grant the only unusual behaviour I can remember about my daughter is that she had a tattoo done. I never saw it myself, it was somewhere on her back." Fox nodded his head and hurried his pace to catch up with Grant.

The journey in the lift down to the ground floor was a tense one. Not a single word was said between the two men until, as the doors were opening, Grant looked at Fox and said, "Have I done something wrong again? You seem agitated."

Before Fox could respond, an equally agitated Dr. Stanridge rushed through the doors into the lift.

"Good morning doctor," said Fox, as both he and Grant walked out of the lift. He received no response from Stanridge, who was frantically searching through his pockets for his office keys.

Grant noticed something fall to the floor and quickly placed one hand against the lift doors to prevent them from closing. He bent down and picked up the black surgical glove, handing it to Stanridge.

"Taking your work home with you, doc?" he asked jokingly.

Stanridge grabbed the glove, snatching it from Grant's grip and placing it back into his jacket pocket.

"Of course not," he snapped back at Grant. "I am a doctor. There are always a pair of these about my person somewhere."

The doors closed, and Fox and Grant looked toward each other.

"Must have had a bad sexual experience last night," said Fox.

"Do you think that glove was involved?" replied Grant and laughed. As he did so, he faked a shiver of disgust. Even Fox had to laugh on this occasion. There were times when he could happily forgive Grant for some of the less funny things he did and said.

------ ------

The young man's screaming had subsided into sobs of pain and fear. He could feel the object that had penetrated his ear, but it had now started to feel like the worst earache he had ever suffered. His torturer's voice spoke again. Neither the foreign object or the seepage of fluid and blood from his ear dampened his words.

"Behold, he cometh with clouds, and every eye shall see him, and they also which pierced him. And all kindreds of the Earth shall wail because of him."

He placed one gloved hand on the head of the nail and pressed it gently downward, angling it so it pointed toward the general area just above the opposite ear from which it was sat. With his other hand, he gave it another quick tap with the metal hammer.

As the nail entered farther into the ear, it severed through the auditory nerve, that, along with the horrendous screams that were even more tortured than the first, and that the young man blacked out because of the lightning bolt of pain that exploded inside his head, it was no wonder that he failed to hear the nail tapper speak again.

"For he will be found of them that tempt him not and sheweth himself unto such as do not distrust him."

He placed the hammer back into the silver tray and gently pressed two fingertips against his victim's neck. He smiled as he felt a strong pulse pumping inside it. He closed his eyes and allowed his mind to wander as he waited for the young man to regain consciousness. *Pain should always be endured, for that is the only way you can learn from it,* he thought to himself. His mind rolled back to his childhood, to the very moment when he had heard those very words spoken to him.

He sat curled up in a tight ball in the corner of his bedroom. His dirty face was streaked with the evidence of tears. He looked up as the bedroom door opened and in walked his older brother, his hero up until a short time ago.

The day had started as many did during the school holidays. It was the early 1970s, the sun was shining, and he was looking forward to hanging out with his older brother and his mates. He always felt special when he was allowed to go with this older group of lads and they always did exciting and daring things. He had been waiting for this particular day for some time now; they had talked about and then carefully planned it, for as he was told: "This was not an adventure on which to get caught."

A makeshift boat had been built using every piece of spare wood they could find. It had been hidden every night in deep undergrowth some yards from the edge of the canal. Now the day was here. The day that they would row their way into the canal basin that would allow them to walk around the Camden Catacombs, an underground web of tunnels that was the monster of all adventures for any young boy. He was nervous and apprehensive, but knew that his older brother would be there to look after him.

The four boys had met up next to the canal after an early Sunday morning breakfast of a few slices of toast and bowls of cereal.

He was the youngest of the four by a good four years, but

Mortimer, or Morty, as he preferred to be called, always insisted that he tag along despite the protests of the other older lads. The short journey across the canal to the opening in the steep embankment that led up to the towpath went without incident. As they entered the large mouth of the entrance, young David became more and more excited. The other boys, in whispered hissed voices, told him to shut up or they would push him into the water. He went quiet for a short while, but as they entered the darkness of the tunnel, he couldn't hold his excitement and again began to see imaginary things, squealing and giggling in a mixture of fear and trepidation.

They floated across the underground canal basin, steered by two planks of wood that had been rudely carved away at to resemble oars and came to a sudden stop with a bump as the raft collided with a low stone wall at the edge of the basin. The older boy, Jason, or "Ren" as he was called, a nickname he was given because of his love of a Japanese horror story character, stepped off the boat first. Using the rope that they had tied to the edge of the raft, he pulled it firmly so that it sat adjacent to the wall and allowed the other boys to step off too. Together they then pulled the boat up onto the stone floor out of the water.

The four boys initially explored their immediate surroundings, using two weak torches to break through the darkness, but after just a few minutes, the older boys had wanted to venture farther. Young David had been reluctant at first, but Morty pleaded with him not to embarrass him in front of his mates and to stop being a "scaredy-cat." All four set off walking around the rabbit warren of tunnels. About a quarter of an hour later, Jason decided that they should split up into groups of two and take a torch each. David would go with him, and Morty and Danny would take the other torch and set off in the other direction.

"Use the chalk to make marks on the walls so that you don't get lost and we will all meet back here in one hour," said Jason, proudly taking on the role of group leader.

David had never liked Jason, he just thought there was something weird about him, but for the sake of his older brother, he didn't make a fuss and went walking off with Jason. "Come on young 'un, I'm going to give you the adventure of your life."

David soon settled down, taking in all that he could see, totally reliant on Jason to shine the torch in the right places. It started to go wrong about twenty minutes into their little venture, when David tripped over one of the metal train tracks that were sunk into the ground. Jason had walked back to him and helped him to get back on his feet, dusting him off and placing his hand on the side of David's fac,e asking him if he was all right. David felt uncomfortable with this because Jason was never nice to him, but he was even more uncomfortable with the way that Jason kept his hand placed on his bottom.

"Let go of my fucking arse gay boy," demanded David, in a young boy's brash but humorous way.

Jason stroked David's forehead saying, "Hey kiddo, don't use language like that, you are a little innocent." His voice then changed to a slightly deeper tone as he rubbed his hand down the crotch of David's jeans saying, "Just the way I like them."

The rest of the memory became a bit of blur. He remembered starting to say something to Jason before the older boy placed his hand over David's mouth. His tone was now completely different as he said, in a weirdly kind but threatening way, "You be quiet now and don't say a word or I will kill your big brother."

He remembered being led to one of the smaller open room areas and roughly pushed into the corner, falling to the floor. Jason sat on top of him, his legs astride David's hips. He remembered the feeling of the elasticated waist of his jeans being grabbed and pulled down to his ankles. As Jason grabbed the top of his underpants he went to say something, but Jason once again placed his hand over David's mouth, much more firmly and roughly than before. "Make one noise and I will kill that faggot of a brother of yours and make you watch before I drown you in the canal, you understand me?" The young David had no doubt that Jason would carry out his threat without a second thought.

As his underpants were pulled down, David didn't make a sound. He felt Jason fumbling around doing something, but David didn't make a sound. Even when he felt cold rough hands pulling the cheeks of his bottom apart, he stayed silent because he didn't want anyone killing his beloved older brother.

When Jason entered him, the pain was excruciating, but he bit his bottom lip, keeping the screams of pain and embarrassment in his head and let the tears smear down his dirty face. For about ten minutes, Jason had his pleasure with young David. Each thrust seeming to be harder and deeper than the one before, but David did as he had been told and stayed silent. When Jason had finished he pulled his own jeans up and reached into his pocket for a paper handkerchief.

He placed it into David's hand and gently said, "Clean yourself up, you've got yourself a little messy back there." David remembered wiping around his bottom. He was sore, in fact, no he was in agony. When he looked at the hanky it was smeared in a clear wet fluid and blood, his blood.

"Let's go find the others," said Jason, with a big happy grin on his face and then losing the smile he looked at David saying, "And remember what I said, not a word, EVER."

The boys met up back at the boat as planned. They floated back across the canal. David remained silent throughout the journey. At one point Morty had asked him if he was all right and David just nodded his head affirmatively. When they reached the opposite bank of the canal, David did not wait for the boat to be secured. He jumped onto the grass verge and ran as fast as he could down the tow path in the direction of his home. Morty asked Jason if David was okay. "Probably a little scared mate," Jason had replied. "You shouldn't have brought him along. The poor kid will probably have all kinds of nightmares tonight."

It had been about four hours later when Morty had returned home to find David curled up in a ball, sitting in the corner of his bedroom. He didn't give David a hug. He didn't ask him any questions. He just said,"Get in the bath and clean yourself up bruv and remember, pain should always be endured, for that is the only way you can learn from it."

David had spent the rest of the school holiday mainly in the house, never going out again with Morty and his mates, and certainly never saw or spoke with Ren again. At the end of the holiday, he returned home to his father and the developing half-brother relationship with Morty came to an end. David never spent another summer, or indeed any time at all, with Morty and their mother. Until recent years, the only thing David could remember about Morty was being told by his father that, "Mortimer has done a really bad thing and you probably won't see him ever again." The last part hadn't proved to be true.

The Messenger heard the young man next to him begin to stir back to consciousness. He once again picked up the hammer. The restrained youth attempted to speak, but all that came were indistinguishable slurs. Behind the black mask, the man gave a smile before saying, "Therefore, he that speaketh unrighteous things cannot be hid, neither shall vengeance when it punisheth, pass him by."

He tapped the hammer against the nail again and it entered farther, this time penetrating through bone and tissue into the base of the brain. The young man's eyes squeezed together, and his mouth shot open in a silent scream. His face distorted to reflect the level of pain he was now suffering and what made it worse, this time, was that he wasn't rescued from the suffering by the embrace of unconscious blackness.

------ ------

Grant headed toward the main exit doors, but Fox stopped him by saying, "Mr. Lambden mentioned something about his daughter getting a tattoo, described it as being something he would say was out of the norm."

"What was it?" asked Grant.

"He never saw it, said it was on her back somewhere," answered Fox.

"Probably just a slag tag," replied Grant flippantly.

"Would you like to find out what it was?" asked Fox unexpectedly.

Grant looked at Fox, initially confused by the question.

"Don't tell me you took photos and didn't include them in the case file you gave me to read?" he responded.

"No," replied Fox matter-of-factly, "we have her body downstairs in the morgue."

"What?" exclaimed Grant, his mouth remaining in an open position for a few seconds after the word had been spoken.

"We have our own morgue in the basement. All the bodies are down there."

Grant thought back to the strange request that Jamie Nickel's father had made, *can I have my son's body back?* Now it didn't seem so obscure.

"Why do you still have all the victims' bodies?" he asked.

"Evidence, why else?" replied Fox, surprised by the question.

"You do realise that there are other victims of these crimes," said Grant, looking at Fox who now had a confused look on his face. "Their families, you knob. They want to bury their loved ones."

Grant was totally exasperated by the lack of compassion that the people of this organisation had.

"You lot think you are real clever fuckers, don't you? The fact is, you couldn't organise a shift rota for a two-man submarine."

It was clear to Grant that he was talking to an emotionless robot.

"Just take me to the fucking morgue," he said.

------ ------

The torture lasted just short of two hours before the young lad let out his final breath. The nail had eventually exited the other side of his skull, just above the opposite ear of which it had entered. The Messenger had struck the hammer six times in total. He felt no relief when it was all over, just an overwhelming sense of justification. He placed a small paper note on the table next to the leg of his victim and began to write on it.

"Now you will know the level of contempt I feel toward you, heathen doctor," he whispered quietly.

His message written, he pushed the note over the head of the nail, which protruded from the ear by about three inches. He lowered his mouth to the dead boy's ear and whispered in a voice that would have sent chills down the spine of the young man had he still been alive:

"Hear me."

------ ------

The downstairs basement was cold. It looked exactly as Grant had always imagined a morgue would look.

Against the left wall stood a bank of silver door-fronted storage cupboards, used to "cold store" the corpses, twenty-one in total laid out in three rows of seven. Each door was numbered with a simple white plastic square, and below each was a red rectangular label. Grant walked past the bank of vaults. Three of the red labels had the names of the dead occupants written on them.

"Thought we had four victims?" said Grant to Fox.

Fox nodded to the far centre of the room where a stainless-steel plinth mounted table sat. The dead body of the fourth victim lay upon it. A hose system hung above the table, and around its base, the floor was a rectangular coverage of grating allowing for water and waste from an autopsy to escape.

As Grant scanned his eyes around the room, he noticed a large wooden cross propped up in the corner of the room. It was smattered with blood stains. It was clearly the one to which victim number four had been nailed. The wall opposite to the bank of body storage cupboards had along its length two sinks, a long work surface measuring around twelve feet and then what had to be the work area for whoever it was who performed the autopsies. A laptop and a desktop computer sat on top of the work surface and a high swivel chair stood in front of them.

"Can we open door number two and take a look at the Lambden girl?" asked Grant.

Fox, without saying a word, turned and walked toward the storage cupboards and opened the door labelled "2." He then slid out the body, which lay beneath a simple looking white sheet.

Fox pulled back the sheet and Grant instantly recognised the girl's face from the incident files photos.

Grant gently placed his hands on the side of the girl's body. "You pull, I'll push," he said to Fox.

Between the two of them, they gently turned the girl onto her side. She was naked under the sheet, so Grant did not have the problem of lifting clothing. The tattoo wasn't on the girls back like her father had thought; it was positioned at the top of her right hip. They both looked at the tattoo, a small rainbow with the letters "HPY" beneath it, which meant nothing to Fox, but Grant was certain that this third sighting of this symbol was now beyond a coincidence and had to be a link. Now, he just had to work out why at least three of the victims loved rainbows, were so happy and yet couldn't spell the word correctly!

Grant covered the body with the sheet and slid the young girl back into the stainless-steel chamber.

"I need to meet with your tech geeks," said Grant, as the door closed silently.

"No Grant, you need to wind your neck in with your demands," countered Fox. "You met Mr. Bloom, which nobody normally gets to do, but as for our tech geeks as you quaintly call, they insist on their anonymity remaining exactly that."

"I don't give two flying fucks what the specky little twats insist on, to be honest." Grant's response clearly demonstrating how fed up he was becoming with the secretive game this organisation kept playing.

"Not going to happen Grant," responded Fox defiantly and stubbornly, "and you need to remember that it was those specky little twats who created the security system that secures your wife inside her room inside our building, and another specky little twat who keeps her imprisoned inside the part of her mind that suits our needs the most."

The anger that appeared immediately on Fox's face was not because of his frustration with Grant, but rather his annoyance with himself for the bit of information his anger had allowed to be disclosed at the end.

Grant didn't react, but Fox knew that this was not because he had not picked up on the words that had been spoken.

"Police station it is then," said Grant, turning swiftly on one heel and heading out of the morgue back toward the lift.

------ ------

The journey to the police station took place in Fox's car, Grant deciding to leave the Dark Horse at their headquarters. It was uneventful and completed in silence, the only notable occurrence being Grant reading and responding to a text, which for reasons that Fox couldn't be bothered to ask about, brought a smile to Grant's face.

As they drove up to the front of the police station, Fox noticed Grant slightly distracted by something outside of the vehicle, but didn't see anything of concern himself.

"Just park outside the front entrance, would you? We won't

be long," said Grant.

Fox, surprised by the sudden and unexpected politeness, changed his intended route from the car park entrance to the front of the building.

"Please promise me that you are not going to put on another display of honesty for the press?" asked Fox, practically begging.

The car parked outside of the police station entrance. The press members were encamped safely at a distance on the other side of the road. Fox felt a little more comfortable with the situation. The men alighted from the car simultaneously. Fox locked the doors with a click of the button on the key fob. Before he could tuck the metal key head away inside the fob and place the key into his pocket, Grant had called his name.

Fox turned to see Grant standing at the front corner of the car, his back facing the throng of press reporters and TV cameras. Grant was holding out his hand, as if to offer a handshake to Fox.

"I don't think this is time to shake hands Grant," said Fox, looking over Grant's shoulder rather than at his face.

"I don't want to shake your hand, I want your fucking car key," hissed Grant.

"Grant, lone male, leather jacket, a cut over the top of it, rapidly approaching from your right, his right hand going to his back pocket," said Fox, quickly as he automatically went into a reaction mode that years of training had prepared him for.

"Any patches?" asked Grant as he took the open car key from Fox's outreached hand.

"Small one, left shoulder, can't make out what it says," replied Fox.

Grant stuck the first finger of his left hand through the plastic loop that attached to the key fob, normally used to hang it up from a hook, and flicking his hand, swung the key around so that it fell against the back of his hand.

"Prospect," said Grant as he spun around, facing his would-be attacker and spotting the blade of the knife as the light reflected off the silver metal, he said, "I hope you're fucking good with that blade you fucking cockwomble."

As the biker thrust the knife toward him, Grant planted his right foot forward and raised his hands to about waist height, bringing them together in a clap like motion. His right hand connected with the back of the biker's hand that was gripping the knife, and his left struck the inside of the wrist. The combined strike forced the attacker's hand to open and the knife flew from his grip. The blade nicked the inside of Grant's left wrist on its journey through the air.

The force and movement of Grant's left hand swung the set of car keys back over his hand. Grant gripped the plastic fob as he felt it fall into the palm of his hand. He stared into the biker's eyes as he gripped the back of his head and with his other hand forced the metal car key into the side of this neck, twisting it as it entered.

Blood sprayed out at an alarming rate and an on looking Fox knew that Grant had connected directly with the carotid artery.

"Thanks for being so predictable," Grant whispered into the ear of the biker as he began to fall to the ground, eventually landing on both knees. The biker held his neck with both hands in an attempt to stem the flow of blood, as Grand said, "Now go and join the other Crippens I sent to hell."

Blood spurted over Grant's jeans and boots as the Prospect

sent by the Crippens fell face down to the ground. Grant looked toward the crowd of reporters and cameras, his face flecked with blood and his left hand, still holding the key used so effectively as a weapon of death, dripping a pool of redness. The cameras clicked as photographers eagerly took as many photos as they could and reporters, slowly recovering from the shocking incident they had just witnessed, turned to the camera operators bringing their microphones to the mouths as they began to report on what had just happened.

Grant cast his eyes to his left. With the exception of Fox, nobody was aware of the leather-jacketed individual speedily walking away from the scene. He headed toward two motorbikes parked down a side street a few metres away—the same motorbikes that just moments earlier had caught Grant's attention and gone unnoticed by Fox.

Grant turned to face Fox and handed him back his car key. Fox retrieved a handkerchief from his inside jacket pocket and wrapped it around the bloodied key.

"I think someone may want that as evidence," he said, looking at Grant. Fox suddenly respected and slightly feared Grant more than he had before.

"Fuck your evidence, fuck your organisation and fuck you Fox." Grant's face was contorted with fierce anger. "You arrange for those drugs going into my wife to be stopped, immediately, or tell Bloom that the next one I kill will be him and then you...you wannabe secret agent motherfucker, I am coming for you."

Grant strode past Fox toward the police station front entrance.

"Where are you going now?" shouted Fox, who had to raise his voice to be heard above the clamour of questions being called out by the reporters.

"Going to get cleaned up," replied Grant, holding up his blood-soaked left hand.

Two police officers ran out of the front doors of the station as Grant approached them with Fox in quick pursuit. One of them grabbed Grant by the arm, saying, "Excuse me, sir, please…" But he didn't get a chance to finish his sentence, as he was stopped in mid-flow by Grant and Fox, Grant telling him to fuck off and die, and Fox shouting to leave Grant be.

Inside the station, Grant came to a halt at the first set of doors. Without even looking in the direction of Fox, he held out his hand toward him.

"Card," he demanded.

Fox didn't argue, simply handing the security swipe card to him.

More police staff members were running down the corridor toward the door as Grant walked through it. The two at the front of them stopped and stared at Grant and his hand dripping with blood. Fox quickly intervened.

"The incident is outside officers; this man was hurt in the process of defending himself."

The police officers carried on, running past Grant and Fox, who was left holding the door open, as Grant made his way toward the sign above a door ahead of him which stated, "Staff Toilet Only (Male)."

Pushing the toilet door open, Grant looked back down the corridor toward Fox.

"You only follow me in here if you plan on sucking my dick," he stated, walking into the toilets and slamming the door behind him.

Thankfully, for Grant, the toilets were empty. He turned

on a hot water tap at one of the sinks and began to scrub his hand. He ripped copious amounts of paper towels out of the dispenser and used them to rigorously wipe the blood from his hand. Streams of blood-stained water ran around the sink and down the plug hole, as he splashed hot water on his face, and only when the water began to burn his skin, did he turn on the cold water tap and hold his now much cleaner hand beneath it.

He held it there for a while, enjoying the cooling effect on his skin. Hands and face still dripping wet, he sat on the floor between two of the sinks and buried his face in his hands. The shock of the attack suddenly hit him. He had been expecting something, but nothing so soon, and certainly nothing as direct. He knew that from the moment that Gus had done as he had asked and got the word out to the new look Crippens that their new leadership, as well as many of the old guard, would want, no, need to hand out some kind of retribution.

Grant had wanted it to be fairly public, but this had just happened in front of the world's cameras and press. He sobbed, gently at first but it built up into a crescendo of tears and anxious gasps for breath, as he realised that indirectly he had put his wife's life in danger, again. Somehow his approach, whilst being devoid of thought or consideration of the outcomes or consequences, and quite frankly, proper planning, had once again resulted in what he was consistently good at, making an impact. Previous military training had always suggested that good planning, preparation and thought would provide a positive result, that keeping a low profile from the enemy would allow you to make more progress, whether in the actual ground covered or in positive relationship building.

Grant wiped his eyes and stood up. As he looked at himself in the mirror, he mentally began to pull himself together. He remembered an old army captain speaking with him, following the end of an escape and evasion exercise. He had been a young man, hot-headed and fit as a butcher's dog. Grant and another young soldier had been the only ones to successfully evaded detection and capture, but as the officer had told him, he had managed it not with guile, deception or skill, but rather with speed, bravado and a bull-headed level of confidence.

"You merely stayed ahead of your hunters," he recalled the captain saying. "You did not follow any of the training given to you by your excellent trainers. In fact, you did the direct opposite and had you been caught, you only succeeded in pissing off your enemy."

At the time, Grant had shrugged his shoulders and simply replied, "Not my fault that they couldn't keep up sir."

"No, it is not Anderson," replied the wise military veteran, "but it was you who left little notes behind you for your would-be captors to find." He was waving a scrap of paper at Grant. "Rather like this one that I believe says you will never catch me, you wankers."

Grant had smiled, remembering the half dozen or so notes he had left behind to antagonise his chasers.

"Good at making an impact, not always a good military tactic," said the captain somberly.

Not a good civilian one either, Grant thought. He had without a doubt blown the cover provided to him by the organisation. He had wanted to send a message to the killer. A message that said, *"hey look at me, look at what I can do."* Thinking about it now, all he had done was hand information to him, information that would undoubtedly make him more careful and certainly more dangerous, should he decide to come for him.

He thought back to one other little gem that the military officer had said to him before handing him over to the instructors, who of course had been his persuasers in the game of evasion and escape, to receive the beating that he probably had deserved.

"Anderson, you will always somehow get by because of your quick wit and ability to think yourself out of a situation."

Fox popped his head around the door and peered into the room.

"You ready to talk now?" he said, preparing himself for a barrage of abuse.

Grant walked toward him and beckoned him inside. When Fox had got within about two feet of him he said, calmly and clearly:

"Fox, when you wake up, tell them that I jumped you and got away, and that you believe that I may have decided that this shit was just too much, and that I probably had already worked out that you lot never had any intention of ever releasing my wife."

Fox's eyebrows ruffled thickly over his eyes as he tried to take in and compute what Grant was saying.

"When I...," were the only words he managed to get out of his mouth before being punched squarely on the bridge of the nose. Fox staggered backward, smacking the back of his head on the door that he had just walked through, which contributed to him being unconscious before he landed face down on the floor.

Grant approached Fox's limp body and crunched his blood

covered boot down on the unconscious agent's hand. When Fox didn't move or react in any way, Grant was convinced that he was truly out for the count. He crouched down next to Fox's head and gently tapped his exposed upper cheek.

"You are a good man Fox, but if you come looking for me, I will send you the way of the Crippens, my friend."

Grant left the gents toilets and made his way, head down, toward the rear entrance of the building, exiting into the sunlight adjacent to the car park. At the front of the building, the scene was one of disorganised chaos. Police were hovering around the now covered body of the dead biker, the press members were screaming out questions and clambering for answers. An overwhelmed DI Gamby stood before the caterwauling crowd of wolves who were the world's press, calling for them to be quiet and remain calm and patient.

Nobody noticed Grant slip out of the front entrance of the car park, through the open gate left that way by the security guards, who were stood on the pavement watching the events unfold and had accidentally left it open. Grant walked away, using the cars as much as he could as cover, and disappeared along a side street at the first opportunity to finally be out of view of any wandering eye or surveying press cameras. No more leaving notes, Grant had finally learned his lesson!

Going Rogue

As pictures and reports began to filter and flow around the world, the police did their best to deal with the aftermath of the incident. Grant distanced himself farther from the police station. He had to think quickly, guessing that once Fox was found, the organisation would shut him down. He took out his mobile and made a call.

"Gus, where is it mate?" he asked.

"On its way like I said, should be arriving in London about now I reckon," replied Gus. "The driver just needs a location to meet you."

Grant told him the location and said that he would be there in around one hour.

"Are you sure you want it delivered to that shithole?" asked Gus.

"I don't have time to argue, Gus. Please just get it done. Oh, and tell the driver to stay with his van and not unload it until I arrive please mate."

Hearing the words "please" and "mate" coming from Grant, Gus knew that he was in some kind of trouble or crisis again.

"You okay?" he asked.

"Easiest answer to that is watch the TV mate. Thanks for your help." Grant ended the call and put the mobile back in his pocket.

As he walked and talked, Grant reached the end of the narrow road he had been walking down, finding himself on a busy main road. He knew immediately he needed a bank. Looking left and right, he saw no wall mounted signs indicating that a bank was close by, so he chose left and began to walk down the road. Just a few minutes later, he saw the familiar blue eagled sign of a high street bank across the other side of the road. Making his way through the moving traffic, he entered the bank's old heavy wooden doors, and made his way to a member of staff dressed in smart organisation attire. The young lady was walking the floor, asking customers if they needed any assistance.

"I could do with some help," said Grant, smiling.

"Certainly sir," she replied. "How can I assist?"

Grant went on to explain that he needed to withdraw quite a large amount of cash, more than a cash machine would allow in one day. He made up a story of being in the middle of completing a private car deal, but the seller wanted cash.

"I would need to call your bank sir. Do you have your bank card and some form of identity with your picture on it, such as a driving license or a passport?" asked the service girl.

Grant handed her his bank card and equally fake driving license. The girl looked at the card and smiled.

"I don't think it will be too much of a problem with this bank, Mr. Garside," she said. "I do know that if you visited their branch in Knightsbridge, you would be able to draw out as much as you wanted."

"Thank you, yes I am aware of that," replied Grant, playing his part of the customer of a high-profile bank. "But the seller of the car is just around the corner and I would hate to lose it by travelling there and back, only to find someone else had got in before me."

"How much would you be requiring sir?" asked the girl.

"£4,000 will suffice," he replied, not knowing if he was pushing his luck with that figure, one that he had plucked out of the air at the point of being asked the question.

"Take a seat Mr. Garside, this shouldn't take long," said the assistant, and made her way through a door to a back office.

She returned only a few minutes later. Her swift return automatically made Grant think that the bank had turned down the request.

"We will just need a couple of signatures sir, and how would you like the cash?" she asked Grant, with a pleased look on her face.

"Err, tens and twenties in an envelope," replied Grant, not quite sure what the protocol was.

"Are you sure sir? That is an awful lot of money to be carrying in an envelope," replied the young girl.

"It'll be okay. I will be handing it over to the car seller in a few minutes," replied Grant.

The girl smiled and asked Grant to follow her to an office.

Twenty-five minutes after entering the bank, Grant was walking out with £4K, less a ten-pound note which he had shoved into his front jeans pocket, in a white sealed envelope that now sat inside his inner jacket pocket.

He walked back up the Edgware Road in the opposite direction to the one he'd been going in before entering the bank. He headed toward the tube station, the sign for which, he had spotted when he had first looked for a bank. Entering the tube station, he first looked at the map on the wall to plot the most straightforward journey to the nearest station to his meeting point, and once done, he purchased the most appropriate, and cheapest, ticket from the automated ticket machine and made his way down to the platforms below.

------ ------

Just a few miles away, on the other side of Regents Park, a man walking his dog alongside the canal saw something strange floating in the water. He immediately called the police to report what he believed to be a dead body floating in the canal close to London Zoo. As he waited for the police to arrive, the sound of sirens already audible, he stared at the floating body. Its head was wrapped inside a plastic material of some description. What he couldn't see was the nail through the victim's head.

------ ------

Grant's journey took much longer than the hour he had told Gus it would take him to meet up with the delivery driver. Hailing a taxi from outside the over ground tube station, Grant was already irritated, to say the least. By the time the taxi pulled up at the retail park in southeast London, he was beside himself with rage. He hated being late, and hurriedly reached into the already torn open envelope. He pulled out a £20 note, handed it to the cab driver, telling him to keep the change.

"Cheers Gov," replied the cabby.

Grant stood outside the fried chicken fast food outlet where he had been dropped off and scanned the area, looking for a large black van in the sea of cars in the car park. He was unable to ignore the large intimidating grey stone high rise blocks in the distance. His gaze was held by the concrete jungle that he had heard so much about over the years, but had never had the displeasure of visiting or even seeing, before today. A voice from behind him broke his attention and, still on edge from the earlier events of the day, he spun around, raising his arms defensively at chest height.

"Easy there mate. I just asked if you were Grant," said the slightly built man who stepped back as Grant turned to face him.

Grant studied the man. He was just as Gus had described—long straggly light brown hair, a thick mass of hair in an out of control goatee style beard that hung down to the middle of his chest and a moustache that was so long and thick, it hid his mouth.

"Are you Snagglepuss?" asked Grant.

The man's eyes squinted slightly and a pained expression flashed across his face.

"My fucking name is Ernie and Gus will be getting a slap for saying my name was anything else," replied the reluctantly nicknamed Snagglepuss. "Now, are you going to help me to unload your heap of shit or what?"

As rakey and lightweight as Ernie looked, Grant didn't see the point of getting on the wrong side of him. He looked as if he had the fighting ability and tenacity of an alley cat.

"Err, yeah certainly Ernie. Didn't mean to offend mate. I am really grateful for your help," said Grant, in an attempt to maintain peace and harmony.

He followed Ernie a few hundred yards to where he had parked his van, in a parking area clearly marked "For Deliveries Only." A traffic warden, or parking offence officer as Grant thought they were now called, was walking around

Ernie's van. He looked up as he saw the two men approaching.

"This your vehicle sir?" he asked Ernie.

Ernie stuck up the middle finger of his right hand in the direction of the traffic warden saying, "Why don't you fuck off, you power crazed turd burglar, before I rip out your eyeballs and piss into the holes."

Undeterred, the official responded back, "It is clearly marked for deliveries only."

"And I am making a fucking delivery," snapped Ernie, "to this shit," he exclaimed pointing in the direction of Grant. "So blame him and give him the ticket or just fuck off."

The traffic official reached for his black plastic covered ticket book, but before he could even get out a pen, Ernie had snatched it from him. He slapped him on the top of his hat with it and threw it away. The warden watched as his pad of power flew through the air and landed about twelve feet away.

"Now, I am going to unload a bike from the back of my van and make my fucking delivery, and if you are still here when that is done, I am going to get into my van and drive right between the cheeks of your arse," said an increasingly angry Ernie.

A passer-by shouted over, "You fucking tell him mate," but Ernie had no time or tolerance for supporters either, shouting back, "You can fuck off too, you nosey cunt."

Ernie made his way to the back of his van, unlocked and opened both doors, and slid out a ramp. Climbing inside the back of the vehicle, he proceeded to unclamp securing straps that had successfully and safely secured the fully repaired Yamaha Midnight Star during its journey from Ernie's garage to London.

"Fucking help me then," shouted Ernie from the back of the van. "Sooner you get your bike back, the faster I can return to the land of normal people. Fucking southerners really piss me off."

Grant hurried into the back of the van and stopped momentarily as he saw for the first time in months the beloved bike he thought was gone for good.

He assisted Ernie in wheeling the bike from the van, although clearly, the slight man needed no help at all. He knew how to handle a bike correctly to maintain its balance when doing the tricky business of loading and unloading. Once off the van, he kicked out the side stand and started to slide the ramp back inside.

Grant reached into the envelope and counted out £200 in crisp £20 notes. He tapped Ernie on the shoulder and held out the money.

"For your troubles Ernie," he said gratefully.

Ernie looked at the money and waved it away.

"Don't need none of that, Gus covered the costs," he responded.

"Please Ernie," Grant said, "for having to spend time down here with these idiots."

The hairy little man grabbed the money and almost tore it out of Grant's hand.

"S'pose it's the least you can do." Ungrateful intonation was all that Grant heard. "Now, your battered helmet is sitting on the passenger seat, did my best with it, but I wouldn't trust it in a crash. I put on an old pair of bike gloves inside it that were sitting around gathering dust. I reckon this money will cover the cost of my additional thoughts and kindness."

With that, he slammed the van doors shut and, looking for

the traffic warden who was now nowhere to be seen, he made his way back to the wheel of the van and drove away.

Grant stood where the van had just been, helmet in hand, which he had just about managed to retrieve before Ernie had driven away. He walked the few feet to the bike and ran his hand over the smooth black tank, walking around it. He could see that Ernie had done an outstanding repair job. He looked at the helmet, which had seen better days. Scrapes and scratches broke up the smooth shiny blackness of it. The chin strap had clearly had some repair done to it and a new visor replaced the cracked one that had been on it following the crash and subsequent beating. The gloves didn't even look like motorbike gloves. Thin black leather with a stud fastening at the wrist, they reminded Grant of the horse riding gloves he remembered his wife wearing many years ago. However, they would do for now.

He sat on the bike and once again ran his hand over the tank.

"Hello you beauty, welcome back to Daddy," he said.

He placed on the helmet and gloves. Grant turned the key that had been hanging in the ignition and pressed the start button. The Midnight Star gunned into a load roaring explosion of action at the first time of asking. Grant sat for a while feeling the rumbling of the engine surge through his body. Now he was ready to catch a killer, he just needed a team again.

As he rode out of the retail park and headed for the large roundabout that took him across the dual carriageway, he once again looked at the imposing and notorious housing estate in front of him. *The man he was about to visit had better be worth the risk and effort,* he thought to himself.

------ ------

A police officer grateful for the opportunity to relieve himself at last after a few hours of standing outside, found a dazed and semi-conscious Fox sat upright on the floor of the gents toilets. The copper knelt down next to Fox and asked him if was all right. A still groggy Fox confirmed that he was.

"What happened?" asked the officer.

"I fell over," replied Fox, rubbing the back of his head and licking and tasting blood on his upper lip.

"Fall on both sides of your head did you?" asked the copper sarcastically.

"I said I fell over," reiterated Fox.

"An assault has obviously happened inside this station sir. I am obliged to report it," responded the officer and went to stand up. Fox grabbed his wrist, preventing him from doing so.

"Let's not make it two assaults officer," he said, tightening his grip around the copper's wrist.

"Help me to my feet, take a leak and forget you ever saw anything."

Doing as he was told, he cautiously watched Fox wash his face out of the corner of his eye as he urinated into the wall-mounted urinal. The copper zipped himself up and washed his hands in the sink next to the one that Fox was using.

"The man outside who was stabbed in the neck. What do you know?" asked Fox.

"I know that he is dead. I know that your colleague who did it is nowhere to be found, and I know that every copper in London is looking for him," replied the police officer, drying his hands on a few paper towels.

"Thank you officer. Now resume your duties, and remember, nothing happened here." The tone of Fox's voice made it very clear that any recollection would almost certainly result in something that the copper wouldn't want to experience.

The police officer left Fox alone inside the gents toilets and once he was absolutely certain that he was alone, Fox made a call from his mobile. The call was answered, but the receiver did not speak.

"Mr. Bloom. Grant has gone rogue, but I don't think we should hang him out to dry yet. Let me find him and try to bring him back in."

"What makes you think you can find him, Mr. Fox?" asked Bloom. "After all, you have clearly lost him once and, to be honest, I don't think you ever had control of him."

"I am asking for one chance, Mr. Bloom. I still believe we need him to catch our killer. If I fail, then do whatever you think is necessary," pleaded Fox.

"I give you twenty-four hours, Mr. Fox. If you have nothing positive to report by then, Mrs. Richardson will die for the second time. I will then allow Dr. Stanridge to use Grant for his next research project. Are we clear?" Bloom's voice was cold and lifeless.

"Yes Mr. Bloom, thank you Mr. Bloom," replied Fox and ended the call. "If Grant doesn't kill you first Mr. Bloom," he said to his own reflection in the mirror.

Before leaving the gents, Fox made one more call. This one was to the Chief Superintendent, who sat a few floors above in his office.

"Call off the manhunt for Dr. Garside now," he said.

"Who the fuck do you think you are ordering me about what to do?" replied the Chief.

"The man who can bring your career and life crashing down around you. Now, do as you are told you bent piece of shit." Fox ended the call without waiting for a response.

Fox knew that he could easily call the tech boys and ask them to locate Grant using the tracking device inside the phone they had given him, but decided that he would call him first and try to persuade him to fall back into line. He made his third call in as many minutes, but this one didn't get a reply.

In a car park, underneath a stationary car, in a retail park near Woolwich, a discarded mobile phone rang…and rang. Its previous owner was, at the time, riding his bike into a southeast London estate, where it was possible to purchase any type of drug that took your fancy, most handguns and automatic assault rifles available on the black market, as well as the services of many thugs more than willing to do your dirty work for you, all within a few minutes of arriving there. That was if you didn't become a victim of the locals before any of that could happen.

—————— ——————

It had taken Grant about fifteen minutes of riding around the concrete rabbit warren of roads and avenues that made up the housing estate, often described as the largest prison in England that didn't have a wall around it, and his journey had not gone unnoticed. No newcomer to this area arrived or left without alerting the undesirables who ran the estate.

Grant pulled off the road and parked his bike on the walkway, directly outside the ground floor flat hoping it was the correct one. A lone youth wearing white trainers, denim jeans and a blue hoodie-style top sat on a low wall just a few feet away from where Grant's bike was parked. He was texting on his phone. Grant knew that he wasn't there by accident, and that the text he was sending was not telling some girl about his undying love for her.

He stayed where he was for a few minutes, sat on his bike, helmet remaining in place, waiting, and he didn't have to wait long. Just a few minutes passed before seven or eight youths arrived on loud high pitched trial bikes and parked up in a half circle around him. Now Grant dismounted his bike and removed his helmet.

"Hello lads," he shouted, trying to be heard above the torrent of noise being made by the youths revving their bike engines to the maximum. One of the young men waved his hand above his head in a circular motion, and all the others pressed the kill switches on their bikes. Instantly, there was an uncomfortable silence.

"As I was saying fellas, hello," said Grant again, not having to shout this time. "I am looking for a man who goes by the name of Shuffler. I believe he lives around here."

"We int knowing no Shuffler geezer innit," replied the youth who had signaled for silence. "What is you doing 'ere man, you five-oh or sumfink?"

"Do I look like I am the police, young man?" replied Grant.

"You's axin' for trouble innit old man," replied the gang's leader, who was now off his bike and walking toward Grant. He was waving his arms about, his fingers in a gun-style position. "You is out of your hood man innit, out of your depf, you know what I means man?"

As the youth approached Grant, his pace and confidence increasing with each step, Grant unobtrusively placed one foot in front of the other and grounded himself, his right hand inside his pocket formed into a fist with the knuckle of the middle finger protruding out. With lightning quick speed, he whipped his hand out of the pocket and with a strong forearm, held it forward in front of him. The forward progressive movement of Grant's arm and the momentum of the youth combined, resulting in Grant's knuckle impacting the centre of the lad's sternum instantly. The youth collapsed to the ground, gasping for breath. Grant was on him like a dog on a bitch in season, snatching the knife from inside his boot and flashing it in front the lad's face, before placing it point first against the side of his eye.

"Don't even blink kid, you might make me slip," Grant told the gang leader.

He looked up toward the others, all of whom remained on their bikes frozen into position, not by fear, but by confusion, because nobody ever stood up to them; nobody ever dared to challenge them.

"Now listen to me kid. I am going to try to speak your language so that you clearly understand me. Nod if you hear me," Grant told the youth, who bobbed his head very slightly.

"Good. Now, I am going into that flat behind me to visit an old friend. That friend is named Shuffler, but you already know that, because you know everyone on this estate. I totally respect that I am on your turf, in your territory, call it whatever you fucking like. But here is where I am, and I am not leaving until I have concluded my business."

Grant kept a sideways look at the other members of the gang, none of whom had moved. "Now, obviously I don't want any damage against me, my bike or my friend, and I fully appreciate that the kind of assurance I need is going to cost me, so this is the point my friend where we do business. Are you ready to talk?" he asked.

Once again, the youth nodded his head and slowly, Grant pulled the knife a few inches away from his eye.

"Rub your chest and get your breath back kid," Grant instructed the young lad.

Eventually, the lad spoke.

"Where you learn that shit?" he asked Grant.

"Salvation Army, instrument protection squad. Now how much?" replied Grant.

"Gonna cost you big style man," answered the youth, some of his brashness returning at the same time as his ability to breathe.

"Yeah, I am sure you think it is, but before you suggest a price, you need to understood a couple of things," Grant informed the lad. "Firstly, I have connections with people who you really don't want to have as your enemy. Secondly, you are coming with me when I speak to my friend. Any misunderstanding about our deal, and you will spend the rest of your life as a eunuch."

The lad thought for a few seconds. Grant truly thought he was thinking about a figure when he replied.

"How you's gonna make me a eunuch man, them tings ain't real is it?"

Grant shook his head in disbelief.

"Not a fucking unicorn you cretin. A eunuch…no bollocks," he said.

The youth smiled and then instantly stopped smiling as the realisation that Grant was threatening to cut off his balls should the deal go sideways.

"Protection is costing you's £500," demanded the youth. To

his surprise, Grant didn't argue.

"A fair price for peace of mind brother. I will leave £100 with the man of your choice. The rest you get when my business with Shuffler is concluded. Agreed?"

The youth nodded and Grant helped him to his feet."Now," said Grant offering his hand, "we shake on it because a man's handshake is his bond." The youth grabbed Grant's hand and they both shook on the deal.

From behind Grant a voice, distantly familiar, spoke out.

"You still one evil bastard, Mr. Richardson."

Grant turned around to see Shuffler stood at the door of the flat he had parked outside of.

"Firm but fair Dawson. Firm but fair," replied a smiling Grant, genuinely happy to see his old servery number one again after so long.

"Yeah whatever guv, you coming in?" replied a laughing Stanley Dawson.

Grant guided the gang leader in front of him and gave him a gentle nudge to indicate that he was to go first.

"Which one of your band of brothers gets to hold on to the hundred?" Grant asked him.

The youth looked over to the others and shouted, "Skid, hold the money bro."

A small kid got off his yellow bike and walked toward Grant, scowling with a look of disrespect on his face. He held out his hand as Grant reached inside his jacket and pulled out a handful of notes from the envelope. He counted out £100 and handed it to Skid.

As the young gang member took the money, he sucked on his teeth, further demonstrating his lack of respect toward Grant.

"Hey Skid," said Grant, "this deal goes south and they will be calling you Skid Mark by the time I have finished with you. Capeesh?"

Skid tucked the money into his back pocket and gave Grant the finger in response.

Grant and the gang leader, who went by the nickname Ghost, entered Shuffler's flat.

——————

In the Bloom Institute morgue, Dr. Stanridge and Fox stood looking at two more dead bodies. The far reaching influence and power of the organisation had once again kicked into action, ensuring that the body of the biker killed by Grant and the body discovered floating in the canal had both ended up under their jurisdiction and control.

The clear plastic wrapping had been removed from the dead boy's head by Stanridge minutes after the body had arrived. While he stood looking at the nail through the head and the note that had been pushed onto the end of it, Fox was admiring the accuracy of Grant's aim into the bikers neck.

"Why is the biker here? He has nothing to do with the case?" asked Stanridge.

"Control of the situation. Simple as that doctor," replied Fox, lowering his face to take a closer look at the wound in the side of the neck. It was not a clean incision. The twisting motion that Grant had made with the key had opened the wound up wide and torn the edges.

"He never goes for a clean kill," said Fox, more to himself than to Stanridge. "Savage, brutal, driven by a deep hatred of something that goes beyond the crimes against his family."

"I would describe it as sadistic," responded Stanridge."Your new little pet project should be locked up forever to make the world a slightly safer place."

Fox stood upright, ignoring the doctor's remark.

"Let's see what message our killer has given us to try to work out this time," he said to Stanridge.

His hand gloved, Dr. Stanridge used a pair of surgical tongs to carefully remove the note from head end of the long nail. He made his way over to the side of the room and placed it down on the desktop. Fox recognised the scrawling handwriting immediately. Whilst not needing any further evidence that this boy was the killer's latest victim, the recognisable writing just affirmed his thoughts. He read the message out loud:

> ***You are not equal to the task of catching me 'Doctor'***
> ***Your taunts are as blunt to me as this nail is to wood.***
> ***You are approaching the end of hope.***

"I would say a personal message to your Dr. Garside, rather than his usual cryptic messages," Stanridge said.

"Still the religious connotation though," replied Fox, silently reading the message again. "A nail in wood, could be referring to Christ being nailed to the cross."

"Whatever it is, your sadistic little dog hasn't produced any results has he?" replied Stanridge, his contempt for Grant not hidden one bit.

"Oh, that is where you are wrong, doctor. This is a break in our killer's pattern. Grant has got a response from him," said

Fox smiling. "My dog, as you like to call him, has wounded his pride."

Fox walked away and began to make his way out of the morgue.

"I don't think we need any medical assistance to work out how this one died Dr. Stanridge, but please carry on, do your stuff and let's see if Grant rattled our killer enough to make him screw up and leave us some tangible evidence."

"And where will you be if I do find something?" asked Stanridge.

"I will be up with the technical scientists, seeing if they have found out anything that will substantiate Grant's suspicions that he has found a common link with our victims."

"What link is that?" asked a suddenly interested Stanridge.

"Something and nothing probably," replied Fox laughing. "Grant thinks our victims might be happy rainbow chasers."

Stanridge waited for about ten minutes after Fox had left the morgue before covering both bodies and making his way out. Entering the lift, he pressed the button to take himself to the third floor.

Returning a Gift and Chasing a Rainbow

The inside of Shuffler's flat was a complete mess, as he rarely left his home these days. He was tied to its confining walls by a combination of conspiracy theories that the state was watching his every movement, and a fear that if he went out, he would once again set fire to something and end up back in prison, this time probably for the rest of his life.

He brushed aside an array of empty cereal boxes and ready meal containers encrusted with the remains of dried on old food.

"Excuse the mess boss," he said apologetically, "been meaning to clear up for a few days now."

It looked more like a few weeks, thought Grant, but he didn't say anything. It was obvious that the old guy was having problems and Grant certainly had no intention of adding to them with some crass remark.

"I'm not boss or guv or Mr. Anderson anymore Stanley," said Grant.

"Call me Shuffler boss, please. You know I like being called Shuffler," he replied.

"Okay, no problem Shuffler, as long as you call me Grant,"

responded Grant.

"Do you get a new name when you become a doctor then?" asked Shuffler.

Grant was totally at a loss by the question. He looked at the kid he brought with him.

"Oi kid, what's your name?" he asked.

"Ghost," the youth replied.

"Wow really? Okay whatever. Ghost, go and put the kettle on and make us some brews."

"Surprised if I is able to find a kettle in dis place," he answered.

"Do you want the rest of that money?" said Grant.

Ghost skulked off muttering to himself, "probably won't be able to find a kitchen in dis hobo crib."

With the kid out of the way, Grant felt more comfortable to talk freely and openly to Dawson.

"Shuffler, what do you mean about me being a doctor?"

"Saw you on the news earlier, guv. That was some move. Was he the killer you have been looking for?" said Shuffler matter-of-factly.

The event being covered by the news, Grant had expected. The fact that they were still referring to him as being a doctor, suggested that the organisation had not exposed him, but how long before somebody else did?

"Shuffler, sit down mate. I need you to focus on what I am about to say to you."

Stanley made his way to a large chair. He picked up two empty pizza boxes and threw them on the floor, slowly easing himself into the now clear chair. He made a grunting noise as he sat and it was obvious to Grant that the old injuries still caused him a huge amount of pain.

"You walk like a man who has taken a beating boss," said Shuffler, doing his best to make himself comfortable.

Grant looked at the beaten up ex-biker/ex-con/arsonist/nice bloke/fucked up conspiracy theorist with a quizzical look.

"I know that pain of a beating, guv. I know the walk of a broken body." Shuffler tapped his temple with his finger as he said it. "Broken body, guv, not a broken brain." He reached forward to the small wooden coffee table in front of him and picked up a small brown bottle. Unscrewing the cap, he took a large glug of its contents.

"Liquid morphine, guv. Couldn't get through a day without it," he told Grant, placing the bottle back on the table. It was the only surface in the room that wasn't covered with rubbish.

"Listen up Shuffler, I ain't no doctor mate. Remember all that stuff you used to talk about back in the nick? All that conspiracy stuff, secret agents, alien shit, the state working in secret to satisfy the needs of the rich and famous? Well, it's all true. Well, maybe not the alien stuff, but the other theories. I am part of it bro, reluctantly may I add, before you try to kill me." Grant waited for a reaction.

"Why you here boss? You in trouble? This ain't no social visit is it. Nobody visits Shuffler these days for sociable reasons." This was not the reply Grant was expecting or really needing.

"Did you hear what I said Shuffler? You were right all along," said Grant, trying his hardest to convince the man of his new-found belief.

"Well, of course I was, guv," replied Shuffler, then adding, "you looking for the heat, guv? Are you needing the help of the flames?"

"I may need your help Shuffler, but only if you are willing to give it," Grant said, with a hint of guilt.

"Well," replied Shuffler with a smile on his face, "I do need to get out more."

At that moment Ghost returned to the living room clearly exasperated.

"I can't find tea, coffee, milk…for fucks sake. I can't find the fucking fridge man."

"Maybe you need to do a bit of tidying up Shuffler," said Grant. All three burst out laughing.

—————— ——————

Dr. Martin D. Stanridge stood outside of the patient's door looking inside the room through the observation glass. To anyone else, it would have seemed that the occupant was sleeping. Stanridge knew him all too well; he knew the small almost undetectable nuances of this man.

"Your head is tilted slightly so I know you are listening," he said. The communication system was open so he knew that Mortimer Church could hear him. There was no reaction from inside the room.

"I'm not coming in Morty, but you have to listen to me," Stanridge's voice was begging, pleading for some kind of acknowledgment.

"They're getting close," he said, but still nothing from The Priest.

"You made a mistake persuading me to convince Mr. Bloom to bring in Grant." This time, he got a response.

"I never make mistakes." Mortimer Church didn't move his position on the bed.

"He is going to make the connections. He is going to discover the tunnels," replied Stanridge.

Church remained in the same position, laying on his side with his back to the door.

"Of course he is, but when we want him to do it, when I need him to do it. How else can he be killed and he Messenger take all the credit?"

"The Crippens almost got him," said Stanridge.

Mortimer Church sat up and then stood. He walked to the door and put his face close up against the glass observation panel. His eyes appeared to be burning with hatred. Locked away in this room, he had no way of hearing about the happenings of the outside world unless his brother relayed the news to him. He tried to listen in to the distant conversations of staff walking around the ward outside of his blank prison, but they were careful, almost fearful of talking whenever they were in the vicinity of his door.

"Never mention their name to me," he hissed, spittle splattering on the inside of the glass. He smiled at the man outside the door, whose face was aching with worry, with fear and pain, the same fear and pain he had witnessed so many years earlier as small boys.

"It is almost time, David. Tonight the Messenger must follow the righteous preachings of the unrighteous," he whispered.

"No," replied Stanridge. "They have tightened up the security. Grant has gone missing. They don't know what he is going to do next."

"He will do what he has always been destined to do, my brother. Follow the crumbs that are laid on the path that will heal us both." Church's voice was hushed, almost soothing in the way that a mother would talk to her baby.

Stanridge turned off the communication system and walked away without replying. As he walked down the corridor, a voice entered his head, his brother's voice.

"Tonight," it whispered.

—————— ——————

Before leaving Shuffler, Grant counted out £400 and handed it to Ghost. He had returned to the kitchen with the youth and easily found the fridge, which contained milk. The coffee had proved much more difficult to find. It was eventually discovered in a cupboard, having for some reason been decanted into a butter dish.

The two men chatted for about thirty minutes while drinking their coffee. Ghost leaned against the frame of the living room door listening to their every word. And with each word, realising that he hadn't even begun to live his life. As he walked down the short hallway toward the front door, Shuffler leading the way, the young lad turned to Grant and said, "Me and the lads can help."

Grant made a noise. The kind that is made when trying to stifle a laugh and it comes out of your nose.

"No disrespect to you and your crew Ghost, but this is grown-up stuff."

Ghost stepped in front of Grant and stood in his way, his street credibility obviously dented by Grant's throwaway remark.

"Your fellow grown-ups got you a gun did they?" he asked. "Cuz I can, in a few minutes. You needs a backup team man, and we can be that."

Grant raised his hand, intending to gently guide Ghost out of the way. The young lad quickly stepped backward, fully expecting another breath stealing knuckle to strike his sternum. Grant opened up his hand calmly, gesticulating to the youth that he intended to harm.

"How about an untraceable phone?" he asked.

Ghost smiled. "On this estate, a three-year-old could get you one."

Shuffler opened the door to allow the other two back on to the estate. Before they passed him, he quickly popped his head out of the door and checked left and right.

"You never know who is watching guv," he said to Grant.

"You better start looking up too Shuffler. I hear they use satellites and drones these days," he smiled and patted Shuffler on the shoulder. "Speak soon," he said.

The moment they were outside the fake street voice returned as Ghost called out, "All good man. Skid, we needs a burner and an invisible dog bro." He was waving the wad of notes triumphantly in the air.

Skid kick-started his bike into action and sped off deep into the heart of the estate, popping a wheelie as he went.

Ghost looked at Grant and winked.

"Two mins, double-o."

They walked together, and Grant grabbed his helmet from where he had left it hanging from the handlebars of his bike. He sat on his bike and waited. The nervous tension between the youths and Grant remained. In an attempt to ease the growing tension that can only be created by nervous young men not quite in control of a situation, Grant asked, "Any of you know anything about rainbows?"

The remaining half a dozen lads were all confused by the

question, one of them retorted angrily, "You taking da piss five-o?"

Grant raised both hands in the air in a mock "I surrender" pose.

"Just trying to piece together a little puzzle bro," he replied. "A picture of a rainbow with the letters H, P and Y beneath it."

Every one of the young bike crew, including Ghost, burst out laughing, whooping and screaming hysterically.They snapped their fingers in the air and slaped their own legs with the backs of their hands. One of them yelled out, "The old dude wants himself a queen bro."

The others joined in.

"You after some pole-smoking action ya fag?"

"Hey Ghost man, yous been hanging wid a butt hugger."

Ghost looked in the direction of Grant. A mixture of embarrassment, humiliation and anger spread across his face.

"Yo, double-o, you an auntie or summit?"

Grant could hear the distinctive high-pitched engine of Skid's bike making his return journey. He looked at Ghost and said, "I was just asking a question, passing the time of day bro."

"Rainbows and dem letters, theys a bender bar up Camden way bro," replied Ghost.

Skid arrived on the scene and, as if to prove the origin of his nickname, skidded the rear tyre of his bike in a wide arc, bringing it to a dramatic halt right next to Grant. He reached inside his jacket, firstly pulling out a pistol, which he slammed into Grant's chest. Grant immediately grabbed it, uncertain as to whether it was loaded or not. As he held it close to his body, the young courier retrieved a mobile. He held it in Grant's direction and slid his thumb down the back of it.

A blade, its base as wide as the phone, which tapered into a sharp point about two inches long, slid out from the body of the phone.

"Whatch'ya rear end Skid bro, the dude is looking for a catcher innit," shouted one of his mates.

Skid initially glanced at the back of his bike believing he was being told that there was a problem with his ride, until he heard the term "catcher." This was a slang term for someone who was on the receiving end of homosexual male sex. The young deliverer of the gun and phone quickly spun his head round to look back at Grant. The situation was returning to the volatile one it had been like upon his arrival. Grant grabbed the phone/knife combination and eased it out of Skid's grip. He looked at Ghost and asked, "Are you saying that this rainbow thing is a club where gay people go?"

"The Happy Club man," replied Ghost, "notorious as a *bear* hangout for picking up newbies to the scene bro."

Grant shook his head in disbelief. Dead bodies, cryptic messages, a whole bloody secret organisation and a case file full of information. Add to that a room full of internet geeks and a police investigation team. Yet it took a gang of baby thugs to identify the link that only he had picked up. The only one he had always suspected, despite it only being a speculative link. He secreted the mobile phone with its covert surprise and reluctantly accepted the handgun.

"How much for the goodies?" he asked, looking at Ghost.

"D'phone is a gift double-o, but d'shooter, dat is gonna make ya a ton lighter man," the young thug replied.

Grant counted out another hundred pounds and handed it to Ghost.

"It's been a profitable day for you," he said smiling.

Ghost waved the money away saying, "Give it to ma bag man bro and we make more in an hour selling bindles to d'smack 'eds around 'ere."

A youth on a red bike rode up alongside Grant and snatched the money out of his hand. He gave Grant the finger as he cruised back around to his position in the pack.

A large black four by four with blacked out windows appeared in the distance at the end of one of the side roads. Ghost glanced up in it's direction.

"Yous need to go now man," he advised Grant.

Looking at the vehicle, Grant suspected that this probably belonged to one of the bigger players of this concrete jungle and decided that the kid's advice was possibly the best he was going to receive that day.

Grant started his bike and rode it in a semi-circle, stopping momentarily next to Ghost.

"Nice doing business with you son," he said.

"Don't come back double-o. Next time we kill yous and sells your ride," replied Ghost, with a rye smile on his face.

"Careful, I am the one with the gun now," said Grant, tapping the front of his jacket.

"And I will have a KK bro," replied Ghost, laughing and imitated holding an automatic rifle toward Grant.

Grant rode away. The small gang of bikers rode in the opposite direction toward the blacked out car. Grant noticed the kid who had taken the money from Grant briefly stop by the back window of the car. He put his arm into the back of the vehicle as the window slid slightly down.

Always have to pay the ferryman, thought Grant, as he rode back toward the dual carriageway grateful to be leaving the estate behind him having only lost a bit of cash.

After only ten minutes or so, Grant spotted a large supermarket to his left and pulled in. He parked the bike at the back of the large car park, which was relatively empty and quiet. He got off his bike and placed his helmet on the seat. Leaning against a set of metal railings, he lit up a cigarette and inhaled the heavenly tasting smoke, swirling it around his mouth before exhaling a large blue-grey cloud back into the air.

He thought about everything that had happened over the past hour or so. The chat with Shuffler, and the unexpected "gifts" and information from the young biker pack. Grant took a piece of paper from his back pocket and transferred the number written on it into the mobile. He tagged the new contact as "Shuffler." He slid his finger down the back of the phone and the blade slid out. It was deadly sharp and its shape was designed to cut into its subject with ease.

What kind of situation would require you to make a call and stab somebody at the same time? he thought to himself, sliding the blade back inside the body of the phone. He placed the phone into the front pocket of his jeans. Using his lighter, he set fire to the small piece of paper, allowing it to float to the pavement as it burned. It occured to him that he was becoming as paranoid as Shuffler.

A sound in the distance caused him to glance to his left. The distinctive noise of a motorbike, tinny and screaming, like the ones he had just left behind could be heard. He watched as he saw the white motorcycle enter the car park and come to a halt. The rider looked around the car park and seconds later, looking in Grants direction, revved the bike again, heading in his direction. Grant instinctively placed his hand in his front pocket and lightly grasped the newly acquired mobile phone.

The lone rider parked his bike adjacent to Grant's. He got off his bike and removed his helmet, all the time looking at Grant.

A young blonde haired skinny youth stood in front him. Immediately, Grant knew that he was no threat. He let go of the mobile and removed his hand from his pocket, turning around so his back rested against the railings. He folded his arms across his chest.

"Did I forget something kid?" he asked.

The young man could not have been more than seventeen or eighteen years old. His scrawniness was largely down to not eating enough and probably some drug usage. His ungloved hands and face were dirty, signifying neglect. It would appear nobody cared enough to remind him to wash. Grant had grown up with kids like this back in times that were less dangerous for kids who spent the majority of their lives hanging around on the streets.

"I think I can help you," replied the youth, his voice timid and devoid of any street accent.

Grant studied the man-child, who now stood in front of him. He had not noticed him before, but Grant appreciated people who could blend into the background. He looked around and listened. He heard no other bikes. The kid had obviously come alone, which could only mean one of two things. He had either been sent by the others to find out more, or he had genuine personal reasons for being in Grant's presence.

Grant threw a mock salute in the direction of the youth.

"So you wanna join up and be a man, do ya?" asked Grant in a mocking "come join Army" bravado voice.

"Fuck you," said the kid, and began to walk back the short

distance to his bike.

Grant walked quickly, and really paced out to get past and beyond the youth, before he could reach his bike and speed away.

"Woah, sorry. I was just having a joke kid," said Grant, holding his hands wide out in front of him but being careful not to place them on the kid's chest.

"Taking the piss you mean, just like the rest of them," came the reply.

"Hey, we just kicked this off on the wrong foot" responded Grant. "What's yer name?" he asked.

The young man took out a crushed pack of cigarettes from his front pocket and fished out the straightest one he could find. He then patted each pocket, front and back, trying to find his lighter. Grant pulled out his own lighter and ignited it in front of the kid's face. The youth placed the cigarette into his mouth and held it close to the lighter being offered to him.

"Thanks," the word was spoken out of a mouthful of exhaled smoke. "My name is Alec, but they call me Halo," he continued, looking down at the ground as he disclosed his nickname.

"Please tell me that's because you jump out of really high planes," said Grant, smiling and immediately realising that his attempt at a joke had gone completely over the kids head.

"No, how could I fucking do that?" replied Halo. He was looking at Grant with a look on his face that almost certainly said, *I think I have made a mistake with this loser*.

"It's because I look so innocent and my mother still calls me her angel," he said clearly embarrassed.

"Hey that's not a bad thing," replied Grant. "You have a mother who loves you. The rest probably have mothers who wished they had swallowed instead."

This time, Halo not only smiled but also laughed. This joke he did understand.

Grant decided to strike while they were on a good level with each other, and asked, "So what makes you think you can help me Alec?" Grant used his given name rather than the nickname he was so ashamed of.

"I was listening to what you were saying back there," he nodded his head toward the direction of the housing estate. "I also watched a video clip of you this morning on my phone. You are that doctor helping the coppers look for that nutfuck killer."

Grant still couldn't fathom out how this kid thought he could be of any help, so he decided on a direct approach.

Okay, Alec, you are a good listener. You like watching downloaded videos and you are a good detective to work out that I am helping the police. How does any of that qualify you to help me?"

"It's not called the Happy Club. That is just a name that is sometimes used by the straights, because gay is an old word for happy. The punters use it because some street artist painted a rainbow on the side wall of the club and daubed his 'tag' at the bottom of it, 'HPY.' All the club-goers adopted it as a symbol, started getting stickers made up and having fucking tattoos done," replied Halo.

Grant thought about those clues. The links that he had fallen upon, all connected to what he was now being told.

"I'm sorry, I appreciate the modern history lesson kid, but I still don't know how you can be of any help," replied Grant.

"I'm guessing you want inside. Into the Rainbow Club, that is. I can get you in."

Now Grant was intrigued.

"You are a young bloke from southeast London. What do you know about a gay club in north London?" he asked.

"Because I am gay," replied Alec, "and older men, men with money, hang around that club looking for young mouths to feed, if you get my gist?" Grant did not need any further explanation of what Alec was telling him.

Grant decided that this was not the time to be coy so decided to be as frank as his potential new ally. "Okay, so you blow rich men down alleyways for chip money. How does that mean you can get me into the club?" he asked.

"Well," said Alec, grinning from ear to ear, "I can get you in through the back door!"

"No pun intended, I bet," said Grant, smiling back at Alec.

——————

Shuffler waited by his window, peering through the filthy net curtain, watching and waiting for the youths to ride away on their bikes. He saw them approach the dark vehicle. He watched as Grant rode away. He continued to wait and watch. The blacked-out vehicle drove away, and the group of bikes rode off into the depths of the estate and still Shuffler waited. He knew that something else would always happen. After nearly ten minutes, when almost beginning to doubt his own convictions, he saw the young lad ride past his window alone.

Now he knew it was safe. He left the window and made his way to the front door collecting his old, torn and dirty leather duster-style coat on the way. He put it on over the vest he was wearing. He double tapped the outside right pocket, instantly recognising the feel and shape of the bottle of Oramorph.

Having a bottle in every room, and every coat pocket, was a rule he adhered to. Before opening the door, he took the bottle out and took a big slug of its contents.

He headed through the estate, heading for the only bus stop that he trusted. It was hidden beneath a thick cover of trees and had high commercial warehouses around it, making it very difficult for satellites or drones to be used to follow his movements. He did his usual "anti-surveillance" trick of doubling back on himself and taking left and right turns when he didn't need to, just to ensure he was not being followed.

After nearly thirty minutes, he arrived at the bus stop, a journey that should have taken even the slow moving Shuffler no more than ten. He was just in time to see the bus he needed turning the corner at the top of the road and lumber its way to the bus shelter. Getting on to the bus, he flashed his bus pass at the driver, carefully and casually covering his name with his thumb but allowing the dated photograph to be seen. The driver just nodded his head without giving the pass even a cursory check. He couldn't give a damn whether it was in date, out of date or even belonged to the old bloke.

The doors of the bus closed. Shuffler went to the first seat available, which happened to be one designated for a disabled passenger and sat down. He was grateful for the additional room afforded for the intended traveler. He sat bolt upright, appearing to be very uncomfortable, both physically and mentally.

An uneventful fifty-minute bus journey later, and Shuffler got off the bus that he never normally had any reason to have to travel on, and made his way toward a taxi rank about half a mile down the road. He leaned into the first cab and handed the driver a scrap of paper with an address on it.

"How much to that address mate and keep it off the clock?" asked Shuffler.

"I don't do jobs off the clock mate," the cab driver replied.

"Look," said Shuffler, "I like to put work into the hands of hard working tax paying men, not snot-nosed ass wipes who drive those private taxis. I have the cash and will pay you up front, so stop wasting my fucking time because you think I am going to fucking mug you off. Name a fucking price, will ya?"

To prove his point, he pulled out the roll of cash that Grant had forced into his hand earlier that day. He must have been holding at least £500.

"Off the clock, it will cost ya a ton 50 mate," said the cab driver, eyeing the wad of cash.

"Deal," said Shuffler counting out the money and slapping £150 into the cabbie's hand. Climbing into the back of the cab he added, "You greedy cunt."

Ninety minutes later, the London taxi pulled up in the leafy suburban area of the address that he had been given.

"Are you sure this is where you need to go to pal?" he asked Shuffler.

His passenger looked around from inside the back of the taxi.

"You are the fucking driver, I gave you the address, so you tell me, are we there?" he replied.

"The satnav lady says we are there pal," the taxi driver responded.

"Fucking satnav," replied Shuffler. "Back in my day we could make our way from Belfast to Fivemiletown without even looking at the sodding map. How much to persuade you to hang around for another thirty minutes?"

Shuffler stepped out of the back of the cab, but before he could even slam the door behind him the cabbie put his foot down and drove away, the backdoor slamming shut as the taxi rushed forwards. He followed the cab's progress down the road.

"Guessing you don't wanna hang around then," he said to the cab driver, who was now too far down the road to hear him, even if he had been interested. He looked across the road at a set of wrought iron, thick set gates, and just knew that this was the place he had been sent to. Despite the intensity of the job he had been asked to do, the only thing that concerned Shuffler was how he was going to get home.

He stayed to the side of the road from where moments earlier the taxi had driven away, and walked approximately two hundred metres beyond the double gates. He then crossed the road and made his way back toward the very same gates. The broken biker who now relied on a mangled body to transport himself around did not, however, have a broken mind or defective observation skills.

Despite what he had been told about the organisation that existed behind those gates, they were lax over their external security. One camera covered the exterior of the gate and was fixed to the area where the communication box was located. Shuffler had experienced this so many times at military bases, a hundred expertly trained soldiers on the inside but one camera watched over by an underpaid security guard was what protected the perimeter. He stopped about twelve feet from the driveway, lit up a rollup, and waited. Despite the unusually cool weather, he was beginning to sweat from the weight of the clothing he wore.

A few minutes later, he started to light up a second cigarette when a black car drove up to the gates and screeched to a halt. The driver's window slid partially down. His arm reached out, the index finger pressing the black button at the bottom centre of the grilled box. Shuffler lit the cigarette and walked behind and then past the car coming to a stop at the opposite wall. He was sure that he had heard the driver say one word before the gates silently swung inwardly open.

The vehicle rapidly made its way forward up the driveway, missing the gates by inches on either side of its wing mirrors. Shuffler's right shoulder missed the gate by a similar distance as he stepped under the gaze of the camera and inside, doubling back on himself to hide among the heavy bushes.

"Fucks," was a really strange password he thought to himself, as he watched the vehicle disappear from his view.

Deciding not to push his luck any further and also not to question the complete incompetency of this organisation, he made his way in the same direction as the vehicle, following the path of the driveway using the cover of the trees and bushes as protection from any cameras up ahead. Despite his vigilance, he spotted none.

Slowed down by the undergrowth, it took about ten minutes to make his way along the driveway before spotting ahead of him a large building, the entrance of which was a solid glass panelled wall just like Grant had described. The black car was parked in front of the entrance doors at an angle alongside three other vehicles, all smartly parked in between the white lines of the marked-out parking spaces.

Shuffler, however, was more interested in the vehicle parked about twenty feet in front of the entrance to the building and the opposite side to the doors from the four cars. The black and chrome of the motorbike shone in the daylight. He scratched the crotch of his jeans as he gazed upon the beauty of something that he had been asked to...he looked down at his own hand scratching his dick through his jeans. "Wrong bro," he told himself, "even by your standards, very fucking wrong."

His hand slid unconsciously to the front right pocket of his jeans, through which he felt the rectangular piece of plastic that Grant had handed over to him.

"What's wrong with keys?" he whispered as he emerged from the cover of the trees.

Kelly entered the arrival time of Fox into the arrivals ledger. He hated his job. He was effectively a glorified receptionist, a door security man at best. He had joined the military at seventeen years of age, completed his infantry training with flying colours, top of his class in every discipline. At twenty-two, after five years of doing nothing exciting, he had applied for SAS selection and failed miserably. This had taught him a valuable lesson in life...only reach for the stars that are within arm's reach.

His battalion had been posted to Northern Ireland, nothing exciting there because *the Troubles* were well and truly over, but it was here that he had discovered a new challenge, for an infantryman with a well above average IQ, this was a star that was more than accessible. He had applied for *The Company* training within two months of arriving in the province, and fourteen weeks later, he had passed and was now classified as an *Operator*.

An expert in surveillance, counter-surveillance, interrogation, hand-to-hand combat with multiple weapons (both issued and not), and a willingness to kill. He had arrived back in Ireland just two weeks before his Battalion left and stayed there for another four years. During those forty-eight months, he had been personally responsible for the deaths of twelve terrorists and the prevention of dozens of bombing and shooting incidents.

However, four years of never being questioned about your actions eventually had to lead to your downfall and it inevitably did for Kelly. He was expelled from 14 Intelligence Company and the British Military for intentionally and unlawfully exploding a vehicle, and endangering the lives of innocent civilians. It had not been a coincidence that the vehicle in question had belonged to the daughter of the Commander-in-Chief of Northern Ireland. She was a lovely young lady, who a few weeks prior to the blowing up of her vehicle, had been caught by her father blowing Kelly.

With the exception of the occasional opportunity to hurt or kill people, Kelly hated his job…unless something unexpected happened.

His gaze was fixated and held upon the character who slowly made his way across the open forecourt, in front of the Bloom Institute's main building, toward the motorbike that had been parked up at the front of the building. Kelly remembered the clear and explicit instructions issued to him and his team by Fox.

"When, not if, when Grant comes to collect that bike, he is to be allowed full and unobstructed access to it."

Kelly followed the progress of the old man. Fox had not mentioned anyone else collecting it.

As Shuffler closed down the distance between himself and the Indian Chief, he began to unbutton the long coat he was wearing. It was fully unbuttoned by the time he straddled his leg across the top of the bike seat. This was a monumental effort for a man who had suffered major spinal and pelvic injuries.

He pressed the ignition button, which in turn powered the bike's engine into action. He began to undo the suicide vest he wore beneath the coat, a task that would have proved impossible for the wearer during the days of its original design. He shrugged the coat off his shoulders, allowing his arms to momentarily slip out of the sleeves so that he could remove the vest from his body and place it on top of the bike's fuel tank. He then placed his arms back inside the coat's sleeves.

Kelly continued to watch this man's actions as the bike was slowly manoeuvred toward the glass doors that sat in the middle of the glass panelled front walls of the reception area within which he sat. Only when the man riding the bike reached inside his coat pocket and pulled out a piece of paper, which he stuck to the glass door, did Kelly make a move toward it. As he walked toward the doors, he watched as the man threw a canvas sleeveless type jacket to the pavement and then ride the bike away from the building.

Two feet away from the glass door, Kelly first looked down at the item on the ground and then looked up at the glass door at a yellow, square piece of paper he now recognised as a Post-It note. It was only upon reading the word written on it that his brain calculated that the canvas piece of clothing on the ground was a suicide vest. The word that had been fixed on the glass door so that it could be read from inside the building, said:

BOOM!!

Kelly ran, heading back toward the reception desk as if hell's own demons were propelling his ass forward. The explosion shattered both glass doors and all six of the glass panels inwards. This assisted his dive toward and over the reception desk. Shards of glass and debris from the torn apart fixtures and fittings covered the floor of the reception area. Its modern décor now ripped apart and partially hidden behind dust and smoke, as Kelly's face appeared above what was left of the reception desk.

The desk remained remarkably intact, considering its positioning within the blast area. Kelly made his way carefully through the open area, stepping over and between the array of debris, toward the now unhindered access to the outside world. He saw no sign of the perpetrator of this attack.

Shuffler was already half way down the drive, heading toward the gate, when the explosion happened. He had just carried on riding, mainly because by turning around, he ran the risk of receiving some minor facial blast damage as well as probably falling off the bike, but also because he was enjoying being back on a bike after so long away from them.

He had shouted out a loud and long "Yeeessssss," as the blast had sounded. The site of the closed gates brought him back to reality. He braked hard, the rear tyre skidding slightly, as the rapid halting of his momentum threatened to tip him over the bars of the bike. He had already planned out his departure as he had entered the grounds. That plan had been based on him leaving on foot because he never really expected to be leaving on this bike. However, like every good Boy Scout, he had come prepared.

He placed the bike's gear system into neutral and rested it onto its side stand. Dismounting the bike with painless ease, he walked the hundred metres or so to the gates. Shuffler reached into his pocket and retrieved the hand grenade that had been there for many weeks. As he wedged the grenade into the gap where the two gates met, he only had two thoughts in his head. The estate where he lived may well be a shithole, but he never ceased to be amazed by what you could get your hands on if you knew the right people; and, he wasn't looking forward to the return of his almost ceaseless pain once the adrenalin dump kicked in.

He pulled the pin and turned quickly, running as fast as his damaged body would allow him into the wooded area at the side of the driveway. Ducking behind a large thick-trunked tree, he hoped that the bike was far enough away so as not to sustain any damage.

Seconds before the grenade exploded, splitting the gates apart and ripping one entirely off its heavy hinges, Shuffler looked toward the bike. Grant had asked him to send a message to this organisation, a message that clearly said, "I don't need you or your gifts," but from the moment he had seen the bike, he knew that he could not intentionally destroy it.

As he waited for the explosive device to detonate, he was conscious that the unpredictable damage capability of a grenade could easily achieve what Grant had asked of him. He closed his eyes and hoped that when he opened them again, the bike would still be undamaged, or at least be roadworthy because he was now beginning to hurt again and could do without being chased on foot by some fairly pissed off individuals, especially that black dude he had watched walking toward his sticky note.

He gave it a few seconds following the second blast he had caused that day and opened his eyes. He smiled as he saw the bike still standing and apparently undamaged as far as he could make out. He hurried toward it, initially worried as the engine was no longer ticking over. He gave the bike a quick once over but could see no damage, and then he remembered the smart little device in his pocket, and realised that the engine must have cut out the moment he was out of range from the bike.

He pressed the ignition switch and she immediately fired up. He drifted through the damaged gates, being careful to steer around the many wrought iron pieces from the exploded gate. Heading left, he carefully opened her up, the wind hit his face and head and he was reminded by nature that he was not wearing a helmet. Even the best Boy Scout can't prepare for every eventuality!

The Chicken and the Fox

A figure appeared at the bottom of the stairs inside the Bloom Institute's now very unwelcoming reception area, and watched as Kelly stepped through the broken glass doors into the outside world, the immediate part of that also covered in shattered glass. He reflected on the fact that Kelly had access to the outside via any of the broken and blown out sections of the building's front wall, yet he had chosen to leave by the doorway.

Human behaviour and mortal predictability were usually flaws Fox looked for when doing his job, but once again Fox had been unprepared for this act of destruction by Grant; a message he had expected, but nothing to this extent.

He scanned the exterior of the building, immediately noticing the absence of the bike. Theft was not something he attributed to Grant. Perhaps a desperate situation had demanded drastic action. He thought again of Grant's situation. He knew that Grant had already latched onto the fact that he had access to money. Fox didn't think he yet knew how much money he could have access to, but for the time being he had allowed full access to continue.

Knowing Grant, he thought that it was probable that he was only spending on what he really needed. The visit to the bank to retrieve cash rather than to leave a bank card user trail had been a clever move, albeit a predictable one. And then Grant had disappeared, no trace anywhere, no CCTV footage, no agent reports, no visuals from any of their resources, until now.

"I am assuming that it was our mutual friend," Fox shouted in the direction of Kelly.

Kelly turned to face Fox, but before he could respond a second, smaller explosion could be heard farther down the drive. Kelly instinctively ducked down and covered his head with his folded arms.

By the time he stood up again, Fox was standing just a few feet away from him, still inside the building.

"By the sound of that, it would seem that our scurrying thief of a little chicken has made good his escape." He looked at Kelly again and asked, "I am right in guessing that Grant has re-emerged?"

"Not unless he has aged by quite a bit, grown a full scraggy beard, developed a really bad gait and changed his fucking face entirely," replied Kelly. His voice was slightly raised, mainly because he was ashamed of himself for ducking down from a blast that could never have caused him any harm. That, and the fact that it had happened in front of Fox, a man who looked down on him and thought him no more worthy than the position he held, a uniformed receptionist.

Fox smiled to himself, quietly pleased that he had been correct. Theft, as he had thought, was not a label applicable to Grant.

"So, our chicken is building a clutch around him again. Now this could get interesting," said Fox out loud. Unintentionally, this statement was audible to Kelly, the man Fox considered to be a failure.

Fox headed back up the stairwell toward the upper lift that would return him to his meeting with Mr. Bloom. He had been bringing Bloom up to date with regards to the situation with Grant, and the new information that the technical team had retrieved from the laptop that Grant had handed to him.

—————— ——————

Leaving the bike where it was, Grant walked toward the supermarket. He needed a top up of his favourite cigars. He wondered if Shuffler had made his move yet. He doubted it, even though it had been a few hours since he had left his friend's flat. Hours that had been filled with interesting conversation with Halo and a few errands set for him to run, useful little errands, but ones that didn't matter if the young lad failed or bottled them. They were more of a test than anything else.

His first problem was finding a place to stay. He needed something low-key, a place that didn't keep a register or at least not one that had any significance or usefulness for anyone trying to find someone. Basically, Grant was looking for a place one grade above a doss house. He needed more money, or to be absolutely accurate, he wanted more money.

He didn't know whether or not the organisation had stopped his access to this, and the only way to find out would involve another visit to a bank, another breadcrumb to the miniscule trail that he had already laid. That could wait for now. He wasn't desperate for cash but would prefer not to leave it until he reached the point where he was. Impulsion normally resulted in mistakes being made. He needed to think about the information and clues that he already had in his possession. At the moment they were like scattered pieces of a jigsaw puzzle.

Grant had started to put together the outside pieces and it was becoming clearer where some of the inside pieces could go, but the whole picture was a long way from making any sense.

The young lady at the tobacco kiosk handed him his tin of cigars, the lighter that he had also requested and his change from the £10 note he had used. He thanked her and asked if the supermarket had a café serving hot food. She pointed toward the sign hanging from the ceiling that said "Café" and an arrow pointing toward the far end of the store.

"Can't see the end of my own nose sometimes, thanks," he said with a smile.

He decided that a big greasy breakfast was called for and while it was probably not going to be as big or as greasy as he liked, it would be at least adequate. His mind was always clearer when rested on a belly full of eggs, bacon, sausage, beans and fried bread. Hopefully by the time he had finished his meal and had another smoke, he may have received a call from either Halo or Shuffler if the gods were on his side.

The call from Halo came just as Grant was wiping his plate clean. The last forkful of fried bread loaded with a few beans and the last slice of sausage were being pushed into his mouth. He answered the phone mid-chew.

"Yeah," was the best greeting Grant could get out of his overfilled mouth.

"Yo man, I know you want to get into the Rainbow, but I hope that isn't cock you are chewing down on," replied the young kid.

Grant paused, chewed, swallowed and paused again before

responding.

"It was a sausage yes, and that is the last gay innuendo you are getting away with kid."

Halo laughed before saying, "Well, mission number one accomplished boss."

The first task he had set Halo was to retrieve his stuff from the apartment where he had spent one night. He had never expected this one to be successful, he just wanted to see how gutsy and committed to helping Halo really was.

"Define accomplished," said Grant.

"I got your stuff dude," came back the straightforward response.

Grant was genuinely shocked into silence, not only by the fact that this young upstart claimed to have achieved what was asked of him, but also by the speed with which it had apparently been done.

"You still there?" asked Halo.

"Err, yeah. So you got all of my stuff out of that apartment?" he asked.

"Well yes and no," said Halo, and then further explained. "I got your stuff, but the guy on the desk had it all packed up and he told me to say to you that you only got this bit of help because he hates you less than the people he works for, but only just."

"Tell me exactly what happened Halo," said Grant.

------ ------

Shuffler made one brief stop on his journey home, which he was completing by sticking to as many leafy suburban roads as he could. He knew that if he hit the main links, he would be stopped for having no helmet within a few minutes. The stop had been brought about on spying a child's bike lying on the road. To be exact, it was laying at the bottom of a driveway of a rather nice looking property. Even more precisely, it was in the middle of the driveway and the small double gates were closed.

The bike had obviously been dropped there by its owner before they had disappeared into their home, or the home of a friend. Either way, none of this was important to Shuffler. The important bit was the piece of equipment loosely hanging by its chin strap from the bike handle, a crash helmet. It was a dark green helmet probably for a twelve-year-old, give or take a year or two, but in Shuffler's head it was a helmet and surely, he thought, in the eyes of the law it had to be better than nothing.

He stopped the bike just past the gates, nipped through them quickly and snatched it. He tried on for size. Snug would have been stretching the truth of the matter. On the way back to his bike, he extended the chin straps as far as they would go and gave the top of the helmet a heavy slap with his hand in an effort to force it a little bit farther onto his head. The plastic clips of the chin strip strained under the effort, as Shuffler forced one into the other. Returning to the bike, he was annoyed to find that it had once again cut out.

"Fucking technology!" he exclaimed. "Fucking keys don't do this. That's why *they* make this shit so that they make sure you cannot make a quick getaway." He looked up toward the sky and raised his fist shaking it in frustration. "I know you can fucking hear me you bastards," he shouted upwards.

An elderly gentleman out taking a leisurely walk stopped to observe the man's strange behaviour.

"Are you alright young man?" he asked kindly.

The strange bicycle helmet wearing, cloud shouting biker walked toward the old man and pointing at his face, and said, "Do you actually need those glasses to see where you are going?"

"They're my reading glasses, but I always keep them on. I might need to read a sign or something," the strolling gentleman replied, somewhat surprised by the response to his question.

Shuffler reached for them and gently removed them by the bridge from the old man's face.

"Well you ain't bloody reading now and my need is more important than yours," said Shuffler, placing the glasses on his own face. *Okay they aren't goggles, but they are just as good a replacement as this helmet,* he thought to himself as he did so.

"But may I enquire how I will get them back?" asked the despectacled gent.

Without turning around Shuffler called out, "Put your name and address on a slip of paper and send it to the 'we don't give a fuck department,' care of the British Secret Services."

He started up the bike again and rode away, leaving the old gentleman trying to figure out what had just occurred as he watched the strangest site he had ever seen in his entire life disappear out of sight down the road.

Back at the Bloom Institute in the data room, a young tech watched the progress of the tracer on the Indian Scout. He noted the time that the bike came to a stop and when it started back on its journey, the red dot flashed at ten second intervals. He picked up the phone and dialled the number for Fox's mobile and passed on the information.

Fox hung up the call and looked over the desk to where Mr.

Bloom sat.

"Good news sir, we are back in control."

------ ------

Grant listened, intently at first but this soon moved on to boredom as Halo's tale became predictable. However, this was the kid's moment, so Grant didn't interrupt.

"Well it was fairly easy to be honest," regaled Halo. "I got to the underground car park entrance you told me about quite quickly. I know lots of shortcuts around that part of town from burgling there. There are lots of narrow ones that our bikes can get through, but the cop cars can't. Anyway, I hung around for a while, but no cars went in or out, so I couldn't sneak in like I planned to do, so I just walked in the front entrance. It's well plush, that place, being a spy or agent or whatever you are must pay well. I might look into it. Well, as soon as I walked in, this guy behind the reception place was right on me, asking me who I was and what I wanted, so I just got honest with him and said that I was a rent boy and was visiting you like."

At this point, Grant really had to work hard not to interject.

"Well, he laughed like a kitten being tickled. The man said he always knew you was a wrong 'un. So, we chatted a little bit, man to man like, and then he went back to the desk thing and came back with a bag and said it was full of your stuff. He has a really bad limp yer know, bit like Shuffler. You must like the cripples, eh? Anyway, he then gave me the message to pass on to you and told me to fuck off and never darken his door again or he would take me to a place of pain that would make my nightmares seem like pleasant afternoon dreams.

The geezer must be into SMA places where they whip you and stick balls in your mouth or something."

A few seconds passed by before Grant realised that Halo had stopped speaking.

"Oh right, well done lad, so where are you now?" he asked.

"Not far from the place you sent me but now I is going to make a couple of calls to get your ass into the Rainbow tonight," replied Halo.

"Tonight!" exclaimed Grant.

"Friday innit?" said Halo nonchalantly as if that would mean something to Grant. "Place will be rammed full of newbies. I just thought that would be the best time for you to do your surveillance spy shit."

"Halo, I am not a spy. I am simply an investigative profile expert assisting the police with a few things," responded Grant.

"Yeah whatever bro," replied Halo. Grant didn't need to be able to see the kid's face to know that he was smiling as he said the words. "I will call you again when I got it set up."

"Okay you do that, leave a voicemail if I don't answer as I may be on the bike," said Grant.

"Yeah okay," replied Halo.

Grant ended the call, wiped his mouth with a paper napkin and left the café, heading back to his bike. As he walked, he checked his phone to see if Shuffler had tried to contact him while he had been talking to Halo, but there were no texts or missed calls. He thought about riding back to Shuffler's place to see if he had returned already. He doubted that his task was going to take such a short time to achieve, so he put that idea aside trusting in his old servery cleaner to get in touch when he could or when he had to.

Grant elected to ride toward Camden and maybe get a few clothes that would blend in a little more in a nightclub. He would also try to find an internet café and do a bit of anonymous internet searching to find digs for a night or two and then meet up with Halo. His thoughts then turned to withdrawing some more from the Bank of Bloom.

------ ------

Shuffler arrived back at his flat quite a few hours after leaving the leafy suburban surroundings that the Bloom Institute stood in. He had travelled on as many back roads and streets as he could possibly get away with. Should further proof be required that the streets of Great Britain needed more police presence then the fact that an ex-con could ride a stolen motorbike while wearing a child's bicycle crash hat and a pair of stolen reading glasses for nearly two hours without being stopped would substantiate the fact.

He got off the bike, opened his front door and then, sitting back astride the bike, pushed it backward into his hallway. It fitted with about four inches to spare on either side of the wing mirrors. This made getting off it a tight squeeze to say the least. Compounded with Shuffler's mobility and flexibility issues, the fact that he managed it with reasonable ease was a testament to the tenacity of the man. He also knew that any motorbike, let alone one of this quality, would last less than an hour parked outside on this estate.

He tilted the bike's handlebars and front wheel sideways and squeezed past to close and double lock and then double bolt the front door. Squeezing once again past the bike, he stroked the tank and the seat as he made his way to his living room. He sat in his favourite chair and took the bottle of Oramorph sat on the small table next to it. He took a heavy glug then rested his head backward and closed his eyes for a moment, allowing the liquid pain relief to flow through his body and do its work.

Shuffler had not been out of his flat or completed so much activity in one period of time for many months, and so it was probably for these reasons mixed in with the adrenalin, the acquisition of a new motorbike and the acute pain he was now suffering with, he omitted to complete his usual conspiracy theory driven safety checks. He was usually religious about them on arriving back home and every night before going to bed. Had all of those factors not come to together at this very moment, Shuffler would have had every reason to shout hallelujah at the top of his voice as his conspiracy theory bullshit all came flying into his life with an acute reality.

The gloved hand pressed heavily against his forehead and ripped his head farther back than it already was. Shuffler felt the cold sharp steel that only the blade of a very sharp knife could produce being held against his throat. He opened his eyes and looked upwards, the only direction he could look, into the white eyes of a face covered with a plain black non-descript balaclava. The voice that belonged to the face hissed at him.

"One move old man and I will cut your throat and won't stop until your head comes away from your body."

In his peripheral vision, Shuffler saw the shadow of another person walk past his left-hand side. Moments later, he sensed someone in front of him. Shuffler assumed it was the person who had produced the silent shadow. Whoever it was spoke.

"Mr. Stanley Dawson, aka Shuffler, aka miserable arsonist

pyromaniac ex-con. How nice to meet you and how easy it was to arrange," said the male voice, calm, strong and comfortable in the controlled situation he had created.

"I don't remember putting it in my diary, oh and you missed out fairly good squaddie in the aka list," replied Shuffler.

"Stanley, really you surprise and disappoint me. Being the conspiracist that you are, I would have thought you of all people should have been expecting this visit," replied the faceless voice.

Shuffler didn't respond. Secretly, he couldn't disagree with the point his visitor had just made.

"Maybe it was the speed with which we were able to find you," said the voice, "so let me explain even though I do not think any of this will come as any surprise to you. With the right amount of access to the right connections, the most up-to-date technology, some clever people and a huge amount of money, anybody can gain access to an unimaginable amount of information, much of it as it is happening in real time. Your previous criminal activity made it very easy to find out your identity, especially after the face recognition systems matched the picture of your face that we lifted from one of many street CCTV cameras that picked you up on your journey home. Once we had that information, it was just as easy to find the connection between yourself and Grant."

"I don't know anyone called Grant," interrupted Shuffler. He instantly regretted it as the hand that was holding his head back suddenly fist slammed itself into his nose. Just as quickly, it returned to its original position on his forehead. The blood instantly began to trickle from his smashed nose down his face.

"Maybe I should call him Officer Richardson for your

convenience," came the reply.

"Oh him," replied Shuffler, spitting out a mouthful of blood.

"Yes him," said the voice. "I can only assume that your recent visit to our research facility, resulting in the willful damage to our building, the thoughtless danger and threat our staff witnessed, and the subsequent theft of company property all add up to the fact that Grant, I'm sorry, Officer Richardson, recently paid you a visit."

"Last time that twat paid me a visit, I was sitting in a prison cell on A-wing, I think," responded Shuffler. He awaited the next strike to his face. It never came.

The hand holding his head back moved at the same time as the knife was taken from his throat. He instinctively changed the position of his head to its natural upright position. He felt the point of the blade press against the back of his exposed neck.

Someone stood in front of him. Shuffler could see the torso of the man but not the face. He didn't want to risk tilting his head upwards because of the new positioning of the blade, so he raised his eyes up as far as they would go in their sockets and managed to see the mouth and chin of the man, which began to move as he spoke again.

"Mr. Dawson, or may I call your Stanley?" he asked.

"Stanley is just fine by me," replied Shuffler.

"Thank you Stanley. I find that a question-and-answer session always produces better results if a relationship can be developed from the onset." The man's voice maintained its threatening undertone. "I work in a world of truth; it is a world that many people cannot comprehend and one that many prefer to pretend does not exist. You, on the other hand, know that my world is real, but the fact that the majority of the people don't want to believe it, makes it very difficult for you to convince them that your conspiracy theories are in fact real. The problem is Stanley, when you work in a world of truth, lies produce ripples and those ripples have consequences. Now the only way to stop the ripples is to make sure that the lies or, to be more precise, the people who tell the lies also face consequences. Does that seem like a fair outcome to your Stanley?"

Shuffler did not respond. The position of the blade at the base of his neck was his sole focus and the man speaking sensed this.

"It's okay Stanley, the man holding you in place will not cause you any damage unless you try to get away from this situation. In fact, the only person likely to cause you harm will, be yourself. So please feel free to answer my question," the interrogator said.

"I've forgotten the question," said Shuffler, hoping that the man didn't think this was a response to buy some time.

"Now that is the level of honesty I like. It is always best to seek clarity before answering crucial and potentially life changing questions. Do you think it fair that liars should face consequences for their dishonesty?" the man repeated the question for Shuffler.

Shuffler answered directly and simply, "Yes."

"Good, that is very good Stanley. So we must both agree that the lie you have just told me about not seeing Grant for some time, I assume that you do know who I am talking about when I address him by that name, does, in fact, require you to face the consequences. Now, in order to save time, I will explain the rules of my question-and-answer session. You will see that they are very easy to understand. I will ask you a series of questions and you, in turn, will answer them. If the answer you give is deemed by myself to be the truth, I will move on to the next question. If I believe you are telling lies, I will hit you around the head and face with the cosh I am currently holding in my right hand."

Shuffler moved his eyeballs downwards and toward his left. In the man's black gloved hands, he could just about make out a small black round-headed object. The man continued to speak.

"Now, knowing that you are about to be struck violently around the head or face, you will instinctively want to get away from that incoming strike, and as you will not know if the strike is going to come from the left or the right, you will want to move your head backward. Now, this is where you run the risk of harming yourself. Should you take that action, you will push yourself against the knife that my colleague is so delicately and yet so firmly, holding against your neck. The blade is being held against your spine between the C1 and C2 vertebrae. Pressure applied enough will almost certainly cause irreparable damage to your spinal cord at that point. Should you live, you will spend the rest of your life as a high-level tetraplegic resulting in you requiring constant care and assistance in every activity of daily life—dressing, eating, bowel and bladder care—all included."

The last word was emphasised as the cosh came crashing into the left side of Shuffler's face, throwing his head violently sideways. This was accompanied by a scream of agonising pain, a spurt of blood from Shuffler's mouth and a tooth flying through the air. Shuffler's head fell forward, but this was only met with a very clear instruction.

"Hold your head up Stanley and think very carefully about

the answer to my next question," said Shuffler's interrogator. As Shuffler raised his head back to the upright position, only stopping when he felt the point of the blade press against his neck again, his torturer stooped down slightly bringing his face into Shuffler's line of sight.

"I have been rude," he said with a smile. "My name is Fox."

—————— ——————

It was early evening, as Grant sat in a cyber café enjoying a coffee and a bacon roll and surfing the internet as a guest user. He had already found a bed and breakfast, which was located less than a mile from where he currently sat and had called them to ensure that they had a room available and were happy to accept payment in cash. His second call had been to Halo, who confirmed that the final task had been completed. They had agreed to meet at Grant's location as soon as Halo could get there. As he sat looking at current news reports pertaining to the serial killer, his mobile vibrated on the table. The name Shuffler flashed up on its screen.

"Hello bro, I hope you are going to tell me that your road trip was a successful one," said Grant, answering the incoming call. He froze in horror as the caller spoke.

"Depends on how you define successful," replied Fox.

"What have you done with Shuffler?" demanded Grant.

"Do not worry Grant. Stanley is fine. However, once again that would probably depend on your definition of fine," said Fox. "Let's put it this way, he is breathing, but struggling with that, if I am honest. Candor is something that Shuffler has learned much about today."

"I should have killed you when I had the chance, but I didn't think you deserved it. I won't be making that mistake again." Grant's voice was quiet because of where he was, but full of vile hatred toward the agent.

"Yes Grant, you should have and I have to say that, considering the effective manner with which you dealt with certain members of the Crippens, that did surprise me."

"What do you want?" Grant asked him.

"The one thing I have always wanted Grant," replied Fox. "You back in the team, working with us, not against us. We were progressing so well before you decided to flee the coop, but I do believe that you now see that the sneaky fox will always win in the end, because he is quite happy killing all the friends of the number one chicken. So it's time to come back in now, little chicken."

Grant seethed as he was forced to listen to the taunting words of this psychopath. He could not see any way out of this, other than agreeing to Fox's demands. However, he did believe that sometimes buying yourself time could result in a good idea making itself known.

"I'll meet you at the police station in the morning," he said, trying his best to sound even more defeated than he actually felt.

"I believe you to be a man of your word Grant," replied Fox, with a smugness you could almost touch.

Grant thought and acted quickly. Leaving the café, he got back on his bike and headed immediately back to Shuffler's flat. He was confident that Fox and his small team of thugs would have left the place as soon as they had got the information they wanted. The traffic was moving slowly, but he made his way steadily through it by filtering whenever he could, twice risking his life as a couple of car drivers purposely steered their vehicles into his intended path.

On both occasions, he thanked the testers for ensuring that he did the "swerve and avoid" maneouvre was to the required standard. On the second occasion, he used his inside elbow to dislodge the car's wing mirror from the side of the car trying to slow down his progress. He heard the driver shout something at him, but couldn't make out what was being said. He knew that it would have been abusive or threatening. In response, he simply lifted his left hand and flicked a single finger back at the inconsiderate prick behind the steering wheel.

Eventually, he arrived outside his friend's home and flicked out the side stand, leaning the bike onto it, leaping from the bike without removing his gloves or helmet. About fifty yards from where he now stood, he saw one of the street bike gang sat on his bike and observing his arrival, he looked in his direction and shouted:

"Touch this bike and I will find you, and when I do, I will cut your face up so bad your own mother won't be able to look at you without puking. Now phone a fucking ambulance."

He didn't wait for a response as he headed toward the front door of Shuffler's flat, seeing immediately that it was slightly ajar. He ran inside calling out the name of his friend, but getting no reply. As he entered the small living room it quickly became apparent why. Even if Shuffler had been conscious, Grant did not think it would have been possible for him to speak.

The old biker's face had been smashed, crushed and lacerated by the beating he had taken. His body was limp and his head hung backward over the chair in which he was sat. Blood was dripping from what was left of his face, a blood covered grotesque mask of pain and horror. Grant cradled the back of Shuffler's neck and head. He gently pushed it forward to a more natural sitting position. He thought he saw a small movement from under the mass of blood, swelling and broken bones. He wiped away some of the blood and once again it was there, a slight flicker of one eyelid. Grant leaned in close to Shuffler.

"Shuffler, can you hear me bro?" he whispered.

To his surprise, his friend attempted to speak but unsurprisingly he couldn't understand what he was trying to say. It was obvious that his jaw was broken, probably in multiple places. Several teeth appeared to be missing or at least loosened, and Shuffler's nose and mouth were full of blood.

"Don't try to speak my friend, an ambulance is on its way," said Grant, making an attempt to carefully wipe away some of the blood. Shuffler ignored his request and tried to speak again.

Grant placed his ear so close to Shuffler's mouth blood transferred itself from one to the other, and just before Grant felt the full weight of Shuffler's head fall against his hand indicating that he was now fully unconscious, Shuffler said one word. Grant was certain that the word spoken was, "Sorry."

An unknown voice broke the silence:

"Hello, is anyone here?" it asked.

"In here," called back Grant, fear and anxiety clearly audible in his voice.

A paramedic entered the room, two bags slung on his shoulder. The expression on his face changed to one of shock as he approached closer and saw the face of the man being supported by Grant.

"What's happened sir?" he asked.

"This man needs a hospital and quick," replied Grant.

The paramedic placed his hand on the back of Shuffler's head saying, "I've got him, you can let go now."

Slowly and reluctantly, Grant moved his hand and moved out of the way as a second paramedic entered the room. Between them, they carefully placed Shuffler's body onto the floor and began to work on him, talking to him as they did so.

"Do you know this gentleman's name?" the second paramedic asked. Grant watched in silence, anger and regret conflicting with each other in his brain.

"Sir," the paramedic asked again, "what's his name?"

"It's Stanley Dawson and he had better make it to an operating table and not a morgue slab!"

"We will do everything we can," said the first paramedic. "Do you know what happened?"

"Yeah," hissed Grant. "Someone just made the biggest mistake of their life. He walked out of the room and back into the fresh air. He wanted to release his anger with a scream, but as he walked out of the front door, he was met by a police officer.

"Hello sir, I am PC Ngodo. Can you tell me what has been going on?"

Grant looked at the copper; a broad and tall young black man looked back at him. Grant did not answer the question, but instead reached into his jacket inside pocket and retrieved a small piece of card. He handed the business card to PC Ngodo, who looked at the sparce information written on it.

"And who or what are C.O.R.T. sir?" the police constable asked.

"The answer to all of your questions, the bastards who did this, the reason I am leaving here without answering any more of your questions and the reason why I can do that," replied Grant.

PC Ngodo looked at the card again and then back at Grant.

"I need you to stay here for a while sir. I will need a statement from you and I am sure that other colleagues of mine will want to ask you a few questions," said the copper, trying to assert his position.

Grant glared at the copper and through gritted teeth said.

"What you need is your fucking problem. What I need is to hand out a bit of justice that is beyond your capability." He began to walk past the policeman, who temporarily stopped his progress by placing a large hand on his shoulder.

Grant's hand, the one farthest from the copper's halting hand, swept upwards and grabbed the copper's wrist. His thumb fell naturally onto the back of the hand, pushing it forward and then upwards toward the side of PC Ngodo's head. As this happened, Grant pushed his inside hand and arm through the bent arm of the copper, grabbing a hold onto his other forearm and dropping both elbows.

The already effective figure of four arm lock tightened. Grant spun his body position so that he ended up at the side of the policeman and facing him. This now enabled him to place the copper's elbow against his chest, locking the hold firmly into place. Grant's face was now only a few inches away from PC Ngodo's ear so he could speak quietly, confident that the copper would be able to hear him with ease.

"Listen grunt, I am leaving and there is fuck all you are going to do about it. Accept that fact and I will not have to introduce you to medical retirement."

"Sir," replied PC Ngodo, who despite being in some pain remained calm and controlled," you are making a big mistake, now let me go."

Grant tightened the arm lock and the copper made a grunting noise as the pain level increased from a four to a five or six.

"Do not assume that your uniform puts you in control of this situation lad. Underneath it you are human, breakable and easily disposed of. Call the number that is scribbled on the back of the card. If that is above your pay grade, give it to one of the plain clothed wankers who are undoubtedly on their way and tell them to do it."

He applied pressure to the arm lock and dropped to one knee, forcing the police officer to fall backward ending up on his back, hitting the ground solidly, but nowhere near as hard as it could have been had Grant not controlled the fall as well as he did.

A voice called out from behind him. Grant recognised it immediately as being the voice of Ghost.

"Use the phone we gave you bro."

Keeping the arm lock in place to maintain control of the fallen officer, Grant looked over his shoulder.

"I am not going to stab a copper," he shouted.

Ghost got off his bike and ran over to where Grant was kneeling.

"Where's the phone?" asked Ghost.

"What part of we are not stabbing a copper are you having trouble understanding?" Grant replied.

"Trust me," pleaded Ghost. For reasons that Grant would never be able to work out, he decided to.

"Right jacket pocket," he said, and then tightened the arm

lock as he felt Ngodo struggling against the restraint.

Ghost took the phone out of Grant's pocket. Grant watched as the young thug pressed two buttons, each one on opposite sides of the top of the phone, simultaneously. A blue electric arc sparked its way between two tiny silver electrodes located at the bottom of the phone.

"I suggest you let go of the filth now," said Ghost, as he pressed the two buttons again and held the device against the neck of PC Ngodo.

Grant released the hold he had restraining the police officer a split second before Ghost made contact with the taser. PC Ngodo clenched his teeth together as his body went into spasm. As the electrical current surged through his body, his muscles contracted involuntarily, as his nervous system went into overdrive. Finally, he let out several screams as the extreme pain registered in his brain.

Ghost handed the phone back to Grant saying, "Now go and I suggest you charge that as soon as possible, that shit drains it bad man."

Grant grabbed the phone and nodded his gratitude back at Ghost.

"Make sure Shuffler makes it into the ambulance...alive would be a bonus," he said.

Ghost nodded, saying, "I'll send one of the boys to the hospital and will let yous know how it goes bro."

Grant looked down at Ngodo, who was now beginning to show signs of recovery. He placed his hand on the chest of the copper, who flinched as if he was expecting another bolt of electricity to rush through his body.

"Why don't you fuckers ever listen to sound advice?"

He stood up, shook Ghost's hand and made his way back to

his bike. Using a combination of throttle, clutch and brake, he spun the bike around and raced away from the scene. The two thoughts racing through his head—hoping Shuffler would be okay and how to kill Fox—were quickly replaced by Halo.

He was now running late, and so after riding away for some time and comfortable that he was far away enough to offer him a reasonable amount of safety and time, he began to look for a place to pull over so that he could call his young helper.

The Secrets of the Rainbow

The two shadowy figures walked along the corridor toward the lift. Neither said a word as they silently passed doors on either side of them. Entering the lift, the taller of the two pressed the button that would take them down to the basement. They had to journey down in order to get back up and eventually out, a journey they had done several times.

They were a reluctant team, brought together by the needs of them both; both sets of needs were similar but different in so many ways, but all led by one emotion: Revenge. As they exited the elevator, one held out his hand as if to indicate the direction of travel that was required. The second of the pair glared at the first.

"I know the fucking way," he snarled, in a manner that reflected the uncaged animal that he was.

Passing through the morgue, the second, slightly shorter and older man, stroked his hand along the stainless steel doors behind which lay the dead bodies or as he preferred to call them, the Celestas, his messengers of death.

"Sleep deeply now my children, you all served him so well," he whispered, as he caressed the doors and then looking toward his accomplice he asked, "Did he get my last message?"

"I have no idea," the other replied. "I think he disappeared before Fox had a chance to tell him that it was meant for him."

"He has to know that the last one was for him. I have to prod the monster inside him, otherwise his fate will not be sealed as prophesised." The reflective shine from the stainless steel doors glinted in The Priest's eyes, making them glow silver, which in turn made his eyeballs look like steel orbs.

"I don't control Fox and I certainly have no control over him," replied the taller man.

"David, I doubt that you can control your own bladder at times you incompetent fool," replied The Priest.

They continued their walk through the Bloom Institute morgue toward the work station area that Grant had noticed when he had been in the room. Next to where the computer was located was a door. Stanridge produced a key from his pocket that was attached to a silver metal clip along with a metal door pass. He unlocked the door and allowed Mortimer to walk through first.

Following him, he locked the door behind them and followed Mortimer down the short corrider, at the end of which was a set of lift doors. This lift was not visible or accessible from any area other than here and the back of Bloom's office. It was Bloom's personal lift, allowing him to enter and leave without being seen by staff, should the occasion need it.

Only two people had the access card for this elevator, Bloom and Fox, or so they thought. It had had taken Stanridge weeks of observation and patience before the opportunity had presented itself, allowing him the chance to get his own access card. A rare mistake by Mr. Bloom had made it possible, when he had left his desk drawer unlocked during a meeting with the doctor and momentarily excused himself to use the toilet.

Stanridge could not believe his luck when he slid open the drawer and there sat a spare access card, identical to the ones that he had seen Bloom and Fox carry. It had to be the one he had been looking for and needed. He had taken it with the intention of trying to get it copied and then returning it as soon as he safely could. All efforts to have a copy made proved impossible. So it was the one he had taken that he now used to access the private lift system.

Reaching the end of its journey, the lift doors opened onto a dark empty corridor. In front of them stood a door that led directly into Bloom's office, but the two men were not interested in that one. They turned left down the corridor toward a door at the end, a simple metal door with a push bar.

It was a fire escape door that opened up into an internal set of stairs that led down to the back of the Bloom Institute building. It had been a necessary requirement when the building had been constructed. One that neither Bloom or Fox had wanted, but had no choice in or control over. Even the most secret of organisations had to comply with the Health and Safety Executive.

It had not been the fire escape persay, that had been the problem. It was the fact that the door must never be secured or locked. Ihe fact that the necessary escape route could not be used as an entry route into the building, or more importantly Bloom's personal office, made it easier to live with.

At the bottom of the stairwell stood the exit door, which led out onto a sheltered patio style area that had been added after the original building had gone through the usual building safety checks. It had been added for two reasons: To give Mr. Bloom a comfortable area to wait, and to keep the fire escape external door invisible from the outside world.

The two half brothers sat in Bloom's waiting area and waited for darkness to fall. The wait was completed in silence and with a nervous discomfort.

------ ------

As Grant reached for his phone to call Halo, it started to ring. He had stopped at a petrol garage, parking behind the main building, so that he didn't have to put up with some nosey do-gooder having a go at him for making a call from a mobile at a petrol station, and also because it put him into an area where there were no cameras.

He answered the call. Fox's voice identified his mood: Annoyed.

"You have time to go and visit our mutual friend Stanley. You have time to assault a police officer, but you don't have the time to meet with me before tomorrow morning?" he said. He paused waiting for a response but Grant remained silent, so Fox continued. "It makes me think you are trying to buy time. It makes me think you are planning something, and that makes me nervous Grant."

The silence was in place for quite a few seconds before Grant spoke.

"I wasn't the most disciplined of soldiers. It could be argued that I wasn't really made for a life in uniform, but the important things it taught me have stayed with me for life: Honour, loyalty and the truth. You have no honour, no loyalty and you left the world of truth many years ago. Not that long ago, I was fuelled with anger, guilt and vengence, and I did the things I did because I had been put into a position where I had nothing to live for. This, as you know, made me dangerous. The mistake you have made is to give me something to live for again. Don't make a second mistake by thinking that this makes me less dangerous because it has done the exact opposite. From the minute you disclosed that my wife was still alive, the only thing driving me on, the one thing consuming my every thought has been how I am going to kill you." Grant spoke calmly. His tone remained menacing. Fox attempted to interrupt but Grant continued to speak, and Fox immediately went quiet again.

"You think you control me because you hold my wife captive, but I lost her once. I buried her. I grieved and I took action to put that grief and anger into a locked box forever. So go ahead Fox, kill her again if you like. It will make no difference to my course of action because I have already dealt with losing her. Now, you can follow me with your technology, but I will always evade you because you are a company man. You think and behave like a man in uniform. You won't admit it, but deep inside you know that you are just following the orders of invisible spineless pricks. I, on the other hand, am a free spirit. An uncontrollable, unpredictable monster. A nightmare that interrupts your sleep and diverts your focus. So remember this Fox, I suffer patiently so that you will patiently suffer."

Grant ended the call and straight away called Halo's number. Fox stared silently at his mobile. Fear was not an emotion he was used to dealing with. The ace card that was Julia Richardson had just been torn up and thrown on the fire. Doing his job of finding the killer had to be put on the back burner for now. His priority had just become the disposal of Grant.

Grant tried twice to get hold of Halo, but there had been no answer. The young lad's phone went straight to the answer phone. Grant chose not to leave a message. The calls alone were enough of a trail of electronic breadcrumbs without leaving a message that could easily be accessed and listened to.

The journeys of three men commenced at roughly the same time as darkness began to fall. The destination was the same for all three, although the routes were different.

Grant started his bike and headed through London directly for the Rainbow Club.

Stanridge and Church left the comfort of the waiting area and got into the unmarked black company van. Stanridge got into the driver's compartment, with Church hidden in the back. They drove away from the back of the building and down the long drive. Simple identity checks were completed before the gates were opened for Stanridge. The security guard had no reason to be suspicious of an important company employee leaving the grounds in a company vehicle.

Fox stood behind one of the still intact glass walls at the front of the Bloom Institute and watched the black van disappear into the darkness as it made its way down the driveway.

He walked over to the security guard and gazed at the same CCTV screen that showed the face of Dr. Stanridge and listened as he told the guard that he was off to collect medical supplies. As the guard pressed the button that made the gates slide open, Fox was wondering why the doctor would be collecting medical supplies at this time of night when they were normally delivered to the Institute.

The doctor's journey went without a hitch and he eventually

parked the van in one of the car parks dotted around Camden Market. The door of the van slid open before Stanridge had even turned off the engine. Mortimer Church exited the van, and quickly checked around the area. Seeing that it was clear, he made his way across the car park, using the few vehicles that were there as cover. He disappeared down the embankment that led to the railway tracks.

Stanridge locked the van and followed Church down the embankment, along the side of the railway line and into the bushes. Entering the catacombs through the long forgotten hidden entrance, they made their way through the maze of tunnels, never getting lost or taking the wrong turn.

They passed the area where, behind the open doorways, resided their still living victims. They both heard the quiet sobbing of one of them, but this time there was no threatening instruction to shut up.

They walked through the larger open expanse that was used to mentally cleanse the captured, and worship and celebrate their work. Both men looked straight ahead, mentally focussed on where they were heading and what was to be done. They only stopped when they came to the end of one of the tunnels and turned left into an area that was completely empty, except for a set of stone steps that led up to a doorway about twenty feet up the far wall.

The door stood out from its old surroundings, as it was visibly modern, a recent addition to the otherwise unchanged catacombs, well, an upgrade more than an addition. The doorway had always existed, as had the stone stairs. Their combination had allowed tunnel workers access to one of the many factory and warehouse buildings that had been built above and around the underground network.

Many of these buildings had long become derelict and had been torn down, but a few that had been deemed structurally capable of being reused had been converted into a variety of different businesses. Behind this particular door now, stood a nightclub, although from the inside, it was not apparent it was a door.

Where the door was situated had been mounted a full length mirror, allowing the revellers to check their appearance before leaving the same-sex toilets. Many of the young gay clientelle of the Rainbow Club had preened and posed in front of this mirror. Many had taken photographs of their own reflective image, but none had realised that on some of those occasions, they were being watched and studied from the other side by way of a three-foot-long and one-foot-deep mirror—a mirror that allowed one way viewing. It also enabled the people watching to put their selection process into place, and choose a time and a victim who would allow the work of The Messenger to continue.

Church now stood on the catacomb side of this one-way mirror looking in. By clubbing standards, it was still early and the toilets on the other side were quiet. A young girl entered one of the cubicles, hitching her skirt up and starting to pull down her knickers before she was even fully inside the toilet cubicle.

He watched in disgust as she didn't bother to close the cubicle door and was grateful that he only had a visual invasion into the club toilets, so that he didn't have to hear the girl's piss squirting into the water inside the toilet bowl. He watched a young boy tuck his penis back into his trousers and walk away from the urinal and toward the mirror. They stood no more than a few inches from each other.

Unware of this fact, he tweezed his eyebrows with his fingers, did a pout pose and then checked down at his trousers to make sure there was no piss spot, the risk of wearing no underwear, but a risk worth taking if a sudden surprise opportunity arose for a casual sexual encounter with a stranger.

Church studied the young man from the other side of the one-way glass, full of hatred and disdain for this individual. He had noticed how the lad had not washed his hands after he had finished relieving himself. He observed the pleasure on the boy's face as he looked at his own reflection, loving who and what he was.

"A stain on an already filthy planet. A vessel already filled with the belief that it is all right to ignore the rules of the righteous," Church whispered his words to Stanridge, who had now joined him at the top of the steps.

"We are here for Grant," the doctor whispered back.

Through gritted teeth, Church looked directly at Stanridge, saying, "The work the Lord has cursed us with, never stops brother." Looking back at the youth who was still preening, posing and smiling in front of the mirror, he smiled and said, "Here is a poor boy who needs my help to put right the wrongs of his life."

Inside the club toilet, the young girl stepped out of the cubicle and looked at the man in front of the mirror.

"Stop posing and pouting you puff," she said laughing.

"I hope you shook your lettuce dry you dirty cow," the young man replied, laughing along with the girl.

The girl pulled up her short skirt showing a flimsy pair of white lace knickers underneath.

"Come and have a free check if you like hunny," she offered, with a cheeky smile on her face.

"No thanks," replied the lad. "You don't have the tackle that I like to unshackle, baby." He cupped his balls through his trousers as he spoke and rotated his hips around in a circular motion.

The girl laughed loudly and then broke out into a fit of girlish giggles.

"You crack me up." She walked toward the lad and standing close to him, cupped his face and kissed him on his nose. "Good to see you again Halo, it's been too long sweety."

Halo turned around and both him and the girl pressed a face cheek against each other and smiled as they looked into the mirror.

The Priest smiled back at them from the other side of the mirror.

—————— ——————

Grant's journey had been less smooth than that of Stanridge and Church. Firstly, the traffic was moving extremely slowly and filtering in London, while never easy, was even more difficult on the Midnight Star, due to its width and weight. Secondly, an incident with a driver who was obviously not a fan of bikers filtering through standstill traffic, had left Grant with no other choice than to quickly leave the main road and most direct route to Camden, and hide for a while. After what had happened outside of Shuffler's place, the last thing he could afford was a meeting with any more coppers.

It had all started when idling in standing traffic. The driver's window of the car he was next to slid down, and the driver flicked his fag butt in the direction of Grant. The burning ember bounced off of his knee on to the road. Not wanting any grief, Grant had looked at the driver and shouted, "Take a bit more care fella. I'm sat on what is effectively a petrol bomb on top of two tyres here."

As the window was wound up, the driver called him a wanker and flicked him the universal fuck off sign. Seething, but with more important matters to attend to, Grant waited for a gap and filtered ahead of the vehicle. It was only a matter of minutes later, when the same car crawled past him on the inside and when he was fully clear of Grant's front tyre, the driver intentionally placed his vehicle in the way of Grant's bike, in an effort to stop or delay him filtering any farther.

Grant bided his time and once again, when a gap presented itself, he filtered through again. This time, he stopped next to the offending driver's vehicle and tapped on the window. The driver made no eye contact with Grant at all, but simply slid one raised finger up against the inside of the glass. Even though the driver was looking forward toward the cars in front, Grant could see the silly smirk all over his face.

Grant pulled his bike slightly forward and slipped it into neutral gear before smashing his gloved left hand in the car's wing mirror. It bent backward and stayed in an askew position until Grant grabbed hold of it and began to thrash it back and forth, until eventually it ripped away from the vehicle's bodywork. He then used it to tap on the driver's window again. The window slid down and the verbal abuse could be heard as it made its downwards movement.

"You filthy biking piece of shit scum, I am going to kick your fucking ass shitless you fucking moron."

Grant tossed the broken wing mirror into the enraged driver's lap. He smiled and said, "Now you know what it's like to have something thoughtlessly tossed at you, don't you?"

As the driver tried to throw the offending wing mirror back at Grant, he was met with the searing pain of one of Grant's leather-clad fingers being poked straight into his eye. He dropped the wing mirror and covered his injured eye with both hands, yelling and screaming in pain.

"Call the police, call the police," he screamed to a car that he was the only person sat inside. Grant looked around and not one other driver was watching the goings-on.

"Come on, get out of the car and fucking kick my ass until it's shitless," shouted Grant.

The window began to slide upwards, but Grant placed his hand on top and with as much strength he could summon he pressed downwards. The mechanism began to squeal and squeak and then the window stopped moving. Despite the driver pressing the button on the inside of the door, it didn't move another inch. The car driver's confidence had disappeared completely. His face was pale and he no longer seemed to have any threats to throw at Grant. He was about to pull away as he saw the traffic begin to slowly move forward, when he heard the driver whisper, "I hope you crash and burn slowly you twat."

Despite the traffic making very slow progress, Grant got off his bike and removed the phone from his pocket. The driver's confidence quickly returned as he saw the phone.

"Go on then prick, call the coppers! I will have a pretty story to tell them about criminal damage and assault," he shouted in Grant's direction.

As Grant walked past the stuck open window, he leaned slightly in and pushed the back of the phone. The driver saw the blade flick out of the top of the phone's casing.

"Fuck!" he exclaimed, as he tried to move over into the passenger seat without undoing his seatbelt.

"Add this to those list of offences you little prick," he said, and made his way to the back of the car, knelt down and slammed the blade into the rear tyre. Standing back up, he walked past the window again, this time saying, "Let's make that a pair shall we?" He subequently gave the front tyre the same treatment.

Sliding the blade back into its housing and secreting it away into his pocket, he climbed back onto his bike. At this point, his attention was drawn to a siren and a set of blue flashing lights way behind him, making slow progress through the almost stand still traffic. Not knowing whether this was in response to his actions or for something totally unconnected, Grant decided to embark on a little bit of more risky filtering, get the shit out of there and find himself a hiding place off the main stretch of road.

Making his way through the traffic and eventually to the kerb side of the road, he took the first left turning he came to, which happened to be a no-entry, but Grant ignored it and roared up it and out of the area of his crime. A few lefts and rights followed in quick succession before Grant noticed a very narrow alleyway just wide enough to get his bike into. He pulled up just beyond it and pushed it backward, about ten feet into the narrow gap between two buildings and turned off his lights, keeping the engine quietly ticking over just in case a quick getaway was required.

For forty-five minutes, he remained there, looking and listening for signs of police activity, but only three cars passed by, none of which had been police vehicles. Eventually, he deemed it safe to get back out on the road although he decided he should take some of the less busy back roads and side streets which, while adding to his journey time would, he hoped, allow for a police free journey.

He arrived at the front of the Rainbow Club about ninety minutes later than he had planned. He called over one of the door staff to ask if there was anywhere he could safely park his bike.

"Just up the side road there mate, on the right. There is an allocated bike parking space, it's free too," the doorman said with a smile. "A bloody miracle in this city."

Grant nodded his head in appreciation and rode the twenty or so yards up the side road until he saw the "motorcycle only" sign. He reversed his bike into a parking position next to the only other bike parked there, which happened to be a 50cc moped. He locked up the bike and only at this point did he give himself the once over, coming to the conclusion that he could not have been more inappropriately dressed for entering a nightclub had he tried to be.

He made his way back to the main entrance of the club and met up again with the same doorman who had directed him to the bike parking area.

"Good evening mate," said Grant, in his most polite and friendly voice. "Two questions if you don't mind?"

"Shoot," replied the doorman.

Remembering the pistol he was carrying, he decided not to follow that instruction literally.

"Firstly, do you have a strict dress code?" he asked with a hopeful please-be-nice-to-me pleading look on his face.

The doorman looked up and down Grant, eventually saying with a smile, "Well at least you aren't wearing trainers."

"Okay," replied Grant, "things are looking up for me I think.

Secondly, I take it your club has a cloakroom where I can safely stash my helmet?"

"Yeah, we do and plenty of other places you can stash your helmet in the Rainbow, but we prefer you take that type of action home with you at the end of a pleasant evening," replied the doorman, firing a suggestive wink toward Grant.

"So I can come in?" asked Grant. "Only I have arranged to meet up with a friend inside."

"Hey listen my friend, the night is young and business is slow, pay the club membership and the entrance fee, play nice and have a good time. I am sure you are going to be popular in there. They like you Village People types," the smile remained on the doorman's face as if it had been permanently tattooed in place.

Grant didn't hang around, just in case the doorman had a change of mind. He joined the short queue and made his way toward the club's entrance doors. When it was his turn to enter, the second and third doormen looked at him and Grant was sure he was going to be turned away and so quickly interjected.

Pointing toward the doorman he had spoken with just minutes earlier he said, "The lad over there said it's all cool. I promise the next time I visit I will be in head to toe in lycra and diamontes."

The taller and much stockier of the pair looked at Grant. There was no smile on this face.

"This is the Rainbow old man, not fucking Strictly." He nodded his head toward the door and Grant made his way toward it, but was halted just a foot or so before he could push it open. The final doorman laid a hand softly onto Grant's forearm, saying, "Just a quick search please sir." He pointed a finger of each hand toward the sky to indicate that he would like Grant to raise his arms.

Externally Grant was cool, calm and obedient. Internally every bit of him was on edge.

Despite carrying a mobile phone that doubled up as a very effective knife and taser unit and a handgun secreted away, the rub down search was completed so pathetically he was confident that he could have sneaked a missile launcher into the club.

He pulled out his wallet as a diversionary tactic only and to show that he was no threat, he opened the wallet and said, "Would you like to check the contents of my manbag, too?"

The stern face of the searching doorman relaxed and he smiled slightly.

"As long as you have enough money and a stock of condoms, you should do okay."

"Thanks for the tip," replied Grant, and then asked, "Now, where do I put my helmet?"

The doorman just laughed. He began to search the next customer as he said to Grant, "Enjoy your night bikerboy, hope it's an eventful one for you."

Grant pushed the door open and entered the Rainbow Club. He had been into some places in his life, but the foyer area alone told him that this was going to be an eye-opener.

Having entered the club, Grant had fully expected to have his sensory organs invaded by the colours of the rainbow, because of the connection to the gay community and it being the name of the club. He was totally surprised at how subtle the interior design was. He had also expected a bit of a dark, grubby place, a back street gay bar with little thought for anything other than grabbing the punters money. Wrong again.

Around the entrance walls were rectangular glass pieces, each etched with images of people enjoying themselves. Some, as you would expect, were bordering on saucy if not mildly erotic, but still very tastefully done. The subtle part was that each piece of glass had been faintly coloured with one of the colours of a rainbow. Two women embracing, two male figures holding hands, a group of three people dancing erotically with each other—clearly all embellishing the nature of the club, but not forcing the clientelles' sexuality down the throat.

Grant had to quietly admit that it had been done very well and unexpectedly; he didn't feel one bit uncomfortable. The lighting had been very cleverly arranged, giving a shimmer to the whole area as it reflected off and through the array of glass panels.

Grant placed his helmet on the counter of the cloakroom where he was greeted by a young girl with a face full of piercings.

"All right to stash this here, or do you only take coats?" he asked.

"No that's fine, I can take your coat too if you like," the girl replied.

Grant shook his head. "I'll keep that with me if it's all the same to you."

"It gets a bit hot in there," said the young girl, nodding her head in the direction of the set of double doors, which Grant assumed was the way into the main club area.

Not as hot as it would get if you found what is hidden in my jacket, Grant thought to himself. Ignoring the girl's advice, he changed the subject.

"I was expecting to be overpowered with strong blues, reds and yellows. Quite subtle really isn't it?"

"You're inside the Rainbow now sugar, it's magical," replied the girl, and picking up Grants helmet, she sashayed away with it. Looking at the counter where the helmet had been seconds ago, he saw a yellow ticket with the numbers 332 printed on it and below the number in small lettering it read "B HPY." Picking it up and shoving it into the back pocket of his jeans, he decided it was time to enter the Rainbow, get himself a drink and, most importantly, try to find Halo. Expecting it to be a bit on the loud side inside the club, he decided to try calling Halo again, but once again, it went to his voicemail. This time he left a message.

"It's me, where are you, you little fuck?"

He placed the phone carefully into the front pocket of his jeans and walked toward the double doors and pushed them open. The place was absolutely bouncing.

Considering the early hour, the mixture of the thudding, throbbing music beat, the buzz from dozens of loud conversations, clinking of glasses and bottles, and the DJ's booming voice all combined to almost knock Grant back as the cacophony of sound hit him. He stepped inside and the doors closed.

The place was dark, but the flashing lights cast shadows everywhere. Initially confused, he stood still for a moment, acclimatising himself to his new surroundings. A few people, who were stood near to the entrance doors, stared at him for a few seconds, but then returned to their own conversations. Grant had expected to attract some attention. His attire guaranteed that, plus he was a new face in the club, so being checked out did not phase him.

He walked to the bar and waited for a short while until he managed to attract the attention of one of the reasonably busy bar staff. The barman, with black spiked hair, approached him. The strobe lighting made his white shirt glow and Grant noticed a patch sewn just above the shirt pocket which read "Serving Crew."

"A beer please," said Grant, raising his voice above the sound of the music.

"Bottled or old school?" called back the barman.

"What's old school?" asked Grant.

"In a glass my friend," replied the barman, surprised by the question.

Now feeling older than his years after discovering that having a beer in a glass had suddenly become old school, Grant decided to try and be modern and asked for a bottle. The barman threw an outreached arm over the bar and held out an open hand. Grant grabbed it and shook it.

"My name is Alex," he said, "you new to the scene?"

"The club scene, no," shouted Grant, even louder as the throbbing beat of the music went up a notch. "The gay scene, absolutely."

Alex stooped down and retrieved a bottle of beer from the low-level chiller and then standing up once again, he deftly unscrewed the cap and placed the bottle on the bar in front of Grant.

"Just come out have you?" he asked Grant.

Grant smiled and took his time to respond.

"I've come out for the night, but not out of the closet. I'm not gay," he eventually said.

Alex placed his hand around Grant's—the one with which he had just picked up the bottle of beer and was about to be raise to his mouth.

"Don't worry handsome, I won't hold that against you."

Grant pulled his hand away from Alex's grip and said, "You won't be holding anything against me pal."

Alex laughed and raised two thumbs at Grant.

"Now that is the kind of response we like in here: Straight, to the point and mildly offensive."

Grant took a gulp of his beer, then looked back at the amiable member of staff and mouthed the word *"Sorry."*

Alex puckered his lips and completed an "air kiss" in Grant's direction.

"Don't ever be sorry, I'm glad you're straight, because I wouldn't want to wake up next to you in the morning." He raised a hand to acknowledge that he had seen another customer waiting to be served and began to walk away from Grant, but halted immediately and spun around to face Grant again as he heard the statement directed at him.

"Maybe you can help though." Grant's voice remained raised and just as he said the next words, the music level drastically lowered, allowing the last part of Grant's sentence to be heard by everyone within ten metres of him. "I am looking for a young lad."

Alex burst out laughing and leaned on the bar to get closer to Grant.

"Now, call me observant if you want, but I am guessing that wasn't for public consumption."

Totally flustered Grant tried to explain, "No…I meant that I am looking for a boy…no, I mean I arranged to meet someone…holy fuck."

Alex laughed again and tried to help Grant out.

"It's okay, you are meeting someone, it's just for a drink,

totally innocent I get it, but you have to admit you have just made yourself more interesting to quite a few people," he said and then asked, "does the young gentleman have a name?"

"He goes by the nickname Halo," replied Grant, grateful to Alex for letting him off the hook so easily.

"Wow, Halo, really?" asked Alex. "Now he is a player. You sure you aren't gay?"

"He's just helping me out with something," replied Grant.

"I bet he is," said Alex cheekily, "little Halo does like to help out the old men."

Before Grant could respond and because Alex could now see that Grant was becoming noticeably uncomfortable with the conversation, he added, "He was in here earlier, haven't seen him for about half an hour or so. Check out the sofa booths around the dance floor or the smoking area, that's out the back," he pointed to the far corner of the room, where Grant could just about make out the shape of a door.

"Thanks, I appreciate that. How much do I owe you for the beer?" said Grant.

"It's on me," replied Alex, "as a way of saying welcome to the Rainbow." He walked away to serve the increasingly impatient customer, who was now waving a twenty pound note in the direction of Alex.

"Yes all right lover," Alex shouted, "it will cost you a lot more than that to buy some time with me."

Grant leaned his back against the bar and took another drink of his beer as he surveyed the area in front of him. There was an eclectic mix of customers, as would be expected in any nightclub but a couple of transvestites, one of them with a beard surrounding a heavily lipsticked pair of lips, certainly left you in no doubt that this was a gay nightclub.

Or they were part of a really over the top stag night.

He continued to scan the dance floor area, but could not see Halo and decided that he needed to take a walk around the area for a closer look at some of the darker areas. Maybe Halo had got bored waiting for him and decided to mingle.

Grant spent about twenty minutes walking around the club popping out to the smoking area too, and had a smoke of a cigar while he was out there. He attracted some attention, a few pleasant greetings and a couple of lude comments, but nothing as bad a he had expected. Eventually, he returned inside and approached one of the booths that were located around two sides of the dance floor.

He sat down on the dark red sofa that curled around the inside of the booth, and placed his bottle of beer on the small round table that sat in the middle of the booth. He had thought that the booth was empty when he first sat down, but as he reached forward to place the bottle on the table, he noticed a small figure in the darkest corner of the booth.

A young female voice said, "Not interested, wrong gender, fuck off."

"And hello to you, too," replied Grant. "I'm a nightclub inspector and am completing a survey to measure the welcoming nature of nightclubs in the area. You have just managed single-handedly to lower the overall rating to a one."

The young girl stood up, raised her skirt and flashed her white skimpy lace knickers.

"Put that in your survey you pervert."

—————— ——————

Fox had made his way to the tech room and asked one of

the operators to track vehicle 26 for him. All the company vehicles were identified by a number that was contained within their vehicle registration plate. They all started with the letters BI, followed by their identity number, ranging currently from 001 to 038, and ended with the letters CRT. The operator casually typed in the letters and numbers BI026CRT and at the same time informed Fox that, "Vehicle 26 has no tracker on it sir, hasn't had for some time."

To support his claim, Fox could see that his screen was blank, except for a road map of an area of London.

"So why am I staring at a road map, but no flashing red light?" he asked.

"The system will always default to the area that the vehicle was last tracked Mr. Fox. That is what it has done," replied the tech operative.

"So, what am I looking at?" asked Fox, becoming increasingly annoyed with having to ask questions.

"The location and time that the vehicle made a journey with its tracker fitted sir," came the response.

"And where and when would that fucking be?" asked Fox, his voice now louder and his mouth about half an inch from the operator's ear.

The operator looked at the screen and studied it for a few seconds, taking in all of the information.

"That would be the Camden area," he said, and then looking at the date located in the bottom right corner of the screen he added, "around five months ago sir."

"Plot the journey of that vehicle for that date. Every place it stopped, how long for, and find out who was driving it," demanded Fox.

"That will take a while Mr. Fox, but the last part is easy. It was driven by Dr. Stanridge. Vehicle 26 is his vehicle, nobody else gets allocated that vehicle," said a rather bemused and confused operator.

Fox also looked slightly confused. No member of staff at the Bloom Institute had a vehicle that was permanently allocated to them, you got what was available.

"Who allocated Dr. Stanridge his own transport?" he asked.

The operator tapped a few more buttons on his keyboard and the screen changed to another page.

"Looks like it was Mr. Bloom himself sir," the young man replied.

Fox didn't react, but simply asked the operator to get the information he had requested as quickly as he could and bring it to his office.

"Make sure you bring it yourself and don't discuss this with anyone else, do you understand?"

The tech guy nodded and started to work on his assignment immediately. In his short time working at this place, he had learned that Fox was the one man you didn't get on the wrong side of.

—————— ——————

Mortimer Church and Dr. Stanridge watched and waited. The young girl had washed her hands and left the same-sex restroom, telling Halo to meet up later for a drink and a dance.

The two men watched Halo start to do a silly little solo dance in front of the mirror until he was joined by a young man, probably in his mid-twenties, wearing a tight red vest top and skin tight grey jeans with slashes down the front of both legs. He openly spread a line of coke along one of the vanity tops between two of the hand basins and snorted the white dust through a short glittery gold straw.

"You want a line, sugar," he asked Halo, who declined saying thanks and maybe later. The coke snorter left, but not before checking in the mirror that his face was clean of all evidence of his drug taking.

"Can't go back out looking a mess now can I?" he said, planting a soft kiss on Halo's left cheek and patting his backside.

All of this happened in full sight and just inches away from Church and Stanridge. The latter visibly cringed as he watched the physical contact taking place, while Church closed his eyes and started to whisper, to himself or a greater being, Stanridge wasn't quite sure.

"The acts of the flesh are obvious, sexual immorality, impurity and debauchery, drunkenness and orgies and the like. I warn you, as I did before, that those who live like this will not inherit the kingdom of my God," the words left the mouth of Mortimer Church like the ramblings of a madman.

"Oh, great master, my soul is weary with sorrow. Strengthen me according to your word, be gracious to me and teach me your law," he finished by drawing the shape of the cross with his finger down the front of his face. The imaginary cross was drawn inverted.

The Priest looked back into the room. It was now empty once more, except for Halo, who was once again engaged in his silly dance, only this time his back was turned to the mirror.

"Put to death, therefore, whatever belongs to your earthly nature: Sexual immorality, lust, desires and greed, which is idolatry. Because of these, the wrath of God is coming," as he finished whispering these words, he slowly and silently slid back the three bolts that locked the door in place. He held out his hand, the palm open and flat, in the direction of Stanridge.

The doctor reached into his pocket and pulled out a small black zipped container. He unzipped it and removed the syringe, placing it into Church's open hand.

Church slowly pushed on the door and it opened inwards. He stepped inside approaching Halo from behind, who didn't realise that he had company until one hand smothered itself over his mouth and the other stuck the needle into the side of his neck and pressed the plunger, injecting the clear liquid into his body.

Trying his best to kick with his legs and flail his arms backward in a failed attempt to get some kind of purchase on his attacker, the large strong frame of Church dragged the now weakening body of Halo back through the door ,which was pulled shut by Stanridge. A smooth, well-practised manoeuvre had been successful again. The doctor looked through the one-way mirror into the toilets, which were now completely empty.

Stanridge looked round to see that his half-brother was starting to struggle, as Halo put in a last-ditch effort to kick, claw and flail his way out of this situation. Normally by now, their victim was completely unconscious, but this one had a little more fight in him. He went to the aid of Church, grabbing the lad's ankles and lifting them from the stone steps and removing the last bit of stability that Halo had.

The drug began to take a hold, and Halo was completely limp by the time Church started to drag him down the stone steps. He was just about conscious enough to hear his attackers' words.

"Welcome, my child, to the world of The Messenger. Your evilness will be used to spread my message with the words I shall use, both on and in your corpse."

Stanridge remained in control of the feet of the young lad, making it easier to transport him to his place of captivity, although he didn't think this one would be staying around for too long.

Had the drug worked as it had previously on all of their other victims, Stanridge would not have been momentarily distracted and would not have had to help The Priest to control and contain the young lad, until he went unconscious and maybe then, he would have correctly secured the door with the three bolts as he had always done in the past. He may also have noticed Halo's slim mobile phone lying on the floor adjacent to the door at the top of the stone steps as he had pulled the door shut.

Behind the Mirror

Gus sat in his office. His daughter, Emma, sat on the opposite side of his desk, having arrived a few minutes beforehand. They discussed the phone call that Gus had received earlier. The conversation was with a young male, who Gus had never heard of, who claimed to be acting on behalf of Grant.

The subject of the conversation both shocked and worried Gus. It sounded as if Grant was possibly well out of his depth, which was almost certainly why he was asking him to put his career in jeopardy. Again, the worry it caused him was because he was being asked to put his daughter at risk. That did not sound like something Grant would ask of him.

"He brought us back together, Dad," said Emma.

Gus's heart put in an extra beat as it always did when Emma called him Dad.

"That doesn't mean that he has the right to put you in a dangerous position," he replied.

"Yes, it does Dad," said Emma. "He saved me from those bastards, remember. I could be dead or even worse, if it hadn't been for him."

"You were not the reason he went to that place. You were simply an added complication," said Gus angrily.

"Yeah, a complication he cared about and factored in,"

replied Emma. "You may not like that fact, but you cannot argue with it."

Gus remained silent momentarily, and then looked toward Emma.

"We could always pretend I never took that call from this Halo character," he said.

"Yes, we could Dad, but how long before I stopped calling you Dad and went back to calling you Gus again? How long before the guilt placed a division between us that would never be repaired? Grant reunited us and ignoring his cry for help could end up destroying our relationship forever." Emma's face was blank, emotionless and expressionless.

"Let me think this through Emma," he asked her.

"But Dad...," Emma's voice trailed off.

"I didn't say no, I just need time to think about how," he replied with a tone that told his daughter that, for now at least, the conversation had come to an end.

——— ———

Grant stared at the young girl who had at last, thankfully, lowered her skirt and sat down again.

"Listen, I am just looking for a young lad," he said.

"Pervert," repeated the girl, almost spitting the word out of her mouth. "I bet you work for the fucking BBC, too."

Grant couldn't help but smirk. He quickly wiped it from his face when he saw the disgust on the girl's face.

"Who I work for is not relevant, but what is, is the particular boy I need to find. He is known as Halo; do you know him?"

The girl's demeanor changed immediately, but it was clear to Grant that her trust levels remained the same. If anything, they had probably decreased.

"What do you want with Halo?" she asked.

"So, you know him?" replied Grant.

"Not until I know what you want him for?" she replied.

"He knows someone who has a bike for sale, said he would put me in touch with him," lied Grant.

"And you walk into a gay bar because you want to buy a bike?" said the girl, disbelieving every word this stranger spoke.

"It's a nice bike," replied Grant.

"More probable that you are looking for a different kind of ride or you are a fucking copper?" she responded.

Grant was becoming impatient and was ready to grab this girl by the scruff of her neck and give her a large dose of attitude. However, he knew that would get his ass kicked out of the club and he would be no nearer to finding Halo.

"Do I look like a copper or even gay come to think of it?" he asked, trying to keep things on a friendly basis.

The girl leaned forward, out of the darkness of the booth and studied Grant.

"You may not look like a copper, but answer this. Do I look fucking gay?"

Grant decided that disclosing a bit more truth might do the trick, and angling himself in the girl's direction he answered, "I think we both agree that our sexuality is not the important thing here. We also agree that I ain't no copper, so I will be upfront with you. Halo could be in trouble. He was doing me a couple of favours, and since then, hasn't been in touch and I can't get him on his phone."

The girl laughed loudly, although over the loud music, Grant just about heard it.

"You tell me you are going to be straight with me and then tell me more lies. Halo looked fine when I last saw him, so why don't you go back under the rock you came from and go fuck yourself." She sat back into the darkness, but Grant could see the whites of her eyes flitting around the room, probably looking for a member of staff or friend she could call upon for some assistance.

Grant slid himself on the sofa, reaching for his mobile. As he did so, he slid out the blade, hastily positioned himself close up and personal to the girl and poked the blade into her upper thigh.

"Look down, keep fucking quiet and you will not get hurt," he ordered.

She looked down and saw the lights glinting off the blade, although the slight pain it was causing her, had already made her brain register that it was a sharp implement.

"If I put this into your leg and twist it, it will rip open your femoral artery, you will bleed out within thirty seconds or less and I will spend that time snogging the face off you, just to stop your screaming. Now, tell me where and when you last saw Halo?" Grant's tone was sinister and frightening. He had stolen that tone from his very first training squadron corporal, who had been an evil bastard, and who had scared the shit out of Grant for many months.

Despite her situation, the girl did not drop the attitude.

"And when I tell you, you will leave and then I will scream," she said.

"Save your breath bitch. Where and when? You have about ten seconds before I send you to lesbian heaven," snarled Grant.

"In the toilets, about an hour ago...," answered the girl,

adding, "…and I would prefer to go to Hell. I've heard it's hotter."

Grant slowly slid the blade back into the phone. He turned the phone around, once again pressing it hard against the girl's body. As he pressed the two buttons either side of the mobile the sparks hit the girl and Grant whispered, "Sleep for a while, Hell will be there forever."

The girl's body went into spasm and Grant had to move slightly away from her as he felt the effects of the electric shock on his own body. He held the taser in place and waited for the girl's body to relax. As her body became limp, he guided her head down into his lap. Her eyes remained open looking up at him. He placed his hand on the back of her head and forced it up sharply, striking it hard against on the table top.

He positioned the girl's unconscious body back into a sitting position, making it look as natural as he could. The darkness provided by the depth of the booth made it easier to do. Throughout the whole process, he kept one eye on the surrounding dance and bar areas, not one person noticed anything. All of them were focused on enjoying themselves.

He noticed a man approaching the booth and so he leaned forward, placing his face in front of the unconscious girl's as if they were kissing. In the blackness, it would be very difficult to see if it was two men or two women kissing. The man walked by without a second glance. Grant wriggled away from the girl, stopping momentarily to sit her back upright, as her body threatened to topple over to the side.

He left the darkness of the booth and made his way through the growing throng of dancing revelers, asking one for directions to the toilet. The person he asked visually examined him in a way one would, having discovered dog shit on their shoe. He pointed toward the far corner of the room and carried on dancing with his group of friends.

Grant walked in the direction he had been shown and found himself in front of a door with two artistic drawings on the front of it. One was of a man and the other of a woman, both drawn with a finger up to their mouths, standing coyly with their legs slightly bent and their underwear around their ankles. The groin area of both figures covered by the T-shirts they were wearing, as if the artist was trying to show a level of decorum.

He pushed the door open, fully expecting to see two doors on the inside, one being the mens' toilets and the other obviously being the ladies. What he actually found was that he was standing just inside the unisex toilet area. A woman walked toward and past him, her makeup freshly applied. She smiled at him and waved.

"Hi, be happy," she said.

Grant held up his fingers in the universal peace sign and replied, "Yeah, you too, babe."

The girl pulled the door open and left. Grant waited for the door to close and then scanned the room. It appeared empty. Nobody stood by the row of urinals or sinks against the wall to his right side. He walked the length of the room, looking into each of the individual cubicles.

He stopped directly in front of the full-length mirror on the far wall. His face showed the strain of the day. He rubbed his eyes, which made no difference at all. He walked to the sinks, turned on the cold water and splashed his face liberally with it from his cupped hands. He looked up at his reflection again, this time in the smaller face mirror on the wall above the sink. He stared intently. Not at his reflection this time, but at the room behind that was also reflected in the mirror.

He walked back toward the larger, full-length mirror and studied the image in it once again. He focussed on the surroundings, the room and its fixtures, rather than his own reflection. Keeping his attention on the mirror, he slowly stepped backward. With each step something didn't compute; it didn't formulate correctly in his brain. He couldn't quite put his finger on it.

He looked to his right and stared at the small sink mirror, and then back at the full-length mirror. Then he got it. The reflected surroundings in the larger mirror were slightly off kilter, as if the mirror had not been attached to the wall correctly. Had something been pushed behind it, causing it to be farther away from the wall on its left-hand side from where Grant was looking at it?

He walked forward, getting close up to it and analysing it further. He pushed his hand against the left side of it. The mirror moved slightly back and the reflection corrected itself, revealing a true image of the room.

That's better, he thought, and removed his hand. The mirror moved away from the wall slightly. Grant looked at the mirror, confused by its actions and repeated pushing it back into place, only to watch it repeat its action the moment he removed his hand. Moving his head at an angle so as to look at the left edge of the mirror, he couldn't tally what he saw with his own eyes.

Following his instinct, Grant curled the fingers of his right hand around and behind the edge of the mirror, and gently pulled it toward him. The mirror/door swung open on its hidden hinges, and Grant stared into the open dark stone space behind it. He went to look behind himself, and stopped halfway, finding himself not looking at a solid object which should have been the back of the mirror. Instead, he was looking through it at the toilet wall on the other side. He waved his hand on the other side of the mirror and was totally amazed at the fact that he could see his own hand waving at him.

"What the fuck?" was all he could muster, as his brain continued to search for answers.

A noise behind him kicked his senses back into action. He swung around and was faced by a confused looking youth staring at him. Thinking quickly Grant said, "Evening, don't worry I'm from maintenance. Seems like we've had a bit of subsidence trouble. Sorry, I need to put this place off limits until the team arrives to fix the problem."

He walked toward the man, waving his hand and arms as if shooing an animal away. The confused and now concerned looking youth quickly left the toilets. Seeing a tall waste bin standing in the corner of the room below a hot air hand dryer, Grant grabbed it. He laid it on its side, wedging it between the door and the wall. It was a fairly snug fit, enough to keep out someone wanting to use the toilet, but nowhere near adequate to prevent a determined entry attempt into the room.

Grant returned to the hole in the far wall. Having got past his initial confusion, he had worked out it was a secret entrance into the nightclub. He looked more closely at the inside of the mirror and saw three slide bolts, obviously intended to secure the door from the inside. None of them had been bolted into their locking positions.

His first thought was that it must be a trap. Then something on the floor just on the other side of the threshold caught his eye. He picked up the mobile phone. Without quite knowing why, but following a gut reaction, once again trusting his instinct, he retrieved his own mobile from his jeans pocket. He found Halo's number in the contacts list. Noticing that the battery level was very low, he pressed the phone screen. Within a few seconds, the mystery mobile phone in his other hand began to ring.

------ ------

Fox drove toward the Camden area of London, following the electronic footprint of Stanridge's last tracked journey. He had no idea why the doctor had disengaged the tracking equipment, if indeed it was him who had done it. As far as Fox was concerned, Stanridge wasn't savvy enough to even think about doing such a thing, let alone being actually capable of doing it.

His other thoughts naturally turned to Grant. *Where he was? What he was doing? And how was he going to stop him, for good*? All of these thoughts were interrupted by his mobile ringing. He let it ring as it was connected to the hands free system of the vehicle that would automatically put it through after three rings.

"Hello Mr. Fox, It's Jenkins. Are you free to talk?" said the voice.

Jenkins was one of the tech room staff. He was a decent bloke to be fair, and one who Fox often relied on to keep him up to date on things.

"What do you have for me Jenkins?" asked Fox.

"We've just been monitoring a call from the Rainbow Club to the local police, something about a man locking himself inside the toilets after blowing up one of the internal walls. Local police are en route sir."

Grant, thought Fox immediately, and then to Jenkins said, "Thanks Jenkins. Use the normal process to call off the local cops, inform them that the bomb squad is on the way and the most they are to do is to put a cordon around the club and evacuate the place," he ordered.

"Yes sir," replied Jenkins and the line went dead.

—————— ——————

Grant gazed at the ringing phone and then cancelled the call on his own phone. His heart dropped in the realisation that Halo was almost certainly in trouble. He began to formulate in his head. Every inch of his existence screamed slow down and think. Prepare for the mission! Put a plan into place, but one little voice whispered inside his head...*the killer has Halo, do something.*

He crossed the threshold of the open gap in the toilet wall and entered the darkened area above the internal stone steps. Grant about-faced and he secured the door, shooting the three securing bolts into place, and began a slow descent down the stairs.

As he took one careful step at a time, he placed his phone into the back pocket of his jeans and relocated the gun into the small of his back, shoving it down the waistband of his jeans, his belt helping to keep it firmly in place. Finally, he deposited Halo's phone on one of the stone steps.

As he got closer to the bottom of the stairs, he looked around the surrounding area. It was obviously some kind of underground chamber. In the distance, tunnels lead into eternal darkness. He had no idea which direction to take, or how large this underground world was.

All he knew was that he had to find Halo, a total innocent in this complete mess. A young lad eager to help and prove himself, one Grant had allowed to do so with no regard to the young man's safety. *SNAFU,* Grant thought to himself, *situation normal—all fucked up.*

He walked away from the bottom of the stairs and crossed the open expanse, treading carefully around debris left behind from years ago. Eventually, he reached the other side, standing between two adjacent tunnels, one leading off to his left and the other to his right. He had no clue which one to take.

There were no signs that it had recently been used. No footprints or signs of someone struggling or being dragged. In the end, he took the one that had a set of narrow gauge rail tracks leading into it.

As he looked down the tunnel, he could see that shafts of natural light shone through from above, small holes in the tunnel ceiling that Grant assumed had been purposely designed to allow some remembrance of the world above into this stone rabbit warren of gloom.

Grateful for the light, he hurried his pace and then suddenly thought, *If I can see my way, I can be more easily seen by unwanted eyes.*

He slowed down once again, conscious of his foot placement and ultra-aware of making a noise. After about two hundred yards of slow painstaking steps, he reached a T-junction. Grant placed his back against the left-hand side wall of the tunnel he had been progressing down. He could see quite a distance up the tunnel heading off to the right.

Nothing appeared to be suspicious, so he carefully peeked around the corner of the wall to look down the tunnel heading off in the opposite direction, once again seeing nothing but emptiness in the silent murkiness.

As he began to change his direction toward the left, he noticed that this new tunnel was less well lit. He looked down to the ground to make sure he wasn't going to step on or kick something that would alert anyone to his presence, and noticed a smudge mark in the dirt. He studied it closely, possibly the sign of a boot or shoe suddenly being turned in the dirt. It was a tentative clue, but it was all that he had. Staying close to the wall, where the darkness was slightly more dense, he made his way farther into this underground secret world, in the knowledge that every step he took would ensure he had less of an idea of his bearings.

He walked for about another ten minutes, occasionally halting when he thought he had heard a noise. Each time he concluded that his mind was playing tricks, as it has a tendency to do when finding oneself in an unknown situation or location, especially one so dark and tense.

Eventually, he reached another large open area, around its walls were gaps, where maybe wide doors should have been, but had long decayed. He also considered that kids could have stolen them, having found this place years ago. The area behind each gap was dark, and this area somehow seemed even more silent than any other that he had travelled through.

Remaining as close to a wall as he could, Grant edged his way toward the closest gap, stopping next to it. Suddenly realising that his pulse rate had increased dramatically and his breathing had accelerated, he stopped and composed himself momentarily, confused why this area had affected him in this way.

He turned his body position so that his chest pressed against the wall and stretching his neck, he poked his head into the open space and peered into the darkness.

------ ------

Fox sat in his parked vehicle next to an alleyway that he was certain he was familiar with. After ending the call between Jenkins and himself, he had decided that he would continue to follow Stanridge's trail before going to the Rainbow club. As far as Fox was concerned, Grant could rot in hell if indeed it was him at the club causing some kind of disturbance. He knew that the bomb squad would not be heading to the scene. Their highly placed contacts would see to that.

They would send a handful of coppers down there and evacuate the club, and put a cordon in place until he arrived, allowing him the space and time to have a look around so that he could ascertain if it was a Grant situation or just a prank call.

He had spent his time after the call with Jenkins scanning the police channels and the radio stations, but there had been no mention of any bomb blast or explosion in any area of London.

Grant had been a letdown, a complete failure to him. Fox was certain that Mr. Bloom would take great pleasure in reminding him of his incompetence, and that the failure had been down to him. As an agent runner, it was part of his job to recruit new and temporary agents for C.O.R.T.

Typically, simple persuasion and the offer of being able to perform a service for their country would work, but

Fox was equally as capable of more strong-arm tactics to force the individual to do the work needed, blackmail being his favourite and most successful. Almost everyone had a skeleton or two hidden away in a cupboard, but Grant was different.

Fox had thought that the offer of being involved in the treatment of Mortimer Church, the man who had tried to kill him, would work but when that failed, he had been left with no other choice to but to play his ace card, the wife. Now, it seemed that Grant didn't even care about her. He appeared quite willing to allow the organisation to kill her, or even worse, subject her to some of the medical treatments devised and handed out by Stanridge. As far as he was concerned, Grant could become the next victim of the serial killer. It would save him having to do it, even though that would have given him a great deal of satisfaction.

Fox brought up the mobile phone screen on the central panel of the dashboard of the vehicle. He rang the number for Jenkins. The call was answered quickly.

"Yes Mr. Fox," answered Jenkins quickly, then adding, "everything has been put into place as per your requirements."

"Good," replied Fox, expecting nothing less. "Jenkins, remind me of the name of the alleyway where we found the last victim. The one hung upside down on the cross."

Not needing any reminder of how the last victim has been discovered, Jenkins replied, "Rose Walk, Mr. Fox."

Fox looked through the windscreen at the sign high up on the alleyway wall.

"Thank you Jenkins," he replied, and ended the call.

Why, he thought, *had Stanridge been in this exact spot in a company vehicle the very night that the victim had apparently been placed at the end of Rose Walk?*

Fox could not bring himself to believe that Dr. Stanridge was the serial killer. The man was a dork, a coward who could only bring suffering to people by injecting them with mind-altering drugs. Fox could never imagine this man actually soiling his hands in any other way, but what other reason could there be for his presence here at that precise time?

He tried to think of any other reason. Could the tracking device timing have been out when Stanridge had driven here following the discovery of the body? Maybe Stanridge had a secret lover, and used the vehicle to have naughty secretive sexual adventures, but then thought *what chance was there of Stanridge finding a woman who would fuck him in the back of a van?* That last thought brought a brief smile to Fox's face.

There was only one conclusion, Stanridge, somehow, no matter how unbelievable, had something to do with these killings. Fox quickly started the car and pulled away from the kerb and began the short journey to the Rainbow Club. His biggest concern now was, if it was Grant at the club and he was following the killer who was Stanridge, he had no doubt that the outcome wouldn't be good for the doctor.

------ ------

Grant scanned the room, allowing his eyes to get used to the even darker interior of the small room. After a few seconds, he observed something in the far-left corner. He blinked a couple of times and rubbed his eyes, allowing them once again to refocus upon the object curled up into a ball in the corner. He saw what resembled a young girl. A mass of dishevelled blonde hair stuck out above a dirty covering that was possibly a blanket or something similar.

Grant did not want to enter the room and so whispered, "Hey, you."

There was no response, other than the person curled up into an even tighter ball.

"Speak to me, what are you doing here?" said Grant, once again in a hushed voice.

A frightened quiet voice responded to his question.

"Please it can't be my turn? I have done everything you have told me to do. I pray all the time. I have stayed clean and I have pleaded for forgiveness for my sins. Please pick someone else."

Grant was shocked by the response; it was obvious that the girl thought he was someone else, someone who was planning to hurt her in some way.

"I am not going to hurt you," Grant whispered, "I am here to take you out of here."

The girl began to sob and through the tears she pleaded.

"Please be silent. He doesn't allow talking. He will hurt you for talking."

Grant did not hear the near silent approach of the person behind him. He did, however, feel the pointed blade of the knife in the back of his neck. A voice behind him said, "The girl is right Dr. Garside."

Grant was violently turned around. His world went blacker than the chambers he was in as a fist punched him hard and squarely in the face.

Levelling the Playing Field

Gus drove up to the gates that prevented unauthorised entrance to the Bloom Institute. Curled up on the floor in the back of the vehicle lay his daughter, Emma. He pressed the button on the intercom and waited.

"The Bloom Institute, how may I help?" a voice crackled from the metal box.

"My name is Sergeant Murphy from the Shropshire Constabulary. I am her to speak with whoever is in charge of this place," replied Gus.

"Do you have an appointment Sergeant Murphy? It is rather late for a meeting with Mr. Bloom," replied the voice.

"No I do not have an appointment," replied Gus, sounding more confident than he was actually feeling. "I am a police officer conducting an investigation into the whereabouts of a wanted criminal, and I have information that suggests that he is in your care so I don't need no appointment son." Gus held his police warrant card up to the camera as he spoke.

There was a slight pause before the silence was broken.

"Well, are you going to open these gates?" demanded Gus.

"Sir, Mr. Bloom is currently in a meeting with a rather important client. I will need to speak with him to see if he can make himself available to speak to you."

"Listen," said Gus, with a louder and more assertive tone,

"I am happy to return here within the hour with a lot more officers and a search warrant. The first thing I will do is throw your sorry ass into a police cell for obstructing an ongoing police investigation and harbouring a known wanted criminal."

There was a further pause of a few seconds and suddenly, the newly erected gates in front of Gus began to open. The moment they were wide enough to drive through, Gus steered the police car past them and up the driveway. Disappearing from the vicinity of the intercom and moving his lips as little as possible he said quietly, "You okay back there, love?"

"Yes, Dad," answered Emma, "are you?"

"No," replied Gus, "I could shit a fucking brick right now."

Arriving at the building, Gus ignored all of the available parking spaces and stopped the vehicle as close as possible to the entrance doors. He stared at the boarded-up windows which had, until recently, been huge glass panels.

Grant's been here, he thought, getting out of the vehicle. He straightened his shirt and walked toward the entrance. Emma waited a few seconds before moving from her curled up position on the car floor. She slowly got onto her hands and knees, carefully allowing herself to raise her head so that she could just about see out of the rear passenger window.

She watched her father walk through the doors. The boarded-up windows reduced her ability to see into the interior of the building by at least seventy-five percent. She saw Gus walk up to the reception desk, but everything to his right was hidden by the wooden boarding.

This was something that either Grant had forgotten to mention, or he had been unaware of when he had discussed the details of the plan with Gus. The problem for Emma was that if the plan was to work, not being able to see Gus meant she may miss the cue for her to get out of the car and commence her role.

It was clear that a conversation was taking place between Gus and the man who sat at the reception desk. She watched as the security man initially stood up and offered his hand as a greeting, as Gus approached, which Gus did not accept. The man sat back down behind the desk and the conversation commenced with Gus gesticulating with his arms as he spoke.

Inside, the conversation which Emma could not hear, had begun slightly agitated and was now verging on angry.

Kelly had stood and held out his hand, fully expecting the police officer to take it. When he didn't, he sat back down as he had been trained to do so, as not appear to be a threat.

"Take me to this Bloom character please," insisted Gus.

"If you would take a seat over there," replied Kelly, indicating with his hand the area where Gus was to sit. "I am still awaiting a response from Mr. Bloom regarding your request."

"It wasn't a request, Kelly," said Gus, leaning over the desk looking at the name badge that Kelly was wearing on his shirt. "If he won't come to me, then you take me to him. I am sure he would prefer the privacy of his office to hear what I have to say anyway."

"As I said Sergeant Murphy, I am waiting to hear from Mr. Bloom," came Kelly's calm response.

Gus looked around the reception foyer, looking for but failing to see signs normally found in company reception area, informing people of the whereabouts of different departments or people. Failing to see any, he pointed toward the lift.

"Just tell me on which floor his office is and I will make my own way," he said, mentally reminding himself that he was supposed to be on official duty and to remain professional and polite.

He walked toward the lift doors and from outside in the car, he disappeared from Emma's view. Emma immediately panicked, unsure as to what to do, as she watched the security guard walk from behind the desk and make his way toward Gus.

As his attention was distracted, she opened the door, slipping out of the car and quietly closing the door behind her, she rushed over to the front of the building stooping behind a small bush to the left of the entrance doors. From here, she had a better view of what was happening inside.

"Excuse me officer, but you are wasting your time," Kelly grabbed the security card hanging from his waist. He pulled the card slightly away from his body, extending the security wire by about two inches. "You need one of these to operate the lifts and doors inside this building sir. The nature of our work is sensitive. We are a government building, I do hope you understand."

"Fine," said Gus, now becoming infuriated. "So you are the keeper of the card. How about wielding that perceived power and use your little swipe card to take me to Bloom, you power-tripping prick?"

An unfazed Kelly remained calm and slowed down his progress toward Gus.

"Not really the response or the type of language I would expect from a police officer sir. Allow me to see your ID card again please?" he asked.

Gus reached inside his jacket and fumbled around inside the pocket, as if trying to find his warrant card. It was actually in his trouser pocket. Kelly took another couple of paces toward Gus and once again asked, "Your ID Sergeant Murphy. Please."

With only two to three feet between himself and Kelly, Gus seized the opportunity. He lunged at the security guard, wrapping his arms around his well-built torso, bear-hug style. Gus allowed his momentum to force both of them to the floor. What followed was something that resembled a schoolyard fight, as Gus used the advantage of his extra weight, even if it was because of fat rather than muscle, to pin Kelly to the floor while doing his best to unclip the security card from its fastening.

Realising what was happening, Kelly tried to stop Gus's attempts to grab his card, only to be met with a roundhouse elbow swing straight into the side of his head and face. With Kelly momentarily dazed, Gus took the few seconds he had bought himself and, at last, unclipped the card throwing it away from the two grappling men. It coasted across the slippery floor.

From outside, Emma saw the card arc through the air and slide across the floor. Without waiting for it to come to a standstill, she moved from her hiding place and rushed through the door into the foyer area, grabbing the card on the run. She headed toward the lift doors, hoping and praying that this would work. She skimmed the card downwards through the reader. Instantly, the doors began to glide open. Hesitant to enter the lift, Emma looked over toward her father.

"Go Emma, go!" screamed Gus, moving his body position so that he now sat higher up the body of the pinned security guard, and then fell forward burying Kelly's face with his ample belly flesh.

Muffled yells and screams came from inside the fleshy prison smothering Kelly. He found himself to be less bothered about the security card and more worried about his ability to breathe.

"I knew it would come in useful for something good," he called out, with a smile on his face as he looked back toward Emma. "Now, go get her girl."

Emma stepped inside the lift and swiped the card again. The card reader was located next to a dark circular button that she didn't recognise. Emma pressed the button with the number three printed on it, the floor that Grant had said his wife was located on. The doors glided closed and the lift began to ascend. Now she was on her own, she could only hope that Gus was able to stay in control of the security guard.

The lift came to a stop and Emma anxiously waited for the doors to open. She suddenly remembered that she needed to use the card to open them. Having done so, the doors opened. Emma popped her head out into the corridor, quickly looking left and right, and then returning her head back inside the lift. The corridor appeared to be empty. Dim ceiling mounted lights provided just about enough light to see both ends.

Just as she was about to swipe the card downwards to close the door, she changed her mind. Leaving them open would save her some vital time on the return journey.

She made her way down the corridor, slowing to glance at each door to check the name of the patient inside, without wasting any more time than she had to. Grant had explained that his wife was being held in the room at the far end of the corridor on the right, just past the nurses' station, but Emma still checked every nameplate in case they had moved her to a different room since Grant had last been here.

As she walked past the nurses' station, her mind and eyes were focussed on the last door on the right of the corridor. She was shocked into stillness by a voice coming from the left and slightly behind her.

"Can I help you?" asked the nurse, surprised to see anyone in this area at this time of the evening.

Emma replied instinctively. Honesty was probably the best policy in this situation.

"Yes, you can open this door for me," she said, pointing at the door behind which was, hopefully, Julia Anderson.

"Sorry I don't recognise you," replied the nurse. "Do you work here?"

"Yes, of course," replied Emma, trying to sound as confident as possible. "I'm a new nursing assistant."

The nurse looked at her suspiciously and moved toward the nursing station desk.

"Well I think I will just call downstairs and speak with security. What is your name please?" she asked.

"My name is not important," replied Emma. Panic, fear and anxiety mixed with anger gave her voice a threatening tone. "What is important is that the security guard you are about to call is lying dead on the floor downstairs, and I am the crazy bitch who killed him."

She put her hand into her jacket pocket and briefly cast her eyes down to it. Looking back up at the nurse she hissed, "If you don't want the same knife I used on him slitting your throat open too, I suggest you press your precious finger against that pad next to that door. Otherwise, I may be tempted to just cut them off as you bleed to death, and use one of them to open the fucking door myself."

The nurse stopped walking and looked at Emma intently, digesting the words and threats she had heard. The silence between the two women was so intense you could almost hear the nurse thinking about what to do next. To Emma's amazement, the nurse began to walk toward the door, never taking her eyes off Emma.

"They pay me well, but not enough to die! Just don't hurt me," said the nurse.

As she made her way slowly toward the door, she placed her left hand into her tunic pocket. Her intention was to press the personal panic alarm. Her hand hovered half in, half out of the pocket, as Emma said, "I need your fucking finger, not a set of keys, so whatever is in that pocket, I suggest you pull it out real slow and place it on the floor."

The nurse reached into the bottom of the tunic pocket pressing the panic button. Grasping the alarm unit with her thumb and first finger, she lifted it from the pocket gently placing it onto the floor.

"Now, place your finger against that pad and open the door," Emma told her.

"Think about what you are doing Miss. This poor unfortunate woman needs professional medical help, something I don't believe you can offer," said the nurse, walking toward the door and pressing her finger against the pad.

"What this woman needs is to be with her husband. What she doesn't need is to be treated like some lab animal, having God knows what pumped into her body to make her forget everything that is important to her," retorted Emma angrily.

"And all the terrible things that have happened to her," the nurse reminded Emma.

"Shit happens, humans deal with it, but not this way. Now,

push the fucking door open before I create a bitch fest on your face." Emma's anger, now reaching boiling point, was in danger of doing some real damage to this institutionalised robot.

The nurse pushed the door open slightly, Emma nodded her head to the right, indicating that she wanted the door fully opened. The nurse cooperated, pushing the door so that it sat flush to the inside wall.

"Now, in you go and behave like this is just a normal thing. Think about that pretty little face of yours before you think about upsetting this lady, understand me?" said Emma.

The nurse entered the room followed by Emma. Julia Anderson lay asleep in her bed. A solution bag hung next to her, a tube leading from it into a needle inserted into her arm.

"Wake her, gently. Then remove that needle from her arm and move to one side," ordered Emma.

The nurse gently shook Julia, placing her hand on her shoulder.

"Evening Julia, my darling. I just need to take this out of your arm." The nurse looked at Emma who nodded approvingly. "Then this young lady is going to take you somewhere."

------ ------

Down in the foyer area of the Bloom Institute, Gus lowered his body mass farther down into Kelly's face. The security guard continued to struggle, piling punch after punch into the ribs and kidney areas of Gus's torso. Gus took the punches, but he was in agony, he remained in the same position, allowing the painful punches to rain in, knowing that with each one, Kelly was tiring himself out more and more.

"Come on Emma. I'm dying here," Gus shouted loudly, even though he knew that his daughter would be unable to hear him.

The kidney punches began to slow and weaken.

------ ------

In Bloom's office, a meeting with a potential new client was taking place. It was a very rich client who worked in the movie industry. This was not the normal type of client who the organisation dealt with. A person from an industry renowned for being unable to keep a secret, but the money this man was offering was just too attractive to turn down without first listening to what he had to say.

The security guard, who would normally have been sat downstairs with Kelly, stood outside the office doors, as requested by the celebrity guest. He did not want to run the risk of anyone walking into the office and discovering him. Phillips did as he was told, regardless of the fact that this basic duty pissed him off massively.

The radio in his pocket vibrated. On looking at it, the red light on the top of the radio unit was flashing rapidly, indicating that a member of staff had pressed their personal panic alarm. He pressed the transmit button and spoke into the radio.

"Kelly, Phillips here. Are you seeing the same PPA activation that I'm looking at?"

He waited but received no response. Pressing the button again he said, "Kelly, if you are on the shitter again and turned the volume down, I am going to feed that turd to you."

Nothing but silence.

Phillips knocked on the office door and opened it slightly. He popped his head through the gap.

Bloom looked up as the door opened and snapped at the security guard.

"I said no interruptions for any reason."

"Sorry Mr. Bloom," apologised Phillips. "I thought I should let you know that I need to go downstairs. There might be a small problem."

Bloom waved his hand dismissively.

"Do whatever it is you idiots do, but disturb us once more, and you will find yourself doing it somewhere else for much less money."

Phillips moved his head back and closed the door.

"Prick," he said under his breath, and began to walk toward the lift at the far end of the corridor.

—————— ——————

Julia Anderson slowly awoke from her part-normal, part-drug-induced sleep, a side effect from the memory distorting drugs. She looked up at the nurse and rubbed her eyes.

"What's going on Sara?" she asked the nurse.

"I need to remove the needle from your arm Julia and then you are going on a short trip," said the nurse, looking at Emma for confirmation that she was saying the right things. Emma nodded her head.

"A short trip?" asked a very confused Julia. "Where am I going?"

Emma spoke before the nurse could reply to Julia's questions.

"Julia, my name is Emma I am going to take you to see...," She paused, remembering what her Dad had told her about Julia not remembering who Grant was. "...to see the doctor. He wants to see you in his private clinic," she lied.

"But Dr. Stanridge always sees me here."

"He wants to try out some new treatment," replied Emma. She noticed Julia Anderson recoil as she said the word treatment. "It's non-invasive, a medical breakthrough by all accounts." Emma was amazed at her ability to think on her feet and lie so quickly as she saw Julia noticeably relax.

"Will Sara be coming with us?" asked Julia.

"Not on this occasion, Julia. She is going to pack up a few of your things and follow later. Dr. Stanridge thinks you may be at his private clinical for a couple of days," replied Emma, looking at the nurse for support even if it was the reluctant type.

The nurse placed her hand on Julia's shoulder saying, "Everything is all right, Julia. I will get a few of your things together and see you later. Let us get you into your wheelchair and this young lady will take you downstairs."

Emma nodded her approval, glad that the nurse had decided to play along.

Sara removed the medication line from the cannula embedded in the flesh of Julia's arm. She helped Julia out of bed and guided her arms into her dressing gown, finally assisting her to stand and walk the few feet to the wheelchair that was sat in the corner of the room.

Emma repositioned herself behind the wheelchair and grasped the handles.

"So, we will see you later Sara," she said to the nurse.

The nurse leaned toward Emma and whispered into her ear, "Within twenty-four hours, the drugs will begin to wear off, and her brain will start to put everything back together. The outcome is unknown."

Emma glared at the nurse wanting to scream, *You are a monster just like the rest of them.* Instead, she smiled and wheeled Julia out of the room. Turning to pull the door shut, she raised the middle finger of her left hand toward the nurse and mouthed the word *bitch.* She closed the door shut, trapping the nurse inside the room. *You see what it feels like for a change,* she thought, as she walked slowly down the corridor toward the lift.

—————— ——————

On the floor above, Phillips swiped his card and looked up at the digital display above the lift doors. The number three did not change to flashing arrows, indicating that the lift was on its way. He used his card again only to get the same outcome. Unwittingly, he had discovered a flaw in the system. It was always made clear to all staff working at the Institute that all lift doors must be closed immediately after use, as it prevented other users calling the lift into action with the fingerprint recognition readers.

It had always been assumed that the swipe cards would override an open-door situation. Emma's decision to leave the lift doors open, purely for time-saving reasons had been a lucky move. The lift remained in its position on the third floor as she made her way toward it.

Phillips started to walk the length of the corridor making his way toward the emergency stairwell.

―――――― ――――――

Downstairs in the reception area, the punches had ceased much to the relief of Gus. He slowly raised his body, exposing the face of the security guard and looked down at him. He grasped Kelly's nose between his finger and thumb, squeezing the nostrils closed, but got no reaction.

"Are you awake?" he asked the apparently unconscious or dead Kelly.

He started to move intending to climb off the guard, when he suddenly decided to do one more check and violently poked his finger into Kelly's right eye. The security screamed out in agony.

The reaction from Gus was the most instinctive thing he had done in years. As he dropped his bodyweight again, he twisted and arched his torso, falling elbow first directly into the face of the half-blinded security guard. Kelly's nose exploded and cracked. His mouth opened slightly, and his head lolled to one side.

Gus sat back up and rubbed his elbow.

"You're not awake any longer are you? You fucker," he said.

Gus stood above the unconscious body of Kelly as the lift doors slid open and his daughter pushed Grant's wife out of it in her wheelchair. He was still breathing quite heavily, and through a mixture of exhaustion and the relief of seeing the two women, he placed his hands on his hips, attempting to get his breath back.

Emma looked at the prostrate body of the unconscious guard, his broken face smothered in blood that leaked from his nose.

"What the hell have you done?" she asked.

"Rendered him unconscious with my belly," replied Gus, standing back upright.

"Fucking hell, I knew it was hefty, but that is impressive," she responded, briefly laughing, grateful for a reason to cut through the tense situation.

She looked down at Julia, who had a mixture of fear and confusion across her face.

"Take me back to my room. I don't know who you people are," she screamed.

Gus stepped in front of the wheelchair and squatted down so that he was at the same eye level as the chair's occupant.

"Listen to me Julia," said Gus, looking into the eyes of the very frightened woman. "We are taking you to see a new doctor. He has known about you and your case from the beginning and has been working with Dr. Stanridge, and now thinks it is the right time for him to be more involved."

Julia looked into Gus's eyes. She saw a level of care and concern that made her want to trust him. She looked up at Emma, who was still stood behind her.

"Young lady, never lie to me again. Do you understand?" she said.

Emma nodded her head, *just like your bloody husband,* she thought.

The three headed toward the exit, but just as they reached it and felt the coldness of the outside air hit them, a voice yelled at them from inside.

"Hey, who the hell are you?"

Phillips stood at the far end of the reception area, just visible to Gus and Emma. He saw his colleague lying unconscious on the floor and quickened his pace to reach the strangers.

"Get her in the car Emma," said Gus. He walked back into

the Bloom Institute.

Gus walked with purpose toward the second security guard he had confronted in a short space of time. Confidently he said, "I am Sergeant Murphy. My colleagues are on their way and a senior detective will be here to head up this case. Now, if you don't mind, I need to take an important witness to a crime scene with me..."

He came face to face with Phillips before finishing his sentence. He was surprised at the impact of the punch he threw. Its effect was greater than it should have been. His fist connected with the chin of Phillips, who reeled backward, and stumbled and fell to the floor. Gus took the opportunity to run back toward the two women and the car, shaking his hand as the pain radiated up into his wrist. The shaking only added to his pain level.

Emma had assisted Julia into the back of the car and was heading quickly toward the front passenger door. Gus shouted his instructions.

"Emma, you drive. I think I've broken my fucking hand."

His daughter changed her direction and went around the front of the vehicle. She got into the driver's seat, just as Gus was climbing into the passenger seat.

Trying to keep his voice as calm as possible, so as not to freak out Julia more than she probably was already, he said, "Get us out of here, NOW."

As the car screamed away, its rear tyres squealing as Emma floored the accelerator pedal, Phillips ran to the phone on the reception desk and pressed the button that would connect to Bloom's direct line.

His office phone rang. Bloom apologetically excused himself to the Hollywood cash cow who he had been wooing.

Picking up the phone, his tone of voice did not hide his annoyance at yet again being disturbed.

"This had better be good, Kelly. I said no interruptions for any reason."

"Mr. Bloom, it's Phillips. Someone has taken the Anderson woman. They are heading for the gate," replied the security man.

"Get them! They must not get away," Bloom lowered his voice as he spoke, not wanting his new potential client to be aware that anything was wrong.

"Kelly is badly hurt Mr. Bloom. We need an ambulance," replied Phillips.

"I don't give a fuck about Kelly," hissed Bloom. "Get that fucking woman back in her room or else you and Kelly will need more than a fucking ambulance."

Phillips slammed the phone down and ran outside. Two company vehicles were parked outside. Phillips grabbed the car keys out of his pocket and pressed the unlock button. The indicators of one car flashed on and off twice, and Phillips got into it and began to drive it down the driveway.

The initial speed from a standstill to acceleration was so dramatic, that at first he almost lost control. The car's right side wheels impacted with the kerb stones momentarily, driving over the damp grassed area, skidding and sliding, before Phillips managed to get it back under control and back on the hard surface. He pushed his foot flat to the floor and the car sped up, reaching sixty miles per hour within a few seconds.

At the other end of the long driveway, Emma was screeching to a halt as they reached the gates, which were once again closed and locked into that position.

"What now?" she asked, looking at Gus. "I really don't think they are going to let us out."

Gus reached into his jacket, fumbling about for a few seconds and then bringing his hand back out, holding a pistol that had been housed in its holster under the copper's armpit.

"I have the keys," he replied, waving the gun in front of Emma's face before remembering that Julia was sat in the back of the car. As he climbed out of the car, he saw Julia reaching for the door handle. As much as he hated doing it, he pointed the pistol at her and said, "Open that door lady, and your life will end before it has a chance to begin all over again."

Julia's hand hovered over the door handle.

"I really fucking mean it Julia," Gus reiterated. Then, addressing Emma, he said, "Lock the doors as soon as I close this door." He got out of the car and slammed the door shut, waiting to hear the sharp clunk, signifying that Emma had done as he had asked.

He looked up the driveway and, in the distance, through the trees, he saw headlights approaching. Running to the gates, he pointed the gun at the centre of them where just visible was a locking bar that slid into place when the gates were automatically locked and in the closed position.

He attempted to pull the trigger and the pain went from a zero to holy-hell level, proving his hand injury was worse than he previously thought. Looking back up the driveway, the headlights were now much closer. He grabbed the gun with his left hand and pointed it at the middle of the gates. Not knowing how accurate his aim would be by firing with his "unnatural" hand, he moved the gun forward to an almost point blank position and pulled the trigger over and over until the ammunition cartridge was emptied.

Dropping the gun to the ground, he used his weak hand to pull at the gate, which moved reluctantly. He gave it a kick and yanked at it again, and this time it moved more easily. Pulling it open, he swung his arm back and forth to give a visual instruction to Emma to drive forward, which she did, just about squeezing the car through the one opened gate. She stopped once she was clear of the gate and, opening her door window, leaned out and screamed, "Get into the car Dad!"

"Go, go!" yelled Gus. "Park down the road, I will be there in a minute."

He knew that he had to try to slow down the pursuing vehicle and began to pull the gate back into a closed position. As he did so, he watched as the car speeding down the driveway got closer and closer and the headlights began to blind him.

Emma drove away, slowly, watching in the rear-view mirror as her father attempted to pull the gates closed. The next thing she witnessed made her instinctively bring the car to a violent halt. As Emma slammed the brake pedal to the floor, in the rear of the vehicle Julia, who was not wearing a seatbelt, was propelled forward, slamming her head and face into the rear of the driver's headrest. She slumped back into her seat, unconscious.

Gus made the decision to leave the gate partially open as the car being driven by Phillips showed no signs of slowing down as it got within a few metres. Unfortunately for him, he made that decision seconds too late. The car slammed into the gates, propelling Gus backward as the gates were forced forward, opening in a direction that they had not been designed to.

The steering wheel spun out of control and Phillips lost his grip. The car continued its journey forward, crossing over the road, hitting the opposite kerb and then a large tree a few feet beyond the pavement. Phillip's head lurched forward, his movement was cut short by the seat belt as the airbag simultaneously activated. His face buried itself into the inflated cushioning device and was propelled backward. The impact with the tree had exploded the windscreen, causing shards of glass to fly in every direction.

Gus lay on the ground, looking toward the car, waiting for the driver to climb out. There was no movement from the smashed-up vehicle. Inside, the body of Phillips sat motionless, his face crushed and lacerated as a result of the impact with the airbag and the flying shards of windscreen glass. His neck had snapped.

Gus attempted to stand up, but an unbelievable level of pain shot through his body, stopping him from moving another inch. He looked down and saw a large patch of blood macerating through his shirt. In the centre of the shirt, a piece of metal protruded out. Part of the now bent and buckled gate had been separated as the car had crashed through it, which was now fully embedded into the upper abdomen of Gus's body. He laid his body down on the grass verge where he now found himself.

"Shit," was the only word he could think of saying.

It's Time to Die

Grant opened his eyes; his head hurt, and his vision took a few seconds to focus. He attempted to bring his hand up to feel the back of his head. The cable tie that had been used to secure his wrists cut into them, causing further unwanted pain. He moved his head slowly, looking around, taking in his environment and immediately knew that he was still in the underground chambers that he had been roaming around for some time.

This familiarity was compounded by another, unexpected cognisance. To his right, he observed a figure who had his back turned to him. The inability to see the man's face did not, however, prevent him from knowing who he was. Dr. Stanridge was involved in some activity, as he stooped over a hospital style instrument trolley, only turning when Grant spoke.

"You are the killer? That, I didn't see coming."

The medical man turned and smiled at Grant.

"How's your head?" he asked.

"Still attached," replied Grant.

"And your humour is still intact," said Stanridge. "You are going to need that."

"So, is this when you try to explain and rationalise what you have done?" asked Grant.

His question was met by another familiarity, a voice that he instantly recognised. The voice resonated from the darkness of the far side of the room.

"I will answer that question if you really feel you need an explanation," it said.

The Priest emerged from the darkness. The black mask and shroud he wore had no impact on Grant knowing who he was.

"What I feel I must firstly express is my surprise and disappointment in your inability to deduce who was responsible, considering all of the clues I delivered in my messages," said The Priest. "But maybe that was because you are not as clever as you believe, combined with your blundering approach to everything that you do. You are blinded to a level of subtlety that you will always be incapable of accessing."

"Have you ever considered that I find your written communication to be the same as your spoken words?" said Grant. "A complete and utter load of bollocks."

The Priest waved his hand dismissively.

"It makes no difference to the outcome; the clues were merely a way of leading you to me. Your ignorance, however, did not prevent that from happening for here you are, thanks to your reluctance to accept assistance and your need to sort things all by yourself," The Priest said pompously. "Did your failure to enact your revenge against a number of Crippens not teach you anything Grant?"

"I got the revenge I needed," retorted a now fuming Grant.

"No Grant. You killed a few insignificant people, but you left things unfinished because you were unable to kill the significant," responded The Priest. "Me. You of all people should know that every action has an equal and opposite reaction." He paused momentarily before adding, "As does every failure to act."

A murmur from the left of Grant broke the tension that had been created by the meeting of these enemies. Grant looked toward the direction of the noise.

Strapped down to a hospital gurney lay a semi-conscious Halo. A tube led into his arm from a medical drip bag. Other than his drowsy appearance, he looked unharmed.

"Let the boy go," said Grant.

It was Dr. Stanridge who responded.

"I think you will find that you are in no position to make requests or demands. The boy will be leaving here soon, as the next carrier of the warnings to the world. Words that will convince the normal decent inhabitants of this planet that we need to rid our lives of these disease-carrying, life destroying aberrations." Stanridge's face was etched in hatred. His brow became more furrowed and face reddened further, as he spat out his venomous words.

"These grotesque chimeras have been allowed to mutate because of an increasingly accepting world. They have forgotten the beginnings of the human race, the beautiful and innocent creation that we once were. An innocence destroyed by monstrosities like him." He pointed in the direction of Halo as if he thought Grant may not know who he was referring to. "A person known to us, a boy trusted by my brother, who was living a life cast upon him by the devil himself, left with no choice but to spread his disease and sickness to me. I was saved from the hell that he wanted me to descend into. My brother helped me to understand that I could fight against these, these…filthy pitiful beings."

"Wow," replied Grant. "Did mummy refuse you a puppy

dog when you were a kid?"

This response did nothing to decrease the level of hatred being demonstrated by Stanridge. The doctor rapidly moved toward Grant and connected with a back handed slap across his mouth.

The Priest intervened by saying, "I would ask you to excuse my brother but not belittle him." For a split-second Grant thought he detected a hint of love in the words that the man spoke and then, focussing on the actual words that had been spoken, he repeated the one word that stuck out.

"Brother?"

The Priest smiled, pleased that he had Grant on the back foot.

"Half-brother to be exact," he replied.

"Please tell me which parent the common denominator was," replied Grant sarcastically, "we really should destroy the DNA that created a couple of freaks like you two."

Mortimer Church removed his mask. Walking forward, he reached a table on which he placed the mask. Next to it were a mobile phone, a small blade and a pistol.

"You dare to arrive armed with a mobile phone hiding a pitiful knife and a pistol, believing that along with your sharp wit, this pathetic armoury would be sufficient to bring a killer of my efficiency to an end? Then have the audacity to call me a freak?" said Church. "You could not even see my real identity hidden in the messages I penned, you brainless moron."

"Somebody once encouraged me to read Dante's 'Divine Comedy,' but I didn't see the point," replied Grant. "Similarly, I didn't see the point in giving your insane ramblings too much of my attention."

"What a pity," said Church. "You would have learned so

much by reading those examples of outstanding literature."

Grant started to respond, for no other reason than to buy more time. Something he had been working on since regaining consciousness, but The Priest stopped him.

"Silence," he called out, the increased volume of his voice almost echoing around the chamber he stood in. "For you and your dirty little assistant, it is time to die."

—————— ——————

Emma got out of the car and ran to where her father was lying.

"Dad, are you all right?" she asked, before seeing the blood spreading outwards through his shirt.

A weakened Gus looked at his daughter. He felt his life slipping away.

"Emma my darling, leave me and get Julia to safety," he grabbed for her hand and held it tightly. "I am so glad you came back into my life."

Emma ripped her hand from his grip and placed her arm around the back of his shoulders.

"Fuck that and fuck you!" she said. It was not quite the response that Gus had been expecting from his daughter to her dying father. "I have already left one man on the roadside to die in my life and I don't intend to repeat it. Now get up, get in that bloody car and let me get you to a hospital."

Gus accepted his daughter's help and raised himself to a seated position, groaning in pain during the process.

"You have spent too much time with Grant," he responded, trying hard to form a smile.

—————— ——————

In a small oak panelled room, Godfrey Lambden sat at a large table. With him were three other people, all of whom were very powerful figures in the political and intelligence world.

"Thank you for joining us, Godfrey," said the Prime Minister. "I believe that you know both Edward and Janet?"

Lambden nodded his head in the direction of the two people who the Prime Minister had just referred to: Edward Pearson, the Home Secretary; and Janet Goodwin-Mayor, the current head of the British Intelligence Agencies.

"Yes, Prime Minister, I do," he replied.

"I would like to begin by thanking you for your recent report on the Bloom Institute and the activities of the C.O.R.T. agents," the Prime Minister said. "I would also like to add that several other pieces of live information and updates have been delivered to Janet. All of this information leaves me with no other option but to announce that it is time for Mr. Bloom to relocate to, shall we say, somewhere other than this country."

Once again, Lambden nodded his head to demonstrate that he was listening and fully understanding what his Prime Minister was saying.

The PM continued addressing the small collective.

"This game, this experiment, has run its course. It is now only right that the work of this agency returns to its rightful place, that being back under the direct control of this government." The PM paused, more for effect than an expectation that his audience would respond at this stage.

"As you are fully aware, Godfrey, it is my intention to

announce your, shall we call it a promotion, to the position of the Head of the Intelligence Agencies as soon as Janet lets me know when she intends to commence her fully deserved retirement. The heavy burden of then steering the brave men and women within those agencies to tackle the growing problem of combating our nation's enemies will fall to you. I see the C.O.R.T. team performing an important role, although maybe not in its current setup."

Lambden waited a short while to ensure that this was the end of the speech and not just another dramatic pause. Satisfied that it was the former, he replied to the Prime Minister.

"I fully understand what is expected of me sir and I trust you have faith in me to execute my duties effectively?"

"Oh, I do Godfrey," the PM replied. "Failure will not be an acceptable outcome."

The Home Secretary stood, as if knowing that the conversation had reached its conclusion. He left the room. Janet delayed her exit by a few moments to shake Lambden's hand and wish him luck, before following Pearson out of the room.

The Prime Minister stood and walked to stand in front of a fireplace that had not seen use for many decades. He looked up at the portrait of the Queen. Sensing that Lambden was still in the room he said, "You may leave now Godfrey. The next time we meet, I need to hear that this awful mess has been cleaned up."

Godfrey Lambden walked out of the room, leaving the Prime Minister to silently pass on his apologies to the image of his Head of State.

—————— ——————

Mortimer Church and his younger half-brother approached Halo in unison. It was almost as if there was an invisible connection between them that did not rely on verbal communication. From behind the metal trolley, to which the young boy was strapped, Stanridge retrieved a large, long handled sledgehammer and a metal pointed spike that was approximately four feet in length.

He placed the spike between Halo's legs, so that the point was millimetres from his groin. It was angled so that it was pointing up toward his heart and right shoulder. Church placed his hand on the butt of the sledgehammer's wooden handle and looked toward Grant.

"The boy will be the harbinger of my next message and will carry it like the Lord's son carried the wound in his side," he said.

Grant remained silent, studying the psychopathic biker closely. Church carried on talking.

"The words that he will carry forth will begin to help with the change that this world needs, a change for good, for a sinless society." He stopped and waited for Grant to speak, but there was no response.

"Are you finally accepting that you are defeated? Do you accept your fate and place your life in the hands of the Lord?" The Priest asked.

Grant cast his eyes over toward Stanridge and then back at Church. Stanridge made no eye contact with him but The Priest's eyes never left Grant's gaze.

"No not really," replied Grant. "Well, I accept that I am probably going to die, fair enough, you have me at a slight disadvantage. I also accept why you want to kill me, after all you failed the first time and that must really, fucking hurt, but what I don't understand is his involvement," Grant nodded in the direction of Stanridge, who was patiently holding the metal stake in place.

"My brother is a victim of the sickness in this world," replied Church, his voice once again raised.

"Oh, I get that," responded Grant, not really knowing where he was going with this conversation, but knowing that he had to buy some extra thinking time. "I get that he was fucked up the arse when he probably wasn't ready for that kind of loving, but it was one of your friends who did it. So I was just wondering if this was just about guilt on your part. Because, let's be honest here, this has nothing to do with God."

"Do you think that your antagonising words will save this boy?" asked Church. "Do you believe that somehow they will save you?"

"No," responded Grant nonchalantly. "I don't think my words will be any more powerful than yours have been so far."

"Yes, so far," interrupted Church. "The fight against evil is a long and testing journey but history will show, as it has done before, that the battle will be won."

"Oh, for fuck's sake. Can we just drop the God's messenger bullshit and at least agree that this is all about you pair being a couple of sick fucked up individuals?" Grant almost screamed the words at Church.

The Priest let go of the sledgehammer. It remained upright on its metal head and walked toward the table upon which sat the gun and mobile phone. Picking up the weapon he slid back the top slider of the gun, loading the first bullet into the chamber and clicked the safety catch downwards. He walked toward Grant and placed the muzzle of the gun against Grant's temple.

Leaning forward, he whispered into Grant's ear, "You are right. This has nothing to do with my brother. It was just an opportunity that was too good to miss. When he reached out to me following your arrival at his hospital, after he had read your file, he realised that I must have had something to do with what happened to you."

The Priest's finger hovered over the trigger of the pistol and then moved slightly toward it, eventually making contact. "I wanted you to watch the suffering of this young wretch merely for my amusement but now I am bored with you. Time to die…Grant," he hissed through clenched teeth.

The mobile phone suddenly began to ring.

Church beckoned his brother over. "Hold this against his head," he said, handing the gun to Stanridge. "If he twitches, shoot him." Martin David Stanridge nodded his head.

Church walked over to the table and looked down at the phone. The name *Muttley* flashed on and off on the phone's screen.

"A mutual friend," said Church, smiling as he looked over at Grant.

The phone continued to ring.

"Do you want your last words, your last message ever spoken to be wasted on this tub of lard?" he asked Grant.

Grant wasn't listening. He was now fully focussing on Stanridge.

"I thought your name was Martin. What happened to David?" he asked.

"Shut up," replied Stanridge, appearing very comfortable handling the gun—far more comfortable than any doctor should have been.

"Which one of you is the Messenger?" Grant continued, trying to goad the medical man. "It can't be you. Are you just the mad man's bitch?"

Stanridge pressed the muzzle of the pistol hard against Grant's temple, who took the pain, refusing to be the weak person in this verbal conflict.

Church walked toward him and stood in front of Grant, holding up the phone, so that Grant could see the screen. A few seconds passed as he watched the familiar name flashing in front of him, before the phone stopped ringing as quickly as it had started.

Church's smile increased, spreading farther across his face.

"In your hour of need, even your friend abandons you. Do you feel alone?" he asked.

"I've been alone for most of my life," replied Grant. "There is nothing wrong with being alone, but the difference between you and me, is that when I need a friend, they will be there, because they want to be, whereas, your so called friends are there because they fear you. They are not friends. They are cowards, potential victims of your cruelty and madness."

The smile disappeared from Church's face as the phone started to ring again.

From his other hand Church produced the blade that he had earlier removed from the phone. He walked behind Grant lightly placing it against Grant's throat and moving it in an arc across the front of his throat as he walked behind him. No cut was made.

"I could kill you anytime I wanted to," said Church, as he bent down and sliced the blade through the plastic restraint that held Grant's wrists together.

"What are you doing?" asked Stanridge, who was ignored

by his brother.

"But before I do, I will allow another person in your life to suffer further misery because of you," said Church, from his position behind Grant. "It is a skill that I admire. One you should embrace, rather than allowing it to fill you full of self-loathing."

Grant moved his hands to the front of him, rubbing his wrists where the restraints had rubbed and cut his skin. The phone appeared in front of him once again. He slowly reached out his hand and took hold of the phone.

"Answer it, say your last words, but if you mention where you are or who else is here, my brother will happily scatter your brains all over this dark, empty prison," said Church.

Grant pressed the answer button and placed it next to his ear, the opposite one to which Stanridge still held the pistol.

"Hello, Gus," he said. He was not expecting the voice that responded.

Emma's voice sounded strained and tired, but despite that, the first thing she asked was if Grant was all right.

"Yeah, I'm fine thanks," he replied, intentionally not identifying the girl by using her name.

"We've got her Grant, we got your wife," Emma said, almost squealing with excitement.

"Well, that is great news. Thank you," replied Grant, his voice as emotionless as if he had just been told that he was being repaid the penny that a friend owed him.

"Grant, did you hear me? Julia, your wife, is fine. She is safe," said Emma, extremely surprised by the empty response from Grant.

"Yes, I understand," he answered. "Anyway, listen Gus, I have a few things to do so you take care and look after that girl of yours." He ended the call and looked at the screen of the phone. The battery life read two percent.

A memory flashed through his mind. Grant had never been a stronger swimmer; he remembered the fear that he had felt when he had first been expected to perform a river crossing during a military training exercise. The words that remained in his head from that moment were the words of his training sergeant, *"If you are going to die Anderson, at least die trying to fucking live."*

The laughter of Stanridge broke him from his thoughts. The doctor was laughing raucously.

"Your chance to make your final message in life worth remembering, and you decide to say that you have a few things to do," he said, mockingly at Grant.

As the hand holding the phone swung around in the direction of Stanridge, Grant moved his finger and thumb, so that they hovered just over the two buttons on the sides of the phone.

"Those were not my last words," said Grant, looking at Stanridge and watching as the laughing stopped and a look of surprise replaced it. "These are…time to die brother fucker."

He slammed the phone into the side of the doctor's neck and pressed his finger and thumb down onto the buttons and delivered the electric shock. He closed his eyes and waited for the bullet to enter his brain.

Surprised and overjoyed at the same time that no blast from a gun was heard, no split-second searing pain was experienced. Just the scream of Stanridge as the pain caused by the electricity zapped through his body and the metallic thud of the gun hitting the floor.

He turned just about in time to see the blade being held by

Church swinging round toward his face. He could do nothing about it as the tip sliced open the flesh just below his right eye. Grant's instinctive movement backward, caused the chair he was sat on to topple back and he and it landed heavily on the floor. As the side of his head hit the floor, he saw the gun lying about two arm's lengths from him. He watched as a hand reached for it and lifted it from the floor.

"Stand up," ordered Church, the gun aimed at Grant.

Grant stood, everything was slightly out of focus and he could only think that the impact of his head against the floor must have been harder than he had first thought. As he stood upright, he staggered backward, almost tripping over the prone body of Stanridge. Managing to stride over him, which put him further off balance, his body struck the wall. Looking over to where Halo lay, he was grateful that whatever drug was being forced into the boy's body was making him largely unaware of what was happening around him. He looked toward Church, who now stood about eight feet or so away from him.

"If I was a decent man, I would offer you a chance for some last words," Church said to Grant. "But I'm not." He pulled the trigger of the gun and the explosive blast of it firing echoed around the chamber.

------ ------

Emma stood in the corridor of the hospital's accident and emergency unit outside of two cubicles. In one, lay her father, and Julia Anderson in the other. The curtains to both cubicles were both drawn shut, blocking her view from whatever was happening behind them. She did not need to see into the cubicles to know that inside one, her father was being treated for a serious wound to his body, and behind the other, a woman was causing confusion to the medical staff tending to her.

She looked down at the phone in her hand, not knowing what to make of the conversation she had just had—a conversation during which she had just told a man that his wife, a woman who until a short while ago he had thought dead, was now safe and being cared for. A conversation that had ended with Grant telling her to look after that girl of his!

She walked into the cubicle where her father lay. A nurse and junior doctor were inspecting his wound and conducting a medical type conversation, which contained words that she could not have hoped to understand in a thousand lifetimes.

"What did he say?" asked Gus.

"Not what you would expect Dad," replied Emma.

"Well was he at least happy?" Gus asked again.

"Not as much as you would expect Dad," said Emma, almost replicating the answer given to Gus's first question.

"He's a complex man," said Gus, laughing and immediately regretting it as a bolt of hot pain surged through his upper body.

—————— ——————

A ringing noise filled Grant's ears as he stood in the same position that he had adopted the moment he realised that Church was going to pull the trigger—arms crossed over his body and his chin tucked into his chest. He thought he had heard a body hit the floor as the gun fired. His mind was convincing him that it must have been his body and what was stood up now was merely his spirit waiting to be guided to a more serene and peaceful location.

He raised his eyes to where Church had been stood as he fired the gun, only to find Fox now stood in his place, the unconscious body of Church laying at his feet. Fox was holding the same gun that had just been fired in his direction, and for some reason was pointing it directly at him. Grant stood upright and addressed Fox, still surprised that he was able to do so.

"How come I'm not dead?" he asked.

"Not as street wise as you think are you?" the agent responded. "It's a well-known tactic used by armed street dealers. The first bullet is a blank so that it prevents the buyer from killing the dealer and taking the goods without paying."

"How do you know the second isn't a blank too?" asked Grant.

"Maybe we should find out," responded Fox, the weapon still pointed toward Grant.

"So, is this how it ends? I escape one killer just to be faced by another?"

"You seem to have forgotten that I am a government agent Grant," Fox replied smiling, the darkness only helping to make the situation to look more sinister.

"Government backed or not, a killer is a killer is a killer," said Grant.

Church lay at the feet of Fox, next to the lump of concrete stone that Fox had used to strike him about the back of the head. He made a groaning noise and moved his head slightly, allowing Grant to see the large hole in his skull that was bleeding profusely. Fox lowered the pistol and pulled the trigger, the bullet entering Church's head through the hole that he had caused just moments earlier. He raised the gun up again to point it back at Grant.

"Well that answers your question about the second bullet and I suppose about me being a cold-hearted killer, too," said Fox.

"So, who gets bullet number three?" Grant asked Fox. "You have three people to choose from."

"Oh, bullet number three has your name all over it Grant," replied Fox. He waved the pistol toward Halo saying, "Shooting a kid strapped to a trolley would prove difficult to justify, and as for Stanridge, well someone has to face a jury and be convicted of these killings." He paused, a smug look on his face, as if pleased with the way that things had turned out.

"The moment you decided not to work for the organisation, you left me with no other choice but to kill you," Fox continued. "You know way too much Grant. There is no way you can be allowed to walk away from this."

Grant was no longer listening to the words being spoken by the psychotic secret agent. His attention had, for the last few seconds, been centred on the small red dot that had appeared on the front of Fox's jacket.

From the corner of an entrance to the large chamber-like room, a gravelly voice called out a simple and direct order.

"Agent Fox, drop the weapon NOW."

Fox looked over toward the direction of the voice, keeping the gun pointed at Grant, but was unable to see anyone, so he looked back at Grant. Raising his eyebrows and tapping the centre of his own chest, Grant nodded his head forward looking straight at the unwavering red dot.

Fox looked down and the smallest of flinches from his trigger finger bought about a lightening reaction from the owner of the voice in the darkness. With a slight change of aim, the bullet flew from the assault rifle and hit Fox in the shoulder causing him to drop the pistol. The bullet shattered his clavicle and exited through the back of his flesh.

As Fox dropped to his knees, holding his wounded shoulder, a number of figures appeared from different angles into the open area, all clad in the same black uniform. Ballistic helmets, large goggles and balaclavas, they honed in on Fox with the exception of one who headed toward Grant and Stanridge. This individual initially kicked the body of the apparently unconscious doctor, which got a guttural throat noise, indicating that the doctor was merely pretending to be out of it.

"One move doctor and it will be the last you make," the armed operative warned, and then looking at Grant he said, "You, hands on the back of your head and drop to your knees."

Doing as he was told, Grant kneeled down, never taking his eyes off the man holding the rifle.

"You do know I am not the guilty one here?" he asked.

"I'm the judge not the jury," came the stern response.

A few feet away, Grant watched as two of the team pushed Fox to a face-down position on the floor, and applied a set of rigid handcuffs to his wrists, which they placed into position, ignorant to the pain that this caused to Fox. Another of the team walked toward Grant, he was pressing a button that was attached to a webbing vest that he wore over the black set of overalls, speaking as he walked.

As he got closer, Grant noticed a tiny microphone running down the side of the man's face.

"Alpha one, situation controlled. One fatality, medics needed for three others, wait out," he said.

Looking at Grant he asked, "Are you injured in any way?"

Grant shook his head to confirm that he was unhurt.

"Alpha one, no change from last transmission, siege area safe for entry."

The man, who Grant assumed was the team leader, lowered his weapon and visibly relaxed. He removed his goggles and helmet, placing the former inside the latter, and then pulled down the half face balaclava to reveal his face. He held out his hand which Grant grabbed, and the man pulled him to his feet.

"Toby McGregor, Team Leader Alpha team. You sure you are okay?"

Grant nodded and finally said something.

"SAS or some other type of specialist team?"

"A mixed bag of misfits and miscreants. As for me, I'm a Bootneck and Oliver says hi," replied McGregor.

"So, what happens now?" Grant asked him.

"Well now you come with us," replied McGregor matter-of-factly.

"Do I get a choice?" asked Grant.

"Yeah of course, you get to choose the easy way or the painful way. Personally, I am hoping you choose the second option," answered McGregor, with no sign that he was joking.

Two of Alpha team were escorting Fox away, who was half walking and half being carried, which was obviously causing him immense pain. The two men escorting him didn't let up in their efforts to carry him, and it seemed to Grant that they were enjoying inflicting the pain.

"Think I will select option one," he said to McGregor.

The team leader's face showed genuine disappointment as he told Grant to follow one of his team, another of which dropped in behind him, as he started to walk. Grant suddenly came to a stop, almost causing the armed guard behind him to walk into him.

“McGregor,” he said. “Somewhere around here there are a number of rooms. At least one contains a person. There may be more.”

“Yeah, we know, now leave my siege area and let the professionals do what they are paid to do,” replied McGregor, walking away from Grant like he had forgotten about him already.

The man behind Grant shoved him in the back and ordered, “Move.”

Grant looked back at him glaring angrily.

“If you didn’t have that fucking rifle,” he said.

“I would have two hands to fucking kill you with,” replied the soldier. “Now fucking move it.”

Don't Look Back

It had been one day short of seven weeks since Grant had been escorted away from the Camden Catacombs. Confused at the time by the sequence of events that had led to that occasion and angry, an emotion he still held onto, about having the opportunity to kill Mortimer Church himself, he felt that Fox had robbed him of that right out of pure spite.

He had been bundled unceremoniously into the back of a van, where he enjoyed the silence of four of the Special Forces team, who would never receive the recognition for their actions that night. He had tried to make conversation during that journey, but had decided that silence was the preferred option when one of the team had asked.

"Can I shoot him now?"

It wasn't that question which had silenced Grant, but the response.

"Not until we receive clearance to do so."

Grant had been a cocky twat most of his life, known for his quick wit and ability to produce an answer for everything. On that journey, he learned a new skill. How to shut up when the situation required it.

He was taken to a meeting with Godfrey Lambden at an unknown location. It had been this meeting that had answered most of his questions.

Lambden explained that his movements had been followed by Alpha team, ever since they had set up their surveillance positions outside of the Rainbow Club and spotted him walking into the building. Their arrival had preceded his by a few hours after Halo had led them, courtesy of a tracking device that Oliver, the apartment concierge, had placed inside Grant's bag of belongings before handing them to Grant's young volunteer assistant.

He further explained that two of the team members had discovered the secret entrance behind the mirror before he had. They had entered the club to ensure that visual surveillance of Halo could take place. They had remained hidden inside the catacombs, waiting for the armed members of Alpha team to arrive, who were under strict orders not to move until he had. It was, unfortunately, the team's fault that Fox had found the entrance to the underground chambers as they had left it open, not thinking that anyone else would be allowed into the club following its evacuation.

Lambden admitted that Fox had proven to be both more resourceful and persuasive than anticipated, but would not be drawn further on that matter.

Grant also learned that the Bloom Institute no longer existed and that Mr. Bloom was, at present, in an unknown location. He assured Grant that every resource available was being used to locate the man. Grant didn't bother pursuing that piece of information, as he knew that Bloom Institute was potentially an embarrassment to the government, and was probably holed up very comfortably, at the expense of the British taxpayers.

Lambden also told Grant that the organisation known as

C.O.R.T. no longer existed as such, and had been swallowed up by the larger networks of the British Intelligence Agencies, a department that was now headed up by him. As for Fox, well Lambden would say nothing more than that he would be personally managing the agent's future.

Grant had asked about Stanridge, to which Lambden would say nothing more than it was the intention of the relevant departments to pursue a criminal case against the man for the murders of the victims at the hands of the entity known as The Messenger, but that currently his defence team was drawing up a defence based upon their client being mentally incapable of facing criminal charges and that they would be requesting an immediate sectioning of their client under the Mental Health Act, and his immediate transfer from the prison he was being held at to a secure and suitable mental care facility.

Finally, the newly appointed head of the Secret Services Agency had thanked Grant for his assistance in the case, and informed him that a bank account in the name of John Richardson had been set up and a considerable amount of funds placed in it.

The only request that Grant made was that the account was changed so that it was in his name, as he no longer knew who Mr. John Richardson was. Lambden had agreed, and the meeting ended abruptly with Grant being returned to the van and driven away.

When Grant exited the vehicle, he found himself outside of the apartment building where he had stayed for one night. Oliver was waiting at the top of the stairs by the entrance door, his face stern and granite like, that was until he turned to walk into the apartment building. Just before he disappeared through the door, he looked over his shoulder and winked at Grant.

Grant discovered that his bike had been parked in the underground car park. When he was informed of this fact by Oliver, the first thing he did was visit his beloved Midnight Star. He ran his hand over the shiny black fuel tank and thanked her, not for the first time, for being such a permanent and loyal part of his life.

Over the next few weeks, he was visited by and also went to see several people. His first visitor was Emma, who arrived in an official car and spent several hours in his apartment telling him about Gus, and her performing the rescue of his wife, and how Gus had sustained, but thankfully survived, a life-threatening injury.

"He will never be able to work again for the police. He is distraught," she explained.

Grant couldn't apologise enough and bleated on about the number of lives he had affected, none in a good way, but Emma would not have any of it. She told him that neither her dad or herself blamed him for anything and after what he had done for them, they could now at least feel that they were even.

This had not stopped Grant arranging for £100,000 being transferred into Gus's bank account, a drop in the ocean compared to the amount that the establishment had paid him. A figure that Grant still described as his hush money.

He had visited both Halo and Gus in their respective hospitals. Halo was full of excited spirit and wouldn't stop asking Grant when their next mission would take place. He had sustained nothing more than a few bumps and bruises, following his initial capture and because of the drugs given to him, could not remember a thing about any of the events that followed, or how close he had come to succumbing to an indescribable death.

Grant gave him no details about any of that, but what he did offer was his support and help to get Halo and his family out of the shithole estate that they lived in, and said that he would cover the cost of a new place, as long as it was well outside of London.

Initially, Halo had turned down the offer saying that the hero worship he had received from his mates was all that he wanted. However, his mother, who had been at the hospital at the time of Grant's visit, told Halo to stop being silly and to turn down such a kind offer would only offend Grant.

He had no idea how much of his money would be spent on a lavish lifestyle for Halo's mother, but at this point, he did not care, as long as the young lad got away from the influences of the estate where he lived. Once that had been achieved, he would control and eventually stop the availability of money. There was no way was he going to allow the greedy uncaring bitch of a whore who Halo called his mother, live the rest of her life on his handouts.

Gus had been low at the beginning of the visit, and quite angry at Grant for what he saw as being treated like a charity case.

"I don't need your blood money. I did what I did because you were responsible for my daughter being returned to my life. I just did the same for you and your wife," he had stated.

After two hours of careful talking, which eventually turned to light hearted banter, Gus was saying things like, "Well it's the bloody least you can do, nearly got killed for you I did. A hundred grand, you got me cheap you tight arsed biker piece of shit."

Finally, Grant plucked up the courage needed to visit Shuffler, probably the one he felt the most guilt about. This old biker had been approached by Grant, who had used his previous good relationship and knowledge of the man to resurrect the desire to be of use again, to not be seen as a useless broken old man. The facial injuries inflicted by Fox were healing, but very slowly. Shuffler was virtually unrecognisable to everyone, except those who really knew him. Grant had stood at the door of Shuffler's hospital room, unable to think of anything to say.

"Do I get to keep the bike?" Shuffler had asked. "Please let me keep the bike."

Grant did not have the guts to tell the beat up old biker that the bike had been taken by Fox's men before the dissolution of their organisation. Grant had told him that of course the bike was his, but that he would find it outside of a new home when he was discharged from the hospital.

"Always fancied living in the countryside," Shuffler had told him. "My old nanna once told me that Derbyshire is bleedin' beautiful."

They chatted for hours, before Grant eventually made his excuses to leave.

Shuffler was discharged about three weeks after Grant met his wife, Julia. Emma had collected him from the hospital and driven him to Derbyshire to move into a little two-bedroom cottage in a small village. Emma had told Grant that Shuffler had sobbed for a good twenty minutes when he discovered the brand new Indian Dark Horse parked in the garage.

The only other visit Grant performed was a very personal one. A visit to a man he knew virtually nothing about, except that he loved his son more than he would ever be willing to admit. He didn't knock on the door, but simply pushed the strip of photo booth photographs through the letterbox and walked away.

As for Julia, his beautiful wife, Grant had not seen her at all. She had been taken to a private rehabilitation clinic called Drake Manor. He had been informed by Lambden's private secretary, via Oliver, that the cost of his wife's recovery would be covered by the State, no matter how long it took or how much it cost.

The only cost to Grant would be that Drake Hall's leading clinical staff had insisted that he did not visit until they gave permission, due to the fragile nature of Julia's health. They felt that an early visit from Grant during the intense therapy and support that she needed, would do more damage than good. Not a day went by, during the nearly seven-week period since her incarceration into that establishment, that Grant did not spend a large part of his time thinking about her and wondering how she was doing.

Most importantly, would she ever accept him back into her life?

The call had come in the morning; the director of Drake Hall himself had called Grant to inform him that a visit would be most welcomed by both his wife's clinical team and Julia herself.

As he looked through his clothing, trying to decide which of his T-shirts would be most appropriate for this important occasion, he realised that he had not felt this nervous since his transfer to Colchester to serve twenty-eight days imprisonment in the military correctional centre for glassing a barman who had refused to serve him any more alcohol.

Grant heard a knock on the apartment door. Leaving his row of shirts on the bed, he went to open it, not even looking at who was there.

"Come in Emma, I'm nearly ready," he said.

"How do you do that?" the girl asked, as she walked into the apartment. She looked at Grant's naked torso and flinched slightly at the number of surgical scars that remained from his numerous interventions required to fix his broken body courtesy of the Crippens.

"One of my many skills," he replied with a grin, deciding not to tell her that Oliver had phoned up to let him know that Emma was on her way. "Unlike my ability to select an acceptable shirt to wear. Come on, you're a woman, help me."

"Said in a totally non-sexist way, suggesting that I am only capable of such things as picking out clothes for a useless turd," replied Emma.

"Eh?" Grant replied, his mind naturally elsewhere. "Yeah, how is Gus?"

Emma ignored him and walked past him to look at the selection of shirts.

"T-shirts? Really? You are going to meet your wife for the first time in God only knows how long, and you are going to wear a tour T-shirt?" Emma looked at the half naked man, who she loved to bits, but could at this precise moment, very easily slap.

"That's how Julia would remember me. At least I think that's how she would," replied Grant.

Emma shook her head in disbelief and asked, "If you were going to see, I don't know, let's say a solicitor, what would you wear?"

Without a second thought Grant pointed at one of the T-shirts.

"That one," he answered as if the answer was obvious.

Emma looked at the T-shirt being identified, a Judas Priest one with a picture of a leather-clad man on the front of it and the words, "Breaking the Law" written underneath.

An exasperated Emma scanned the selection of shirts, none of which, in her opinion, were suitable for the occasion. However, deciding that this was all she had to work with, she discarded all that were skull related or suggested that the wearer should take a Highway to Hell, and picked up the one with a large brightly covered alien spaceship on the front.

"This one will have to do," she said, picking up the shirt and throwing it at Grant.

He pulled on the shirt and held out his arm.

"So?" he asked Emma.

"So, I'm glad I am not married to you," she replied. "Come on, let's go."

They both walked out of the apartment. Grant picked up his leather jacket and bike helmet.

"Why are you taking those?" Emma asked him.

"I'm going on the bike," he said.

"I give up," said Emma, walking out of the room. Grant followed, thinking that he would never be able to understand women.

He followed Emma, who led the way in her car to Drake Hall, which stood in the middle of an area of sprawling land, and yet still managed to leave visitors with a feeling of intimacy and well-being.

They parked their respective vehicles outside of the main building, and as Emma got out of her car, she watched Grant take off his helmet and light up one of his favoured small cigars. His hands were shaking slightly as he held the lighter up to the tip of the cigar.

As Emma approached him, Grant took a deep draw on the cigar and inhaled deeply.

"What if she doesn't want to see me?" he asked.

This demonstration of vulnerability from a man who had previously shown nothing but a gung-ho devil-may-care attitude to everything he did, bought an aching pain to Emma's heart.

"She cannot wait to see you Grant," Emma responded. "She is still delicate and vulnerable, but she is learning to cope. For the past three weeks, she has been talking about nothing but you, how she worries about you, and how much she loves you."

Grant's eyes shone with the moisture that had suddenly filled them.

"You have seen her? Spoken to her?" he asked.

"I've been visiting her twice a week for the past five weeks Grant," replied Emma, much to his surprise. "She asked to see me, said she needed to speak with someone who loved you almost as much as she does."

Grant's chest started to rise and fall rapidly as a mixture of fear, joy, anxiety, sadness and guilt took over his body, causing his chest to tighten and his heart to beat so rapidly that he thought it was going to explode out of his body. The tears flowed down his face as he said, "I don't deserve that level of love from anyone. I am not a good man Emma. I am bad news."

"No, you don't. No you're not, and yes you are," replied Emma. She hugged him tightly and whispered into his ear, "There is something about you that people cannot help loving."

He pulled gently away from Emma's embrace and sniffed twice loudly, wiping his nose and eyes with the same sleeve of his jacket. He stuck out his chin and gulped the tears back to where they belonged—back into what he knew was a dark heart.

"Stop being such a soppy fucking cow, you'll turn me soft," he said, forcing a smile onto his face.

Emma grabbed the tip of his goatee beard and tugged it left and right.

"There's our big tough teddy bear," she said laughing. "Now come on, it's time to face your greatest challenge."

They both walked toward and then through the large wooden double doors into Drake Hall.

------ ------

Two weeks later, Grant parked his bike outside the entrance doors to Drake Hall, a spare helmet secured to the back of his bike.

He had spent every day visiting his wife since that first meeting accompanied by Emma, the only one that she had attended.

There had been tough and emotional moments. Tears had been shed and angry words and accusations had been thrown around mainly, and quite correctly, toward him. Julia's first words to him when he had first walked into her room had been a question.

"I believe that I am expected to call you Grant?"

"You can call me whatever you like," he had answered, to which his wife had replied, "You know I don't like to use bad language in public."

He knew that his wife was starting to cope when during a long period of silence between them she asked, "You actually buried me?"

"Well obviously not," he replied. "But yes, we had a funeral."

"Please tell me that lots of people attended and that they were terribly upset."

They both laughed uncontrollably and for some time, for which Grant was grateful. He had not wanted to tell her that there had only been eleven mourners, and that six of those had been the coffin bearers provided by the funeral directors.

This was no reflection on how little she was thought of, but more of how many people he had told he didn't want to attend and exactly the reasons why. They were friends who they were unlikely ever to repair relationships with.

Julia found it extremely difficult to talk about their daughter and impossible to talk about the crime that had been committed against them both. Grant didn't push on either subject.

At the beginning of visit number twenty-five that had happened on day thirteen, he was taken aback and filled with relief at the same time when his wife asked, "Can I leave here now please?"

They had both looked at the therapist, who had been a constant presence during all of the visits. She had looked down at the notes that she had been making and then looked up at Julia's pleading eyes.

"I will have to clear it with the clinical director, but I don't see any reason why not," she said.

The senior therapist left the room, leaving Grant and Julia alone for the first time.

"Do I need to hire a car?" he had asked.

"Well unless things have really changed dramatically, it was and always has been my understanding that you don't do cars," his wife replied.

They held each other; it was the first contact between them, except for holding each other's hand a few times, since Grant had been allowed to see her. It felt so good that he didn't want to ever let go.

Eventually, in a strained voice, Julia said, "You are crushing me Grant."

Grant relaxed his hold around his wife and whispered sorry into her ear, "You can let me go now darling and you have no reason to say sorry…for anything."

He began to cry, softly and quietly at first and then it felt like every bit of moisture in his body decided to evacuate through his eyes. He cried like he had never cried in his life, while his wife, a woman who had suffered unspeakable things, held him and stopped his from collapsing onto the floor. If she had let him go, Grant knew that he would never have gotten back up again. At that moment, he had no doubt whatsoever that his wife had found the strength to hold his life together.

He stood next to his bike and watched as Julia, accompanied for the final time by her therapist, appeared at the doors of Drake Hall. They hugged and finally Julia walked toward Grant. He handed her a leather jacket that he had bought the night before and secured inside his side pannier, along with the spare helmet that had a pair of gloves inside it.

"Unlike you to travel light," he said to her.

"It's time to start a new life, babe," she replied smiling. Grant thought he detected something fake or strained in that smile, but shook away the feeling, putting it down to the monumental occasion.

She put on the jacket, helmet and gloves, waited for Grant

to get on the bike and then, placing one foot on the rear foot plate, straddled her leg over the bike seat behind her husband.

Grant pulled away and steered the bike slowly down the driveway. He briefly looked back over his shoulder as he felt his wife place her arms around his waist.

"Are you okay darling?" he called out.

"Don't look back Grant, just ride," she shouted back.

Lightning Source UK Ltd.
Milton Keynes UK
UKHW01f1944180518
322856UK00001B/7/P